# MAYA - ILLUSION

Book Three in the Series

## Behind The Smile

*The Story of Lek, A Bar Girl in Pattaya*

by

## OWEN JONES

# Copyright

# Contact Details

BlueSky: owen-author.bsky.social
Facebook: AngunJones
Instagram: owen_author
LinkedIn: owencerijones
Pinterest: owen_author
TikTok: @owen_author
X: @owen_author
Blog: Megan Publishing Services

Join our newsletter for insider information on Owen Jones' books and writing by entering your email address here:
https://meganpublishingservices.com

# Behind The Smile Series

*The Story of Lek, a Bar Girl in Pattaya*

Daddy's Hobby
ISBN: 978-1-0683538-3-3
An Exciting Future
ISBN: 978-1-0683538-6-4
Maya – Illusion
ISBN: 978-1-0683538-7-1
The Lady in the Tree
Stepping Stones
The Dream
The Beginning

# Dedication

This book is dedicated to my wife and her family, who have always taken care of me in the most wonderful manner, affording me the time and space to take up this career of writing. No-one could have made me feel more welcome and part of their family than they have. I have loved every minute of my life in Thailand, and the reason for that lies largely with them.

# Acknowledgments

The cover was created by GetCovers.

# Inspirational Quotes

Believe not in anything simply because you have heard it,
Believe not in anything simply because it was spoken and rumoured by many,
Believe not in anything simply because it was found written in your religious texts,
Believe not in anything merely on the authority of teachers and elders,
Believe not in traditions because they have been handed down for generations,
But after observation and analysis, if anything agrees with reason and is conducive to the good and benefit of one and all, accept it and live up to it.
**Gautama Buddha**

------

Great Spirit, whose voice is on the wind, hear me.
Let me grow in strength and knowledge.
Make me ever behold the red and purple sunset.
May my hands respect the things you have given me.
Teach me the secrets hidden under every leaf and stone, as you have taught people for ages past.
Let me use my strength, not to be greater than my brother, but to fight my greatest enemy – myself.
Let me always come before you with clean hands and an open heart, that as my Earthly span fades like the sunset, my Spirit shall return to you without shame.
(Based on a traditional **Sioux prayer**)

------

"I do not seek to walk in the footsteps of the Wise People of old; I seek what they sought".
**Matsuo Basho**

"Have I not commanded you? Be strong and courageous. Do not be afraid; do not be discouraged, for the LORD your God will be with you wherever you go".
**Joshua 1:9**

------

"Whatever misfortune befalls you [people], it is because of what your own hands have done- God forgives much-"
**Quran 42:30**

------

Myself when young did eagerly frequent
Doctor and Saint, and heard great Argument
About it and about; but oft-times
Came out, by the same Door as in I went.
**Omar Khayyam**
The Rubaiyat XXIX.

------

# Contents

MAYA - ILLUSION..................................................................i

Copyright.............................................................................ii

Contact Details...................................................................iii

Behind The Smile Series....................................................iv

Dedication...........................................................................v

Acknowledgments..............................................................vi

Inspirational Quotes..........................................................vii

Contents.............................................................................ix

1 A BOLT FROM THE BLUE...........................................1

2 THE VISA RUN TO LAOS............................................13

3 THE DEATH OF A NEIGHBOUR.................................27

4 THE FRUIT GARDEN...................................................39

5 ONE HUNDRED DAYS.................................................53

6 THE FAMILY BUSINESSES........................................65

7 SCHOOL SUMMER HOLIDAYS.................................77

8 SONGKHRAN...............................................................89

9 AYR'S BUSINESS PLANS............................................109

10 TOPPING OUT............................................................119

11 RISING PROSPERITY FOR BAAN SUAY?.............131

12 HIGH SOCIETY..........................................................137

13 LOCAL FALANG COMMUNITY...............................145

14 ANOTHER ONE BITES THE DUST..........................155

15 IN SICKNESS AND IN HEALTH...............................165

16 A TREE FALLS ND TIME STANDS STILL..............177

17 THE BUSINESS TRIP.................................................185

18 CRAIG'S BOOK...........................................................201

19 WOOLLEN WEDDING ANNIVERSARY.................209

20 THE PARTY SEASON BEGINS..................................219
21 A CHANGE IN FORTUNE..........................................231
22 THE SANUK EMPLOYMENT AGENCY.................243
23 OPERATION 'SALVAGE'............................................257
24 CHRISTMAS AND NEW YEAR.................................269
25 MAYA - ILLUSION...................................................279
GLOSSARY....................................................................293
THE LADY IN THE TREE............................................295
ABOUT THE AUTHOR.................................................309
Other Books by Owen Jones.......................................313

# 1 A BOLT FROM THE BLUE

Lek was waiting in Craig's study.

She had been building up the courage for this moment for days and at the precise moment that she had chosen to do it, he had gone to the toilet. She knew that if he didn't get back soon, she would be in tears before she could tell him her news.

She heard the flush go, so she steeled herself, but then the shower started. He would have to pick just this moment to have a shower too, she thought, but to be fair, he didn't know that she wanted to speak to him. They spoke so seldom to each other these days.

Lek started to dust his desk with her handkerchief and tidy his bits and pieces for something to distract her, but she could feel the tears welling up in her eyes already. What the Hell was he doing in there?

She went into the kitchen and poured Craig his second daily cup of coffee, took it back into the office, cleared a space for it among the clutter on his desk and carefully put it down.

Clack! The bolt was thrown on the bathroom door with the sound of a rifle being cocked.

As he came into the office moments later, he was surprised to see Lek standing there – she would normally have left the house hours ago to embark on her quotidian routine tour of friends for coffee and then lunch.

"Hello, telak, how are you this morning?" He kissed her on the temple and sat down. "Thanks for the coffee. Just what I need."

That was it, she was crying. Tears flowed down her face although unaccompanied by any sounds of sobbing at all.

"Oh, Craig, my darling! I am so unhappy... I think that I must go back to Pattaya and start work in Daddy's Hobby again, if Beou will have me. I am so sorry, my dear."

"I don't understand... 'if Beou will have you'. We have talked about your going to the city to get a job. The costs of our living in a city would outweigh what you could earn..."

"No, dear. I don't mean that we go to Pattaya... I mean that I go alone. I can live in a cheap room; share with other girls, like I did before. You... you cannot come with me. You must stay here..."

"What? You are telling me that you want to go back to Pattaya to work in a bar and that I should just sit here and wait at home?"

"Yes, but not wait... I will not come back... You can stay here... get a divorce.... go... wherever you like. You can find a new lady, a good lady to take care of you and I will... I don't know what I will do, but it will be without you. I am so sorry."

Once she had spoken, Lek regained her composure and the tears ceased to flow, but as the magnitude of what Lek has just said sank in, Craig began to cry.

It had been so unexpected. He had seen no signs. Not a dicky bird. He looked up at Lek, who was calmly staring back into his watery eyes.

"But why, Lek? What has brought this on now? I just don't understand."

"I don't know where to start, Craig, but I have been unhappy for some time. I expected more than this. I thought... I spent ten years waiting for my hero to rescue me and all the time I worked and put up with crap, but worked on and dreamed of a better life. Then I met you and I thought that my dreams had come true... I am not saying this well. It is not your fault, but I expected more and I want more than.... than this.

"We have been together for about eight years and married for five or six years, but I am poorer now than when I was working. I know that that it is not your fault, Craig, you work hard, but... well, you know, we have nothing and I don't want to live like that.

"Soom has been at university for a year now and it costs... I want my daughter to go to university and I cannot see how we can afford it on the money you earn. I tried to better myself too… I went back to school, but there is no work for people like me here in Baan Suay. If we had a car, maybe I could get a job somewhere near, but... not have.

"I do not have a choice, Craig. My family means everything to me and my daughter more than all that put together. I am so sorry."

Craig thought before replying, his tears had also dried up, "So, I do not count as family after eight years? How long does it take to become a member of your family if you're not born Thai? You know that I gave up my friends and my family to come here – or at least I put them after you... and now you are saying 'bye bye'? I can see that you want Soom to have a better life, so do I, but you also know that I sit here working for fifteen hours a day, while you go out and socialise or whatever."

"I am not blaming you, my dear. You did a very brave thing to come to try to help me and my family, but it has not worked out and now we must move on. I am very sorry."

"Way! I did not come here to rescue you and help your family, I came here because I loved you and thought you loved me. Helping your family was secondary to me. I always told you that I would do whatever I could to help your family and I have, not that they have ever asked for anything."

"Yes, I know, but I did not understand the differences between falang and Thai then, same as you did not understand. It was just a big accident..."

"What? Us falling in love was a 'big accident'? My coming over here, building a house that I will never own and working fifteen hours a day for eight years is just a 'big accident'?

"Lek, Lek, Lek, you hurt me now very much..."

"OK, lovely accident, but now my daughter must have money and I don't have. You have?... No? So I must go get. Or can you go get? If you cannot, I must. My mother cannot give, my family cannot give. You think that Soom must work on weekends and at night? She cannot make enough money in a hamburger bar to pay for university, so what you want her to do? Work in a bar same me before?

"I kill someone first. I steal from someone first... but I go to work first and kill and steal later... If you have a good idea, Craig, please tell me, because I don't want to go away again."

Now they were both crying and Craig stood up to hug his wife, his mind racing with possibilities to save their marriage.

After a few moments, Lek pulled away, "I am sorry, Craig, but it is no good getting close and crying. Something has to be done and if I am going to go away, this is not helping either of us. You understand why I must do this and I understand that you cannot help me.

"I will leave in two days. Do you want me to move out now?"

"No, no, not yet, Lek... I think that you ought to at least tell me the costs and the shortfall. I have never asked you because you always seemed to have everything in hand and now you hit me with this! Or do you actually want to go?"

"I do not lie to you, my husband, but it is true that I do not, or have not always told you the truth one hundred percent. I tried to many times, maybe every time in the beginning, but the language was between us and … well, it was easier not to.

"When I worked in Daddy's Hobby, I did lots of things that I did not want to do because I had to do them. I do not want to say any more about that unless you ask me and that is your right, I think.

"Anyway, I saved some money for Soom's education. Goong also left me 500,000 Baht when she died four or five years ago. I gave some of it to her family, but kept most of it.

"I don't have much of it left now. I was bored here for years with nothing to do and gambled a lot of it away on cards. I paid Soom's university fees last year and I have supplemented the money that you gave me for food for several years.

"Now, I cannot pay Soom's university fees when they come up next year and cannot buy her the clothes, books and laptop that she needs right now to be comfortable with her studies. I don't want her to look poor in university! She is the first person in my family to go to university and I want to give her every chance.

"That may mean losing you... but I will do it, if I have to, my darling, because I don't know what else I can do."

A few tears escaped her eyes, but she quickly wiped them away with her hand.

Craig was looking down at the beautifully-tiled floor, feeling like a total failure.

"So, you have paid the fees for now, right?" he said not meeting her eyes. "When do you need more money for Soom?"

"About six months. I pay university fees two times a year, but I give Soom money for her room and living every month."

"So you have six months?"

"No, I must start working now to give Soom money every month and then more fees in six months. If I wait, it is too late."

"OK, Lek... I wish that you had brought this up before, but, please give me a few hours to think about the problem, before you do anything quickly. Let's say that you have... two weeks, eh? Can you wait two weeks?"

Lek nodded and put her hand on his shoulder, "Sure, I can wait two weeks."

Craig was still shell-shocked. He put his hand to hers and patted it a few times, slowly. "I wish you had told me your problem before, Lek, I really do. Now, it's hurry, hurry, hurry, but thanks for... Er, well, we have two weeks, eh? ... What are your plans for today?"

"It has taken me days to say this... I don't have any plans now. Do you?"

"No, but I know that right now, work is not the answer... Why don't you go off to your mother's and I'll have a think?"

Lek was glad of the excuse to get out and be alone, and, having recovered somewhat from the initial shock, so was Craig.

After Lek had left, he finished his cold coffee in one, packed up his laptop and went to the shop where he did a lot of his thinking. The office was for slog work, but Nong's shop was for deep cogitation, usually over a few ice-cold beers. Watching the people in the village coming and going, carrying out their daily lives had always had a calming, yet inspirational effect upon him.

He sat down at the one table outside the shop and waited for Nong to notice him. He had been drinking at Nong's shop for eight years, but they still could not talk to each other in any meaningful way. Nong appeared not to have an aptitude for English and Craig had spent most of his time trying to earn money rather than learn Thai.

As he was staring out before himself, he heard Nong say, "Hello Mr. Craig, how are you today?" in Thai.

"Sabaai dee, kap - I'm fine thanks. Khun duay, mai? You too?"

"Yes, thank you. The beer is very cold today."

Nong always said that, but then the beer was always cold too.

Craig slouched in the bench seat and stretched his feet out in front of himself. He thought with a smile, that if he smoked, this would be a two-pipe problem, as Sherlock Holmes would have said.

"Why hadn't she mentioned it before? Why the sudden crisis? The real bottom line was, if she believed in karma, as she insisted she did, why did she think that she could change her daughter's karma?" It did not make sense now, although Lek's news had hit him like a bullet.

The problem was that Lek seemed to be sure that her only way forward was to go back to work in a bar. So, whether she was right or wrong in her religious philosophy, she would probably leave him in fourteen days.

Craig knew that Lek had an iron will. If that was what she had said she would do, that was what she would do, unless there was a very good reason not to. And the only reason that was good enough was money, so he needed a supply of money.

Or he needed to shed the chains that held him and Lek together – he needed to stop loving her.

Money or love?

That was the dilemma.

Lek had already decided that she would choose money, although not for entirely selfish reasons. Selfishness was in there though, he was sure. He knew that she would not be able to bear the shame of having to withdraw Soom from university for lack of funds.

Although that was the mechanics of the situation, it did not help his predicament. He loved Lek, but he was being offered an honourable way out. No-one would blame him for cutting and running now. Lek had told him that he was on his own.

Craig wondered for a little while whether Lek was offering him this easy exit because she had found someone new, but he dismissed the idea as much for lack of evidence as the fact that it would have hurt him too much to countenance it. He believed that Lek was genuinely concerned about her daughter's future and that helped him with the next choice, which was whether he should stay or go.

That would take another beer. It was not that he didn't want to stay. It was more a question of whether this problem would erupt again over an unrelated issue like Soom's first home, Soom's first car, Soom's babies, when she had them, which she inevitably would. Soom had been brought up by her grandmother as had Lek and he knew that Lek was looking forward to the role in her turn.

Craig, however, was not, yet the likelihood of it coming to pass was only three or four years away.

Nong saw the empty bottle and swiftly brought another one.

The ultimate decision was between selling everything that he had left in the UK, looking after Soom's children and staying with Lek in the village that he had come to call home or to call it a day and move on.

It was a tough one.

∞

Lek had gone to her Mum's house, which was just over the lane from their place, less than half-way to Nong's shop. She hadn't discussed her predicament with anyone yet, because so much depended on Craig, but she was ready to bite the bullet and go back to work if things worked out that way.

She was prepared to accept her own bad Fate, but she was not prepared to allow Fate to affect Soom's future, if she could do anything about it.

If Craig fell by the wayside, then so be it. The ball was in his court now. She had given him an out and a two-week period to come up with a solution. There was nothing more to do than steel herself again and wait for what her Karma would throw at her. She did care about Craig, but she cared more about Soom and she cared nothing for herself.

After the dreams she had had for and the nightmares she had had about Soom's future over the last eighteen years, Lek was not about to leave anything to something as intangible as Fate. Her daughter might not be clever enough to pass the examinations, that was something else, but she would sit them, shortage of money notwithstanding.

She sat with her mother, but her mother could see that she was troubled, so she cut and peeled some fruit for them both and pretended to be busy until her daughter made the first move.

"What would you think if I moved to Bangkok, Mum, to be closer to Soom if she needs me? I think that I can be more use there than here now. What do you reckon?"

"I reckon that that is your decision, Lek, but what does Craig think about it? He is your husband and therefore the one you should be asking this question, not me."

"Yes, I know, but... I'm just not sure..."

"I never followed you around when you were growing up. Did I do wrong? Why do you think that you have to be at your daughter's side and not your husband's?"

"Soom has her own mistakes to make like we all did and still do – it is part of growing up. Will you be there when she meets her first lover too?"

"I would like to be, yes! And if he's not good enough I'd..."

Lek could see her mother's smiling eyes although no mirth showed around her mouth.

"You can only do what you can do. You could not be here for the first part of Soom's life, but that is not so bad. I did my best and you were here for the last eight years. Soom is a good, level-headed, intelligent girl, now is the time to give her some headroom – let her practice what she has learned – don't keep her hemmed in.

"She may start to think that you think that she's stupid and you don't want that do you? Not when she is in a big Bangkok university with all the rich kids. They will give her enough complexes already.

"What is your true concern?"

"Money, Mum, if I am honest. I want the university fees for the full, four-year term of the course in my bank account right now, so that I know that money will not stop her staying at university. I want to see it, in a bank book."

"Yes, I see. We would all like enough money in the bank to be safe, but that is not how it is for working class people like us, unfortunately. What does Craig have to say about it all?"

She didn't want to say that she hadn't consulted him or that she was thinking seriously of going back to work, so she said, "He doesn't want to live in Bangkok. Nor do I really, since I don't know anyone there except Chalita and her husband and I couldn't just hang around with them all the time. Sis has her own life to lead. Maybe I could live in Pattaya, it's only an hour or so away.

"Craig doesn't think we can afford to live in a city and he's probably right. I would have to find a job to pay the rent and most of the university fees..."

"I see," said her mother slowly. "Like that is it? How old are you now? Thirty-nine, forty? Not old certainly, but getting old to be doing some types of job, don't you think? Your job opportunities would be limited by your qualifications, lack of experience and age, I imagine. What sort of work did you have in mind?"

"I don't know Mum. I only know bar work and basic bookkeeping. Perhaps I could get a job as a cashier in a bar, or a receptionist in a hotel or working the till in a shop."

"Don't you need qualifications to be a bookkeeper these days? I think you do, unless your family gives you a job. Have you spoken to Beou about it?"

"No, not yet. I just told Craig and he's gone to Nong's to think about it and get drunk, I suppose. He took it rather badly although I did kind of hit him with it out of the blue."

"It is a shock to me, I can't imagine what he is going through. He gave up everything to come here to be with you. All his friends, his family, his connections... and now you are dumping him. Not a very nice prospect, is it? Now that he's spent most of his money too. It makes you look heartless, my dear, although I know you are only thinking about the security of Soom's future.

"However, you are married now and you and Craig must work as a team. This may sound like your concern alone, but it is not. We might not be able to help you financially, but we would miss you if you left again. It has been so..., so homely, like the good old days, having you around again for the last eight or nine years.

"Then there is Soom. Have you asked her about your idea of moving down with her? Perhaps she was looking forward to a lot more freedom. That is one of the perks of going away to study, isn't it? To learn about life in the 'real world', learning to stand on your own two feet? And she'll have you hanging around criticising her every mistake.

"If you want the advice of an old woman, I would say not to abandon the people who love you the most. Look for ways that we, or you and Craig can sort this problem out together. Talk to him properly, don't just tell him 'this is how it is going to be...'. He has his pride too and if you push him into a corner, he may leave you and I think that you would regret that sooner or later. Probably sooner too.

"Soom would miss Craig too. Well, we all would. We have all become fond of him and his funny little ways. He's a breath of fresh air sometimes."

"Do you think that I should go to him now, Mum?"

"That is up to you, Lek, but maybe it is better if he thinks things through on his own for a little while longer. Give him an hour longer and that will give you time to think what to say to him and cook him something nice. What is his favourite? Oh, yes, Paneng. Put some of your love into a Paneng for him and if he's not back by the time it's ready, take him a bowl to the shop."

"Thanks, Mum, you always know what to say just at the right moment... whereas I, well I just rush in and... Do I get that from Dad? I'll give it a shot. Do you fancy some curry too? I'll make enough for all of us."

∞

Craig was well into his fourth pint when Lek appeared at his side. He actually smelled her coming before he saw her, or at least he had caught a whiff of his favourite Thai meal being cooked somewhere near by.

"Hello, telak. I have brought you something to eat. You not eat all day and drinking with no food is no good." As soon as she had mentioned drinking and an implied criticism, she regretted it.

"Who cares? Go to Bangkok, then you won't have to watch, will you?"

"I did not mean anything, my dear, honestly. May I sit down and join you? I think I need a few beers too."

"I don't need a few beers, I want a few beers... Sure sit down, what do you want? A Leo? Nong! Can I have a Leo, a glass, some ice and another Chang, please?"

Lek was unwrapping her parcel of food and two dishes that already had servings of white, fluffy rice in them. She passed the bowl of curry, a bowl of rice and a spoon to Craig, so that he could serve himself first in the traditional way.

"Thank you. It smells very nice. Thanks, Nong. Cheers, my dear, bottoms up! When are you off? Oh, yes, in two weeks..."

"I want to talk to you about that, Craig. I am so sorry that I sprang it on you so suddenly like that. It must have been a terrible shock. I should have been more... more subtle. Is that the right word?"

"Well, it's one of them and you certainly were not it."

"Yes, I know and I am sorry." She put some more curry into Craig's bowl before taking a little for herself. "You understand the problem though, despite

10

my inept way of putting it, so I have come to you now for advice. You have more experience in money matters than I. I am only a blunt farm girl at heart, what do you think that we could do together as a family to solve this crisis?"

Craig knew that he was being buttered up, but he also knew that it was Lek's way of apologising. It was very rare for her, or any Thai for that matter, to actually say the word 'sorry' and she had said it at least six times that day already – she preferred to show it in deeds.

"I know how important Soom's education is to you. I know how much you blame your own previous circumstances on your own lack of a formal education and I know that you don't want the same for Soom. An education with papers – qualifications – is like a guarantee. I know you think all that and I agree with you.

"So, I propose using my visa guarantee money to help you and Soom. That takes the pressure off for now. It means that I will not get a twelve-month visa extension next month, but maybe it's time we had a holiday anyway. We could go to Laos – Vientiane – for a holiday and pick up a three-month visa while we're there. I have a few ideas for replacing the visa money, but there is no rush for that. How much do you need right now for Soom?"

"I give her twelve thousand Baht every month for expenses. Later I will need sixty thousand, but not right now. In six weeks. I have most of that money, but then I have no reserves for if there is a problem. That is what worries me."

"Yes, OK, Lek. Tell Soom that you will transfer the money into her bank account on Monday and in the meantime, we can start planning our holiday to Laos. Cheers! I mean it, cheer up. We both need to."

Lek felt a lot happier now that the foreseeable problem had been sorted out. She had a year to find next year's payment and she still had fifty thousand in the bank.

Craig could see that the storm had passed but the sky was definitely still very overcast.

# Maya - Illusion

# 2 THE VISA RUN TO LAOS

Vientiane, the capital of Laos was not actually all that far away, as the crow flies, but getting there was a very different story unless one flew, which Lek and Craig decided against for financial reasons. Lek took the bus into Phitsanulok with one of her girlfriends to buy the bus tickets the day before they were about to leave. This too was not a long journey, but it could easily take six hours to get there and back. Lek liked to take a friend so that they could make a day of it – do some shopping and eat lunch somewhere nice. This was the plan for the day also.

Lek and Craig had been getting on a lot better since he had given her a hundred thousand Baht – a quarter of the money that he needed to keep in a Thai bank in order to qualify for a twelve-month visa extension. It troubled him, but at least his 'family' was stable again for a while and everyone was happy or to be accurate: Soom was ecstatic, Lek appeared happy and Craig was pretending to be happy.

Lek had postponed her plans to go back to work indefinitely, which was a relief to Craig, although he was all too aware that he had had to pay her a hundred thousand Baht to keep her. Not an ideal arrangement, but it did give him time to think about what to do next and he did feel that the two ladies in his life had earned the right to a year's stability, even if he did decide to leave them high and dry the following year.

There was no question about it, Craig was feeling terribly hurt that Lek had been prepared to leave him at two days' notice after they had been together for eight years. He just didn't know what to do about it just yet and he wanted to help Soom stay in university. The kid had never had much and was genuinely nice. He often wondered whether Lek had been like that before going to Pattaya. He knew that she was a very popular woman, she often seemed to be the life and soul of the party, but she was often a different person when they were alone. Especially the last couple of years. Maybe she had grown bitter through disappointment, but disappointment with what? With him?

He had always done his best and no-one had ever suggested otherwise. When people left for the fields at seven or seven-thirty in the morning, his office light was always on and when they went to bed at nine, ten or eleven at night, his light was still burning. All the neighbours knew that and Lek had said she was very proud that he was such a hard worker. But it was true that the long hours had not translated into a good salary.

He had spent all his saving and everything he had earned keeping the three of them together and now it seemed that Lek had been topping up the house-keeping money with her own savings too.

He could think of only one thing to do: sell the flat in his home town of Barry, South Wales and live off that. He and Lek had been hoping to keep the flat for their retirement. It was not worth a lot of money, but if it had continued to rise in value for ten years, it would have seen him out and left Lek with a few million baht too.

Now it would have to go and there would be no welcome boost to the retirement fund for either of them, unless Fate pulled its fickle finger out.

It began to dawn on him that Lek had been trying to get him to sell the house, so that she wouldn't have to go back to work. It was possible, because it would have been out of character for Lek to ask anyone to do anything as momentous as sell a house just to help her. She was far too independent for that. The more Craig thought about it, the more it made sense that that was what Lek had wanted all along.

∞

Lek and her friend Su waited until nine for the eight o'clock bus and so arrived at the bus station at ten-thirty. They had bought the two bus tickets ten minutes later and had about four hours to enjoy themselves before the next bus went there way. Lek made it clear that she would have to get some money from an ATM.

"I don't have much money on me, I'm afraid, but Craig gave me a hundred thousand the other day, so we can take some of that, go for lunch – on me of course – and then we'll have a look around the shops."

Su was pretty much in awe of her friend and always had been, but a hundred thousand Baht was about nine months salary to her, so this was very impressive stuff.

"Let me see... we can spend five thousand today and I'll take ten thousand to Laos with me. I've never been there, but they must have some decent shops, mustn't they? Have you ever been there, Su?"

"No, not me Pee Lek. I've only left the province once and that was to go to Bangkok for a few days when we got married fifteen years ago. We stayed with the old man's auntie. It was nice enough though. I haven't even got a passport and wouldn't know how to get one. Have you got a passport, Pee Lek?"

"Oh, yes, we went to Wales a few years ago, remember. I know Thais can enter Cambodia and Laos without a passport, but you can't fly to Europe without one."

Lek was not the sort of person to rub people's noses in her apparent good fortune, but she did like to milk situations for the maximum amount of face she could get out of them. It was a habit she had gotten into after returning from Pattaya with Craig, when her reputation in the village was at a pretty low ebb and so was her self-esteem.

They took seats in a nice but not posh restaurant, after all, Lek didn't want to embarrass her friend whose table manners left a lot to be desired.

"Order what you like, Su, it's my treat to say 'thanks' for coming with me today. It's so boring doing it alone. It's very reasonable here too – good food, but not expensive."

Su thought it was expensive, but she didn't say so as she had her pride too.

However, she referred to her friend as 'Pee', not because Lek was older than her – they had been in school together – but because Lek appeared to be of higher status than she was. In general, 'pee' means 'You are older than I and I am being polite', but it can also refer to status, although age confers status too. The 'opposite' is 'Nong', which is a polite way of referring to a younger person or someone of lower status.

∞

The first stage of the journey was to get from Baan Suay to the bus station. Lek hired one of her friends to take them at seven o'clock in order to catch the

VIP bus at nine. The driver took his wife and family in the back of the pick-up for a trip out to the big city, which they probably didn't do from one month to the next. Once at the bus station, Lek treated them all to a meal and paid the petrol money.

Displaying largesse was one of her favourite jobs – she would have made a great Santa Claus, if he had been a woman.

The next stage, was the actual six-hour bus ride to Udon Thani through the mountains, but as it would be dark, there was nothing to see. Lek had taken her travel-sickness pills as usual, because she suffered from even the shortest car journey. The only problem was that they tended to make her lose her mind for several hours. She was well aware of the problem and would tell Craig when they were working, effectively putting him in charge of her well-being until she came down off them.

Lek invariably fell asleep on long journeys so the tablets were only a problem when they had to change vehicles. As they passed through Loei, Lek popped up from under her travelling blanket and peered past Craig out of the window. She looked him in the face from a few inches away, rubbed her eyes and stared out of the window again.

"If I met someone from here I would not know what to call him," she said and flopped back in her seat.

"Do you mean: 'Do you mean that you don't know where are we?'" he asked.

"That's it," she replied.

And she was asleep again before he could tell her. He had often regretted not keeping a collection of the odd things that Lek had said and done while stoned on travel-sickness pills.

They arrived in Udon Thani shortly after three and had to wait two hours for the bus to Nong Khai, a city near the Laos border. That took an hour, so at six- fifteen, they took a twenty-minute taxi ride to the border.

Craig was leading Lek around, carrying his laptop and dragging their case, so he was relieved to find the customs channels virtually clear. They filled in the exit papers and went straight through to where they had to get another bus over the long 'Friendship Bridge' in order to cross the Mekong into Laos.

Then it was more faffing about with immigration and entry visas and a taxi to a hotel that Craig had booked on the Internet. Lao is very similar to Thai, so

Craig had no problem telling the taxi driver the name of the hotel, which was situated on the 'Water Front' in the centre of Vientiane.

They were stripping off, going for a shower in their room at ten a.m. After a journey of five hundred kilometres which had taken thirteen hours. Craig was shattered, but Lek was starting to come down. Craig decided to leave the visa for the following day.

They were both tired, hungry, thirsty and inquisitive, but they settled for setting the phone alarm for one o'clock and taking a nap. However, when one o'clock came, they were both raring to go outside and see what Vientiane was like. Lek had some preconceptions of Laos and had met many people from there, but Craig had no idea what to expect. Their first impression as they left the hotel was that it was very clean.

Old but clean, in the way that proud, poor people might wear old clothes and even have an old car, but keep them in the best possible condition. A lot of the street signs still bore their old colonial names in French, although Laos had been communist for decades. Lek was amused by the way Lao used the Thai language. She kept pointing differences out to Craig, who knew enough Thai to understand what she was talking about.

The only thing that Craig remembered about Laos was that it was the most bombed country of all time and that its mostly rural population of about six and a half million were still regularly finding landmines and packets of cyanide dropped by the Americans in the Seventies, so he was surprised to hear so many American accents there.

There were also a lot of French people, presumably tourists. Lek chose a restaurant-cum-bar within a hundred yards of the hotel and they sat down. Lek took the menu and made noises as she read it, Craig ordered a Beer Lao, which he had never tried before and a spa for Lek.

"I have no idea how hot this food will be, telak, so I will order two Thai dishes and some spare ribs for you. OK?"

"Yes, that's fine. Do you want to try this Lao beer? It's quite nice."

She took a sip and agreed.

"I'll wait for tonight or I'll be asleep again soon. I can't drink in the afternoons any more. It makes me too sleepy."

"You're getting old, that's what it is."

She knew it was true, but did not want to hear it.

"You can get a new lady if you want. Maybe a Lao lady and stay here..."

They both regretted it. It didn't take much to cause an argument these days. They both found it hard to talk together for more than fifteen minutes without one of them passing a snide comment or getting angry over the smallest thing. Conversation was like picking your way through a minefield. Craig often didn't say anything at all for fear of the consequences.

He wondered if Lek was going through an early menopause. He had heard that hormones in food were causing girls to become fertile earlier and women to become menopausal earlier too. Or at least, he thought that he had read it. He couldn't remember at that precise moment. Perhaps he had dreamed it. It made sense though. If women were born with all the eggs they would ever have and they started using them earlier, the supply would run out earlier too. It sounded feasible, but he had no idea really.

Maybe they had a million eggs and could never use them all up.

Or maybe they went off.

Lek was hoping that this vacation would be a second honeymoon. She didn't like to suggest it, but she was hoping that Craig would try to make it something romantic, something special. They had not decided how long they would stay, but they had both forgone birthday parties that month. Craig's on the 14th. had not been important, but Lek's fortieth on the 12th. had been a milestone.

It was just that the atmosphere had not been right, although the family had urged them to have a joint celebration, like they usually did. Thai Mothers' Day is also on the 12th, but they didn't even do much for that – just a small meal at Mum's. Surely everyone knew that they were going through a very rough patch.

The Seven-Year Itch a year early.

They had plenty of time – they could stay away as long as money allowed, but then they were sort of trying to spend less money, although they were not trying very hard and Craig had not mentioned being frugal on holiday.

She made up her mind to try to be extra nice to him and not find fault with everything he said. She looked up from the menu and smiled at him.

"I will have a glass of beer with you darling. Thank you."

She called the waiter and placed the order while Craig poured her a drink.

"Cheers! Have you noticed that they don't say 'Sawasdee, ka' here? They say 'Sabaidee' instead. I have noticed that they don't say 'ka' or 'kap' very often at all."

"I hadn't noticed the 'sabaidee', but I had noticed the 'ka' thing, because Thais put 'ka' or 'kap' on the end of most sentences..."

"That is because we are polite. There is nothing wrong with politeness..."

"I didn't say there was, did I? I just assumed it was a regional practice, like in the UK, Londoners say 'sir' more often than we do in Wales. It doesn't make them more or less polite. It's just their way. Maybe the communists made them drop 'ka' here because everyone is supposed to be equal, whereas in Thailand they are definitely not. You have a class structured society, like the UK does, with royalty and all that, but communist countries don't.

"Their class structure is built on party membership and having a good job in the civil service".

But Lek had already stopped listening. She didn't waste any time at all worrying or even thinking about things that didn't concern her or her family and she certainly didn't care about the social structure in Laos. She just could not understand why Craig was interested in just about everything, it seemed such a waste of time.

"I emailed my brother last night and asked him to put my flat on the market. If I am lucky, the tenant will buy it, so there might be a quick sale. Well, quick for Britain. British solicitors are not known for doing anything quickly. It could still take two or three months."

"But, I thought that you were keeping that for when we are older."

"Look, if I don't have money to eat and drink, I won't get a lot older, will I? Yes, I wanted to keep it for another ten years or so too, but things haven't worked out like that. I didn't create the recession. I couldn't predict that people would spend less on the Internet or that the Thai baht would become nearly forty percent stronger or that inflation would hit Thailand as it has. Even you say how quickly prices are rising in Thailand. Food has shot up, hasn't it?"

"Yes. I know it is not your fault. It's just that I thought we would have the house to sell when we are older... Now we will be poor when we are old. That is not something nice to look forward to. I will have thirty years to think about how poor I will be when I am old."

"And me! Not only you! I used to have a house and in three months I will not. Jeez, woman listen to yourself... I, I, I, poor me. What about me? It's my house you will be eating for the next ten years, don't forget that. Don't be so bloody selfish."

"But you can go home and the government will take care of you, my government will not take care of me. I will be working until the day I die. It is something that I have wanted to talk to you about for a long time, because it worries me."

"Did you think of that when you were playing cards all day?"

And they were fighting again already. Both seemed to realise it at the same time, because they both fell silent. Craig pretended to read the label on the beer bottle and Lek looked around the walls. The waitress bringing the food broke the awkward silence, giving them a chance to try again.

"One more beer, please," said Craig. "How is the food, Lek?"

"Do you want to try? It is alright. Not so hot as I like. A bit boring."

Craig took the proffered spoonful of curry and rice in his mouth.

"It's OK. Not as hot as you like, I know, but it is all right for me. Maybe they make it like that here because of all the foreign visitors."

"What about all the Thai foreigners? Don't we count? I have heard before that Lao food is not as hot as Thai food, now I know that it is true."

Craig thought that it would be hard for any country's food to be hotter than Thailand's, but he judged it prudent not to say so at that juncture in time.

After the meal, they walked up and down the Waterfront for a few hours. Lek bought a parasol to shield her skin from the sun and then they went back to the hotel for a rest.

Lek lay on the bed, watched TV, dozed and pretended to be dozing, while Craig checked his web sites, answered his emails and wrote an article on travelling to Laos for his web site on Thailand. She didn't want to talk lest it led to more squabbling, especially since they had had such a pleasant walk along the bank of the Mekong.

It seemed to her that everything that she had done had been for nothing. Nearly twenty years before, she had gone to work in Pattaya because the bank was threatening to foreclose on the farm, due to a loan that her father had taken out on it, but now that she needed money, where was the farm to help her?

She had worked in the sex tourism industry for ten years and actually saved money for her daughter's education, but she had squandered it playing cards. Well, not all of it, but most. Her friend Goong had left her a lot of money, but now it was all gone and with nothing to show for it.

She had relied on Craig to save her and to be fair to him, he was doing, and always had done his best, but they were still broke and now he was having to sell their pension fund ten years early. Again through no fault of his own, but it did now mean that they always would be hard up.

Nothing that she had hoped for and dreamed about was going to come about, except that Soom would go to university and sit the exams. It was something, but it was only a small fraction of what she had wanted. The books were right, it was all Maya. Hopes and dreams were all illusion. There was nothing you could do to change your future. Nothing helped except your behaviour towards others. People got what they deserved, they got their Karma. The rest was all smoke and mirrors – Maya.

What had she achieved? She wanted to cry, but it was beneath her dignity. Not many people and certainly not many things could make her cry.

Not any more, not after ten years in Pattaya.

She looked at Craig's back. Eight years older. Eight years of slaving over a machine working on a medium that would cease to exist if there were no electricity. She couldn't even remember how many web sites he had now. There was something sad about that. She ought to know what her husband was working so hard at, but it was all pointless too since it was not paying for their lifestyle, which was not lavish by any Western standards. She would never have the jet-set lifestyle that she had thought having a foreign husband ensured.

She had been so stupid and if it wasn't for Soom, she would happily be dead. Her mother could take care of Soom, as she always had and if she faked an accidental death, her life assurance would pay Soom a million baht, which would see her through university and buy her a good job.

That was something else that Craig didn't know about yet. It was one of those embarrassing things that Thais only discussed with Thais. They were ashamed to admit them to foreigners. Corruption. No matter how well Soom did at university, she would never get a very good job if she didn't have the money to buy her one.

And they didn't have any money and they didn't have any reserves or a pension pot. Soom would discover bitter disillusionment early in life, when she realised that university had ensured her an office job, but not a good one. There were several glass ceilings that only money could smash and they didn't have any and never would have.

She was too old to go back to 'work' and earn good money now, but in five or ten years, she would have no chance at all of working in Pattaya. If she were going, she would have to go now or forever hold her peace. Could she rely on Craig to get her out of this awful situation? She would truly be happy to go to sleep now and not wake up again.

Craig woke Lek up at seven o'clock as it was getting dark outside.

"What's the matter? Why are you waking me up? Oh! I forgot. We're in Laos. What time is it?"

"Seven. There are a lot of people walking around outside. Shall we go out and have a look? Are you hungry?"

"Yes, OK. I'll just brush my teeth. Five minutes."

"OK, Lek. Say, don't you think we should get some Lao money, some 'Kip'? We paid in Baht this afternoon, but I think they just round everything up when you pay in Baht. Let's get five thousand Baht's worth and see how it goes. I can pay for the hotel by credit card. I don't know about the visa. What do you think?"

He could hear her gargling in the toilet. When she came into the room, he asked what she thought of the plan.

"I couldn't hear a word of what you were saying! I only heard 'blub, blub, blub, blub, blub'. You knew I was brushing my teeth, why were you talking to me? What did you say?"

He told her again.

"Yes, OK. We can get some Kip. You have very many Kip for one Baht, I think. You want to get now, tonight?"

"Sure, as soon as possible, eh? Do you have my new Lloyds ATM card? The green one they sent me last month?"

"Yes." She rummaged in her bag and handed it to him.

"And the PIN – you know the number – security."

"I don't have. You not give to me. You have."

Craig wanted to blame Lek, but he couldn't remember having given it to her. She might be right, but that made the card useless.

"Oh, shit. We cannot take money from the UK bank. Do you have your card?"

"No. I not take any gold or cards with me, I think it is not safe in Laos, because I do not know here."

"Right... so we cannot get any money from the banks and we are on holiday in Laos. Great! I'm not blaming you... I am just saying. I am thinking aloud. How much money do you have?"

"Thai money?"

"What else? Do you have any Chinese?"

Lek was already counting out some notes. "A little more than seven thousand Baht."

"OK, the visa costs nineteen hundred, I believe, so we have money to last for now, but we either have to go home early or.... This is bloody daft, eh? Who goes abroad with no money, eh? Only us! Come on, let's go out. We can change a thousand Baht and enjoy ourselves. We can deal with it all tomorrow. Are you ready? Come on then, my dear."

They turned left out of the hotel and walked the three hundred yards to the bureau de change that they had spotted earlier in the day. The exchange rate was two hundred and fifty-one Kip to the Baht and Lek was as delighted as a child at Christmas to be given a quarter of a million Kip for her one thousand Baht note.

She felt very rich and very superior, which were sensations that she was not accustomed to.

"Look at all this money, Craig! Look!"

"Yes, Lek, it's a thousand Baht in Kip. The numbers don't matter, it is the value that counts."

But she wasn't listening again, just counting the notes over and over.

"Where do you want to eat, dear?" asked Craig.

"Oh, we can eat anywhere with this sort of money," she replied. "How about that open-air restaurant on the pavement near the hotel? The food looked very nice and they had the big prawns that you like."

So, they walked back towards the hotel and sat at an empty table in the restaurant area. When the waiter came, Craig ordered two beer Lao's, ice and a glass. When that had arrived, Lek went with the waiter to select the food that she wanted cooked for them.

Lek was in her element, but Craig was feeling rather stupid for not having checked his ATM cards.

The food that Lek picked was fit for a king. They had a dozen huge prawns, a large, steamed, pink river fish, spare ribs, salad and shellfish. Just as they were struggling to get to the end of it all, Craig ordered another round of beer. The waiter looked at his watch and said:

"It is nine o' clock. We close now. Everything in Vientiane close now, but you can have one more, if you are quick. You must finish before I clean everything away... OK?"

Craig agreed. Lek and Craig stared at each other.

"Surely, the capital city of Laos doesn't close at nine thirty, Lek?"

"That is what he said. Look around you. Lights are going out, people are going home."

Lek spoke to the waiter when he returned with the beers and the bill. He confirmed that the city did indeed close at nine thirty by order of the government. Lek was not all that bothered, because she normally went to bed at nine thirty anyway, but she was shocked when she saw the bill of a hundred and eight-five thousand Kip.

∞

They rose at seven thirty, showered and went down for breakfast. There were both Thai and 'European' styles, so they were both happy with that. Then they went back to the room, picked up their paperwork for the visa and went back down. Another surprise awaited them- they needed sixty thousand Kip to get to the embassy and back in a broken-down, tuk-tuk motorbike taxi, so they had to change another thousand Baht. Lek was not so impressed with the two hundred and fifty thousand Kip she collected after seeing how fast it could run through her fingers.

At the Thai embassy, Craig collected his form, filled it in, stuck his two photos on it and waited for his number to be called. When it was, he went up to the counter. The immigration official looked over his document quickly and said:

"Marriage certificate."

Craig called for Lek, who came running, as she hated to keep officials waiting. They talked. Lek looked in her bag. Then said something and the official said:

"Next!" A man tried to take Craig's place at the counter.

"Hey! Stop pushing! Wait your bloody turn! Excuse me, what is the problem with my application?"

"Your wife no have marriage certificate and no have house book. I cannot gib you non-immigrant 'O' visa. Next!"

"No, wait! So what can I do about it?"

"You can go back and get all your papers I need. Next!"

"But that will take a day or more..."

"Not my problem. I must see papers. You not have papers. What can I do? Next!"

"Isn't there anything I can do? How about if I change my application for a two-month tourist visa?"

"No can do, I know what you want now already. I cannot do that. Next!"

"This is crazy!"

"Send your wife home get. You can go too or wait here in Vientiane, now please go. Next!"

Craig turned to glare at the man who was hovering behind him. He backed off a little.

"OK, I can accept fax of papers this one time, because I see you have long visa before. Now go. Next!"

Craig bumped the next guy in the queue as he exited the line.

"Isn't it bloody marvellous? Why do I need to prove I'm married to get that visa. Your ID has your name 'Williams' on it; your passport has bloody 'Williams' in it. It's not a very common name in Thailand, is it? Do they think I searched Thailand for a Thai woman called Williams so I could get a ninety-day visa instead of a sixty-day one? Jesus! That makes me so angry. Well, now we are stuck here. Tomorrow is Friday, so if we hand the forms in then, we won't get them back until Monday. OK, back to the hotel.

"And we don't have any money! Shit, shit, shit, shit, sodding shit!"

Back in their room, Lek phoned her mother to go into their house to get the documents and fax them to their hotel. Her mother was pretty worried about taking on such a hi-tech venture, but she assured Lek that she would get it done with someone's help. Meanwhile, Craig Skyped his friend in Barry, Blond Billy, and asked him to lend them £300 for a week or so. Billy agreed to wire the money care of the hotel.

The money actually arrived before the paperwork from Thailand, but they eventually had everything they needed and Lek went back to the bureau de change with $420 to exchange some of it for a million Kip. Holding a million Kip had as much effect on her as two hundred and fifty thousand had the day before.

In the afternoon, they went for a walk along the Mekong again and then back to the hotel. It was really too hot to do much and there didn't seem much to do anyway.

In the evening, they ate at a different, but similar outdoor restaurant and the bill at nine thirty was about the same. Lek concluded that Vientiane was a lot more expensive than Bangkok and if she could have gone home the next day she would have, but there was still the visa to get.

The visa application went smoothly enough, although the transaction could not be completed in one day. It has to be applied for on one day and collected the following business day, which meant staying until Monday. They both reckoned that they would have had enough of Vientiane by then to make going back home no hardship.

Lao people were friendly enough and Vientiane was easier for Westerners that most Thai cities including most areas of Bangkok, but there was so little to do and it was so expensive.

On Monday morning, they got up just in time not to miss breakfast, ate slowly and then checked out. They booked a taxi to the bridge but asked him to wait at the embassy first. The embassy opened for the collection of visas after lunch at one-thirty, so they had plenty of time to start their long-winded return trip home.

Sitting in the bus to Phitsanulok, both were analysing their 'holiday'. Both thought that it had gone well considering and both felt better for having spent so much time alone away from Lek's distractions in the village. As she felt the tablets kicking in again, Lek reached out under the blanket and took Craig's hand and he squeezed it back.

# 3 THE DEATH OF A NEIGHBOUR

Lek and Craig both benefited from their trip to Laos in that their relationship grew closer and they started spending some time with each other again. Craig still had to work all day, but Lek made a point of meeting him at Nong's for a couple of hours at five o'clock every day, whereas these meetings had dropped to once of twice a week over the previous year and even then Lek had spent most of the time on the phone talking to her daughter in Bangkok or her cousin in Pattaya.

Craig had actually wished she would stop coming, because he found it distracting and unsettling to have her talking loudly in a language he couldn't understand to people he couldn't see when he was out for a relaxing break between two long sessions of work. More than once he had reminded her that it was a mobile phone, so why didn't she 'walk over there' and chat to her family.

It hadn't helped their relationship any, but it had been at rock bottom anyway.

Now she was being 'nice' to him again, but he couldn't help wondering how long it would last. Craig was sure that either she was menopausal or worried about something and the 'something' could only be her daughter or money or both.

"How are your web sites doing, my dear?"

"I have a hundred and fifty-two now, but the global recession is still hitting them badly," he replied somewhat shocked at the sudden interest. This was probably the second time she had asked about his work in eight years.

"I'm thinking of scaling back to a hundred web sites or less, because I cannot write enough articles every month to keep them all looking fresh. At one five-hundred-word article a week for each site that would mean writing twenty-two articles a day or eleven thousand words a day. That is unsustainable..."

Craig looked up but he could see that he had lost her.

"If I am going to be writing... Lek, Lek! If I am going to be writing eleven thousand words a day for web sites, I might as well write a book, mightn't I?" he joked.

"Yes, dear. You could write a book on Thailand. Write some stories. Maybe they sell better than web sites."

"I was joking. I've never written a book in my life... I wouldn't know where to start. Writing five-hundred-word articles on interesting topics is easy enough, when you get into the swing of it. I can do five a day for a few days, but I can write three a day for ever. However, three a day means twenty-one a week which will only support twenty-one web sites, but twenty-one average web sites won't provide enough income to support us."

Craig loved to talk about his work, but no-one else in the village shared his interest and he never met anyone else. Or rarely, so whenever anyone showed the slightest interest, he tended to go over the top, as he was now. Lek tried to maintain a level of interest, but she had no idea what he was talking about.

"Darling, you know me. I care about people: my family and my friends, I know nothing about machines and computers. It just goes in this ear and out that one, but nothing sticks. I am stupid, I have no education. I never go high school and never go to university. My mother not have money to send me. That is why I want Soom to go. I don't want her stupid like me, I want her clever like you."

It always broke his heart to hear her talking about herself like that.

"You went back to school a few years ago, didn't you? I thought that was for high school."

"Yes, now, at the age of forty, I can prove that I am as clever as a sixteen-year-year old. Great! I am still twenty-four years behind. Do you think anyone wants to give a job to a forty year old woman with the brain of a sixteen-year-old? No, I am on the scrap heap. I am even not fit enough to work in the rice fields like women half my age again. My Mum is sixty-er, er... something and she can still work in the fields all day if she has to, but I would not last one hour and you would not last ten minutes."

She started laughing at the thought of him planting or cutting rice by hand. She found the mental image of Craig up to his ankles in mud hilarious. "I am sorry," she said with a hand before her mouth, "but when I think of you..., you standing in sloppy mud planting rice, complaining about your bad back and wanting a cold beer because there is no shade... Oh, my Buddha. You are very funny. Ha, ha, ha, ha, ha!

"You working with all the old ladies and they are working faster than you and you complaining and wanting a chair, a beer and an umbrella in the wet rice field... Oh, my Buddha."

It was nice to see her laugh again. She touched his hand, clinked glasses and put hers to her lips. At the last moment she had to put the glass down again as another mental image caused a laughing fit.

"Oh, I must tell my Mum later! I will tell her that you want to help her in the field next time, but she must take a chair and some beer for you." And she was laughing again. Craig didn't mind in the slightest being the butt of her jokes – anything to see her laugh again, He wished she would do it every day.

"Oh, Lek, that money we borrowed from Billy in Barry. I had forgotten all about it. Had you? Anyway, I sent it back to him by PayPal today and thanked him very much. He pulled us out of the shit there big time, didn't he?"

"Yes. How stupid we were. I liked Billy the first time we met him in O'Brien's. And the other guys we used to sit with on market day when it was freezing cold outside... Look at the time, Soom will be thinking that I have forgotten her."

At six o'clock Lek always phoned her daughter. It was their designated time; it was the time she should be arriving in her bedsit from university or 'school' as Craig called it. Lek would never demean such a respected establishment of higher education with the word 'school', although she had respect for schools in their place. She realised that Craig could be so flippant about university because he had attended one and familiarity breeds contempt, as they say, but she didn't like him using that term when referring to Soom's university.

Lek looked forward to phoning Soom every day, so took up her mobile and rang her.

"Hello, where are you now?" - the standard greeting - "Have you eaten yet? Good... Are you well? How did university go today? Good.... Good. Me? I'm fine. Yes, he's all right too. He's sitting here with me now, drinking beer. Soom says 'Hello'. He says 'Hello to you too'. What are you going to do tonight? Yes, that's right... Do your homework, read a bit, watch TV for a while and then early to bed

"Tomorrow is another day. You want to be fit and bright for every day in university. You have worked hard to get there, now you have to work hard to stay there. You will do that, I know you will..

"OK, yes, OK. Phone me if you need anything at any time of the night or day. We are well, don't worry about us. Gran is fine too. She sends her love. Yes, OK, thank you. We miss you too. Bye-bye for now. Bye...

"That was Soom. She says she misses us... and you. I mean including you. She is doing well though. I miss her too. I want to go down to see her. Maybe stay with her for a few days, what do you think?"

"If you stay with her in her bedsit, then I can't go. That's what I think, but I don't mind, if you want to go on your own. I can survive here alone, on my own, with absolutely no-one to talk to for two days, if that is what you want.

"I know how much you miss her. I don't mind, really! I'm only joking with you. Look, it's, er, Tuesday today, so why don't you go down on Friday morning, stay the weekend while she's off school and comeback on Monday morning?"

"University, dear. Soom finished school last year – nearly eighteen months ago. She does go in on Saturday morning for private lessons, but that is a good suggestion of yours. OK, I'll book a seat in the minibus and leave on Friday. Thank you for understanding, darling." She cupped her mouth and whispered the words 'I love you. Choop, choop.' "You would only be bored in Bangkok anyway. It's no good you coming, is it?"

It was true that Craig did not like big cities, but he said, "Yeah, right! I'd be bored rigid what with all those bars, girls, strip joints, A-Go-Go bars and everything. I mean... you get too much of that around here.... Enough to last a man a lifetime."

Lek thought he was joking, but even after eight years, she was rarely completely sure. They both had such different senses of humour and Thai humour was different from the British variety anyway. Probably Asian was different to European in general. So she put on a weak smile and studied his face.

"Only joking. I'm happy for you to go and I'm happy to stay here. All alone, while you're out going everywhere in Bangkok. Boring old Bangkok. While I live in up in Baan Suay, the only place I've ever lived without a pub."

Now she knew he was joking. Maybe speaking the truth in jest, but that was his way. He didn't mind her going and didn't mind staying at home.

"OK, thank you my dear. I'll let Soom have a shower and then ring her with the good news. I am really looking forward to it. Isn't it exciting? We haven't been separated for more than a few hours for eight years."

He had had his little joke, so he didn't push his luck. He just smiled back at her. He was wondering if he could get his friend Murray to come around and take him out in the car. He had never explored the local village 'bars' – if there were any.

Just as Lek was about to phone her daughter, Nong came running out.

"Lek! Lek! There has been an accident. Mrs. Ng just told me that a petrol tanker has knocked two local ladies off their motorcycle in the lane. One is dead and the other has less than a ten percent chance of pulling through. Who is it?"

"Oh, how awful! But how would I know? I've been sitting here for the last hour." She told Craig about the accident."

"But no-one knows who they are?"

"I think some people know, but we don't know," she replied, wondering whom she could phone to find out who the victims were.

Nong spoke up after making a phone call. It never took her long to know the local gossip, it was why she was always busy, people called in for groceries and to find out what was going on. In the absence of a local paper or radio station, Nong was the repository of all local knowledge.

"One was that young Mrs. Ma who lives... lived just round the corner. The one with two young children and another on the way. She's the one that died outright and the other one was your next-door neighbour, Joy. They'd been out shopping apparently and were coming back through the lane when BANG! Head on into a petrol tanker making deliveries around the villages.

"He was actually due here, but was redirected down the lane by road-workers. The driver is beside himself with grief. The doctor had to sedate him. Joy is in hospital, but she was dragged a little way by the truck so she's in a very bad way. They think she'll die. Just a ten percent chance of pulling through."

Craig couldn't follow much of the conversation, but he could see other women gathering at the shop to discuss it. When Lek started explaining to

Craig, Nong darted off, anxious to tell the others what she knew and maybe learn a few more details.

When Lek got up to join the other women, Craig slipped into the shop and helped himself to another Chang. He knew that there would be no decent service for at least an hour and he didn't mind helping out. Eagle-eyed Nong spotted him in her peripheral vision and nodded him her consent.

Craig was roused from his daydreams, by a collective sharp intake of breath, but he could guess what had happened.

When she had all the information there was to be had, Lek rejoined Craig. "Joy just died too. Isn't that just awful? Ma had two young children and was just pregnant with a third and Joy, well, she is or was a grandmother, but only fifty years old and looking after her daughter's baby... and her husband's not well. I know you don't like him much, but you used to get on well with Joy, didn't you?"

"Yes..., we never actually spoke because we couldn't, but when she saw me sitting here she always used to shout 'go home'. I used to like to think that she meant 'go home to your wife' and not 'go back to Britain'. She probably didn't know any other words in English. Yes, I liked her... she used to ask me to dance at parties, remember?"

"Yes, I liked her too. You realise what this means, eh? I won't be going to Bangkok this weekend. Not if they have the normal seven-day ceremony. Still, Bangkok will still be there next week, so no rush.

"Perhaps, Soom ought to come back to pay her respects. She has known Joy all her life. I must phone her now. Are you all right for ten minutes?" She inspected his bottle, "OK, I'll get you a fresh one first. I think I'll have one too. It's no good waiting for Nong, I'll get them myself."

As soon as Lek had sat down, she was back on the phone to Soom.

"Soom can't come back until Friday. She finishes early on Fridays and can cancel her..., what name did you say again? Her 'tutorial' on Saturday morning, then, if she goes back on Sunday afternoon, she won't miss any classes, so that's all right, isn't it? Maybe I could go back with her. Couldn't I?"

"Well, obviously you could, but you won't see much of her during the week and if you only get to see her every few months, why use up your visit so soon after she has come home? Why not leave it a month and then go down? That way you see her twice in two months. Sounds better to me."

"Yes, maybe you are right. We'll see what happens."

"Well, when Soom goes back, Joy's funeral will not yet be over, so that is another reason to put it off for a while. Look, I'm not trying to stop you going... I know that it is going to happen one day, but I want you to get the maximum effect from your visits. That is all. Think about it."

There was no longer a bristle of gossip among the twenty or so women gathered at the shop, they had become hushed. Talking in whispers out of respect for the double fatality. Two women, one in her twenties and one just turned fifty dead, killed not a hundred metres from the safety of their homes by a truck that shouldn't have been there, that had never travelled that route before. Two husbands and three children left behind and one baby dead with its mother, still unborn.

People talked in hushed voices about who or what had sent the petrol tanker to kill these women and wreck the peace of their families for months, years and decades to come. People talked of never going down the lane at night again lest they should come across the ghosts of Joy and Ma walking back and fore along that isolated lane doomed forever to keep trying to get home to their children.

When they left Nong's at seven o'clock it was already beginning to get dark. Lek clung to Craig's arm, petrified that she would meet Joy looking for someone to take care of her family in her absence. When they entered their garden, they could see the family gathering next door.

One group of men were putting out rows of chairs, erecting awnings and blocking the lane to cars, while another group were setting up the P.A. that would relay the monks' ceremony to those sitting outside and play the funeral music.

They had already brought Joy back from the hospital and half a dozen older women were preparing her body to lie in the refrigerated casket, which would be its final resting place for its last seven days on Earth.

"I want to go to Bangkok now, Craig. I am scared. What can I say to Joy, if I see her with her head smashed in and she asks me to help take care of her family?"

"She never hurt you when she was alive, did she? So why do you think she is going to try now?

"If you meet her, just say 'Hello' and if she asks you to take care of her family, tell you can't because you're going on holiday to Bangkok soon. I'm sure she'll understand. She's not stupid and has family nearby anyway. Advise her to ask them. Tell her I'm a handful."

"You are never serious. This is serious..."

"Hold on a minute. OK, I like to joke, I accept that, but I am being serous about Joy. If she asks you, just tell her that you are too busy to do a good job. Tell her to ask someone else. What's wrong with that? That is what you would have said if she had asked you yesterday when she was alive, so why not say it now? Nothing has changed except she hasn't got a body any more."

"Oh, don't say that. Oh, my Buddha. I won't sleep for a week until she's gone. I know it. Oh, my Buddha..."

"Look at it this way. With all the worry, sleepless nights and helping out next door, you will probably loose those extra pounds you have been putting on, won't you?"

"Oh, thank you very much. I'm scared and depressed and you call me fat!"

"Joke, my dear. Just a joke."

She tried to smile.

"But, it might work. Every cloud has a silver lining, so they say," he added as he nipped into his office.

Lek was truly worried about Joy's ghost, or 'Pi' in Thai. She had been to hundreds of funerals before but never because of such a violent, unexpected death involving a close neighbour and friend. She went next door to pay her final respects before the monks arrived at about seven thirty.

After the four monks had performed their duties for the first day, which took about thirty minutes, a rushed meal was passed around those who remained behind - about fifty people. It was a very quiet affair compared to average funerals – the whole village was in deep shock. Nobody liked to voice their thoughts about the evil spirit that had caused the petrol tanker to be in the lane and to kill, on its one and only re-routing down there, two women who had made that journey hundreds of times safely before.

Attendees at the funeral wanted to get home early in case there was an evil spirit lurking in the shadows.

When Lek went home at nine o'clock, she had a friend walk her up the drive to her front door even though it was only fifteen yards, the lights were on and

Craig was working in his office. He had never seen her that affected by a death – not even that of one of her best friend, Goong, six years before. Goong had died at an even younger age than Joy, but she had been ill for a while, accepted her Fate – even welcomed it - and had had time to sort out her affairs.

She hovered about in Craig's office, talking incessantly about one thing and another, but mostly about things that she would not normally concern him with. Then it dawned on Craig that Lek was frightened to go to bed alone in the dark. Actually, it was much worse that that, she was even too frightened to shower alone, so Craig did the right thing: he shut his computer down and suggested an early night. Lek leaped at the chance and held on to him tightly all night.

Craig got to sleep with difficulty, as had been the case since he was an infant, but Lek didn't remember sleeping at all, which was most unlike her. She was waiting for her friend and neighbour to come walking through the wall looking as if she had been dragged through a hedge backwards.

∞

Whatever state of consciousness they were both in, they were immediately aware when the lorry-load of huge speakers roared into life at five a.m. the next day The speakers were less than twenty yards away, but their purpose was to call any women in the whole village who wanted to help prepare food for the evening's ceremony. This was a cathartic event for people who were grieving. Instead of sitting at home alone while the men were in the fields working, they could sit together, chop, peel and prepare vegetables and meat and generally keep each other company.

Lek jumped out of bed and prepared to join in. There was no way Craig could sleep again, so he just started work. He understood that this had to be done and it didn't bother him in the slightest. Lek was showered, dressed and out of the house in fifteen minutes, which Craig did resent a little, wanting to ask whether she had seen Joy's Pi in the night.

Later he was glad that he hadn't had the opportunity, deciding that it would probably have caused a problem. Sometimes, he just didn't know when it was inappropriate to make a joke.

The music was turned down a lot when they had most of the helpers that they were expecting, about thirty minutes later, which made it feel less like having his head in a kettle drum at a Jamaican beach party. Craig just got on with the daily routine of checking and answering his email and writing relevant articles for his web sites, but when he got up to put the hot water on to make his coffee, he remembered what Lek had said the evening before about writing a book on or set in Thailand.

He knew that Lek had no idea of his writing skills- how could she? She had never read any of his work because she couldn't read English and none of her friends could have told her either. It was an intriguing idea and one that he may never have come up with on his own. At least, he hadn't so far in his fifty-eight years. He took his coffee back to his desk and got back into his routine.

Another routine was established too for the duration of the funeral ceremony of seven days. Lek brought him some lunch from the funeral at about two o'clock and met him in Nong's at five. He would then have to escort her to the house next door for fear of Joy's Pi, he would go back to work and she would stay there until about nine, when someone would walk her home. Craig could follow all the events from his office and sometimes he went to sit on the patio to concentrate on the monks chanting at about seven thirty.

On the fifth day, Joy's body was cremated at the usual time of three o'clock. Her friend had been cremated the day before. Craig could hear gunfire and fireworks coming from the Wat and the final acts of the ceremony were completed on the seventh day of her death.

Soom was back for the actual cremation which pleased her mother and Joy's family. Death is taken very seriously in a Thai village despite the fact that they don't fear it as Buddhists. Lek saw it as part of Soom's training, that she should learn and observe the traditions that made sense to her and to Lek. Anything that could improve one's Karma made ultimate sense. She wanted her daughter to have the best chance in life by using every tool at her disposal: physical, metaphysical and spiritual.

Normally, Lek would have played cards every night after a funeral, but she did not at this one. Whether that was because she was scared of ghosts and wanted to be home or whether she was trying to be nice, Craig never knew. In fact it was for both reasons in equal measure. She was not afraid of death, but she had been shocked by how sudden it could come and she wanted to be around to see her grandchildren.

The death of those two women had had a profound effect on her.

And so had the way Craig had talked about ghosts

# Maya - Illusion

# 4 THE FRUIT GARDEN

Lek was feeling a lot happier in herself than she had done for months. The extra injection of cash from the sale of Craig's property had helped, despite the fact that she hadn't wanted to go down that route. She had wanted to save her cake and eat it and she realised that now. Her philosophy had always been to live in the present and let Karma take care of the future and she could see that she had lost the plot for a few months – taken her eye off the ball called life with its ups and downs sent to try everyone, not only her and her family.

Maybe the trip to Laos had helped too. She definitely thought that it had and she was especially pleased with how they had solved the crisis of their marriage papers and shortage of money together and so smoothly. What could have so easily been a disaster leading to a big row and days of bad feeling had become nothing when they had worked on it together.

The crisis had dissolved before them like smoke before wind.

The sudden death of her life-long friend Joy had also had an effect. Joy was ten years older than herself and was just beginning to discover the contentment of grand-parenthood. A life on Earth, but not a life, snuffed out when all that happiness was just before her.

She also thought about her own actions over the last eight years. In the beginning, she hadn't contributed one penny to the family kitty and not worked for one hour in paid employment. Not only that, but she had squandered the small fortune left to her by Goong on playing silly games of cards because she was bored and wanted to show the others that she too had money to burn; that she hadn't worked in Pattaya for nothing; that she was as good as the best of them.

However, she could see now that she had been on a fool's errand. People had enjoyed taking her money from her and probably laughed at her behind her back. The wolves in sheep's clothing; the sneers behind the smiles. This was truly the illusion that Goong had warned her about. No, reminded her about, for hadn't she been taught not to chase illusions all her life? Not only that, but she had learned the lesson long ago and had it thrust down her throat day in and day out in Pattaya.

How had she come to drop her guard in Baan Suay? Maybe it was because she was home again and felt warm and protected with her friends and family about her. The wolves had still got her though, hadn't they? She had stopped looking out for them, but they hadn't taken their eyes off her and they had skinned her alive.

And now Craig had to sell their pension.

Lek was good at self-criticism, she had had years of practice in Pattaya, and low self-esteem. She had dreaded Soom finding out what she had been doing down there. How silly that was too. It was odds on that someone would tell her one day, if they hadn't already. She could only rely on Soom's common sense on that one.

As she saw it, the only problem that mattered was the one she could solve now. Not the one she should have solved last year or even the one she might have to solve next year – how could she best move forwards right now.

It was late September and she knew that adult learning classes would be starting up very soon, so she took herself off to the mayor's office to see what she could find out. She saw no shame in going back to school. She had done it before a few years ago and finished after gaining her high school diploma, but at the moment she could not remember for the life of her why she had stopped.

In any case, she was now ready to carry on and as Goong had reminded her, the proverb was: 'When the pupil is ready, the teacher will appear'. The teacher had appeared before and she had faith that he or she would appear again. She took a deep breath, and walked up the mayor's drive to look for him.

"Hello, Mr. Mayor, I'm looking for someone who can give me some advice about adult learning classes."

"Hi, Lek. Sure, you need my wife. She's around here somewhere, just go on through and look for her. Fancy one of the teachers, do you?"

"No, I want your job," she said as she walked past her old friend.

The mayor was chuckling, he had always liked Lek, even when they were at school.

Lek found Jan in the vegetable patch behind the house collecting bits and pieces for their evening meal.

"Hi, Lek, nice to see you. Is this a social visit? It seems like we haven't had a nice chat for ages. Come, sit down in the garden." Jan led the way to a round stone table with a curved bench seat at the edge of each quadrant. She called her daughter to bring them some iced water. "How are things with you and that lovely husband of yours?"

"We are well, thank you, Jan. It's just me. I think it's time I took up my education again and Nic said to ask you."

"Where did you see him?"

"He's sitting out the front doing some paperwork, I think."

"Oh, you saw him just now, did you? Ah, I see. I thought you meant round and about. Sorry about that. Um, let me think... We definitely have plans for adult classes starting two weeks Saturday. The same sort of thing you did before. Nine till three with an hour for lunch at twelve. That's the one you're talking about, aren't you?"

"Yes. Last time I got the certificate I should have gotten when I was sixteen, er, twenty-four years ago." She mumbled the last part in a comic way.

"Yes, time flies, doesn't it, but it didn't seem to matter in those sleepy Seventies and Eighties. However, things are very different now aren't they? Education is everything now. I wish that there were more men and women who missed out the first time round going back to catch up now. The number of people who can't read properly.... well, that's another subject for another time.

"What is it that you want to learn? Any preferences?"

"I really don't know, Jan. I can read as well as anyone; my handwriting is abysmal, but that's just sloppiness, I think. I can add up, basic maths, that sort of thing. I worked in Beou's bar in Pattaya as a cashier for years. We had to balance the books, regulate the stock, invoices, and all that... What do kids learn after that?"

"A hell of a lot of them don't know that much to be honest with you, but they would have a more rounded education like reading literature, cooking — well, there's no need for you to learn that, I know - er, computers nowadays, of course... I'm not sure to be honest with you.

"They would start specialising in order to go to university. By the way, how is your darling Soom doing in Bangkok?"

"She's great! She came back two weeks ago for Joy's funeral, but only for two nights..."

"Wasn't that awful? The whole village is still in shock about that. It's the children, I feel sorry for, of course...."

"Anyway, where were we? Yes, are you thinking of going to university?"

"What me? In university? No, nothing like that... University! Me? The very idea... No, I just don't want to feel stupid... and I do. Craig went to university and now Soom is at university and I? I left school at twelve... It has bothered me all my life... Well, since I was twelve anyway and a lot since I was twenty..."

"But it was the way in those days. Parents didn't realise the value of education and a lot of the ones who did, couldn't afford to send their kids to school... It was just the way it was and now it's different."

"I suppose so... So, can I do a general course to bring me up to the brain power of an eighteen year old, so to speak?"

"I don't think that there are such courses, Lek. I think that you have to specialise now. You could take two courses, say, computers and Thai literature. Or maths and computers... or ... I'll tell you what, I'll find you a list, then you can think about it, can't you?"

"Yes, thanks, Jan. I'll be off now then and will wait to hear from you. Thanks for your time. See you soon." She went out the way she had come in and tapped the mayor's table when he didn't glance up: "Bye, Nic."

"Yes, bye, Lek. Did you find Jan? Good. Come back soon. Don't be a stranger. We are here to serve the people."

She smiled at him warmly, but he had said it with such practised sincerity that she wasn't sure whether he was pulling her leg or not.

"Right, thanks, see you.." and she walked back up onto the road to go home, phase one of her plan having been put into action.

∞

Craig was already sitting in Nong's reading a document on marketing on his laptop, when Lek arrived at five o'clock.

"Hello, telak, do you want another beer? OK. Nong! Aow eek nung quat, ka! - 'another bottle of beer, please'." She sat down opposite him and waited for him to close his computer down. "How has your day been, Craig?"

He was quite taken aback by this unusual question from Lek, but tried not to show it.

"I'm fine thanks. The Internet is working well – I can't expect much more really, can I? There is nothing to change around here and nothing changes. It is generally 'a very good place to be'. It is the best place I have ever lived and I love it here. How has your day been?" he asked feeling that they were playing some sort of game.

"I have been thinking about taking some courses in school. What do you think?"

"I think it's a great idea. I thought the same last time too. What do you want to learn?"

"That's the problem... I don't know. I went to find out about it today. There are courses starting in a couple of weeks, but I thought that I could just pick up from where I left off. You know, learn from sixteen to eighteen, but the gumnan's wife said that it doesn't work like that. I would have to specialise like they do in school at that age before going to university."

"Is that what you want to do, go to university?"

"No. I don't think so. There's no point, is there? Me, in university?! I just want to learn something. Jan suggested computers or Thai literature..."

"If you want to, why not? I could help you with computers, if you ever need it, but I know nothing about Thai literature

"No, nor do I really. I don't know if I'd like it. I have only read magazines and newspapers since I left school and only text books while I was there. I've never read any literature in my life."

"Yes, I see. That is a tough one. When teenagers get to fourteen, they have – in the UK, in my day at least – they had to choose eight subjects to specialise in for two years. Most kids choose their favourites or what they were best at and some choose subjects so that they could get a special job. Then most kids at eighteen would specialise even more in three of the eight to go to university.

"So it is harder for you, because you don't have any subjects to pick from. What do you like doing?"

"I like being with young children"

"That's a start then. Go down to the school one day and ask them what qualifications you would need to be able to join their staff. Job done."

Lek was quite impressed with how easy Craig made it seem, but she still had twenty-six years of shame telling her that she was too stupid to be a teacher.

'Thanks, telak, I'll do that. It sounds like good advice. I would probably need more than a few hours of Saturday morning classes to be a teacher though, but I'll ask. There is something else too.

"I would like to be a teacher, but that might take years and I want to make some money now. I want to put some money into the family. Help pay for Soom's education. I know that it is too late to save your house, but it is not too late to do something."

"No, it is never too late. What do you have in mind?"

"I was talking to Mum this morning. She has a small piece of land over there, not far away... I thought that I could plant some trees, bushes and things on it and sell fruit. If I buy three or four year old fruit trees, they will make fruit in fifteen or eighteen months. Maybe I could do something else there too. She will sell me the land cheap It is nearly two rai, and she wants fifty thousand Baht."

"I see. Can you pay every month for one year?"

"Yes, I think so, but that will not help. It will not make money in one year. Or maybe a little bit, but not five thousand per month."

"Do you have the money?"

"Yes, but it is all that I have and I am using that to pay Soom's living expenses every month."

"So, you want to use some of the money from the house to buy some land for yourself from your own mother? Is that right? Because I can never own land in Thailand, can I?"

"If you put it like that, it sounds horrible. You make me look bad. I am only thinking of helping pay. I don't want you to sell your house to buy land for me – that is not my idea.

"OK, you could lend me the money to buy the land."

"But if I did that it would be the same as paying your mother slowly."

"No, not the same. I cannot pay my mother slowly. She is old, it is good if she has some money now and I will start pay you every month next year, when I have fruit."

Craig didn't like the sound of it, but he would be getting a fair amount of money soon and it was hard to refuse to lend his wife £1,200 for two years.

44

OK. You've got it, but the money won't be here until the end of October, I think. Maybe a little longer."

Lek jumped up, ran around the table and kissed him in public.

"I am so happy that you waai-jai – uh, believe me."

"No, trust me."

"Yes, darling, I do trust you... Thank you. Can I buy you one more beer? I am so happy that I will have one with you and I will pay for that myself too."

Lek looked at Craig as she sat down again and he could not help but be amazed at the way his wife operated.

∞

The following morning, Lek told her mother what had transpired the evening before.

"But, Lek, do you have enough money to plant the land. It is no good to you unless you can buy trees and bushes for it and from what you have told me, it would be pretty difficult to go back to Craig again for yet more money."

"No, Mum, I could not do that easily at all, but there is another way. You told me yesterday, that if I waited long enough, I would inherit the land anyway and I said that I would rather have it now – buy it now – and give you a little nest egg. Well, I know that you don't spend much, so I was thinking that if I gave you twenty thousand now, I could use thirty thousand to plant trees and do some work and then I could pay you back over the following year at two and a half thousand a month.

"Would that be all right with you, Mum?"

"Er, yes... You are right, I don't have any plans for the money. I probably wouldn't even spend it. Maybe buy a few things for around the house, get some new clothes and fix the toilet roof... I don't need twenty thousand for that, so why not? Yes, sure, if you like."

"You are a really, special Mum. You know that, Mum? This is what I intend to do. Do you have some paper and a pencil?

"Right, thanks. I'm thinking of putting a cheap concrete-block shed here, in the corner for growing mushrooms in and here, I'll have rows of mapang – they are all the rage now and sell for a hundred Baht a kilo! Bananas only sell for seven Baht! I can get a hundred or more in here, see? Three metres apart, I think, but I have to check and then chilli plants in between the bushes or trees, whatever they are.

"What do you think, Mum?"

"I think that that looks like a very feasible plan. And thirty thousand will cover it?"

"Yes, it should do, but I'll try for a discount anyway, obviously." She grinned broadly at her mother and eventually her mother smiled back.

"Or you could become my partner, Mum, and we'll split the profits fifty-fifty."

She slapped Lek's arm gently, "Get away with you. I'm too old for new business ventures. You're on your own, unless you want to ask someone else, but I wouldn't. One person can handle this alone quite easily, but two would be falling over each other."

"Yes, you're probably right, Mum. I wouldn't want to share the profits with anyone but you anyway. It is a good idea and it is thanks to you – and Craig – that we can get the project off the ground so quickly, so why should we share that with anyone else?

"I think I'll go and look at mapang trees and see if Don can start building the shed too. Might as well get on with it, eh? The sooner the plants are in the ground, the sooner the money is in the bank. Thanks again, Mum, I'll see you later. I should be back by five to meet Craig at Nong's, so if you see him, will you try to tell him that? I don't want to go back into the house now. I can't wait to get started

"I haven't been so excited for... I don't know, ages."

"Oh, Lek, I almost forgot. Jan, the mayor's wife, came by earlier to see me about something and she asked me if I could give you these papers. They are to do with the courses available at the school. She said to tell you that people who are interested should go for registration at the school on Monday 8th October and that classes would start the following Saturday or the one after that."

∞

Lek had had a very productive day and couldn't wait to tell Craig the news – to show off a little. She really wanted him to see her as a fully contributing partner in their relationship. She was aware that that small piece of land wouldn't make them rich, but it would be a start and who knew? If Fate dealt the right hand, she might be able to expand. She had to try very hard not to imagine having hundreds of rai in five years time. She turned a corner on to the main road home and a speeding lorry missed her by twelve inches.

She was shaking badly, but she wanted to get to Nong's as soon as possible. On arrival, she collapsed into a heap on the bench and wept out loud.

"Whatever is the matter, Lek, what has happened?"

"Give me a brandy, please. I have good news, but I have shock, just now. I nearly die same Joy."

Craig ordered a half bottle of brandy from Nong, who also brought a glass, ice and soda, which was how most locals drank Regency Brandy.

"Whatever has happened, Lek," asked Nong, virtually pushing Craig aside and taking charge."

Lek explained, and satisfied with the latest gossip in town, Nong moved off.

"What happened, Lek?"

"I have had a fantastic day. Mum is happy about selling me the land and she likes my plans about what to do with it, so I went out today to look at fruit. I talked to farmers and chang and I was coming back very happy to tell you, when a truck nearly hit me same Joy. Not his fault, I was daydreaming, but I am OK now. I want to tell you about my idea. I want to know what you think."

They were sitting down at the table opposite each other and clinked glasses. Lek showed him her rough sketch of the plot and the rows of trees and bushes. She showed him where the hut would go and hoped for his approval.

"What you think?"

"I am no farmer, Lek, but I can see that you have thought about it and if your mother thinks that it will work, then your opinion and hers are good enough for me. I wish you all the best, but try harder to stay alive to enjoy it, please."

Thy clinked glasses again.

"One more thing. There are many kinds of mapang and I want you to come with me tomorrow to the nursery to choose one or two varieties to plant. Will you do that?"

"Sure, I'd love to. Thanks very much. You know, you have had more success today – in one day – than I have had this month. What is the shed for? Tools?"

"No, well, maybe a few, but I want to grow mushrooms in there. You love mushrooms, so I want to grow special mushrooms for your dinner."

"Magic mushrooms?"

"I don't understand. I know 'magic' and I know 'mushrooms', but I do not know magic mushrooms. You cannot grow by magic, just with water and flower food. Maybe ask Buddha for help."

"No, I'm only joking, dear. Magic mushrooms are the same as ganja. People eat and see colours and everything. Like acid trip. Like hippies. They grow in the grass in Wales and everywhere in Europe."

"Ah, joking again... I don't like drugs. Only whisky, beer and brandy... and some more, like tequila..."

"Yes, I know, don't worry. I was only joking. Forget it. It's a very good idea. I love mushrooms and toadstools if they're not poisonous, but if you are running a business, we will buy the mushrooms that we eat from you. When you have big money, we can eat them for free. OK?"

"OK, telak, OK, good idea. Nothing for free when we start."

∞

The next day they went to the nursery shortly after lunch, despite it being Lek's least favourite time of the day, but she wore a crash helmet to keep the sun off her face, add-on sleeves and gloves to keep the sun off her arms, and socks. She worked hard to keep her skin as pale as possible, as did most women, so she wasn't going to ruin a month's work by going out for two hours in the Thai midday heat.

At the nursery, they were treated like visiting dignitaries, but Lek was going to spend up to twenty thousand Baht, so it was a big sale by any standard in rural Thailand. First they were introduced to all the family, who worked on the farm-nursery and then Craig was asked if he would prefer a beer or tea – he chose beer and Lek had tea. They were seated under a canopy of grapes on vines and served a dozen coin-sized slices of mapang arranged in pairs. Lek explained that these were the varieties grown at the farm.

48

They chose four of the six and then eight more pieces were brought. Lek wanted it narrowed down to two, which they did after a short debate. Lek took it very seriously and Craig tried to as well, but it reminded him of TV wine critics going on about minor subtleties that most people wouldn't notice. For his part, he just chose the sweetest varieties, the ones that tasted most like a ripe mango, but Lek found one of the slightly more bitter ones more thirst quenching.

Lek chose the sweetest and the least bitter varieties. The husband of the farm, stood at a respectful distance making noises and answering Lek's questions like a good sommelier should. When she had made her final choices, a dozen of each was brought on a plate by the owner's wife to prove that the quality and flavour were consistent.

When Lek had agreed the deal by word of mouth, they were brought a large carrier bag containing six bags of mapang, one of each variety, to eat at home. That bag full alone was worth six hundred Baht in a food market. Lek put all her gear back on, everybody waaied everybody several times and they headed off back to the village.

Craig wanted to stop at Nong's, Lek sighed inwardly and acquiesced.

"So what was said there exactly? I know there was more going on than I understood. It all seemed a very civilised way of doing business, I must say."

Lek was as pleased as Punch. "Yesterday, I told the farmer that I had a plot of land that I wanted to put about one hundred mapang on. I showed him my drawing and told him the rough size. Today we chose the varieties. Tomorrow, he will come and look at the land and tell me what I need to do to it and how to set it out and then he will select a hundred trees of two metres and delver them when I am ready."

"Sounds great, so when will you put them in the ground?"

"It depends, I don't think that there is a problem with the land, so maybe we can start the day after tomorrow. I will need help to dig the holes... and I have asked chang to build a shed for my mushrooms. I must check when he will start."

Craig was really pleased to see Lek looking so happy. He wanted to hug her, but he knew that although he could get away with doing that in public once in a blue moon, he could not at the moment, so he just sat there and admired her.

∞

Lek was up early, as usual the following day, but she didn't stop to do any housework or water her plants. She had other plans for the day. She wore similar protection from the sun as the day before, but she replaced the crash helmet with a T-shirt over her head, leaving just a slit for her eyes by tying the shirt sleeves behind her head in the old Thai-farmer style and she wore a wide-brimmed raffia hat on top. She looked like a Mexican ninja, but very fetching. She had an appointment with the mapang farmer to survey her land. He turned up within the expected bounds of punctuality in Thailand and they walked the field together.

"The soil is good, Lek. Very good. You should do well here..."

"It is... was my mother's land. She grew bananas here for decades, but nothing for the last five or six years. I suppose all the leaves from the trees have rotted down..."

"Yes... there is a slight fall to over there. What is there?" They walked over. "As I suspected, a bit of a bog, where your water drains to. Is that your land too?"

"No, but they have never complained about it getting water-logged..."

"Well, it will get pretty wet when it rains, I imagine, but the good news is, that your hundred trees will soak up any spare moisture from now on, so that will cease to be a worry..."

Lek never had worried about it and nor had anyone else, but it was comforting to know that it never would be a problem either.

"Er, which way do you suggest I plant the rows of trees?"

"Oh, you want them running across here... the first row between us and the bog and so on behind us. That way, any excess water flows onto the trees and gets sucked up. If you have them running the other way the water may by-pass the trees in the early years before the roots have spread. Once they are three metres high it won't matter a rat's arse... hmm, sorry, it won't matter at all."

Lek carried on walking, pretending not to have heard his slip of the tongue. "So, you don't think I need to do anything then?"

"I wouldn't go that far, no. You don't need to do anything, but you could dig a foot down in the lines where you are planting and turn the soil over... get this leaf mulch in the soil to help the roots, but you could just put a spadeful of rotted cow muck in there instead. Here's a tip, when you dig out for the saplings, put the spoil to the side, so as to make walk-ways between the rows.

"That'll encourage the rainwater to flow around the roots and keep your feet dry when you're inspecting them in wet weather, although these buggers love rain.. the more the better. Sorry for my bad language, miss, I'm used to mixing in the fields and all..."

"Don't worry about it, I've heard worse. Well, thank you very much for your advice. When can I have the saplings?"

"How do you want them? Ten a day starting tomorrow? Just say the word."

"Right... there will be three of us on spades, do you think five a day each and we can make the walkways as we go?"

"Certainly, Khun Lek, there's no need to kill yourselves is there? Five a day each is a fair clip, so I'll deliver 30 every two days, then if you want to do more you can… but don't leave 'em standing more than that. I'll wrap the roots in plastic, but you'll have to get them in the ground pretty fast and get them well-watered in. If you over-run, phone me and I'll put off delivery for a day. OK?"

"Sure, thank you very much for all your help and advice. Give your wife my regards and say that my husband asked me to say 'thank you' for the hospitality we were shown yesterday."

"OK, miss, I mean Khun Lek. Thanks for doing business with us too."

∞

Lek and her employee friends worked every day until five and so did the bricklayer, chang. At five, they would have a perfunctory wash in the field and Lek would take them to Nong's to join Craig. Lek bought the drink, a bottle of whisky, and a few packets of crisps and they would sit there talking loudly like the crew off a yacht that had just put in after a day at sea.

It often annoyed Craig that they spoiled the peacefulness of his only two hours off a day, especially when he couldn't understand what they were saying and so felt left out, but he pretended to be having a pleasant time and hoped that he nodded and shook his head at the right times. He didn't want to appear a miserable sod, which of course he wasn't.

Not normally, anyway.

Lek looked forward to the hour drinking with her workmates and then the hour bringing Craig up to date with what had happen during the day. They had been scared by snakes, threatened by scorpions, seen beautiful birds that didn't come into the village and even seen a pangolin in the area by the bog – a big lizard that bore a passing resemblance to a juvenile Komodo Dragon. Don, the bricklayer had wanted to take it home to eat, but Lek had claimed rights over it and scared it away.

On the eighth day, Craig was invited to go and look at their handiwork. He was very impressed that so much could be accomplished in a week, considering how long it had taken the builders to convert their house several years before.

"I'm impressed, Lek. I didn't see it before, but this is really nice. I hope you do well here. He gave her a big hug and the other people there awkwardly pretended not to notice.

That evening in Nong's, over a celebratory bottle of beer Chang – it was the only alcoholic drink that Nong served that had bubbles in it – Lek revealed the second item of which she was very proud:

"Telak, you remember I told you that I wanted to go back to school to get the brain of an eighteen year old? Well, I signed up for a Saturday morning course yesterday and today Jan phoned me to say that they had more than the minimum number of students to begin the course.

"Guess what I am going to be studying?"

"Er, um, teaching? Nursery school assistant? Child Care? I don't know, I give up."

"Business Administration," she announced proudly.

# 5 ONE HUNDRED DAYS

Lek had not felt so empowered since she had stopped working in Pattaya. She loved Craig, as far as she understood the definition of the word, because she had no doubt that love meant different things to different people. Her idea of love did not entail any restriction of freedom. The only thing that stopped her doing absolutely anything she wanted, was that she didn't want to hurt Craig's feelings.

She had already told him several times over the years that if she caught him playing about, she would take him for every penny he had and then dump him and she knew people who could advise her how to do it.

However, she did feel 'beholden' to him, because he had worked so hard for nearly a decade and had spent all his savings on them and was now selling his house too. She felt that she would never have done that for anyone except Soom, not even her mother, whom she loved dearly.

In Pattaya she had been in charge of her life in a way that would never have been possible in Baan Suay – heck, it wasn't even possible now. People in the village worked hard, but there was little entertainment during the day, so those not at work watched TV and gossiped and then told their family when they came home and then they talked about it in their turn the following day in the fields.

She hated the gossip and the scrutiny. When she had first gone back seven or eight years before, it had been even worse, because people had held her 'job' against her. It was easier now, because she had 'proved' herself and the villagers had mellowed a little with the departure of so many young girls to the cities to seek their fortunes.

Lek knew how that worked and she knew what most of them would be doing, if not by day then by night and on the weekends.

In 'her day', twenty years before, those who went away, usually went to fulfil a goal. She had gone to save the family farm from foreclosure, but these days most girls went because they wanted the deposit for a car or wanted to leave the country with a foreign husband. She had wanted both of those things, but had fallen in love with Craig and he had fallen in love with Thailand and she had wanted to stick by her daughter at least until Soom didn't need her any more.

Now that Soom was at university in Bangkok five hundred kilometres away, her life seemed empty. Yes, she had Craig, but it was not the same. He was working all day and didn't enjoy the same party lifestyle that she did, but he didn't often get jealous about it and she knew where he was.

Now things were different again though, she had a business, albeit a small one and she was studying, even if it was only four hours a week. She felt that she had regained some control over her life, although her philosophy and her religion told her that Karma ruled destiny. That was a deep one for her at the moment, so she was going to go with the flow; be as good a person as possible; and throw herself into her work and studies.

And she did so. With a vengeance. Lek did the housework including the garden in the early morning as the sun was coming up; she studied a bit with Craig in his office in the afternoon and she watered her Suan – her market garden in the evening so that the sun would not boil the leaves of her precious trees, which were little more than bushes, but bore so much hope. This meant that she could not always be there for evening drinks in Nong's, but Craig understood and, hey, you can't have everything.

She was happy with the way things were turning out. The bushes had not died, which had been a danger, but it was past and her school work was not as hard as she had expected, largely because she had helped out with the administration of her cousin's bar for so many years and had helped her parents with the paperwork on their farm before that.

In fact, the point of the course was to help small farmers cope with the modern requirements of the Thai government. Increasingly, the government wanted proof, documents, evidence, receipts, wage slips et cetera and most Thais knew nothing of these things in the villages. Lek did have prior knowledge from the bar, so she was actually a few steps ahead of her classmates who ranged in age from fifteen years younger to fifteen years older than herself.

She loved being one of the smartest in the class after thinking that she was one of the thickest for miles around for decades. It was doing her self-confidence and her self-esteem a power of good.

The course did not include computers, that would have frightened most of the farmers off joining, but she did want to ask Craig to teach her the basics of email and Facebook, so that she could keep in touch with Soom who used them extensively, as all young people were doing in Thailand. Facebook was like an epidemic and she wanted to know what it was all about too.

She made a point of being there for the five o'clock drinks that day.

"Telak, I want to have a Facebook page and an email address, do you know how to set that up for me?"

"Yes, Lek, I can show you how to do that. I can either do it for you or show you. It's not difficult, when you know how, like most things. We can do it tonight or tomorrow, if you like."

"Tonight would suit me, darling, if you are not too busy.

"Lek, I just offered. If you want, we can take a few bottles home and I'll show you when we have finished this one."

"Yes, please! I am anxious to learn. It will save money too, telak, if I can email Soom instead of phoning her every evening. In fact, while we are drinking up, I'll phone her and ask her to text you her Facebook page and email address. You will need those, won't you?"

"I know her Facebook page already, but you can ask for her email address. That would help."

Lek got on the phone immediately, but that was nothing new – she only needed half an excuse to phone someone up and none at all where Soom was concerned.

When they got home, Craig set up his laptop while Lek poured him a beer and got an extra chair so that she could sit by him.

"Right, the first thing to do, is decide what you want your Facebook page to be called. You can change it later, but it is better to get it right the first time."

He let her think about that for a while.

"Lek and My Garden," she said.

"Yes, you could have that, but, I don't know..."

"Lek in Baan Suay"

"Again, yes but..., I don't know, I always try for something memorable and 'Baan Suay' – I may be wrong – but no-one has ever heard of it..."

"Lek in Pattaya'..."

"OK, let's go with that for now. Like I said, you can change it later if you want."

Craig showed her step by step, how to set up her Facebook page called http://facebook.com/LekInPattaya and then they moved on to the email.

"I can set you up with Hotmail or Yahoo or add you to one of my web sites, if you want."

"What is the difference?"

"Most good names on Hotmail and Yahoo have already been taken and free addresses look juvenile and amateurish anyway, but if you use one of my sites, you can have any name you like, except Craig, and it looks professional."

"OK, I'll go with you."

He showed her a list of his web sites.

"Pick one that you like..."

"How about this one?"

"Sure, 'Behind The Smile' it is. And your name?"

"'LekinPattaya'"

"There is no reason to use your Facebook name. That is a different thing, you can be 'Lek Williams' or just 'Lek' here on my domain if you like."

"OK, 'Lek'."

"So, on the Internet, that becomes 'Lek' – they prefer small letters – and your 'street address' is 'behind-the-smile.org' so your full email address is now 'lek@behind-the-smile.org'. Easy, wasn't it?"

"You made it look easy, yes, but I don't know whether I could do that on my own."

"Look, Lek, no-one is born with the knowledge. We all have to learn what we know. Fifteen years ago, I didn't know how to create an email address, last year, I didn't know how to create a Facebook page, I still don't know what Instagram is all about, so you just find out, if you're interested, don't you?

"You never saw the need for email or Facebook before today or a few days ago, now you do. Maybe your Mum will see a need for it next month. Or maybe not. It doesn't matter, does it? I can't change a nappy, but not having had any kids and not likely to either, that doesn't matter either, does it? No-one can know everything. You pick what you need and leave the rest. Don't worry that you don't know what other people know."

"I can see what you are saying, but it is easy for you to say because you do know. Now I want to know too."

"Lek, some people want to build clocks, some people only want to know how they work and even more just want to tell the time. Use the Internet as a tool, if you want, by all means, but let others do the spade-work, if you don't want to learn how to. On the other hand, learn how it all works if that's what you want.

"I can teach you a lot of it, but really, you don't need to know how a clock works to read the time from it."

"OK... so, now I have an email address and a Facebook?"

"Yes. You just tell people that your Facebook address is 'Lek in Pattaya' and that your email address is Lek at Behind The Smile dot org – it is that simple. No need to explain anything, if they don't understand then they wouldn't know how to use the information anyway.

"So, if people ask me my email address, I say: 'Lek at Behind The Smile dot org' and my Facebook is Lek in Pattaya... It is that easy... Really..?"

"So, I can send Soom an email now? And put a message on her Facebook?"

"Yes, like this for email.... and like this for Facebook.... Now just type something and click here. This is in English and click here to change the keyboard, this thing, into Thai."

"Wow, and that is free?"

"It is for you... but I had to buy a computer and I pay TOT six hundred Baht every month for the Internet, and I pay every year for the domain name – the behind-the-smile.org bit - but after that it is free, yes."

∞

Lek found out over the following few weeks that she was not really interested in knowing how the clock worked, but she did wanted to tell the time and often. It seemed that whenever, Craig got to up to get a cup of coffee, Lek was at his computer when he got back. It was easy to see what her next Christmas present should be.

Saturday school was a joy to her. She didn't need to be able to use a computer for it because they did all their work with figures on a traditional paper spreadsheet, but Craig showed her how to transfer all the figures to Excel and let the computer take care of the calculations for her.

She was soon hooked. Lek went from being one of the most atechnical people in the world, to one of the most knowledgeable about using a computer in the village. At least among those over twenty-five years of age and not that that was difficult in a village which had only acquired its first computer a few years before, but it was a big achievement nevertheless and one which she would have said would have been impossible a month before.

She passed her first end of term exams at the top of the class and derived great pleasure from helping those in her form who were struggling to keep up. Craig was very proud of her and when Soom came back for the end of term break just before Christmas, she was flabbergasted at the transformation in her mother.

When Craig bought her a laptop, she and Soom spent all day setting it up together and copying programmes from Craig's and Soom's computers. Soom's English was pretty good, but she did all her computing in Thai, mainly because the teachers and her fellow pupils could not speak English so well, but Lek did not have that problem, so she wanted her computer set up in English.

Craig was dismayed that Soom was having to dumb down to doing everything in Thai instead of English, not because the Thai language was deficient, but because it was restrictive. He had met dozens of bright computer kids in Thailand who could not converse about their computers in English even though they had learned the English terminology. Their pronunciation was just so bad and they had learned that from their teachers.. Computer became 'com'; programme, 'progra'; monitor was 'scee'; keyboard 'keybo'; hard drive was 'ha dive' - it seemed such a waste.

Those kids would forever only ever be able to work in Thailand for low wages. He wanted Soom to speak correctly and learn computers in English, but the quality of the teaching staff was such that she was being taught wrong – nobody in the world would ever understand her except Thais. He was glad that Lek was avoiding this trap, although it meant learning a whole raft of new terminology, which she could either learn  correctly or badly.

The converse was that no Thais would be able to understand her now, although the rest of the world would, not that she had any plans to be an International, jet-setting computer wizard yet.

Soom, Lek and Craig were able to have three-way discussions on computer-related topics for the first time ever, not that many people would find that enviable.

∞

Their sixth wedding anniversary was on the 20th of November, but they didn't want to make a big fuss about it. More important in the practical sense was that Craig's three-month visa would expire the same day. That would be a clash for ever more unless they changed it so Lek asked one of her cousins to take them to Naan for the day on the 14th of November to get a visa.

Neither of them had been to Naan before although the province was less than three hundred kilometres away and none of the three expected to enjoy the trip. It was all up mountain on the western side and mostly down mountain on the east, but the scenery was fantastic.

They left at six a.m arrived at eleven, were done by noon and on the way back. Lek and Craig wished that they had gone alone, because that remote mountain province was just the sort of place they liked to explore.

They arrived back in Baan Suay at six fifteen and they took the driver to Nong's for a 'thank you' drink, although he didn't stay long as it was not a place he felt happy drinking in. Most people in the village felt like that, and so did Lek to a certain degree. Villagers preferred to drink at home.

As the driver was leaving, Craig asked Lek to tell him that they would put him up for a night in the city of Naan, if he took them next time, but Lek didn't look keen and may have said something else.

Lek gave him three thousand Baht for his trouble and he went away a happy man.

∞

Other than Lek and her computer and Soom coming home for a fortnight, Christmas was a washout for Craig, but that was neither a surprise nor a disappointment. He had become used to it. When he had first arrived in the village, no-one had even known what Christmas, or 'Kisma', Day was. They were all Buddhists, so why should they? But gradually, over the years a few people had cottoned on and some even surprised him by wishing him 'Happy Kisma'. He rarely said it first to anyone over the age of ten, because the youngsters were normally told in school about big days in all major religions.

Craig did his annual tour of the village hot spots during the morning, drinking a beer in each of the five local shops, telling those who were curious why he was out drinking so early, what day it was. Most were none the wiser when they walked away bemused.

There were now two Internet Cafes in the village, which created two fifty-metre radius Wi-Fi hotspots. Luckily for Craig, there was a shop in each of them and the owners had been good enough to give him their passwords so that he could surf from outside. One covered Nong's shop and the other was at the far end of the village about five hundred metres away, which gave him a good excuse to get the only exercise he ever got.

They had almost totally given up celebrating Christmas. In the beginning, when Soom had been younger, it was fun to decorate the patio with trimmings and lights that played tunes, but when they broke, they were not replaced and no-one missed them. Craig had also used to cook a Christmas Dinner of roast chicken, roast potatoes and the like. Soom and Lek would eat some out of politeness, but he had always eaten most of it himself and cold, so he stopped. Likewise with cakes.

For the first few years he had baked a couple of cakes on Christmas morning, but one year he had used mono-sodium glutamate instead of salt and they were as hard as concrete. Not even Bpom and Bpouy, the dogs, would eat them. Everybody, including Craig, had had a good laugh, but he didn't cook any more at Christmas ever again. Their wedding had been the last time, six years before.

There was a baker in the village now anyway who would make bread in the European style at twenty-four hours' notice and fantastic chocolate cakes and pizzas. Bread had been something that Craig had missed badly, now he only needed a dairy farmer to make some cheese and he would be as happy as a skylark.

Despite the fact that Christmas was not a time for celebration in Baan Suay and the surrounding area, there were normally more parties than would be usual in the West. This had always come as a surprise to Craig, even though he had been there some years. December is also Thailand's winter, so the 'cool' evenings were ideal for garden parties and the New Year was the perfect excuse. Cool in Thailand though meant about 25°c, so there was no hardship.

The parties started in late November to early December and there were dozens of them. Craig liked to limit them to two a week, but Lek often went to four. The village council held a party, the town council too; the schools all held parties and so did many businesses, most of which allowed friends of employees or customers. The banks held them and local government agencies did as well. Big farmers held them and so did the church charities.

Then New Year's Eve, every family held their own party then. In the midst of all this merry-making, one family had a more sombre task to perform, because it was one hundred days since Joy's death on the 27th of December. Thais take the One Hundred Days funeral celebration very seriously and so it was with Joy's family too.

Lek responded to the call to action at five o'clock in the morning and went next door to help cook for the monks and guests, who would arrive at about ten, since the monks had to finish eating for the day before noon. The monks chanted for the departed spirit of Joy and the well-wishers prayed for her happiness in the afterlife, then the monks went back to the Wat and the music, food and card-playing began.

Lek actually wanted to leave at that point and get on with some studying on her new computer, but her friends hadn't got used to her new ways and persuaded her to share a bottle of whiskey and play cards. Craig watched disapprovingly from the desk in his office. She knew what he was thinking, but did not feel that she could do anything about it. Craig didn't mind too much about the odd occasion either, but he didn't want it to become a habit, because the only two women he knew who played cards regularly were outrageous liars and always broke.

He had lent one of them five hundred Baht for her daughter's birthday party years previously on Lek's advice, but he had never seen the money again. After months of her saying 'I'll pay you next week', Craig had told Lek to tell her to 'get stuffed'. Lek hadn't said that, of course, she would never be so rude, but she did arrange for her friend to work three days in the house garden at half rate to pay it off. She had never asked them to lend her money again.

Joy's family gave Joy a second day of remembrance with the monks which followed the same pattern as the first and then she was left to carry on with whatever her future had in store for her.

∞

Thailand celebrates three New Year's Eves. In general, the Chinese New Year is the least celebrated, then there is the Western 31st December and the biggest by far is the old Thai New Year in April. However, the Western New Year is still pretty big by any standards.

Lek went to her mother's house to start preparing for the party at seven a.m. and there were already people – family and elderly neighbours - there by then. Some were even drinking alcohol too, but then the Thais are not hypocritical about that sort of thing. They work hard and if they have a day off, they make the most of it by doing whatever they like no matter what anyone thinks.

This would be one of those days, but not for Craig. New Year's Day had always been just another day for him, but not so with Lek. She had always celebrated it with her family before she had gone away and she had earned more on that night in Pattaya than any other too. People were more generous when they were drunk and there were not many sober foreigners in Pattaya on New Year's Eve. Practically every bar had its balloons out and a pig roasting.

In the village they settled for a dozen different dishes of food and a couple of chickens, but in fact the fayre was better than in most Pattaya bars.

However, it was an all-day affair and shortly after midnight, most people were ready to go to bed. Most people except Lek and her cousin Beou that was. Beou had missed Joy's funeral for one reason and another, so she had come for the Hundred Days and stayed for New Year. She had said that she would be back in Pattaya for the next day, so they wanted to chat together for an hour or so. Craig thought it best to take a couple of bottles home with him and leave them to it.

Lek and Beou talked about the 'good old days' mostly.. They talked about some of the idiots that they had had come to the bar, the antics that some of the drunks had got up to, like falling off their stools or giving all their money to one of the girls that they had fallen in love with for the moment.

They talked about holidays they had had together on the islands near Pattaya – the 'firm's outings' as they called them and those that had been paid for by wealthy or crazy patrons. Some of the Arabs had been extremely well-off and one man in particular thought nothing of closing the bar for the afternoon and taking all the staff to Ko Lang a few miles off the coast.

They also talked about old colleagues, those that had done well, those that had done not so well and those that were no longer with them, like Goong. Goong's father had passed away a long time ago, but her brothers still held Lek, Ayr and Beou responsible for 'taking' her to Pattaya with them, even though she had told them and everyone else that it was her idea – that she had wanted to go, because she couldn't bear the thought of decades of boredom and drudgery living and working in an isolated village.

They had chosen not to believe her and stuck to their own version of 'reality'. Neither of the women knew whether the brothers knew that she was now 'on the other side' because they wouldn't even recognise Lek's existence, nor Beou's. Goong's father had died in ignorance, because that had been Goong's express wish and it seemed rather pointless to tell the brothers now anyway.

They had assumed, or at least were telling everybody that Goong had married a wealthy American and was living in New York. They said that they were proud of her for doing so well, despite having been 'led astray by her friends'. Their logic did not extend to explaining how she would have met such a man if she had stayed in Baan Suay, where Craig was the only falang that anyone could remember seeing there in decades.

They were drinking Thai style, whiskey out of a shared shot glass, but Beou filled it up, raised it to Goong, said, "Wherever you may be, friend' and drank half of it. She passed the glass to Lek, who repeated the toast to their absent sister and added: "May you always be as beautiful as the last time I saw you".

The mood became down-beat, not quite solemn, after that, but they were both a little drunk and lost in their private meanderings down their private lanes of memories, so they said goodnight and went to their respective homes.

# 6 THE FAMILY BUSINESSES

The family finances were still not on a firm footing, despite the money from the sale of Craig's flat. They were still spending more than they were earning. The vast majority of this shortfall was due to Soom's university fees and the cost of her upkeep in Bangkok. Her small apartment in a girls-only guest-house cost more per month than some girls of her age even earned in a month at a straight job.

Then there was the school uniform, not so much a uniform as a dress code: sky-blue or white blouse and navy shorts, slacks or skirt. Basically, Soom had needed a new wardrobe in order to fit in with the mostly rich kids who normally populated the classrooms of Thai universities, especially the loftier ones in Bangkok, one of which Soom was attending.

She had also needed quite a few course books, a laptop and the de-rigueur iPad. Craig had always contended that the iPad was not one of the items necessary to study at university, but Lek wanted her to have everything she wanted and so had lost the argument. Not that he had argued very hard, he understood the desire to appear the same as everyone else, the need to fit in in people and especially in young people away from home.

Soom was now mixing with the sons and daughters of the rich and influential, quite a few brackets up from her own origins and it would have been the social kiss of death to admit that her parents could not afford something that her colleagues took for granted.

This cost a small fortune by Thai standards, although it was well below the cost of a European university education. Still, Craig didn't begrudge her the expense, because she had worked hard to get the necessary grades to qualify for entry to this, her dream choice. Other universities would have been cheaper.

The family businesses, such as they were, consisted of Lek's suan of fruit trees and bushes and her mushrooms and Craig's web sites and other related Internet activities.

Craig had been slow to realise how astute, or lucky, Lek's timing had been. She had planted her suan as the cool period had started, when the rainy season would help with the irrigation of her bushes and trees. There was no better time of the year to have done it.

The heat of May and June would have made it harder for the saplings to survive and the mini monsoon of July and August would have made working in the suan very difficult, but September and October were just about the best compromise you could get. None of the items planted had died or suffered much and now, in late January, as the temperature started to rise again, they were well enough established to survive, assuming that they got enough water and as Lek had had mains water laid on, that would not be a problem.

Craig's admiration for Lek grew and grew. Little did he know that she would have tried to make the garden work no matter what season they had found themselves in because she was desperate for something to do, but she had realised that it was a good time of the year also. There was still enough of a farmer about her to know the seasons and how to grow things, even if she and her family had specialised more in rice for generations.

Lek's suan had a hundred and twelve mapang bushes in it, which had not produced any fruit yet, but neither had they been expected to. The farmer from the nursery had said that some plants might produce a few fruit the following year in March, April or May, but that she should not count of it. However, twelve months later, there should be enough to sell and the year after that twice as many and that the crop might double in size every year for the next ten years, so it was a question of just making sure they got enough water and food so that they had a chance to grow.

However, although the mapang were definitely the cash crop, she was making pin money from other crops in the suan. Most of the 'fence' surrounding the field was dense bamboo, which was cut down young as food or allowed to grow older to order. Bamboo was used to make many things in Thailand like sala or garden shelters, scaffolding and other light structures. The bamboo grew quickly, so could be grown to two, three or even six metre lengths within months.

Bamboo, or elephant food, as Lek liked to call it, became a larger part of their regular diet in those cost-cutting days. Craig liked it the way Lek prepared it, boiled first alone to soften it and then lightly fried with pounded garlic, chillis and other spices all tossed in a beaten egg - it wasn't an omelette, because there wasn't enough egg to bind it. Served with fresh rice, it made a really lovely meal which soon became one of Craig's favourites. Not only did it reduce the cholesterol and raise the amount of roughage in their diet, but it saved a few Baht too.

As Lek said: 'Look what it does for elephants!'

Just inside the 'fence' was a ring of mangoes, coconuts and bananas. These crops were not worth much as the area around Baan Suay was famous for them and every garden had its own trees. However, the mango trees produced enough fruit twice a year to provide all their fruit for those months and although the bananas only cropped once a year, they produced so many bananas that they rotted before the could all be eaten.

It was customary to give the excess away, barter them with strangers or make a kind of toffee which would keep almost indefinitely. Lek's mother was an acknowledged expert in the village for making mango, banana and pineapple toffees, although pineapples didn't grow locally.

Coconuts kept for ages in their outer husks, which people used as kindling to start their cooking fires. Most people still cooked on an open fire or a gas ring in the garden in the traditional way, so that the cooking smells didn't taint the house and its contents. The chillis that grew between the bushes also grew well in the area and Lek was able to sell dozens of kilos of the small, red-hot chillis called 'mouse-shit' chillis, although Lek and most Thais could eat them like Westerners eat popcorn.

There was also a very ready supply of the bush called 'cha-om'. When cooked, it smelled like an open sewer to Craig and many Thais agreed, but they loved it for its slight bitterness all the same. It was added to soups and stews or chewed raw to clean the teeth after a meal in the fields. Lek sold bags of it, which Craig was glad of, because otherwise she would have brought it home to eat.

However, the star of Lek's garden at the time was the mushroom shed. It had been a stroke of genius, because she was the only one doing it for miles around, although it was obvious that that exclusivity would not last long. Lek produced fungi and mushrooms of all sizes and types, according to the season, in the darkness of her humid shed, although a lot of the popular varieties grew all year around, since the climate didn't vary much around Baan Suay anyway.

People flocked to her for her mushrooms. On a harvest day, she would sell out in thirty or forty minutes. Three or four kilos gone at twenty Baht per hundred grammes, ten or twelve times a month. The mushrooms paid for Soom's accommodation and pocket money on their own and she wished that she had had a bigger shed built. She intended to build another.

Ideas for expansion included flowers, orchids and other 'unusual' 'hanging plants' that many Thai housewives liked to use to decorate their homes and dining areas. It seemed that the more Lek did, the more she thought of doing. It was certainly true in her case that success bred success.

Lek was on a roll for the first time since she had met Craig, although she would not have phrased it like that to him, even if the thought had crossed her mind.

Craig's contribution to the family finances came solely from his Internet work and savings, which included the sale of his house. Craig had about a hundred and fifty web sites of varying quality. Google's Panda update had hit him quite hard, because he couldn't write enough articles to keep them 'fresh' enough to stay at the top of search results, so he was paring them down working on the Pareto Principle, which stated that eighty percent of the effects came from twenty percent of the causes or that his top thirty web sites were producing eighty percent of his revenue. In fact, they weren't but it wasn't far enough off to argue about.

Craig decided to abandon a hundred web sites as they came up for their annual renewal and concentrate on his best performers. However, even running just fifty web sites was a mammoth task for one person, because it would mean writing seven, five-hundred word articles a day, which exceeded his maximum sustainable output. One day, he knew that he would have to lose another twenty.

However, on the plus side, he had always built web sites of at least five pages, with twenty supporting articles for each, so dropping a hundred web sites would give him twenty-five hundred, five-hundred-word articles to do with as he liked. Losing another twenty gave another five hundred. All he had to do now was figure out what to do with those three thousand unique articles.

The web sites had paid for daily living costs for the last five or six years, but the income had not extended to health insurance, visa expenses and holidays (and now university fees). This was the shortfall that had depleted his savings and cost him his flat. Lek's income helped, but it was still only twenty-five percent of what Soom needed for university, so until the mapang came on line, it was up to Craig to provide the money. His savings would cover that, but it did produce a very precarious situation.

One avenue open to him was the sale of those redundant articles to other web masters as PLR articles, which meant that the purchasers had the right to publish them under their own names. He had already begun to bundle articles on the same subject into ebooks on niche subjects and they were selling. Not in large quantities yet, but enough to show that money could be made there and that his articles would not go to waste.

He was making about two ebooks a week with fifteen articles in each, so he had the potential to make about two hundred ebooks and sell them multiple times each at about $5 net revenue to himself. If he retained eighty percent of the revenue from his web sites as predicted by the Pareto Rule and grew his ebook income, he thought that they could survive until the mapang could help out, but it was still iffy. Very iffy.

They needed yet more streams of income. Craig thought of eBay, but although that might work in Pattaya with its big markets, it was a lot more difficult in the countryside. He thought that he could provide a bespoke article-writing service of some sort. If a webmaster needed a set of articles on a niche subject he could write them and sell them with copyright. He might even be able to create websites for people, although there were Asians doing that already who would charge less than he and do a better job. No, he could see that a lot of his potential to earn depended on his ability to write well in English.

He had seen many web sites over the years with an appalling standard of English, obviously created by people whose second-language was English. There was also probably a market for those who could write but didn't have the time. Creating on line publicity was an on-going process as he knew only too well.

Then there was the time that Lek had thought that he had said that he was going to write a book. He was certainly not shy of writing now and was having some success with his web sites and ebooks, so why not put a few hours a day into writing a novel too? That would definitely take a different thought process though - one long, sustained story of eighty-five to a hundred thousand words was a different kettle of fish to a string of five-hundred-word articles.

Craig foresaw that continuity could be a problem if he stopped writing for a long period of time. Or should he keep notes? He had no idea, but he decided to start thinking about it and writing down some ideas when he next went to Nong's. It was an interesting idea to write a novel, but very risky. He wouldn't know whether his book would sell until after having spent hundreds of hours on it.

Hundreds of hours, the equivalent of five weeks work. Could he afford to lose five weeks work for no pay? Certainly not, but he still had money in the bank to tide them over, so if he was ever going to try it, now was the time.

Lek also had ideas of extending herself. She was still top of her class and she had lost her natural fear for computers now, so she was thinking about giving private lessons. She also thought that Craig could teach English, using the computer and the Internet as the focal point. They could even teach as a partnership to say ten or so people on a Saturday morning.

Her idea was not to just teach English in the conventional way, using colours, parts of the body, kitchen items, etc, but to teach computer terminology with the correct pronunciation and teach how to go on line and use the Internet. As Craig had told her, not everyone wants to know how the clock works, most people only want to know the time.

She could show them that or they both could.

Both of them came to these conclusions separately, but at roughly the same time. That was not anything wondrous, since they were close although they had had their rough patches, and money was an issue, so it was inevitable that they would both be thinking of ways to improve their financial health. Besides, they both knew that the inevitable outcome of doing nothing would be that Craig would be deported for insufficient funds and if he had no money, then he could not take Lek back to the UK either, which meant enforced separation and neither of them could bring themselves to contemplate that prospect.

It was there though, as large as life, looming over them a few years into the future, if they didn't do something effective to prevent it happening now.

Craig got to Nong's first, as he usually did, but instead of setting up his computer he took a notebook and pen out of his bag and wrote the date on a clean page. After a few minutes, in which Nong brought his beer, glass and ice, he wrote 'Ideas for a Novel' in the centre of the top line.

It would not have looked much to an onlooker, but to Craig it was momentous, because it meant that he was seriously going to try to write a novel and, given his circumstances, it would have to be a popular one. He sat back, pen in one hand, pint glass in the other and stared at the enormity of the implications. He was going to try to be a successful novelist as the result of a chance comment from someone, all right, his wife, when she had misheard him say something.

What gall to think that he could become a writer! He wondered what it would entail. After all, he had 'written' since he was in school and he had written letters since he had left home. Then he had written  thousands of articles for his web sites... Did that make him a writer already? He certainly didn't feel like writer. He wouldn't have had the temerity to put 'Writer' in his passport under profession.

What had he put last time? Ah, yes, 'Retired'. He hadn't known what he was then either and still didn't. He could probably safely describe himself as a marketer or better still, a webmaster, but even that sounded a bit airy-fairy. 'Marketer' would do for now, but when would he become a writer? Or an author?

That sounded even grander and even further out of his reach. He decided to stick with the goal to become a writer for now, because it sounded more attainable and turned his attention back to the almost blank sheet of paper before him.

Craig decided to come back to the story ideas later and so left fifteen blank lines and wrote 'Genres'. He wanted to try the most popular ones so he wrote: Romance; Detective; Murder; Mystery; Sci-Fi and Werewolves and Vampires on separate lines underneath each other. He wasn't sure whether they were actual recognised genres, but he knew that they were very popular subjects.

He thought about each one and put a tick before romance; mystery and werewolves and vampires. He wasn't sure he could write a detective novel and murder involved detective work, and he wasn't sure about sci-fi. He still liked Star Trek, but his knowledge of advanced propulsion theory had not advanced since then. He sat back to think about titles and then wrote:

"Mr. Fu's Mysterious Rice Crop Circles"
"The Mysterious Rice Crop Circles of Mr Fu"
"The Mystery of Mr. Fu's Rice Crop Circles"

Feeling that he had played that title out, he skipped a line and opened the inverted commas, willing the pen to perform its own mystery and suggest a title to him.... A few sips of beer later, he wrote:

"Mr. Fu and The Cow Girl"
"The Forbidden Love Life of Mrs. Fu"
"Miss Fu Goes to Town"

Another bottle later and he was enjoying the task:

"The Fu Family Vampire Alliance"
"The Fu Werewolves Declare War"
"What Became of the Family Fu?"

He was quite proud of his hour's work and also of the fact that he had thought to choose a name that was unknown to him locally. As he took another sip leaning back from the table, he saw Lek pulling up on her motorcycle. He watched her dismount – she was still beautiful and he loved looking at her.

"What's the matter? What are you looking at?"

"You, telak."

"Why? Have I got something on me?"

"No, you look fine. You are beautiful..."

"And you're drunk."

She sat down and said, "How has your day been, darling? Did you find the food I left you? Was it all right? Good. How long have you been here?"

She looked around for bottles, because Nong always cleared up after they had left every night.

"Only two? Good boy... I'll have one with you."

She shouted up two bottles, which Nong brought immediately.

"No computer today, Craig? What's the matter? Is it kaput? I can't remember seeing you without your nose stuck in that thing for years."

"I have decided to do as you suggested and try to write a novel – a book – a story."

"As I suggested? I didn't suggest that, I thought you were already writing a book...."

"I have compiled a few books, yes, but not written a story book – a novel. You gave me that idea a few weeks ago, but I'm sure you misunderstood me or perhaps I misunderstood you... anyway, that doesn't matter now. I am going to write a novel."

"What about?"

" I'm not sure yet, but I think I'll set it in Thailand and probably in the countryside. What do you think?"

"Thais will not be able to read it, so they will not buy it. You will not sell many books and it will be a waste of time. Why not write about the UK or America?"

"Mmm, well... First, I don't expect Thais to buy it. I expect falang to buy it and second many people write about the UK and I have never been to America. However, I am here, so it seems to make sense to me to write about that, 'though I could easily be wrong. I often am and this will be my first attempt, if your overwhelming enthusiasm doesn't put me off."

"Pardon?"

"Look, never mind now. Shall I read you my ideas?"

"Yes, please. You start already?"

"I started an hour ago with some ideas, that's all. He read them to her with a pause for effect after each."

"Who is Mr. Fu?"

"I don't know. There is no Mr. Fu, I made him up."

"Mmm, it is not a real Thai name, it is more Chinese. I thought you said you want to write about Thailand. And do you think that Mrs. Fu wants you to tell stories about her and her geek?"

"I don't know a Mrs. Fu... or her lovers. It's just a story in my head and it's not even that yet. Why? Is there a Fu family in the village?"

"No, not in this village, but maybe nearby. I don't know, but if you write lies about them they can take you to saan, er court, and you must pay big money. You must be careful with this in Thailand."

"Aw, come on, dear. It's a story! When you see a film on TV and the lady is called Lek, you don't think it's about you, do you? You don't go to see your lawyer the next day. Come on now..."

"OK, maybe, but you must be careful. Do you think that you can write a story about growing rice? I think you only know enough for two pages not a book, but don't worry too much about that, I know lots about rice and I can teach you. However, it is not Thai to grow rice in circles. I have never seen such rice fields in Asia..."

"Maybe in Australia. I hear that they grow rice over there too.

"You can see that we grow it in square fields, so if you change that, I think you can write a book on rice with my help... and maybe change Fu to a Thai name. We can do something there for sure.

"Er, what is this vampire and werewolves you talk about? I have heard the words before, but I do not remember."

"They are 'mythical' creatures. Stories about people who can turn into animals at night. The werewolf is a person who can turn into a wolf when there is a full moon. He runs alone or with his friends and kills and eats people and the vampire is a person who is dead, but comes alive at night as a bat and sucks blood from your throat.

"Do you have them in Thailand? I mean stories about them?"

"Oh, yes! I have seen films about Dracula and those wolves. Only Hollywood films, you know, and Thai films, but many people believe in them. We have many good and many bad spirits in Thailand that is why we have the 'Spirit House' in the garden. They can live in there if they want to, but not come live with us.

"What do you know about them? You see one already? I am scared that if you write about this, people think you know too much or maybe vampires and werewolves come to see you, because you call them. Are you sure this is a good idea, my telak?"

"I'm not sure any more after ten minutes with you, but before you sat down I thought that it had some potential, yes. I don't know why I told you. I should have predicted this. You are so superstitious, aren't you?"

"I believe in ghosts – good ghosts and bad ghosts – and these are bad ghosts. I do not want them in our house. I am very scared of them. Do you want them to come after us and make our life horrible, dear? Because they can, if you don't take care."

"No, if they exist, I don't want them in our house either. Look, I'll tell you what... You tell me all you know about good and bad ghosts in Thailand and I will promise to only write my book when I am sitting here in Nong's shop. Then, if I attract any nasty ghosts, Nong will have to deal with them OK? But for Heaven's sake don't tell her or she might ban me."

"Craig, you believe in ghosts, I know that you do, we have talked about it many times. You are not frightened of them, but I am. I know the old saying: 'Be frightened of the living, not the dead', but I am still scared. I cannot help it and now you have worried me very much.

"Maybe if you only write your story in Nong's shop we will be safe. I think that is OK, but do not work on it in our house or in our garden and never if I am sitting with you, alright? I know you think that I am stupid for believing this, but you never know and it is better not to find out. Don't tell people about your book, eh?

"Tell no-one. Not even Murray, because he will tell El and she will tell others because she will be scared like me. So, you write your book if you have to, in Nong's shop, and, er..., we'll leave it like that for now.

"I wish I had never given you the idea and encouragement to write a book now. If I knew then that you were going to write about Chinese people and their lovers or bad ghosts, I would have kept quiet... Me and my big mouth."

She ordered another beer each for them Craig would have thought it funny if he hadn't seen how much it had affected his wife, but it had never occurred to him that she would take it this badly or even badly at all. In fact, he had hoped that she would be pleased.

Lek was really worried. Craig's revelation had brought the incident with Joy back to the forefront of her mind and she was praying that he hadn't inadvertently woken her up or called her to him. She didn't mention the reason to Craig, but that was why she insisted on going home before dark and why she stayed talking to Craig in his office until he realised that he wouldn't get any more work done that night and went to bed early with Lek close beside him.

# 7 SCHOOL SUMMER HOLIDAYS

The winter in Thailand is a short and very mild one. By the second week of January, it is already a lot warmer than at Christmas and by March, it is too hot for children to attend school, since very few rural schools have air conditioning. Therefore, the school summer holidays start sometime around the middle of March and go on until early June, by which time the great monsoon has usually started. The rainfall is enough to sufficiently lower the ambient temperature so that children can study again.

Therefore, late February and early March is a stressful time for students and pupils because it is end of year examination time. Lek had no problems with her class work. If there had been such a thing as a second or even third year in her studies, she was already qualified to attend them. However, there was not, so she had been lobbying her friends at the mayor's house to find someone to teach computers.

Nic and Jan were keen on the idea, but they thought that it would be difficult to find a suitable teacher, because computing was still only just beginning to filter down from the elite to the masses and teachers were still in short supply. Who would want to teach the subject in a village on a Saturday morning for low wages? Lek understood the problem, but had no ready solution. Craig's Thai wasn't good enough and her knowledge was not deep enough either.

Lek passed top of her class as everyone had predicted and everyone that she had coached passed too. In fact, only two participants failed and they were two teenage boys whose parents had forced them to make a last ditch effort to try to stay in day school and make something of themselves, but they weren't interested.

Lek felt both sorry for and angry with them. Maybe they were not academically-gifted but they had parents who cared and had the money to keep them in school and here she was, trying to do what she should have done twenty-odd years ago. She felt like giving them a good slap and a history lesson from her past, but that would never have done.

Soom was to come home from university too. Her exams had been far more comprehensive, so she would not get her results for another six weeks, but she was confident that she had passed them. She usually did, coming somewhere in the top five or six for most subjects.

Soom was studying Systems Analysis and Computer Science, which involved some programming or coding; the study of the uses of computer hardware including peripherals and a look at what the future may have in store for mankind in that field; English language; mathematics; systems analysis and design and a few peripheral subject in less detail like logic and the history of data processing.

She had just finished her second year out of four and was loving it. She enjoyed the course, which she found taxing but within her capabilities and she enjoyed the freedom. She also enjoyed having her own money, although she was well aware where it came from and that Craig had had to work for it. She was also only paid monthly by her mother, so she didn't have the opportunity to go wild – ever.

'Going wild' for Soom meant paying for her own bottle of beer on Saturday night and her own slap-up meal once a month. Still, it was far more than she had ever had in her life in the village before, when her every move had been watched by dozens of well-meaning aunties and uncles.

It made her feel very grown-up and trusted. She didn't know it, and probably never would, but she would never suffer the crises of low self-esteem and confidence that her mother had endured until quite recently, although Lek had learned to hide it very well too.

Soom brightened the lives of everyone who knew her – she had inherited that knack from Lek, so when she returned to Baan Suay for three months, it was not only Craig, Lek and her grandmother who were affected.

She was also not the only student to return – there were dozens of them. Teenagers who had been in school together since they were six were returning home from places like Chiang Mai, Phitsanulok, Phrae, Udon, Bangkok and elsewhere. It was a fantastic time for the kids, but it brought some of them back to reality with a bump. In the village, they had to muck in again and mix with people who were not being stuffed with new knowledge everyday.

Some found that hard, but Lek and her mother had done a good job on Soom, who was a very sensible and helpful girl by any standards.

Craig didn't see her often now, because sometimes she stayed in her room in Bangkok for religious or even half-term holidays or went to stay with her Aunty Chalita on the other side of the city. Lek went down to stay whenever finances allowed but it was cheaper for her to go alone, because she would sleep on Soom's bed with her.

Obviously, Craig couldn't do that, so they would have had to run to the expense of a hotel. When she came bounding into Craig's office with her mother minutes after arrival in the village, Craig had said, "Wow, Soom, you're all grown up!". Soom had beamed at him proudly, but Lek had slapped his arm. Later she told him off, "You are not supposed to notice those things in your daughter." He had tried to make light of it by asking 'What things?' in an innocent voice, but Lek was having none of it. "You know what I mean," she had replied, "I never want to hear you talk like that about your family again."

He hadn't meant it as anything more than a compliment, but Lek was fiercely protective of her daughter.

Soom went back to her old room at her grandmother's, which Craig thought odd, but as Lek said: "That was her home when I wasn't here and when I was. The same as my grandmother brought me up. It is normal."

But Craig thought he noticed a tone of sadness in Lek's voice.

Just a slight one.

∞

Soom would be the centre of Lek's attention for the foreseeable future. There was nothing that was too much trouble to do for her, although to be fair to Soom, who did not actually ask for much, most of it originated from Lek. Lek took her shopping; took her out for lunch; took her to visit friends on her motorbike and did everything that a doting mother would like to be able to do within financial constraints.

Time was not a problem – they both had bags of that and nor was the weather, because even getting caught in a thunderstorm was only like having a warm shower. The only one who might have suffered from all this was Craig. A couple of times a week, Lek's mother brought him over a take-away from the shop on Lek's telephoned instructions. It usually went along the lines of: "Mum, you couldn't do me a favour again could you? Soom and I are over-running, could you take something from Ron's to Craig, please? I'll pay you back later. Thanks."

Sometimes the message was more honest and said that they were having such a lovely time that they didn't want to come back just yet.

Craig didn't mind too much, especially in the first week or so, but he hated to see or think that he saw sympathy or even pity in the eyes of Nong and Lek's mother. Mum would hand him his food on a plate and say apologetically: "Lek is busy with Soom... You OK?" in pigeon Thai so that he could understand. Nong was a bit more forthright: "Lek not sitting with you again tonight? Where is she today?"

That was what was getting on his nerves. The sympathy and the pity, because the village women knew that that would not be done to a Thai man – he just would not tolerate it. But then a Thai man had transport and knew where to go to teach his wife to 'behave'. Not only was Craig not able to do those things, he didn't even want to.

Soom began to pick up on the problem long before Lek acknowledged it. Lek knew that she was pushing Craig a bit far, but she also knew that he would understand why, but Soom didn't know that and her sympathies started to favour Craig. She started making excuses for not going on trips. She said that she had to write a dissertation or pre-read the course books for next year. Lek would never suspect such motives for staying home, never argue with them, and not only not feel hurt, but feel immensely proud that Soom was taking her studies so seriously.

The truth was though that Soom did not want problems between her parents and thought that Lek was being a little unfair. Most people thought that she was being very unfair and Craig had seen it all before. So he just got on with his work, but in his head, he was trying to resign himself to the worst-case scenario, that is that he would be going home alone broke in a few years time.

He had created a new work schedule to accommodate his new book-writing venture. It was a sandwich of: emails, Twitter, Facebook and web sites until four p.m; then book-writing until seven over a few beers at Nong's; followed by another layer of the mornings activities, but in the evening, he allowed himself to listen to BBC Radio 4 and 4 Extra while working. Listening to the radio over the Internet didn't have a great effect on his output, but it did create a more relaxed atmosphere.

He was working seventeen hours a day most days now: from seven a.m. until at least midnight, but there was nothing else to do so it seemed logical to carry on trying to postpone the inevitable day of departure. Lek invited him to the parties she attended regularly, but he declined all but three or four a month at most.

After the initial over-reaction to Soom's home-coming had died down, they stayed locally a lot more which meant that they all three of them saw more of each other, or to put it more accurately, the two women saw more of Craig and vice-versa. They started working on Lek's suan together and at midday they would both go to Mum's house and cook a meal for themselves, Mum and Craig.

It was almost invariably Soom who brought it over to Craig. She always put the plate or plates on his desk and gave a little curtsy in the old Thai style. Craig had seen it done before but never so correctly, so olde worlde. He wanted to say that there was no need for it, but it was obvious that Soom derived pleasure from being so dutiful, so correct, so respectful. Maybe that was the right word – respectful.

Maybe she realised that her own father should have been paying for her education and that Craig was going it voluntarily and feeling the pinch because of it to boot. She was certainly not dull and she had lived in Bangkok for two years, which was a pretty tough teacher in itself.

God knew what she had seen going on there, but neither God nor Soom were telling at the moment.

∞

One day, Lek came into the office quite excited:

"Guess what! Ayr is coming back for a few days! She can't stay long because she has promised Beou that she will be in Daddy's Hobby to man the till at Songkhran, but she can stay in Baan Suay for a few days! Isn't that great?"

"Yes, dear. It sure is. We haven't been down to Pattaya for … er, a year or two? Jeez, is it that long already? And I can't remember the last time I saw her up here... two or three years? Maybe more?

"Yes, it will be nice to see her again. When is she arriving?"

"This evening, I think, but maybe tonight. I am not sure which bus she is on, but I doubt that we will see her until tomorrow anyway. She will want to see her family first, shower and sleep and all that... You know. But it is great news, isn't it?

"I must get Soom to help me give the house a good going-over and tidy up the garden. We can't have her seeing us like this, can we?"

"Why ever not? I have to see us 'like this' every day!"

"Yes, but you don't count, you live here. Half this mess is yours anyway. You should take more interest in the house. You are here all day, I am not, so most of this mess is yours, not mine."

The irony in what she had just said escaped her now that she was on a mission.

"What mess?"

"All this dust and your office is very untidy..."

"Yes all right dear... I'll try to stop shedding so much skin and making so much dust, but there is nothing that I can do about the office or my desk. I need all these things to be where they are. So do what you like out there in the rest of the house and in the garden, but leave the office alone. I'm sure that Ayr will forgive me or you can just tell her that I'm an untidy falang."

Lek knew that that was all the help that she would get from Craig, so she phoned the thirty yards to her mother's house to enrol Soom's assistance in the big clean-up.

They started inside and thankfully left the office until last. Craig used the opportunity to have a shower and he noticed that it and the kitchen were gleaming in a way that he hadn't seen for a long time, he wondered why Lek was going to so much trouble to impress her oldest friend – one of the Three Musketeers that had gone to Pattaya together twenty years before. When he went back into his office, they had washed the floor tiles and the inside of the windows and Lek was cleaning the outside. Soom was tidying his desk.

"Mum wanted to tidy your desk, but I said that I would do it. I haven't really moved anything, because I know how personal a desk top is. I'm just pretending really, because I know that Mum would have put all your stuff in the draw.

"Now that you're back, I'll go and help her and say that you said you needed everything where it is. Is that OK?"

"Yes... That is perfect. Thanks, dear."

"That's OK." She smiled, performed another little curtsy and soon appeared outside the window helping Lek, who whispered something to her, they both looked at him and began to laugh.

Craig knew far better than to think that it was anything more than a good-natured wind-up from his wife.

He had always liked to watch Lek working in the garden and now he was enjoying watching mother and daughter so obviously enjoying one another's company.

'Sanuk' they called it in Thai – it meant fun at work, pleasure with one's co-workers or comrades, camaraderie, or group enjoyment.

∞

The following afternoon, Lek instructed Craig that lunch would be served in the garden at two o'clock.

It was put so formally that he didn't know whether it was a joke or not. He was used to eating at his desk.

Lek laid out clean clothes for him. He had noticed Lek and Soom cooking in the garden earlier.

As the time approached, Lek went in to shower and Soom went home to do the same.

"Have you had a shower yet, telak?"

"Yes, my dear, and two minutes before I go outside, I will change my clothes. Is that all right?"

"Yes... Perfect...," he heard just before the bathroom door locked.

Craig had guessed that this had something to do with Ayr, but he didn't know why the preparations were so elaborate, but then he was used to being only half in the know. It seemed to be the way Thai women treated falang, because he had heard many men complain about it. Maybe they were the same with Thai men too, but if they were, he had never heard a Thai man complain about it. The one thing he did know was that it certainly was not only Lek who behaved in this way.

When Lek came out of the shower, she was wearing a towel and singing. She was looking forward to seeing her old Musketeer friend again and very curious about the man that Ayr had said she was bringing with her. Ayr had always been the only one of the three who had never seemed to want to settle down. She herself had had Craig, Goong had had something going with Will, but Ayr had never been 'close' to anyone, as far as she knew and they had been friends since kindergarten.

Ayr had said that she was bringing a man back, so that meant someone special, but she had also said that she wanted to play the situation by ear. Ayr was obviously walking on eggshells with this one. The question was, did that mean she liked him or needed him? Lek only had to wait an hour before she would be able to judge for herself.

Naturally, she had not told Craig any of this because first, it was none of his concern; second, there was no guarantee that he would show up and third, he wouldn't care anyway. He took things as they came and didn't bother too much about what anyone else thought. Sometimes, she even wondered whether he worried about what she thought, but she had decided to give him the benefit of the doubt on that one many years before.

She put on her make-up as carefully as she always had done when she wore any, which was not often these days as she had had her eyebrows and a line around her eyes tattooed regularly for the last few years. It saved quite a bit of work on a daily, routine basis in the village. She had also had her lips outlined a few years before, but Craig had actually noticed that, so it must have been garish and she hadn't been too keen on it either, so she had let that fade out.

She wore a new white top with embroidered dragons up each front side and knee-length shorts with lace frills at the end of the legs and a floral pattern embroidered on one of the rear pockets. She thought she still had a nice bum and that that drew a little attention to it.

Once dressed, she checked herself in the mirror and went to see how Craig was getting on.

"Are you ready, darling? They will be here in a moment. Come on, get off that computer, put your shirt on and let's go outside. You can have a beer in the garden and I'll take your fan out too. Come on, move!"

"Yes, all right... You said two o'clock and it's only ten to... and Thais are always late anyway... Who are 'they'?"

"They? Did I say 'they'... well, Ayr may have a friend with her, but Soom will be here soon too, so come on! Please, go now."

She put his clean shirt on his keyboard and took his fan outside.

Craig had to follow Lek out as they had no air-con and it was sweltering indoors without a fan.

"Now, you sit there, Craig. Here is a cold beer for you and a glass with ice. Now where is Soom …?"

"Look, Lek, it is nice and cold, so I'll just drink it straight from the bottle, you can save..."

"Just drink it from the glass with the ice... OK?"

"OK, if that's what you want." He took a rebellious swig from the bottle.

"It is. Thank you. Best behaviour today. I want everything right for Ayr, so you just take care... They're here..."

Lek ran down to the lane garden gate and opened it for her friend. A man was taking off a crash helmet and walking towards them.

"Oh, it is so good to see you again, Ayr," there was no physical contact as normal between Thais, but not even a waai as they had dropped that habit between themselves decades before.

"This is my friend Ross, he is from Australia"

He waaied Lek and Craig who had got up to stand behind Lek.

"Come on in, Ross, don't stand in the lane."

Ross put his hand to Ayr's back to encourage her to go first and as she came through the gate, Craig took her hand and kissed her on each cheek as he always had done with Lek's best friends. Then he shook hands warmly with Craig, who responded likewise.

"Can I get you a beer, Ross?" Lek was already talking to Ayr a few feet away in a lowered tone.

"He seems lovely, Ayr. Is this your 'special friend'? He is very polite, isn't he? And very distinguished too."

Ross was about sixty-five years of age, with a weathered complexion and a full head of grey, white and dark hair that looked almost steel coloured. He was tall, at least six feet two and stood bolt up-right with a military bearing, although his clothing was like Craig's – very casual. However, Ross' clothes had sharp lines ironed into them which said that he had ironed them himself as Craig had never seen clothes come back from even a laundry that immaculate.

"Cheers, mate!" said Craig.

Ross held his bottle up and took a swig, before looking round to see where Ayr was. He waved the bottle at the ladies and then took another, smaller drink.

Both men were well aware that Lek and Ayr were talking about Ross, although they were pretending to be busy with the food.

And the women knew that the men knew, but didn't care.

It was normal

"So, Craig, have you lived up here long?"

"About eight years now, I think. Maybe a bit less, I came over from Wales about eight years ago, but we stayed in Pattaya for a while. How about you?"

"Wales, eh? Rugby... I've been coming to Thailand on and off for twenty years, I reckon. I still can't speak the lingo though. How is your Thai?"

"Worse than yours, I imagine. I spend most of my time working – on the computer, the Internet... web sites, that sort of thing. It keeps me off the streets, out of the boozer and the wolf from the door, you know..."

"Yes... I'd imagine a guy would need a hobby up here. Excuse the French, but there's bugger all to do, is there."

"I don't know why we need to excuse the French, but no, there isn't much to do. As someone told me once... 'there is only work here, you have to make your own pleasure' or something very like that anyway. But it is true.

"My way is to live in my head, work and try to learn Thai in my spare time. It suits me, but I don't seem to get much spare time... hence the poor Thai. What do you like to do?"

"I can do computers, but I like to be outside. I like to look after myself. I'm retired now though, so I don't burn calories at work any more. I walk, swim, run and climb a bit, you know..."

"Yesss...," said Craig slowly. "How long are you both here for? Ross is a Welsh name as far as I know... were your family from Wales originally?"

"Ye-as, they were! From near Snowdon, you know, the mountain? It has one of those weird Welsh names... oh, no offence, but I could never remember it. North Wales, anyway, 'though the country's so small, I don't know how they know what is north, south, east or west."

Ross was pleased with his joke, but it sounded like one that he had made many times before, although probably not in front of many Welsh people.

"It's big enough for us to know which way is up and which way down, y'know. Still, which part of Oz are you from then?"

Ross was just about to say, when Lek, Ayr and Soom started putting dishes of food on the table. Ross stood up and Lek told him to sit down again, which he did.

The meal started out with a little too much formality with the women trying to impress Ross and Ross trying to behave like a perfect gentleman, but as the drinks went down and the ladies saw that Craig and Ross were getting on well, everybody let their hair down and had a good time.

"What do you think of bamboo, Ross?"

"I like it..."

"Yes, so do I. It has become one of my favourites and the dish we had today came from my wife's own garden, Not this one, but one over there. Anyway, I'm not sure what vitamins are in it, but Lek calls it 'Elephant Food' and look at them!

"I tend to think of it as a gut-cleaner. The haute cuisine equivalent of the rifle pull-through. Eating a handful of that is like poking a piece of four by two down your throat and out your backside.

"What do you think?"

"Um, er, um, I thought it was very nice. I had never thought of it in the terms that you describe..."

"Look, don't worry. Lek knows that it's one of my favourites. Just relax, Ross."

However, Craig knew that he had to do something to break the tension that he had unwittingly caused.

He spoke to Ayr, avoiding Lek's steady gaze, but smiling back at Soom, who was grinning from ear to ear beside her mother out of her direct vision.

"It is lovely to see you back in the village, Ayr, but how is life in Pattaya?"

Ayr knew what he was up to and was willing to help.

"It's OK, but everyday the same. A little bit boring now. Twenty years more, it is enough, you know? Maybe I want to look for something new. Maybe come back to Baan Suay, but is big decision, you know? I cannot do quickly.

"I hear what you say to Ross, I the same. I must work. I cannot stop yet, but do what? I am old lady now and cannot work in the field same as before... and I don't want to too."

Craig picked up the baton gratefully and ran with it:

"Oh, Ayr, you are the same age as Lek, you are not old. Neither of you look much over thirty. Certainly not like us old crocks over here. Do they look old to you, Ross?"

"No, of course not. They are both in their prime...." Craig had known that Ross' gallantry would not let him down. Ayr smiled at Craig, knowing that he had got out of that one pretty well, and Lek smiled at Ross for the compliment. Not that she had been fooled into anything, it was just her conditioning from birth to be polite and please men, and from ten years doing the same in Pattaya. It was almost impossible for her to behave in any other way

Soom just thought that the whole situation was all very funny, but tried not to show it.

# 8 SONGKHRAN

The morning after the afternoon with Ayr and Ross, Craig tried to find out some more details from Lek.

"That was a lovely afternoon and evening, yesterday, Lek. It is easy to get out of the habit of entertaining – at least, it is for me. I suppose I've become a bit of a hermit now. I don't go anywhere and hardly want to anyway. Different for you, you still get about...

"Ayr said that she had sort of had enough of Pattaya and might come back here to live. What do you think? With Ross?"

"I don't know, telak. You know me, I don't talk about what I don't know. I am not the same as falang – always want to know this or want to know that or guessing or asking.

"Why do you want to know? Is it your business? Do you really care? Why do you falang ask so many silly, pointless questions?

"When Ayr is ready, she will tell you, if she wants you to know. That is my advice to you and it is not the first time that I have recommended minding your own business in Thailand, is it?"

It certainly was not, but Craig was naturally curious and liked to speculate. Lek was the opposite and could wait until she was told, which she had been, but she was not at liberty to tell Craig – not that he had anyone to tell anyway.

"OK, fair enough, I won't ask again," and then sotto voce, "at least for a while...

"Are you going into the market today, Lek?"

"Yes, I was going to ask Soom to come with me..."

"Well, why don't you ask me instead? I haven't been anywhere for months. I fancy sitting in Ben's shop, doing the crossword and watching the shoppers. I may even write a bit of my book... When you are not there, of course."

"So, you sit drinking and I have to go shopping alone. If I take Soom we do everything together and have sanuk..."

"Look, one time in several months is not much to ask, is it? I like, even need to get out of the village sometimes too. Anyway, you are bound to see someone in there you know. Phone Su and ask her when she's going in. You can meet up."

"Yes, all right, you win, but you must shower now. I want to go before the sun gets too strong."

"OK, great. I'll be ten minutes."

He felt as happy as a child going on a school day trip.

Once in Phichai, Craig left Lek locking the bike outside the coffee shop and went in alone.

"Hello, Ben, how are you? Long time no see..."

Ben turned, a big smile on her face, and waaied.

"Hello, Khun Craig. I am fine. How are you? Where is Pee Lek?"

"She's..., uh, she was just there. Probably gone to the bank. She won't be long. She wants to go to the market and I'm going to sit here and read the paper, which reminds me, I'd better do that now in case someone else gets it. Wait a moment... I'll have a cold Chang, please."

He nipped next door to the newspaper stand and bought the last copy. The vendor recognised Craig and waaied with a big smile. Craig waaied back and returned to Ben's. He saw his beer, although not his wife, but sat down anyway.

"I don't know where Lek has got to... She must have met someone I suppose. Thanks for the beer."

"You want me phone her? I have the number."

"No, it's OK, thanks, Ben, she'll be here when she's good and ready."

"Pardon," she said coming over to the table, "when?"

"'When she's good and ready', it's an expression, a saying, it means 'in her own time'. She will be here when she wants to come."

"Yes, I see. I think so too. When she is good and ready"

Ben spoke the best English of any Thai he had met in the area in eight years, except Lek, but unlike Lek, she liked to practice reading English too. Craig had often left the fashion page for her to read over the years and he was looking for it now, if it was still a feature of the Tuesday edition.

"Here Ben, a present for you. Some homework."

She smiled broadly at the joke. If she had more English-speaking customers, she would soon be speaking English really well as she must have done at one time before she got rusty. There were virtually zero tourists in this area.

"Any falang about, Ben?"

"Yes, I did see one new face two days ago. A big man from England, but he did not stay long. He was angry, I think. I tried to say hello, but he didn't want to talk and he left after one quick coffee. Maybe he has go already. Maybe stop here for a little time and drive on to Chiang Mai. You see this sometimes."

Lek came in. They greeted each other and Lek sat down.

"An iced coffee, please, Ben. I'm tired already. I went over to the bank, bumped into a friend outside and got chatting, but that sun! It can wear you out just by standing in it. I was trying to get away or get her to move into he shade, but she works outside all day, so the heat doesn't affect her so much.

"Right, I can't sit here gossiping all morning or the market will be closed. I've only got an hour as it is. See you both later." She drank some coffee and left.

Ben had a steady stream of customers to serve, but it didn't take long to put a ladle of whatever they wanted in a dish or serve a drink. All the hard work – the buying in, chopping, peeling and cooking was done before six a.m. Lunch was actually near the end of her working day. She usually sold what she had, cleared up and went home at about three, but she liked falang, so if there was one in, she would stay open and chat. Murray was her most regular falang customer.

"How is Murray? Is he about?"

"No, Murray went back to Canada two weeks ago. It is too hot for him here in the summer and he say Canada is very beautiful in spring. El not go though, she may come in later."

Ben pointed to the entrance with her chin. It was a white foreigner – a falang. He nodded briefly at Craig, but sat as far away as possible, which was only about four yards. Craig went back to his paper. The bloke still looked angry, or maybe he was always grumpy. Craig didn't care, he had never been the first one to talk to foreigners anyway.

About thirty minutes later, he heard:

"You'm from 'round 'ere? I say, are you from 'round 'ere?"

Craig looked up, a Brummy accent, or from around about Birmingham anyway.

"Yeah, I live about fifteen miles away."

"Shit 'ole, in'it?"

"What is?"

"This place. It's a dump. I hate it, me."

"Each to his own," he said and went back to his paper.

"I've got to stay another thirteen days 'cause my wife is from a village nearby and this is the only place to come for miles around. Is that my paper you got there from the news stand outside. The Bangkok Post?"

"Did you order a paper?"

"No, but I've been here four days and there's always been one there for me."

"It is the Bangkok Post from there, yes, but he has been buying one copy for at least eight years and it goes to the first one who asks for it. You were too late today and you may be a few more times in the next fortnight too."

"Like I said, a shit 'ole. No regular English papers, no English food or beer, no English TV. It's a dump, no wonder no-one comes 'ere. All they got is that Thai piss that you're drinking. You like that stuff do you?"

"I don't want to be rude, but I don't get a lot of free time, so I'd be grateful if you would just let me read my paper and enjoy my beer in peace. OK?"

"Please yourself. Just trying to be sociable..."

Craig neither raised his head nor answered him and a few minutes later, he heard him leave.

"What a horrible man, Ben! That was the prick from the other day? Sorry, I meant the man from the other day?" but Ben hadn't caught the word and wouldn't have understood it anyway.

"Yes. Did he say he stay here thirteen more days?"

"Yes. I probably won't see him again, I don't come to Phichai often, but I think you will. Look, here is two hundred Baht... I want you to buy the Bangkok Post every morning early for the next eight days, but put them in your bag, eh? Don't let him see them and tell the newspaper man to say that a falang bought them. OK. You can give them to Lek for me later.

"I don't care about the news, I just want them for the puzzles and to upset our angry old man. Maybe he'll stop coming into town for a paper after a while."

Ben put her hand before her mouth and chuckled, then said,

"Just like a stone or a lizard get energy from the sun, miserable, unhappy, angry people take energy from the happy. It is best to avoid them."

She couldn't wait to tell Lek and El her story.

∞

As Songkhran approached, the level of excitement increased in the village on a daily basis. Most Thais would have no hesitation in saying that it was their favourite festival by far. It also attracted many tourists to Thailand, although they only saw the commercialised, city version of it, which was often 'enhanced' just for them. Most places celebrated Songkhran for three days, but it went on for ten days in Pattaya and more than three days in a few other places too.

Songkhran was the original Thai New Year, defunct now because Thailand followed the Western New Year on January 1st officially, but the people still celebrated their own ancient version just as the Chinese did. Some foreigners called it the 'Water Festival', but then some foreigners called Loy Krathong in November the 'Water Festival' too or 'The Festival of Light'. Craig found it easier to stick to the Thai name for Thai New Year. It was his favourite festival too.

Songkhran started always on the 14th of April, which made it the only Thai festival that was not variable depending on the moon. The village was sure to swell by twenty to thirty percent as factories and government offices closed for the holidays and people went home to celebrate with their families.

Craig had had three Songkhrans in Pattaya, but he had not enjoyed them. The Thais were fine – well, most of them, but the falang went crazy. They actually became a public nuisance. They missed the point of the ceremony completely, thinking it was just about partying all day, totally ignoring the religious aspect. Every year, Songkhran was one of those times when you knew you were going to feel ashamed to be a foreigner several times.

Songkhran in the village was totally different. Kids under the age of about twelve would throw water on you, if they knew you or if you encouraged them to. People would ask permission to smear your cheeks with wet, scented talcum powder. Dousing someone with water was an act of kindness in the scorching sun and a sign that you were willing to give them water in a period that was essentially a drought.

Rubbing talc on the face, wet so that it would stick longer, was an act of wishing someone good luck for the following year. These were acts of kindness to Thais, but the falang had turned them into signs of derision, because they didn't understand what was really going on. They hadn't bothered to find out and the bar girls didn't want to spoil the boys' fun, in case they went elsewhere.

One year, the local government in Pattaya had threatened to ban the sale of alcohol over Songkhran if the foreigners didn't behave themselves with more decorum and recognise that it was essentially a religious festival, albeit part Buddhist and part pre-Buddhist.

Lek and all her friends and family really enjoyed this time of the year far more than any other. Lek actually saved a little money every week for a few months before the New Year, so that she would not be short at the wrong time, but then that was a habit that she and most other poor Thais had had since they were school children.

Chalita and Deo would be coming back as they always did and Beou would stay for four days and then have five or six days of it in Pattaya too. It was part of the job to be there for this the busiest or joint busiest time of the year, but she also made a fortune.

Songkhran was an especially poignant time of the year for arable farmers, which was still the vast majority of the population, because it was a plea to God for the Heavens to open up and send the Great Monsoon, which would not only fill rivers, reservoirs and ponds, but saturate the soil thus raising the water table. The Great Monsoon had come in early to mid May for centuries, but was now less predictable, but only a little less.

∞

Lek's family arrived back in the village on the 13th, so the New Year's celebrations started for them, as it did for most families, the day before New

Year's Eve, but it was a very low-key start as they were tired from driving so far. All the family gathered in Mum's garden on and around the big outside table and chopped and peeled vegetables, while sharing a bottle or two of whisky.

Lek was there, but Craig only popped in to say hello on his way home from Nong's. He was of the firm conviction that their parties went far smoother without his being there, because then no-one had to be concerned whether he could understand or not. He knew that it certainly made things easier for Lek, because she had told him so many times.

He didn't mind, the coming three days of excess would be plenty enough for him. He preferred to go back and write another article or maybe indulge in his new-found pleasure: Columbo on the Internet. He had liked Columbo the American cop series as a teenager and he had recently discovered, quite by chance, a web site that showed episodes of Columbo back to back twenty-four hours a day, every day. He had heard of such sites before, but it was only recently that his connection speed was sufficiently fast to watch them in full streaming video

He didn't want to become addicted to them because he knew that he could waste days and eventually weeks just watching Columbo re-runs, he was that starved of TV entertainment that he enjoyed. He thought he might watch one or two episodes back to back while typing up some articles that he had written in a notebook a while before.

Lek came in pretty early for a family gathering with her rarely-seen close relatives, but as she pointed out, she had to be out again before six o'clock. She went to bed at eleven o'clock, but Craig watched four episodes until two a.m. He hadn't watched so much TV since they were last in Pattaya well over a year ago and he had enjoyed this more anyway.

After a quick shower, he reluctantly joined Lek in bed and was soon fast asleep.

After what seemed like a few minutes sleep to both of them, came the loud music that they knew would come at five-thirty. Not as loud as for a funeral or a weeding, but pretty loud when it was coming from a neighbour – Mum's house. It was not only coming from there either, most of the families in Baan Suay were getting ready for the big day before the very big day. Lek was away like a starter's hare as usual, but Craig thought he might take his computer to bed with him and watch some more Columbo.

"Craig, not coming over for breakfast?" asked Chalita, Lek's sister. "He can sit with the men over there and have an early beer."

"He does love his beer, that's true, and he doesn't mind getting up early either, but his first few drinks of the day are usually coffee," replied Lek. "Anyway, I don't want to teach him any bad habits. If he's not here by lunch time or when we get back from the temple, I'll go and get him. He doesn't eat Thai food for breakfast either. Only toast and yoghurt, but he'd just as soon have nothing until lunch. Strange, isn't he?"

They both laughed. It was almost inconceivable to them that someone would not want to eat if there was food available.

"That reminds me. I ordered him four loaves of bread yesterday. Soom, will you go and collect the bread for Craig and put it in our fridge for him? Thanks. Here is the money."

Lek took random nips of Thai whisky as she passed food from the women cooking it to the men eating it. Neither Chalita nor their mother drank alcohol, but Lek made up for them. They just didn't know where she put it all and how she could still walk about, but that was nothing new.

When Soom returned, Lek asked, "How was Craig?"

"I don't know, Mum, I think he's in bed watching the TV. I heard something, but didn't see him. I don't think he even knew I was there."

Lek had to go and investigate, because it wasn't like Craig not to be working already.

She found him propped up on the bed with his computer on his lap, watching a film.

"What is that?" she asked as she perched on the edge of the bed so she could watch too.

"It's Columbo. Do you know him? Policeman, American, from the Seventies, Eighties and maybe Nineties?"

"Yes, I remember him. I used to like him too. Where did you get the DVD's?"

"This is not DVD, it is live off the Internet. Great, isn't it? People can do this for years in some countries, but now TOT is fast enough too. I only found out a few days ago. I love Columbo."

"OK, Soom said she heard the TV in the bedroom, so I had to come and check. I thought maybe you sick and take TV come in here. Very good. I must go back to my family now. You come when you want, but we go to the Wat at ten o'clock. Come back maybe twelve o'clock. Bye, telak," and she kissed him lightly on the lips, before she left.

"He's sitting up in bed watching old TV films on his computer. No DVD's though, from the Internet. I didn't even know that that was possible."

"Sure, Mum, if your connection is fast enough, that is faster than about 7 Mbits a second. We've had it in some areas of Bangkok for a while now and I can get super-fast access at uni, over 15 Mbits on a good day, but TOT has started rolling the service out all over Thailand. I guess we are just lucky in this area to be one of the first to get it."

"Will you listen to my daughter speak! That's how Craig speaks. I thought I didn't understand it because he was speaking in English, but I don't understand it in my own language either! You are bright, Soom, at least I know that you are learning something down there in Bangkok, even if I don't understand what it is."

"Aw, Mum, it's just technical stuff," replied Soom embarrassed.

"I'm sure it is." said her uncle Deo, "Can you explain to us thickos what it all means? That's a challenge and a half, isn't it, Soom?"

"I'll have a go, uncle. Megabits per second is the number of pieces of data or information that are being sent per second in thousands. Let's say that a film runs at twenty-five frames a second, most do, and each frame takes one thousand pieces of information, then you need a speed of 25 Mbits/s to watch the film or it will appear jerky."

"7 Mb/s doesn't seem fast enough then", put in Chalita.

"No, but they compress the data. Let's say that Mum, Gran, Craig and some others wanted to send me birthday presents – I wish – they could send them separately in five boxes, or they could send them in one together. So I would get one packet instead of five packets. You can do this with data too.

"The sending computer wraps data into parcels and the receiving computer unwraps them again. So at 7 Mb/s with a compression ratio of 5:1, the receiver is actually getting 35,000 bits or 35 frames. So, it plays 25 and builds up a store of 10 every second. Of course, you need fast computers to be able to do all this."

Soom's grandmother said, "Even I understood that."

Lek was as proud as an exceptionally proud peahen.

∞

Craig decided to go looking for everyone at noon. He walked past Mum's house but hoped that they were working to Thai time and would not be there, although Lek had said they would be. He was in luck, they had not gotten back from the Wat yet, so he walked on to Nong's shop to see who was about.

After eight Songkhran's he knew better that to take his computer or even his wallet, so he put a few hundred Baht and the folded crossword section from a newspaper into a resealable plastic bag and set off. The kids around the corner knew that he wouldn't mind, so they threw water at his legs. A few other kids squirted him with water pistols, but he was dry again within an hour.

He sat at Nong's and waited with his crossword.

Nong brought out a silver bowl and asked if she could put water on him. He agreed and she tipped a cupful from the bowl down the back of his neck. He thanked her and she went away happy.

From time to time, girls visiting the shop would ask if they could put talc, which they kept in mini washing up liquid bottles, on his face. He loved it. Crag was happy to sit there all day, he didn't mind in the slightest.

∞

Lek and her family had taken the cars to the Wat and when they were invited to a party to celebrate the initiation into the monkhood of the son of one of their acquaintances, their plans evaporated.

They passed Craig still sitting in Nong's shop at four-thirty and waved guiltily, but there was no need, because he was happier where he was.

Lek went back to the shop to see how he was getting on.

"So, sorry, telak. We were invited to a party for a boy becoming a monk and everyone want to go. Are you OK? Happy?"

"Happy might be a bit strong, but I am all right. I'm just sitting here on my own as usual keeping myself amused as usual. Just an ordinary day with more water and talcum powder."

"Who put powder on you?"

"Some girls came by and did it."

"Young girls or old girls?"

"I don't know, how old is an old girl?"

"Sixteen, seventeen, eighteen, you know, what I mean."

"I'm not always sure what you mean. No. In English 'old girl' usually refers to an old lady. You could say 'elderly teenager' but no-one ever would. 'Young lady' might be best. But, yes, about that age about seventeen, I suppose."

"Did you know them?"

"No, I don't think so. Maybe they are here on holiday. I don't know. Shall I get their telephone numbers next time?"

"I am not jealous. You know me."

"Yes, darling, I know you. Look, if you want to go and sit with your family, take three beers for me and I will come there before it gets dark. I'll just sit here and see if anyone else comes along."

Lek, slapped his shoulder and left.

Craig kept his word, but only just. He arrived about five minutes before darkness fell, but with a few more bottles, which always helped. He said 'hello' to Deo first, but that didn't last long as neither of them spoke the other's language. Deo was their brother-in-law and was a thoroughly decent man. He had not wanted to be a farmer, so had moved to Bangkok after he had married Lek's sister.

He had worked hard, as had his wife, and after twenty years, without paying any bribes, he was a line manager on a very good wage. He enjoyed sport and had been a good football player, but that was behind him now. He was one of those people who enjoyed life and accepted whatever it dealt him. Deo knew no English and had no intention of learning any. They liked each other, they were brothers-in-arms, each with a Suksawat sister for a wife.

Then he spoke to Chalita, who looked a lot like Lek and who also spoke English quite well, Craig suspected, but she always seemed as if she needed a week's practice with a native speaker. She struggled for words, but knew them when reminded, a little like Ben.

And finally he sat with Beou and Lek – The Inseparables. It was easy to talk to them as Beou's English was almost as good as Lek's. The three of them were friends, but he knew that Lek out-ranked him and always would, although Beou always referred to him as cousin these days and had done off and on for about eight years.

As last time, when they were all three together at the Western New Year, Craig went home early and left them to it.

∞

Lek hadn't got in before he went to bed and she wasn't there when he woke up to the sound of music from his mother-in-law's house. Either she had not come home or left even earlier than normal. It was pretty typical for Songkhran, especially if Beou was back. It had never happened at any other time of the year or when anyone else was involved.

He had a quick wash, brushed his teeth and went over to find out what was going on. Staying out all night, even at her mother's house was not to be encouraged. He was working himself up for a big argument and, although it would mean that he would lose a lot of face, he was beyond caring.

As he opened the gate to the lane that separated their house from Mum's, Lek was coming through a gap in the hedge made for that purpose.

"Where the hell have you been all night?"

"Sorry, telak, must go to the toilet quickly, talk to you later," she said and she hurried past him. Craig continued on through the hedge. As he rounded the corner to the seating area, he saw her two brothers, brother-in-law and sister sitting there stern-faced as if waiting for him.

"Lek bai non nee gap Beou. Mao maak maak. Mai dee, eh?"

Craig understood, but Chalita translated just in case:

"Lek sleep here with Beou," she said, pointing at the table on which the men were seated. "Both peoples very, very drunk. Not nice. Eh?"

"Mai dee," he agreed, pulling up a chair.

Deo handed him a Chang from a small fridge situated on the table, Chalita took it from him, opened it and passed it back.

"Pee sao dirm lao maak maak Songkhran," said Long the elder of Lek's brothers.

"My big sister drinks a lot of whisky at Songkhran," put in Chalita.

"Tang atit, tuk atit... All week, every week not only at Songkhran" replied Craig and wished he hadn't because it sounded too critical, although they all knew that it was true. He didn't know how to finish the sentence in Thai. He hoped that someone would change the subject, otherwise he thought that he would have to leave. He didn't want to discuss Lek even with her closest family, because it seemed disloyal somehow, although they were exactly the people with whom he should be talking, because they were the only ones she would listen to.

The younger brother, Ngat, who always wore a big smile said:

"Pee Lek dirm tang wan, ther tuk khon dirm maak maak Songkhran..."

"Lek does drink every day, but everyone drinks too much at Songkhran."

Everyone nodded sagely and Craig hoped that that would be an end to it. So did everyone else, but they knew that there were still two days to go, so doubted it.

Back at home, Lek had finished being sick in the toilet bowl, had brushed her teeth and was lying on the floor with the TV and a fan on snoring loudly.

At ten o'clock, everyone bar Mum, who stayed behind cooking, started the kilometre trek to the Wat, from where a procession would march around the village. Craig parted from their company at Nong's, but knew that they would meet up again at about noon when the procession usually got to the shop. It was 42°c and most people were dripping wet from perspiration and having had water thrown at or put on them.

More than half of the people he saw had a bottle of whisky, large or small, with them. There were six 'old girls', as Lek had called them, sitting at 'his table' when he arrived. As he walked up they started giggling behind their hands. Normally they would have got up and left at first sight of him, because it did not do for girls of their age to mix with men they were not related to.

"Sabaai dee Bpee Mai, poo ying, Happy New Year, ladies" he said. "Nang ni dai, mai? May I sit here?"

They all wished him a Happy New Year and waaied him. One of the girls shifted up a lot more than necessary as a token gesture to propriety. Craig waaied back before sitting on the very edge of the bench as a mark of respect to the nearest girl.

One of them said, "Happy New Year, Mr Craig. Do you like Thai New Year very much?"

Nong was busy, but she had seen Craig and brought him a bottle, no glass and no ice, but he knew the score. Nong didn't want her glasses to go walkies.

"Yes, very much, thank you. And you?" he replied to the girl that he had seen at a few of Soom's parties when she was still in school. As he looked around the six faces, you knew that he had seen them all before, but only in school uniform. They looked a lot different in wet shorts and wet T-shirts. They were drinking a large bottle of coke from plastic cups. One of the girls pulled a 'ben' – a half bottle of whisky out of the front of her shorts, giggled, took the top off and offered it to Craig for a swig.

"Dirm bia, kap – I drink beer, thanks. Lao keng maak maak phom – Whisky is too strong for me." They all giggled again. By rights, he should have taken it so as not to cause offence, but he hoped that this was an acceptable excuse.

As she poured a little into each cup, he was thinking that most boys of her age would have given an arm to hold that bottle after where it had been. She lifted up her T-shirt and put it back.

When they left half an hour later, one of the girls got a pitcher of water from the butt and asked if she could wet him. He didn't mind, so all the girls had a go and then they huddled around to dab watery talc on his face. As they were all around him and no-one could see, one of the girls looked around and then pulled her bottle out from her shorts and handed it to Craig.

"Please Mr. Craig, for good luck, happy New Year."

He could not refuse a second time so he took the bottle and a short swig. They clapped hands as he handed it back. Then the other five wanted him to have a drink for good luck. He was pretty glad that Lek was not about, because she would have shooed these chicks away like a farmer's wife.

With their bens safely stowed, they danced off to join the procession.

Ngat was right, everybody drank at Songkhran and some of the women got a little naughty, but he had never seen any trouble in the village in eight years.

Beou came minutes later with Soom. She hugged him and put a cheek to him to be kissed, then the other one. Beou had stopped caring about propriety a long time ago and the rules were relaxed at New Year anyway, probably because everyone was half cut. Craig got more kisses on the cheek on this one day every year that on all the other three hundred and sixty-four combined.

They waaied him and sat down, "Want a drink?" said Beou, holding out a full bottle of whisky. He took it – in for a penny, he thought. "Thanks. I would have been offended if you had refused after accepting drinks from those girls. I might even have got jealous. Where is Lek?"

"I don't know. Last time I saw her she was running towards the house. Maybe she's still there. The others are in the procession by now, I imagine. We all left together about forty-five minutes ago."

"Yes, Lek's mum said. You'd wait here, like you do every year, I suppose? At your writer's table..."

"Ah, you've heard about the book then?"

"Of course! Lek was telling me about it last night and she made herself so scared that she wouldn't walk home alone at that hour. Three or four o'clock, I think it was. I said 'Well, don't look at me, I'm not walking you home'. Next thing I knew I was waking up. The family was getting up so I went home and left her there asleep.

"What is it about? Want another beer? Nong! A beer for Craig."

"Stories about witches, werewolves and vampires are very popular in the West at the moment – maybe they always have been – so I thought that I would try to write one in my spare time."

"And it's about ghosts in this village?"

"No, did Lek tell you that?"

"I'm not sure to be honest. We were both drunk. Is it about this village?"

"No, I will set it in a made-up, a story village in Thailand, but not a real village."

"Oh, good. I think that Lek is worried about that. Why don't you talk to her about the book? Put her mind at ease."

"She has never shown the slightest interest in it. Never even asked one question about it."

"Well, try talking to her about it, Craig. It will help. I'm off to join the procession now. Are you coming, Soom? See you in an hour."

"No, Aunty Beou, I'll wait here for Mum with Craig, thanks."

"Bye-bye, Beou. Cheers," he said holding up the beer she had bought him.

"Well, Soom, how are you enjoying Songkhran this year?"

"Very well, thank you. And you?"

"Sure. It's the best day of the year. Always is. It doesn't get any better than this in Baan Suay, does it?"

Soom smiled broadly. She understood what he was saying after having spent two years as a student in Bangkok. Previous to that though, she would not have. She had seen that there was more in the world than Baan Suay had to offer however lovely it was there. She was becoming too big for the village, as her mother had, before she shoehorned herself back into the box that was society in Baan Suay.

After six years of trying, she had still not completely managed it. It was obvious that the place drove her mad sometimes, as it did Craig, and then they had to get out. That had usually meant a trip to Pattaya, but now they could go to Bangkok to visit Soom or to Naan for the annual visa.

"Tell me more about writing, please, Craig."

"What do you mean, Soom?"

"What is it like to write so much, to have web sites and to write a real book... how you say that?"

"A novel? I don't really know, you know. I've only just started my first novel, but I like writing it. You are writing a story and you can make the story go anywhere you want. In the right story, you could even be Supergirl or sprout wings and fly. It is fun.

"On the other hand, sometimes I get stuck into writing and a few hours later, I realise that I have written a few thousand words and taken the story down a path that I had not intended. The story or the characters, the people in the story, have done what they wanted to do and not what I was going to make them do.

"It is a strange sensation – like being taken over. When it's like that, I am just pushing the keys and typing their story for them, but it is then that the story sounds best and that the most work gets done.

"I was scared of writing a book – I suppose everyone is. It's a big project, but a book is made up of chapters, so if you want a book of a hundred thousand words and say, twenty-five chapters, you can aim for roughly four thousand words a chapter. If four  words a day sounds a lot, aim for two thousand and your book will be written in fifty days. In two months, it will be on the shelf. At that rate, you could go from never having written a book in your life to having written six in one year.

"How many people do you know that have written a book? And how many do you know who have written six?"

"You make it sound easy."

"Well, I have not finished my first book either yet... I am just telling you how I stopped being afraid of writing a book... Break a big project like that down into parts that are not intimidating, er frightening or scary.

"It is the same with your degree. If someone gave you all the books, papers and coursework and said come back in four years and I'll give you an exam, you would not finish it, but by taking the lessons one at a time, day by day, it becomes manageable and less formidable, er, less scary, less frightening a task.

"And web sites, well, they are a much smaller project anyway, but they are on-going, they are never finished, whereas a book, once published, is done and finished with."

"Yes, thank you. I go now. I hear people start to come with the music. I think I go get Mum."

"Yes, OK, Soom, see you later." He was not sure whether he had bored her or helped her, but she had asked.

Sitting alone, still thinking about writing, it occurred to him that he had become the writers' equivalent of a goldfish after years of writing five-hundred-word articles and wondered whether mind-expanding drugs would help him hold a full-length plot in his head, because he was having problems with continuity.

Soom woke her mother up.

"Come on, Mum, wake up. The procession has started and everyone is out there except you".

"I want to die... Ohhhh... my head hurts…"

"Charming way to see your mother, I must say... Come on get up or I'll go back without you. I'll sit with Craig and Beou and some normal people and have some fun and you can stew in your pit on your own…"

Lek could hear that Soom was on the verge of tears and felt ashamed of herself: "OK, Soom, I'm only play-acting. Look, I'm up! Give me five minutes for a shower and I'll be with you. Make the bed for me, will you, darling? Thanks".

She walked to the bathroom without staggering, but it took a lot of effort. The cool shower blew away a lot of the cobwebs, but she knew that she was still not completely sober. She would have to be careful with Soom watching her. She didn't want to start setting a bad example now, since everything that she had been doing for the past eight years had been done to give Soom the right impression of her; to give her a good role model to aspire too, but Soom knew about drinking now and Lek thought it was time that she tackled that vice in herself too next, especially when Soom was around.

Not over Songkhran though! Nobody could expect that of anybody.

She put on some old, but stylishly bright and frilly party-type clothing and went out into the kitchen.

"Well, will I do?"

"Yes, Mum, you look lovely. Here is a plastic bag for your phone and money. Come on, the music is near now..."

They locked the door behind them and danced down the garden path in Indian file and then side-by-side to Nong's shop where there was quite a crowd already gathered to wait for the procession.

"Soom, the head of the procession is still a couple of hundred metres away, so we have about twenty minutes before it gets to Nong's, shall we sit with Craig till it gets here?"

"Yes, OK, Mum."

When they were seated, Lek ordered a bottle of beer, a bottle of Coke and a ben of whisky. Soom said, "I was asking Craig about writing before... Aren't you just so jealous of him being able to write books and things? I want to do the same after university, as a hobby, of course".

"No, darling. I am not jealous. Why would I be? I have a husband who can write. It would be no good if we all did the same things, would it? Stick to what you are good at. Push yourself and experiment, by all means, but it doesn't do any good to be envious or jealous.

"You are good at computers, so stick with that until you get your degree and a good job and then you can try to write a book, if you like. You have plenty of time – all your life – to write books, my dear.

"Are you all right here, Craig? We are going to join the front of the people, what do you call it? 'Procession'? Yes? No? OK, see you later. Maybe in the Wat later... Bye."

"Bye-bye both" and Soom took her mother's arm as they danced off to join the head of the dancing snake of people. A home-made water canon was parked fifty metres in front of the crowd ready to cool everybody off as they danced past.

Craig sat alone, although people often came to put water or wet talc on him or just to clink bottles. Others tried to get him up to dance, but years ago he had developed a routine which suited him. Bringing up the rear would be a pick-up with a few monks in it followed by another with a statue of Buddha and a monk in it. When this had passed him, he would walk on through and past the throng of people until he got to the next watering hole and he would wait for it again. He could do this three times before the procession got back to the Wat.

It meant that he could dance for a bit, say hello to people and watch everything from the comfort of a stool in a bar, or a shop at any rate. By the time they reached the last shop, many people would have joined him. The difference was that he would have a chair. He passed Lek, Soom and the rest of the family three times too.

When the procession passed the final shop, most of the people drinking there tagged onto the end of the crowd and danced into the grounds of the Wat, where there were stalls, sideshows and music to keep them amused. Craig stayed behind and was soon joined by the boss' pretty daughter Bum, whom he had known for years.

"How are you, Bum? Did you enjoy that?"

"Oh, very good for business, Khun Craig, but I very tired now. Stand up and cook all day. Now I want to sit down and rest. Then I must make everything clean again. Can I sit here, talk to you and have one kapong?"

"A tin – of course, you can. Put it on my bill."

"No, excuse my English. I not ask you buy for me. My father give me for working. I only want ask if you want sit alone or if I can sit here too little bit."

"OK, up to you about the beer, but please do join me. Take the weight off your feet. How is your family? I see them here today, but not now."

"No, they too old now They go inside, eat and sleep little bit. I make clean when I drink finish this tin."

Craig had actually wanted to join his family, but he was too polite to get up and go until Bum had finished her break. He had always liked her anyway, she was a good kid.

Lek, Soom, her family and some friends were dancing when they spotted Craig, thirty minutes later, picking his way through the crowd, looking for them in the grounds of the Wat. Soom went to get him.

"You come late. Everything finish now. Maybe everybody wants to go home in fifteen minutes. Do you want to come back with us or what do you want to do. I think that we will be going very soon. People are starting to get tired and want to eat now."

"That's all right. No problem. I remember the score from last year. Show's over, so people will go home and collapse. I don't have a problem with that. I'll come back with you and maybe stop in Nong's for an hour or maybe just go home and have a few more beers at my desk. I won't be far. No need to worry."

Most people, including Lek and Beou, were asleep by nine o'clock and didn't rise until ten the next day, which was the quietest of the three days of Songkhran, when people tried to shake off their hangovers in preparation for the routine day job the day after.

The village was as quiet as a graveyard all the next day. Craig was one of the only people to be seen on the street as he was walking to Nong's as usual, except for kids throwing water, where he was joined by Soom for more talk about writing and commercial web sites.

Craig took it as a sign that he had not bored her to tears and was thankful for it.

# 9 AYR'S BUSINESS PLANS

A week after Songkhran, when things had gotten back to normal, Lek received a phone call from her old friend Ayr.

"Hi Lek. I'm back in the village, staying at Mum and Dad's. Do you have time for a chat? OK, great, I only arrived last night, so I'm taking it easy today – yes, I'm on my own, but Ross may come over in a few days. I just want to get together and have a chat. No problem if Craig is there. It's not really hush-hush or anything. How about, er, two thirty? Would that suit you? OK, see you then."

Lek told Craig that Ayr was coming around but without Ross and that he could join them in the garden 'if he wanted', but he was more concerned about getting some work done. Lek filled in the time with a general clean-up, but nothing like she would have done if Ayr had been bringing 'a friend'.

When Ayr arrived, Craig went out to greet her, but was soon back at his desk. They sat at the table in the garden kitchen. Lek pushed some vegetables towards Ayr and they started peeling and chopping together.

"It's really nice to see you again Ayr. So you have finally gone and done it?"

"Yep! That is me and Pattaya finished. I am back home for the foreseeable, as they say. Unless my plans go completely tits up, I am back for good."

"Excellent! I will have a comrade again. It has been lonely without you, poor old Goong and Beou. I will admit to you that I have gone over the top sometimes... It has been, no, it is so hard to come back and I have been here for what, six or seven years now and I still miss something... you all, I guess... not the men, for sure, but the sanuk, the sorority, we were the Three Musketeers. We were... sisters-in-arms, all for one and all that shit and... I miss it so much..."

"I know, Big Sister, I know... I have missed you... and Goong, for a long time too, but we are together again now. Pass me some more veg, I need something to do with my hands. I gave up smoking when I left Daddy's Hobby. I thought I might need to get fit again..."

"Why? What do you have in mind?"

"Well, that is one of the reasons why I wanted to talk to you. You have your ear to the ground up here, you know what's going on. My parents were smart in their day, but they... I don't know... I think that they are happily retired and glad to be out of it, but they still think that twenty thousand Baht for a rai of prime rice land is expensive. Whereas we know that it is treble that now.

"So I am looking for some help. I have saved a nice nest egg and I still have the money that Goong left me... so my plan is to buy some land to grow rice and build a shop to sell the stuff that a rice farmer needs. Maybe even do tool hire too.

"Now I have the money to do all that on a fairly small scale, but if someone were to come in with me, I would have some spending money, be able to buy more land which will make that side of it more viable and make the shop easier.

"Ross has offered to come in with me, but I don't know. He'll be flitting off here and there and that'll leave me on my own running the show. I would prefer a partner who is here nearly all the time, someone that I can trust.

"What do you think?"

"I think it's a great plan, but... are you asking me to be your partner?"

"I suppose I am, yes. What do you think?"

"I think that you are a wonderful woman and a wonderful friend and I can't think of anyone I would rather work with or kiss right now than you!"

"I'm glad you think like that, Big Sister, because nor can I."

"OK, Ayr, I will be honest with you. I have been a stupid cow with the money that Goong left me and I haven't worked since I left Daddy's Hobby. Craig has supported me and Soom all the way.

"I would love to be able to go in with you and pay my way again. However, it will have to be with Craig's money. Lent by him to me, so there is no comeback on you or the business and I will pay him back with our earnings.

"So, I will have to tell him everything and hope for the best. Do you still want me as a partner now that you know how bloody stupid I have been?"

"Sure I do, Big Sister, especially now. That was hard to admit, but it doesn't make me trust you any less. Do you want to call him out here now or talk to him later?"

"I suppose we could call him out now, eh? Strike while the iron is hot, keep a moving truck rolling and all that... Hang on a sec, I'll just go and get him."

Lek opened the fly screen to his office window.

"Telak, do you want a short rest? Come have a beer and talk with Ayr and me."

"Yes, OK. Good idea."

Lek opened a cold beer Chang and Ayr put some ice in a glass.

"Just as you like it, Craig, neh? What are you doing now working in there? You can sit with us like old days, neh?"

"So, good to see you again, Ayr, what are you doing up here again so soon?"

"I was born here. This is my home."

"Yes, sorry, I didn't mean that, but you never used to come back often and now..."

"Then and now are different times, Craig. At one time I lived here, then I did not and now I do again."

"Wow, you have moved back? Finished with Pattaya?"

"Yes. I have finished with Pattaya for living and for working, but maybe not for holiday, neh?"

"So, what are you going to do here or is Ross going to move up with you?"

"That is what I have been talking to my old friend Lek about. I have ideas for a small business and want her to be my partner."

They talked about Ayr's business plan and Craig was impressed. When he had finished his beer, he went back to work accompanied by Lek.

"Did you mean it, telak? You will lend me the money to go in with Ayr?"

"Yes. I think that she is level-headed and has a good idea. You yourself talked about a shop selling goods to farmers a few years ago, but we didn't have enough money. Now we do and you have a friend to work with. Go for it, but please, tell everything as it happens, all right?"

"Yes, thank you, telak, you will not regret this." And she went back to join Ayr who had seen, but not heard all the goings-on through the office window and fly screen.

"So, that's a green light then?" said Ayr.

"It looks that way, Little Sister, we are in business again!" and they high-fived each other

"OK, back to reality. Where do you want us to start, Ayr, as this is your show?"

"I had my eye on that bit of scrub land next to Nong's for the shop. You know, the bit where they used to hold a market every Monday morning for a while? Do you think that she would sell it to us? Or rent, but I personally would rather buy. I have never owned any land before. I'm forty-odd years of age and never owned any land or had my own house or husband or kids. Sad, isn't it?"

"You can make up for it now, can't you?"

"You watch, Pee Lek, I bloody well will too. We'll make such a go of this business that they'll all want to marry me - even the schoolboys!

"Not that I really want to get married anyway... A couple of lovers wouldn't hurt though would it? A few toy-boys? None of those rough-handed old farmers... A couple of nice, well-mannered university students would be all right though, eh?"

"Sounds good, but not for me, Ayr, I'm more than happy with Craig. My only problem is I get bitchy sometimes and he gets short-tempered. I was wondering... was I like that in Pattaya too?"

"No, Big Sister, of course not. You're just bored up here with nothing to do but talk to farmers' wives who know more about superstition than they do about the world outside the village.

"You are cramped in, you have brain-cramp," and she laughed at her own description. "Brain-cramp, that's what it is. Well, we'll sort that out. Why don't we start now? Let's go round and talk to Nong... See if she'll sell us that bit of land. Craig won't mind, will he?"

"No, he won't mind... He'll be wanting to go round there himself in about an hour and a half. I'll go and tell him that we'll wait for him there."

They sat at what had come to be called 'Craig's Office' and Lek called Nong over.

"Two tins of beer Chang, please, Nong, and do you have a few minutes for a chat?"

"Sure, the next rush will be the kids coming home from school. It can be very quiet in the afternoon."

Nong brought the beer and sat down. "How are you doing, Ayr? I hear rumours that you are back for good this time... Finished in Pattaya, have you?"

"Yes, finished down there now. You can get bored with all that sex in luxury hotels, you know. It's OK for the first ten years, but after that, same old, same old...

"So, I've made my fortune and now I want a proper job. I've had my fun, now I want to put something back into the community like you have... Open a shop to help people... I was thinking of putting an American-style convenience store just down the road. You know, open all day and all night..."

Nong was visibly shaken, she said, "I don't want to put you off, but there is no room for a shop like that in this small village. There's just not enough trade, is there, Lek? You know the score, Lek. Tell Ayr."

"Well, I don't know, Nong. Ayr has a lot of new ideas from the city. Maybe a '7-11' is just what Baan Suay needs... Something new..."

Nong was getting palpitations at the thought of all that competition. "You can see, just look around you... the place is dead in the afternoons..."

"Yes," said Ayr, "maybe you're right, but I have to have something to do. What if I put a shop on that piece of land next to yours? Not a grocery store of course, yours serves the community more than adequately, but, say, a farmers' supply store selling fertilizer, pest poison, tools, that sort of thing..."

"Oh , yes. That's a much better idea. We need something like that, sure enough. That's an excellent idea."

"I think you're right, Nong, and people coming to my shop might call in at yours while they are there. That would help your trade too, wouldn't it?

Farmers wouldn't have to leave the village to get their supplies and buy their groceries out of town, they could just use us two."

Nong was already calculating how much a shop like that next to hers might increase her turnover. "Yes, it might help me a little at that."

"I have an option on old Dtum's plot just down the road for the '7-11', but you have persuaded me now that that's a bad idea, 'though, I don't want to put my farmer' store down there... Would you sell me that bit of land there, next to yours? It is yours, isn't it? That way, you could benefit from my customers, like you said."

"I may sell it. How much is it worth to you and your new business?"

"I'm not sure, Nong. There are no services and I would have to build a shop and stock it... how about twenty-five thousand?"

"Ha, if I wanted to give it away, my family would take it off my hands. A hundred thousand."

"No, I can have a '7-11' for less than that and they would stock it for me and lend me money... Thirty thousand."

"I couldn't, my father left me that land and he'd turn over in his grave, if I let it go that cheaply... Eighty."

"Forty. Think of your increased turnover and better security with two of us living so close. We would be neighbours. Two single, eligible young women like us... we could have a riot, me and you?"

"Fifty and that is my final offer."

They shook hands and that was that.

"Have a beer with us Nong to celebrate."

"I don't drink alcohol as a rule, but I suppose I don't sell land every day as a rule either. OK, I'll have a beer with you, neighbour."

Nong fetched three tins of Chang and put them on Ayr's bill.

They sealed the deal with a drink and agreed to go to Phichai the next day to complete the land transfer or as soon as they could after the mayor had finished his side of the paperwork.

When Craig appeared at four thirty, Nong got up to be ready for the rush of school children. She also knew that they would probably start speaking English and she didn't want to appear uneducated.

"We just bought that piece of land, Craig. That is where our new shop is going to go. You should have seen Ayr in action. She played Nong like a violin. I nearly believed her myself!

"That was a good touch about the '7-11'. You should have heard her, Craig. Ayr told Nong that she was going to build a '7-11' just down the road. Nong's face looked so worried... I thought she was going to have a heart-attack! What's next in your master plan, Ayr?"

"We need to secure that land before Nong changes her mind. I suppose it's too late to do anything this evening, but we could make an appointment for tomorrow.

"I'll tell you what. I'll go and talk with Nong for a minute and then go and see Nic and I'll phone you later. There's no need for you to come. Stay here and have a chat with your lovely husband. I'm feeling a bit tired anyway after all the moving, packing, loading, unpacking et cetera of the last few days, so I'm going to have an early night. You can tell Craig the details.

"Take care both. I'll phone you later, Lek, and see you both tomorrow."

∞

All three parties met in the mayor's house at nine a.m. Jan and the gardener witnessed the purchase which was made in cash that Ayr provided. Lek had promised to pay her share when they went into Phichai later that day. Nong was only mildly surprised to discover that Lek was in on the deal, but it made no difference to her. She would have liked more money for the land, but it was a fair price and she would benefit from the extra trade and security, so all in all she was quite satisfied with the transaction.

With the three signatures on the mayor's title deed, the land now officially belonged to Ayr and Lek, but they still had to get it recorded in the Land Registry in Phichai, which the two friends decided to do immediately. Nong went back to her shop, which her mother was running in her absence, wondering how much of it she would allow herself to spend on frivolity. It would not be much, because she was really quite a miser.

It didn't take long to conclude their business at the government offices, nor to withdraw the money for Ayr from the ATM and then they were sitting in Ben's coffee shop with a notepad and pen, which Lek had brought with her.

"That all went very smoothly, didn't it? Let's take it as a good omen," said Lek. "What's next? We need a building and suppliers, I suppose."

"Yes, well, this is where you will know more than I do. I've been out of touch for quite a while. Which brands of fertilizer et cetera do your family use and do you know any good builders?"

She wrote a few names down off the top of her head.

"I've heard people mention these brands, but I can ask my brothers and my mother. If you ask around too, we should get on top of that one quite easily. As for builders... I only know the people who built our house. Chang lives across the road, a bit up, from Nong's. He did a good job on our house and I do have some experience with how he works.

"We got on well enough, but building the house was a nightmare for my relationship with Craig. I don't know how we survived it. I wanted to kill him every day, I think, and he probably felt the same.

"Maybe not, he's not as hot-tempered as I am, but we fought like cat and dog every day for ages and ages."

"Maybe, we should not use him if he's so slow..."

"Maybe, it wouldn't hurt to get a few quotes, but you need to pin him down on a timeline. We mucked him about a lot. Either I wasn't happy with our design or Craig wasn't happy with something... We kept changing our minds. I think we drove him crazy too."

"Well, the shop will be just a shoebox basically, but maybe with a small day-room, a toilet and kitchen in the back. What do you think?"

"Where are you going to live, Ayr? Why not stay in the shop?"

"I thought I would stay at Mum and Dad's so as not to complicate things between us, but as being as you are suggesting it – I would love to. I can pay rent or just pay for that part of the building myself. Thank you partner," and they high-fived.

"If it's what you want, we can ask Chang to give us a quote on the basic shop with a day-room, small kitchen and toilet, then we both pay for all that fifty-fifty. Then, you say: 'Oh, and how much extra for this... and you show him what you want done. The extra is your extra bill. Easy, eh?"

"It is with the two us working together, yes. So far anyway."

"I've got an idea. Ben! Ayr and I need a builder, do you know a decent one?"

"We get all sorts in here, Lek. Let me think... I might know one or two. Do you want me to give them your number when I see them?"

"Your number or mine, Ayr?"

"It doesn't matter really, does it? We'll meet them together anyway."

"OK, Ben, give them my number. You still have it, don't you? That's easier then."

As they rode back to Baan Suay on Ayr's motorbike together, Lek was thinking that she wouldn't mind moving in with Ayr again. She could let Craig keep the house and she could move in with her old room-mate again. Times had been tough then, almost twenty years ago, not financially so much, but they had had so much fun. Where was all the fun in life now?

Ayr was a fast driver, so the wind made it difficult to talk. Lek leaned forward, put her arms around her friend's waist and squeezed her:

"I'm so glad that you are back, I have missed you, you know," she shouted near Ayr's right ear. Ayr tapped the hands around her waist in agreement.

Once in Baan Suay, they stopped in Nong's to survey their new plot of land. "Let's design our shop, shall we?"

"Sure, why not? And when Craig gets here, he can have a look at it – he was in building or something before, wasn't he? And then when we see Chang come home, you can call him over, if you don't mind, Lek?"

"No, sounds fine. Where's that book and pen gone? Ah, here it is... This is going to be fun. Nong! Two cold, red Birdy coffees and two pieces of banana cake, please, for your new neighbours. I wish I was moving in with you Ayr... I really do. It would be like old times again. Well, not completely, but you know what I mean. Nong, can I have a rule too please?

"OK, the plot is about twice as long as it is wide, so we can imagine the page as our land. It's not quite the right proportions, but it's not far off.

"Then we put a line down each side of the page to give us a border around us of, say, two metres... like this and space for parking in the front... say, four metres... That leaves us with this much ground area.

"What do you think?"

"I think you could have been an architect. That all sounds logical."

"How much space would you like at the back for yourself?"

"Don't worry about me. The business has to come first."

"OK, but how much would you like?"

"Say, six metres...? I don't know. I'm used to pokey box rooms. I'd probably get lost in six metres."

"OK, so we leave six metres at the back for storage, sitting, a garden and cooking; six metres for you inside; three metres for us inside and four metres for parking out the front. That makes... nineteen leaving us with about twenty-three for the shop and twenty wide minus four for borders... makes twenty-three by sixteen metres for the shop.

"That sounds plenty big enough to me."

"It sounds bloody massive."

"We don't have to build on all of it, but those are roughly the dimensions that we have to play with. Come on, let's go and pace it out. See what it looks like."

They worked out the four corners of the building and poked sticks in the ground to mark the spots and went back to their table.

"See, it's not that much bigger than Nong's house-shop, is it? Surprising really?"

"I'm amazed at you, Lek. Where did you learn to do all that?"

"Ah, I picked it up from Craig and Chang when we were building and designing and endlessly redesigning our house. It is hard to imagine a building from a drawing, but when you mark things out, it becomes a lot clearer... a lot easier to visualize."

"Now we can transfer that to paper and carry on. If the front is a roller shutter, that will give the shop plenty of light and we could add a window in each side wall... like this... and two counters like this... with a lift-up centre piece for access. A door to our rest room, like this, the toilet here and a door and two windows again and two interior walls to partition it off from the shop and your accommodation and a door to access your rooms and our part is more or less done except for details.

"Now you do the same for your space. Well, I don't mean right now, but this is how you draw it out for a builder to understand and work from. These marks mean a window, these a door. This a European toilet and this a hand-basin. I can't remember a shower, but I'm sure Craig will know."

When Craig arrived, he showed them the symbol of a spray of water to denote a shower and said that they could mark out any areas that required tiling with squares, but for the rest, it just needed redrawing more neatly, now that they knew where everything was going. He also suggested photocopying the basic layout a dozen times so that they would not have to keep redrawing the basic design if the altered anything minor.

When Chang arrived home from work, Lek went to ask him to join them and Craig moved from where they were sitting to his 'office' on the other side of the shop to let them continue in their adventure alone.

They explained their ideas to Chang and bought him a beer to wet his whistle, they also sent one over to Craig. Chang promised to have a better look at the sketch over the following couple of days and get back to them. One other builder recommended by Ben phoned and arranged to collect a drawing from Ayr the next day.

Maya - Illusion

# 10 TOPPING OUT

It took a week to get the two tenders back, so Ayr and Lek spent that time sorting out suppliers. When the quotes came in, there was not much between them, so they chose the local contractor because he would be easier to contact in case of problems. Being local, he would also be more worried about his reputation. They accepted a price of ninety-five thousand Baht for the basic design and thirty thousand Baht for Ayr's extension. Chang began work the next day without any form of contract except a verbal go-ahead, as was normal in a village like Baan Suay.

He promised to have the building useable in six weeks time which the ladies were happy with. This gave them ample time to sort out background details like creditworthiness, a bank account, credit cards and transport for deliveries etc.

They were both there to watch the first shovelful of earth come out of the ground for the footings and at five o'clock, all those with any connection to the project were invited to share a bottle of whisky and a  simple meal at Nong's that Lek and Ayr had prepared in Nong's outdoor kitchen during the afternoon. Craig was as proud of the ladies as they were of themselves. The mayor joined in for a few whiskeys too as he had stopped off to congratulate the entrepreneurs while passing by.

Lek roped Craig in to show her how to set up and run spreadsheets for accounts and stock control. She also got him to create the shell of a web site, which she then learned how to control and populate with articles on farming in Thai. However, she had to go back to Ayr for a company name to use as the web site URL as they didn't yet have one.

They thought and thought about it and came up with several names in Thai such as: 'Rovers Return', 'Thaigirls' Return', 'Green Supplies', 'Eco Warrior' and 'Daddy's Job', but Craig pointed out that the web site should reflect the nature of their business, so they went with 'Farming Supplies', which they thought was boring but accurate. That domain name had already been taken, so they added the word 'Northern' to it, making 'Northern Farming Supplies'.

Lek shared her new knowledge with Ayr and spent a day or two teaching her how to use the spreadsheets and web site. Ayr was very nervous about using a computer for anything more than Facebook, but like Lek, she soon got the hang of operating one.

They both started writing articles in Thai which they then posted to their web site in order to give farmers practical advice, increase sales and improve the site's page rank. Both of them were amazed that they were using computers in ways that they thought only whizz-kids could, just a short while ago, especially Ayr, who was feeling the same elation that Lek had experienced six months previously. Lek enjoyed teaching Ayr how to use the computer for spreadsheets and Ayr enjoyed learning.

As a useful exercise, they tracked all the materials used and man-hours expended on the job and matched them against their invoices in excel. Craig was able to help out when needed, but that was not very often at all, besides which they were working with documents written in Thai, which he couldn't read.

The basic design of the building was shoebox-like and so pretty simple. This meant that there were very few alterations, so work progressed far more quickly than it had done on Lek's own property. The only constraint was the number of courses of blockwork that it was safe to lay one on top of another in a day. However, since, the external walls were quite long, they rarely hit the maximum. Progress was pleasingly rapid.

The partners loved to stand within the walls of their shop in the evenings and sense how the building was growing up. Both Ayr and Lek took a special interest in the design of Ayr's flat. They both wanted Ayr's first real home of her own to be both cosy and practical.

It was quite easy for them to make a splash on the internet, because so few businesses had a presence on line in their area. After writing half a dozen articles each on practical aspects of farming in their province, their web site was one of the most popular for miles around. They also set up twitter, Facebook and LinkedIn accounts and spent some spare time each tweeting, and posting comments within a few weeks, they already had several hundred followers, even if most of them were local school children.

One of their most popular articles was on the return of the heron to an area some fifty kilometres west of Baan Suay. One farmer with a lot of connected fields had stopped using pesticides as an experiment and found that wild birds did almost as good a job at controlling snails as chemicals did. The following year, other farmers had joined the experiment and the number of herons increased to such a level that they did as good a job as the poisons, but free of charge.

Lek remembered when farmers hadn't used much pesticide for killing snails in Baan Suay too, but mostly because they hadn't been able to afford it. However, as the region had prospered and the pesticide companies became more aggressive with their advertising, the application of them had increased. Lek thought that they should encourage the diminished use of poisons in their area too. Although it meant a loss of sales, it did mean increased kudos which she hoped would mean more profits from other farming-related items.

Judging by the comments that were coming in, few people had noticed the increased absence of herons, but regretted it now that it had been pointed out to them. Lek asked Craig to help her create a flier on the computer with their web site address and contact details on the bottom. It gave just enough details about saving money on pesticides and helping the environment to make people curious enough to visit their web site or shop itself. They had five hundred printed and handed them out far and wide. Also mentioned on the flier was the free party on opening day with surprise artistes, free product samples and free refreshments all day from nine till six.

During all this activity, Lek didn't have much time for her new fruit garden, but then there was not a lot to do either. The mapang wouldn't start fruiting until the season came around in March the following year, but the other fruit trees and the chilli peppers needed harvesting or at least checking every week, which Lek could find the time to do. If anything needed picking, she paid her friend Su to do it for her, unless it was the coconuts and then they called in the man Lek called 'the tortoise', because he was so strong. He had fallen out of trees dozens of times, but had never suffered serious injury.

Soom was also able to help out from time to time, but she was due back in university in the second week of June to start her third year and really needed to do some preparatory work for it, although she was pleased to help her mother out as much as she could especially picking the chillis and the mushrooms. She was too frightened of snakes to want to have anything to do with the banana trees, which were often the chosen home of poisonous green pit vipers that were hard to spot by the untrained eye.

It was far safer to stick to the chillis and mushrooms and let Su do the rest because she was used to it, thought Soom.

Lek did spend some time on her mushrooms, although they only needed cutting three weeks after a new batch was started and then every day or two for a couple of weeks. They also needed watering every evening which Lek took care of herself. The money from the mushrooms still made up the majority of her contribution to the family finances, although they had had the money from the sale of the flat through some time before.

The last fortnight before the grand opening day and topping out ceremony was hectic indeed. They had already selected their suppliers, but as the news spread that a new farmers' supply centre was opening, more sales reps came every day on the off chance of finding a new regular outlet. Ayr and Lek used every trick they could think of to wangle free samples and free gifts out of these reps.

They accumulated bottles of whiskey and beer; caps and t-shirts; pens and pencils; stationery; penknives; packets of seeds and several other gadgets, some of which they kept for themselves, like the two miniature radios and two jackets they received from two successful suppliers' reps.

They also got their mothers to prepare tureens of curry and rice and hundreds of small, traditional Thai cakes. They bought a box of crisps and a few hundred paper cups and plates and plastic spoons from Nong, although they could have bought them cheaper from a wholesalers themselves. Nong was as excited about the forthcoming 'topping out ceremony' as Lek and Ayr. She anticipated a steady stream of extra customers all day for that day.

When the time came for Soom to go back to Bangkok, Lek wanted to accompany her, but Soom said that she was quite capable and that her mother was needed in the shop more. Soom for her part would have liked to stay for opening day, but that would have been impossible given both her own and her parents' respect for education. There was no way that they would have let her miss the opening two weeks of the first term of the year.

So when the sad day of departure came, Lek assured Soom that she had put the tuition fees and her first month's allowance into her account, slipped her a few thousand for herself and drove her to the bus stop on her bike. Craig had also given her a few thousand baht, so she was feeling quite wealthy, although she knew that the money wouldn't prevent the intense homesickness that she always felt for a week after going back. They both promised to write and phone every day and they both knew that they would both keep those promises. Skype's free video link would be a godsend that they had never enjoyed together before.

When Lek waved Soom goodbye as the bus departed, she couldn't help but shed a tear and she knew that Soom would be crying too. Lek hurried back to the shop for something to do to take her mind of her sense of loss.

She didn't neglect Craig as much as either of them had thought that she would, because Ayr had suggested right from the beginning that they take a break at noon when the builders stopped for lunch and went back to Lek's house to cook. Often, Soom had done some preparatory peeling, slicing or pounding, but there was no real need as many Thai dishes can be prepared and cooked by one chef within twenty minutes. With Ayr, Lek and Soom on the job, it had been a dead cinch to get a meal on the table by twelve-thirty at which time, if not before, Craig usually came out to join them. He also saw his family at four thirty when he went down for his regular drink. They would then usually join him at about six o'clock when the builders went home after a bite to eat and a drink.

So, on the whole, they were seeing more of each other now than they had been used to for the last four or five years or even longer. Even when the shop was open for business in the future, he would be able to go there for his lunch, which was all he needed, not being accustomed to eating much more than fruit in the evenings anyway. All in all, it looked to both of them as if the shop was going to usher in an era of stability and contentment for their relationship, even if what it would do for their finances was still unclear.

Ayr and Lek wanted to put on music and a few acts to attract people and keep them there while they read various pieces of literature like leaflets, fliers, and coupons for time-limited special offers, but they didn't want to spend much money on it. Ayr came up with the idea of providing a small stage and a PA system, so that people could perform their own routines if they wanted to. All performers were allowed a free drink and food and the best two, decided by questionnaire, would each receive five hundred baht. They also hired a local troupe of dancing girls from the village and nearby.

CD music was to begin at nine a.m. And the girls were to do a thirty-minute routine every hour until six o'clock. The intervening periods would be filled with impromptu singers or musicians and if none turned up then there would be karaoke which always went down well. They didn't see the need to hire the village security squad, because Ayr and Lek reckoned that they could deal with any freeloaders themselves after years of running free bar parties in Pattaya.

Two days before the launch, chang said that due to the extras and alterations, he was likely to over-run by a day or so. However, he also had a solution. He suggested ceasing work on the flat and putting all his men and women onto decorating the shop and putting up shelves. The partners agreed readily and the morning before the opening everything except Ayr's shower room and kitchen was complete. Some of the reps had stored their orders nearby so that the shop could be loaded up as soon as necessary while others had already delivered to Ayr's father's barn.

On the eve of the opening, Lek, Ayr and Craig stood proudly in the shop checking details, but it looked perfect. The sacks of feed and seed were piled down the left of the central isle and the smaller items were on shelves in rows down the other side. At the end of each side was a counter with a reconditioned till on it. When the raised centre of the counter was dropped, it looked like one counter with a till at each end. They were not sure whether this was a good set-up, but it seemed about right. Only time and experience would tell.

The stage had already been erected outside, and tables and chairs, hired from the Wat, had been put in place. The alcohol was stacked in their day room and that could be sealed by locking the door behind the counter and the one leading to Ayr's room. The food was in containers on every square inch of counter space and there were fans on it to keep it as cool as possible. The curries would need to be reboiled before serving, but that was no problem.

There was nothing left to do but lock up and retire to Nong's for a drink with chang and his people.

However, neither Ayr nor Lek could enjoy themselves. They couldn't help trying to think of things that they might have forgotten. In the middle of one toast to the prosperity of the enterprise, Lek whispered to Ayr:

"Soft drinks! We haven't ordered any soft drinks."

"True, trust us to forget that. Still, there won't be many people drinking lemonade tomorrow when there is free beer and whisky for the asking, but you are right. We do need some. Not to worry, though, eh? Nong will sell it to us at retail as we need it or we can get someone to go into town in the morning, buy boxes of the stuff and have most of it left over for weeks.

"Let's just enjoy ourselves for now, though, Lek. We can deal with that tomorrow. There is another thing too, a shop sign with our name on it. Anyway, bottoms up, partner!"

They did not stay out drinking long, but they didn't get much sleep either. All three of them were awake hours before they had to get up. Lek was keen to get to the shop, but because Ayr was sleeping there for the first time, she didn't want to disturb her friend. Little did she know that Ayr couldn't sleep either. Craig was as nervous as either of them, because he wanted them to have a successful day. However, he was more certain of their ability to throw a party than they were at that precise moment.

Lek couldn't wait any longer than seven a.m, she just had to get round there. In case Ayr was still in bed, Craig said that he would be there in an hour. As it happened, Ayr had been trying to find things to do since six o'clock. She had dusted every surface, brushed every floor and cleaned up outside after the night winds had blown papers and bits and pieces onto their forecourt.

When Lek arrived, she was starting to polish the dust off the front display window.

"Why didn't you phone me, Ayr, I've been awake for hours. I would have loved to help." She steadied the step-ladder as Ayr mounted it.

"I thought that you would be wrapped around that husband of yours, fast asleep. I probably would be if i had one. As it was, well, i suffer from sleeplessness in a new bed. It was homely in there though, even though they haven't quite finished everything off yet.

"To be totally honest with you, big sister, i don't think that there is anything more we can do except have breakfast. We're selling to farmers, not royalty and farmers are used to a bit of dust. If we didn't have a bit of dust here and there they would probably be scared to come in, so let's put this stuff away and eat.

"Something in our stomachs might kill the butterflies, eh?"

When Craig arrived, they had eaten rice soup and had prepared an omelette mix for the three of them. They called Nong over to join them in their back yard.

"Want some omelette, Nong? There's plenty here... Or rice soup? We've got a gallon of that left. There's about two gallons of curry too heating up on the stove. Just say the word or help yourself."

Nong got up and noseied around, pleased to be invited to do so. She looked under every lid and every cloth, before taking a bowl of rice soup.

"Very tasty... Just what you need in the morning... I'll have a bit of that omelette too when it's cooked, if you have enough."

"Sure, neighbour," sad Ayr, "we're going to be feeding the five thousand today, if we get our way. What is one more? Anyway, you are most welcome. We appreciate all the help you have given us... We wouldn't even be here even, if it wasn't for you, would we, Lek?"

"no, no, we would not. Any time we can help you, just ask, Nong, and we'll be there. We lady-entrepreneurs should stick together, shouldn't we? After all, there aren't many of us about! The men outnumber us by a long way... Power to women! That's what i say... Don't you, Lek?"

"Yes, power to women! Don't you agree, Craig?"

Craig had no idea what they were talking about, but when Lek told him to just say 'yes' he did and stabbed his clenched fist into the air.

At eight-thirty, they cleared away the breakfast things and opened up early. They just couldn't wait any longer. They put a kettle on for coffee and put buying a coffee machine on the list for 'must have soon', uncovered some of the food, but left the cling film on and powered up the tills in hopeful expectation.

The DJ and the dancing girls arrived at eight forty-five. Ayr showed the girls into her quarters so they could get changed and the DJ set up his equipment. They started their first set, just five minutes late, which was pretty good by local time-keeping standards.

Just before nine o'clock, Lek's brothers, long and Ngat entered the shop.

"Jill and the other girls are looking good out there. You should have asked me to be DJ. You could have saved a bit there. And i could have helped the girls get changed. You know, helped them with those awkward zips and fasteners." Said Ngat.

"We want to be your first customers, if the price is right," said long.

"What are you looking for?" Asked Lek.

"We read what you said about pesticide for the snails and think that that is really good advice, so we talked to a few of the farmers with fields around ours and we're going to give it a try. See if we can get the birds back too. Storks, weren't they, you said?"

"Herons."

"Yeah, well, see if we can attract any birds back that eat snails," added Ngat, "but we still need something to kill insects, don't we? So, we could do with a couple of gallons of that. Or are you breeding birds that eat them too?"

"We're working on that one," put in Ayr. "there are a few species that we have in mind for an intensive breeding programme... Like the pink spotted African fly catcher, but we need an importers license. Yes... The problem is they are very territorial and kill farmers too..."

They all laughed, but wouldn't put it past Ayr to be doing something like that. She was as keen as mustard.

Lek continued, "we have sourced this pesticide which is very specific... It only kills flies, which includes bees of course, but it kills on contact and is only active for about twenty minutes, so it will kill the mosquitoes and rice flies that are living in your crop, but will not harm visiting species outside that time span. It is unusual too, in that it is completely harmless to amphibians and fish, which are your main allies in combating mosquito larvae, as you know.

"It is competitively priced and covers the same acreage as the more common, old-fashioned pesticides."

"It is 50b more per gallon!"

"Like I said, it is competitively priced, but yes, it is ten baht per litre more expensive, which works out to approximately twenty-five baht per rai and you get to keep all your fish and frogs and the bees live another day, unless they fly onto the fields of less progressive, less far-thinking farmers.

"Surely, you're not going to let fifty baht a month stop you from moving with the times and setting a good example, are you?"

The brothers looked at each other and then at Lek and Ayr, "well, if you put it like that, sis, i don't see how we can refuse, do you Ngat?"

"No, Long, we could try it. See if it works, can't we? OK, two gallons for now. We'll try it tonight, after the party's over. Oh, we could do with a new hose for the sprayer and two pairs of gloves too.

"Are you going to do monthly accounts, sis?"

"We will be setting up monthly accounts for regular customers who spend over five thousand baht per month. Subject to a credit check, but to obtain these special prices today and until the weekend, all transactions must be in cash."

"OK, but can you put them aside for us?"

Lek gave them the receipt took their money and gave their change.

"No, don't be lazy. Take them round to Mum's. It's only a few hundred yards away and then come back."

"Last of the big spenders," laughed Lek as they walked out the door with their purchases.

"It was thoughtful of them to break the ice for us like that," said Ayr. "Now where are the rest."

Long and Ngat came hurrying back. "We're not going in today, not until after you close anyway. It's better to spray at dusk when the rice flies are roosting and the mosquitoes are just waking up thinking abut breakfast. We decided last night that we would like to be here for you.

"We can help carry purchases out to the pick-ups, move stock about, move loafers on, kick out drunks... That sort of thing. You don't know who is going to turn up or what is going to happen, do you?"

Lek was proud of them, but Ayr said "thanks, lads, that is really sweet of you. We appreciate your support, don't we, Lek?

"Why don't you move the sun-shade a little and sit outside? Look as if you're enjoying yourselves... See if you can get others to join you. We'll bring you something to eat and drink in a minute."

Lek and Ayr put curry and rice on two plates, poured two cups of 'Cuba Libra', took two promotional baseball caps, then wore one each too, and went outside to give them to the brothers.

"Service with a smile," said Lek as they put the refreshments and caps down. "Now get to work and draw those punters in."

There were several people standing around watching the stage, so Ayr took a few leaflets and handed them out. There was no need for targeting, everyone in Baan Suay was either a farmer, a retired farmer or a child and most of the children were in school, which was why they had not chosen a Saturday or Sunday to open.

As confidence grew in the surrounding people, some entered the shop and had a look around, many bought or ordered something, but some just sat down out of the heat of the sun and watched the girls. Within the first hour of business they had sold 10,000 baht's worth of supplies. Most of it was to friends and relatives, but it was a great start and far more than their highest expectation.

In fact, they had tried to make a sales forecast and had entered it into excel as an exercise. They had predicted one thousand baht every hour until lunch; three thousand baht in the lunch hour; two thousand baht hour after lunch and five thousand baht in the closing hour; making nineteen thousand baht in total. The special offers would reduce the profit margins a little and the extra overheads would wipe out the rest, but if that forecast was accurate, they would come out quits financially, but with a lot or happy customers and bags of goodwill.

Everyone got a business card with their on and off line contact details and Lek's laptop displayed their web site all day behind the counter where no visitor could miss it. They told everyone that orders could be placed on line by any customer who joined their mailing list. She gave a flier to everyone with full details of how to register, so that they could get their children to help them when they got home.

Business was extremely good, far exceeding their wildest expectations. By mid-afternoon, they were already on the phone to the reps looking for new stock early the next day. Some reps had depots nearby and were able to deliver immediately. Those that did stayed to enjoy the party.

One of them was an excellent amateur stand-up comedian and entertained the crowd for a full half-hour break while the girls had a coffee. He sang songs, told jokes, and imitated a few prime ministers and film stars. He got a huge round of applause. Lek wondered whether they could book him for their next promotional do.

They closed officially at six, but there were still people there at seven o'clock. Long and Ngat had left a couple of hours before to do their spraying, but Lek's mother helped them tidy up.

"What an amazing day! We took fifty-six thousand baht and change. Fifty-six thousand, two hundred and thirty-two baht to be exact, which means that we actually made some money today. I don't know how much yet, but once we enter all the invoices and receipts, the spreadsheet will tell us to the satang.

"However, that will have to wait for tomorrow because i am dead beat. How about you, Ayr?"

"Me too. I'm ready for bed. Let's lock up and start again tomorrow. What time?"

"Eight-thirty?"

"Right. Good night then, partner."

They pulled the shutter down and Ayr locked it, before going around the back to let herself into her room.

# 11 RISING PROSPERITY FOR BAAN SUAY?

The following morning, Lek was at the shop at eight fifteen, but it was already open.

"You're open early, Ayr? Couldn't sleep again? I slept like a log."

"So, did I until seven o'clock when tapping on the shutter woke me up. It was old Leng wanting gloves, a belt for his PTO and a gallon of the pesticide 'like what you sold Long yesterday'.

"So, nine o'clock opening looks like it'll have to be seven o'clock. I don't mind starting at seven. You can come in at nine and I'll take two hours off during the day. What do you think? You can come in at seven sometimes so I can have a lie-in."

"Yes, that's fine by me. I don't mind starting at seven either. I'm usually watering the garden by six thirty anyway. Right, I'll start on the invoices and receipts. Do you want me to show you how to do that?"

"No, not just yet. Tomorrow. I'm going to clean up a bit, then have a shower. I haven't done anything today. I want a shower desperately and to put some make-up on. We've taken 3,240B already this morning and we haven't even opened yet, so to speak."

Lek got a real kick out of entering the receipts and invoices. The net profit from sales was 12,330B less electricity and drawings. She couldn't wait to tell Ayr. When Ayr returned to the shop front, she was not greatly surprised by the news, but was just as pleased as Lek.

"We won't get that every day, I shouldn't imagine. Maybe half that, but that's still great news. Now, we were saying that we needed a sign and I think we need a land line phone too. Then we can have our own broadband Internet connection – we do need that, don't we - and a phone with a fax machine?

"It is all very well accepting Internet orders but more people still use faxes at the moment. When the farmers of Baan Suay move to the Internet, we will be ready for them, but we need a fax at the moment. It would also be helpful for placing orders, wouldn't it?"

"And a coffee machine. I agree about the fax too."

"Right, well can you hold the fort and I'll pop out to order a phone line and get a coffee machine and I'll ask my uncle if he'll come around to talk to you about the sign.

"I'll see you in an hour or so. You will be all right, will you? Not nervous?"

"A little, but I'll soon get the hang of it again. It can't be more difficult than running a bar, can it? Same sort of thing really."

"You'll be OK, don't worry. You'll probably know anyone that comes in. See you soon."

Lek enjoyed being in charge behind a counter again. She enjoyed the repartee with the customers and she enjoyed the flirting which she considered part of the job. She had known all along that she missed that, but now she was sure of it. Ayr was right too, she knew everyone that came in.

People bought rolls of nylon netting, wicker mats, coils of rope and pesticide most often, although this was only their second day. She liked the way that people took her into their confidence and discussed their requirements with her. When the shop was empty, she read the suppliers' literature and went on line using the Wi-Fi link from the cyber café across the road to look for more products and more ideas.

When Ayr came back, she had served a dozen customers and was designing a shop sign in 'MS Paint'.

"What do you think? We have to add the new phone number of course. Did they allocate you one in the shop?"

"Yes," Ayr pushed a piece of paper across the counter to Lek. "Very good. So what will you do with that? Print it off and give it to my uncle?"

"Yes, that was the general idea. I'll just add this number... here and push this... and hey presto, it's on this memory stick, which we can take to the Internet shop across the road and get printed out for 2B. Easy when you know how, isn't it?

"As Craig says, no-one is born with the knowledge – we all have to learn what we want to know in life."

"Well, I wouldn't argue with that. By the way, here's that coffee machine. Better run a pot full through it first to clean it out."

"OK, I'll do that now and while it's boiling, I'll get this printed out. I won't be a minute."

When she returned, Ayr took the print-out, nodded and said:

"Lek, I want to buy some land. That has always been the second part of my plan. However, I know that money is still tight with you, so would you mind terribly if I bought land alone? I want about ten rai at the moment, so I want to invest 500-600k Baht. You can't match that, can you?"

Lek couldn't match it or anything like it and she did feel hurt not to be able to be part of her friend's second phase, but she hoped that she didn't show it.

"No, Ayr, it's your money," she said, "You have to use it as you see fit. I spent mine on other things, as you know. Squandered most of it. That is my stupid fault. I'm just really grateful that you let me in on this part of the business," and it was true, she was.

"Maybe, as we make money and I save, we can buy a few rai together later on?"

"Oh, thank you, Lek. I've been ever so worried that I would hurt your feelings and I don't want to do that for the world. Yes, we can buy land together another time. We've got years ahead of us."

"You see, I see Baan Suay as really taking off. There is so much potential here with three crops of high-quality rice a year. The government has raised the price of a ton of rice from 6,500 to 7,500B and I believe that it will go a lot higher. Maybe even double over the next few years. If scientists ever develop a faster-growing strain of rice, we may get four crops a year. In fact, the best farmers, on the best land are already achieving that in a good year, so it's not just a fantasy.

"And I want to be in on it. You have been here a long time, maybe you don't see what I see, but I feel a buzz here. Look at all the new cars, the babies, the extensions and even new houses. They are everywhere. There is already a mini boom on in the area and we have just the right shop to help the farmers and ourselves make a fortune.

"As they said about the Californian 49'ers, it was the guys that sold the shovels that made the most regular money and that is us right here.

"There is so much more we could do too. Where is the next generation of farmers around here? There isn't one, because as soon as they are old enough, kids go looking for work in a city. No-one wants to be a farmer any more, or more accurately, no-one wants to work on a farm any more., but they don't mind owning the land, do they? No! And someone has to... and someone has to work it, no matter how mechanised we are.

"Do you see what that means, Lek? The farms will need to import labour... either from poorer parts of Thailand or from Laos and Cambodia. How are they going to get here? Through an agency – our agency... and where are they going to stay? Why, in our guest house or our hotel, of course. There is a huge future for this region and I believe that we are well-positioned to exploit it. What do you think?"

"To be honest, Ayr, I'm flabbergasted. There has been so much going on in that head of yours while I've just sat here and moaned for years. You astound and excite me and I want to be part of it with you."

"That is what I want to, Big Sister. Not only that, but it is too much for one person to do alone. A shop, fields, an agency and a hotel and who knows what else we'll come up with?"

"What you'll come up with you mean... My idea was a fruit garden..."

"Maybe the time just wasn't right or you were just not used to looking for opportunities... Don't worry about where you have been or where you are now, think about where you are going! And we are going places, you and me!

"We are going to make a great team and before very long, we'll be employing people too."

Lek did not have trouble taking it all in, she was just so surprised that she hadn't seen what Ayr had and what seemed as plain as the nose on her face now. She was determined not to let her friend down.

"Yes, I have read about the diversion of food resources into bio-fuel, but it didn't occur to me that we were part of that... Come to think of it though, we do produce bio-fuel too, don't we?" said Lek.

"Yes, we do and with the West in deep poo-poo, they will be cutting back on oil imports and trying to make their own. Or encouraging other countries to make it for them. Couple that with rising populations and increased prosperity in the East, especially in India and China and food is going to rise in price dramatically.

"I know I'm making this sound as if I'm making it up, but Pattaya is a lot quieter these days, so while I was sitting there waiting for customers, I read newspapers. I never used to, but it is too quiet not to these days. The papers have been full of these sort of predictions for years now. I'm just applying what I've read to our village.

"I should imagine that other people are doing the same in other parts of Thailand. We're just lucky that we were the first to catch on here. That was why Ross and I came back before Songkhran... to suss the place out. Ross agrees that this place is ideal for this type of venture. He wanted to come in with me, but I preferred to work with you.

"He is setting up joint ventures like these all the time. He funds them and Thais run them. He does it in Australia too wherever he sees the opportunity.

"So it is not that I am so clever as to have thought of it, just clever enough to have seen the sense of it and bored enough with Pattaya to take a risk and give it a go.

"Just look at the mess the West is in and look at how well Asia is doing. If I had the money, I would build a street of modern houses for the kids of the farmers who are going to come back here when they realise how much daddy is making, but want to live in a modern bungalow, but that is a chapter in the story that we may miss for lack of finance. You never know though, if we do really well at this, the bank may be prepared to lend us some money in a year or two's time. Something to bear in mind for the future. After the hotel, that is..." and she laughed out loud.

Lek just had to laugh too. Ayr was so optimistic and her enthusiasm was so infectious. In fact, she was bordering on manic.

"Who would have thought that a couple of old working girls would become tycoons under the noses of the people who despised them for decades? We'll show the stuck-up sods, won't we, Big Sister? They have looked down their noses at us for years and we have stolen this gold-mine business out from under their stuck-up noses. I just can't wait."

Lek put her arm around her friend's shoulder, but she felt a little uncomfortable about doing all this for revenge.

She just wanted some money again and a car.

# 12 HIGH SOCIETY

Both Lek and Ayr loved their new job and they threw themselves into it. Within weeks they were one of the biggest suppliers in their own little area. Lek's family and friends used them for all their purchases and so did Ayr's. It was safe to say that there was no-one in Baan Suay who did not buy most of their supplies from them and new customers from surrounding villages were coming to check them out almost every day. Success brought a heady feeling, which they both enjoyed.

The suppliers' reps gave them targets for increased discounts and they hit them every time. When they got a bigger discount, they would pass a third to a half onto their customers in one way or another. Sometimes it was to all customers, sometimes to account-holders and sometimes to farmers who themselves had hit purchase targets. They both enjoyed working out how they would reward loyal customers and entice new ones, so it became part of a regular brain-storming session, often over a few drinks after work and sometimes Craig was invited to give his opinions too.

Customers perceived them as two beautiful, single, middle-aged women, even those who knew Craig, and so did the reps. They were often invited to customers' private family functions, like weddings and initiations into the monkhood, but Craig was always told in such a way that he wouldn't find it appealing. Reps invited them to parties for salespeople and product launches and they loved to go.

Lek felt that Craig would hold them back and he probably would have to. His inability to speak Thai was stifling to conversation, when Lek had to stop and translate most of it for him. In all fairness this was not only Craig's fault, he was still trying to support his family by devoting all his time to work. Learning Thai came a poor second, but the decision to approach life in Thailand like that was beginning to work against him.

Most of these functions took place on Friday, Saturday and Sunday afternoons. Since their shop was open seven days a week despite the fact that most farmers didn't work on Sundays, they had to have a stand-in. Lek's mother stood in the breach for most of these times, but one of Ayr's aunties helped out too in order to keep the money circulating more fairly between the two families.

The business didn't suffer from their attendance at these parties and functions. Indeed, quite the contrary. They were networking like professionals although they were not aware of the term at the time. They met all the big, local farmers and farming contractors. They met local politicians and became friendly with many in the local high society, which was usually shortened to 'Hi-So', using the English words rather than the Thai equivalent.

Their beauty, ability to speak English, knowledge of computers and status as budding high-fliers made them interesting party guests. Lek was often asked whether she was married and to her credit, she never denied it, although when asked what he did for a living, she was want to say rather optimistically that he was a successful webmaster and author.

Lek was frequently asked whether her husband would give English lessons to advanced foreign-language students, but she always replied that he was a shy recluse, although that she would ask him, which of course she never did.

Both women received many advances from their hosts and some of their customers and suppliers. Lek had never accepted, but she was sure that Ayr had. She didn't have a problem with that. Lek was happy that she was married again, now that she had a regular income. Sometimes, she felt sorry for Craig, but she didn't know what she could do about it. Every now and again, she tried to do something special for him like buying him a dozen bars of his beloved chocolate or putting fresh flowers from the garden in a vase on his desk while he was out of the room.

Lek knew that Craig was a sucker for such simple demonstrations that he was always in her thoughts.

At one of their brain-storming sessions on how to share out an extra 2.5% discount, Ayr asked Lek a question:

"What do you think about our own discount?"

"How do you mean?"

"Well, we are making pretty good money and it is going to start showing up in our taxes soon, so why don't we allow ourselves to buy what we want at, say, just 1% over cost? Or enough just to cover our overheads? I buy a lot of stuff every month and so does your family, so I would make a saving and you could either keep the extra or pass it on to your family.

"What do you think? To keep it fair, we could limit the maximum amount to 5,000 each per month or 10,000 each per month."

"Sounds fine by me. Do you want me to check some figures tonight?"

"Sure, take your time, but why let the taxman have it? That's what I say. Or we could just remove our own purchases from the system completely and pay for our own stuff ourselves and leave the company out of it all together."

"I'll take a look at the spreadsheet, have a think and get back to you, Ayr."

They left it there, but Lek was not feeling one hundred percent right about the idea. She didn't want to get involved with anything shady. She was happy with the amount of money she was making and didn't want to complicate things or rock the boat.

They often met foreign men at the Hi-So dos that they attended, because many of the foreigners in the area that had so far eluded them were teachers or married to women, who had returned from working abroad and bought land or a business with their savings. Many of these men were in the same position as Craig, that is, they were unaware that there were any other foreigners living nearby.

Many of the teachers were young and anxious to move on to a bigger city where the night life and anonymity were better. No foreigner was able to take advantage of what little night life there was in the area without everyone talking about it the next day, especially if he were a teacher. The headmasters of local schools had already had to warn several young foreign teachers that it was not acceptable behaviour to appear drunk in public or date school girls, even if they were over the age of consent.

None of this would be a problem in cities like Pattaya or Bangkok, where everyone was just part of a huge crowd.

Lek tried to improve the social lives of one or two of these young men mostly because she felt sorry for them, but also because she knew how much they contributed to the educational system. If it were not for them, the standard of spoken English roundabouts would be dismal. Not only that, but one or two headmasters and several teachers that she had met socially had asked her to ask Craig to try to help them out by encouraging friends to come to the area to teach, because the turnover was so great. Craig was not impressed, but didn't know anyone that would be interested anyway.

Lek wanted Craig to befriend those who were already there, but after so long being virtually alone, Craig was not particularly interested in playing host to a load of bored teachers, as h put it, although he did go out of his way sometimes.

A little out of his way and not often.

Lek would try to steer him into going to Ben's on a Saturday or Sunday every now and then, and she would make sure that the teachers knew about it. She would also invite them to her house or the shop if there was a party or function going on, although not many came to the house as Baan Suay was not easy for them to find and there was no public transport at all.

Lek herself had never learned to drive a car and was ambivalent about learning now, although some days it seemed a priority to her and other times quite unimportant. Craig could drive, but didn't like to in Thailand 'because of all the crazy motorcyclists'. Lek could understand that, but other people coped, she thought. When she wanted to go to Phichai or even Phitsanulok, one of her brothers or Ayr were usually willing to help out. Once in Phichai there were taxis by the railway station that would take her back home and it was better than drinking and driving.

All in all, she knew that she was safer not having a car, because she drank too much or at least too often and the temptation to drive home under the influence would one day be irresistible. She knew that, but socially, people couldn't understand why she didn't have one and she found that rather embarrassing. She always had done. People had been asking her for years why Craig hadn't bought her a car.

In the days when they could not afford one, the embarrassment of these questions was actually painful, but now that she could buy one if she wanted, it was just annoying. Status and social trappings were far more important in village life than in a city, where no-one knows anyone.

Lek did invite Craig to some of the parties she went to and Craig took her up on the offers sometimes too. She thought that he was becoming grumpier as he got older and told him so. Craig thought that she was probably right, but didn't explain that he didn't like not being able to support his family himself.

It wasn't that he was jealous of Lek's success; quite the contrary, he was very proud of her; and it wasn't the fact that she could and did treat him far more often than he treated her. It was just that he was working hard too and always had and still success eluded him. He felt that the world owed him a living wage as recompense for all the effort he put in, but the world did not seem to agree and this made him grumpy.

Lek often had to cover up for Craig's lack of Thai social graces too. This wasn't because he was rude or uncouth, he was just ignorant of their ways. It hadn't mattered so much in the company that they normally kept, but at the Hi-So parties, a higher level of etiquette was expected. Lek knew that she should have taught him better Thai manners earlier, but there it was, she had not and now it was irksome.

In fact, she was more bothered about it than anyone else, because most people realised that Crag just was not aware of the higher social graces in Thailand and so turned a blind eye. Lek, however, could not because it embarrassed her. At the wedding of the daughter of the mayor of a nearby town, the meal was what is known in Thailand as a 'Chinese Table'. That is, six to eight friends, or even strangers, sit at a table and the food and drink provided is shared by everyone. Every table gets the same. This is typically six to eight dishes of different styles of food: fried rice, a large fish, a leg of pork, two or three curries and two or three other dishes.

Craig had eaten everything that Lek had selected for him, which was their usual tactic, so that he got only the food that she knew he could or would eat. However, noticing that his plate was empty one man pushed a dish of something towards him saying 'Try that. It is delicious'.

He put some on his plate and then put some in his mouth. It was a red-hot chilli curry. The helpful man asked: 'Lovely, neh? Have some more' and spooned more onto Craig's plate. Lek could see that Craig was having difficulties. He couldn't swallow the food or didn't want to and couldn't speak. When the man asked again: 'Nice, neh?', Craig had swallowed the mouthful and said without thinking: 'I'm sorry, but it is too hot for me'.

The man called the waitress over and said that there was a problem, because the food was too hot for a foreigner. A few sentences were exchanged and the waitress brought three bowls of the food that the man had seen Craig enjoying earlier. 'There,' he said, 'I apologise for our mistake. This food is for you alone.

They watched him all evening and Lek warned that he had to finish at least two of the bowls to be polite. He knew himself better than to finish the third or he would get more.

Later, the wedding cake was brought around and shortly after that the happy couple visited every table for their gift. When the bride had asked Craig whether he had enjoyed the food, he replied 'The cake was lovely'. Lek jumped in to rescue him immediately with: 'My husband liked all the food, but he especially liked the wedding cake because it reminded him of his mother's cooking. Isn't that true, darling?'. He nodded realising his faux pas. Honour was saved and the bride and groom moved on smiling.

Craig's little errors were not usually serious, but she had to keep an eye or an ear on him at all times when he was in public. There had been one occasion a few years before that could have turned very nasty. Lek had gone to the Ladies; Craig wanted a bag of 'karapow' (boiled water-plant roots)from a passing barrow boy. In his best Thai he had asked how much they were, but the man had guessed that he spoke English and replied 'Five Baht'. Thinking that the man could speak English, Craig had asked for 'One bag'. The man had thrown down the bag of karapow that he held in his hand expecting to sell, spat on the floor and advanced on Craig with an ugly sneer on his face. 'Five Baht, not one Baht,' he growled. Lek and Nong had got there just in time to sort out the misunderstanding.

Lek had been warning Craig not to speak to strangers for years but he had always insisted on trying, despite quite a few 'misunderstandings' of this nature over the years, even with Lek herself. There had been one that lasted four or five years when they were first together.

Craig had had the habit of saying 'For God's Sake!' when frustrated by a situation. He had started doing it in an effort to cut down on swearing, which he had picked up when he was younger. However, Lek had thought that he was saying 'F*** God!' and had found it so embarrassing and uncouth that she wouldn't talk to him for hours afterwards.

For years Craig had suspected that something was wrong, but couldn't work out what it was, because Lek had always walked away and refused to speak to him. One day, he had grabbed her arm and made her explain. She shook free and would only say: 'You know what you say. In Thailand we never speak about God like that. You are very lucky! If some Thai man hear you say these bad words, he box you in hospital.'

Immediately, Craig could hear how the words must have sounded to Lek. He had tried to explain but she would just not listen.

"I not say 'F*** God' – Listen: 'Fer' God's Sake!' 'Fer' is sloppy for 'for' – 'FOR GOD's SAKE' means 'For the Sake of God'. 'Sake' – it is a very old word. It means 'good' or something like that."

But Lek had thought that he was trying to wriggle out of heinous blasphemy: "I not sure," she had said, "I ask my friend later."

"No, you won't ask your bloody Thai friends later!" he had exploded, "They know even less English than you do. Come here."

It had taken him twenty minutes on the Internet to prove that he was right and that it was a common, everyday expression among millions of English-speaking people all over the world. However, she didn't like the expression, but never reacted in the same way again.

Craig had wondered at the thought that they had had hundreds of icy patches because he had used that phrase, which Lek had misinterpreted, but was too proud or stubborn or ashamed to ask him to explain.

Lek had never apologised for her mistake and never given any indication that she was aware how many hundreds of hours of frosty atmosphere her mistake was responsible for. Like many Thais, she saw apologies as a waste of time. She had often said to Craig when he had apologised to her, words to the effect of 'Do your words change anything? Are they a guarantee that you will not do it again? So, please do not waste them on me. Show me, by never doing it again and thinking before you hurt me next time'.

And there was definitely one thing that you could say about Lek and that was that she practised what she preached.

In fact, Lek's command of the English language had varied throughout their eight years together, although the general pattern was always upwards. In the short term the problem always came after staying in the village for a long time, and in the long term it came from staying in Thailand for a longer time. In short, lack of practice with good native speakers was to blame.

They were in such a period at that moment and it crossed Craig's mind that Lek's English was getting worse. She was starting to leave out letters that were difficult for her to pronounce especially the last consonants of syllables. She was like some F1 hybrid plant that was reverting back to the original. In Pattaya her English had been good, but it had improved a lot when she was on holiday in the UK, now it was definitely getting worse again. Maybe watching some English-language TV would help it improve, he thought, because he had no plans to go back to the UK for the foreseeable future.

As Fate would have it, a partial remedy was at hand.

# 13 LOCAL FALANG COMMUNITY

Murray, a friend that Craig and Lek had met five or six years before, was in the habit of spending six months in Canada with his family during the Thai summer, but usually came back to Thailand shortly before his birthday in September.

Craig emailed him every now and again and they arranged to meet up in Ben's Coffee Shop for a few beers and a chat one Saturday morning.

"Hiya, Murray, how are you doing, me ol' mate?" He waaied at Ben, "Good morning, Ben."

"Hello, Craig," replied Murray, getting up to shake hands. "How the devil have you been?"

"Ah, you know. OK. Nothing changes around here. How was Canada?"

"Beautiful, beautiful, Craig, you ought to see it in the Spring. I go back every year, because the Thai Summer is too hot for me and it's nice to see the family, but I love the Spring in Canada too."

"El tells me it was a hot one this year. Where is that lovely wife of yours?"

"She went to get some money and, oh, I don't know... She won't be long, she's looking forward to seeing you again. Ben, two beers, please."

When the bottles arrived, Murray automatically peeled part of the front label on his bottle down, a habit that had become unconscious now. He did it so it was easier to count how much he had drunk and how many he had to pay for.

"Actually, Murray, I said that nothing has happened, but I suppose it has really. Has El not told you that Lek has opened a shop with one of her friends?"

"No, at least, I don't remember her saying that, and I think I would have remembered. What sort of shop? Clothing? Fashion? That sort of stuff here in Phichai?"

It was a fair question, when falang bought a shop for their wives to keep them busy or and earn some money, it was usually either a clothing shop or a hairdressers.

145

"No, I know what you mean, but their shop sells farming stuff like fertilizers, seeds, sprays, chemicals all that sort of thing. It's only been open a few months but it's doing really well. I won't say much more because it is Lek's story. She'll tell you if you ask her.

"Then for myself, I started writing a book."

"Things have changed quite a bit then and you said nothing had happened. What is the book about? What made you want to write a book?"

"It came about because Lek misheard me and thought I was already writing one, so I thought, 'Yeah, why not? Good idea'. It's a ghost story. Supernatural. I'm trying to work in some werewolves and the odd vampire, because stories like that seem to be trending at the moment. What do you reckon?"

"I wouldn't know, Craig... I don't read a lot of books... I'm more a newspaper guy, and I read them on the Internet now anyway. Sounds like a good idea to write what a lot of people are reading now though. Good luck with it. I'll buy a copy when it's finished. I'll be your first customer and you can sign it for me."

"Really? OK, you're on." They shook on it and Murray said:

"Yes sir, 'You can tell a lie on credit or the truth for cash... Just think about it a minute...'"

Craig did, "Yes, good one, I like that..."

"It's my favourite saying of the moment, that is. You can tell a lie on credit or the truth for cash..."

"A bit like: 'A hero only dies once, but a coward dies a thousand times.'"

"Yes, same sort of idea. That's it, you got the gist... I knew you would."

At that moment, Lek and El came in carrying shopping. Craig and El, Murray and Lek exchanged waais and greetings. Craig rarely hugged El, but did sometimes or shook hands when the situation called for it. He had discovered long ago that it was best to let the woman set the pace on the physical contact front. Murray jumped up and hugged Lek. She was more used to foreigners and never minded a hug from friends or a kiss on the cheek, if she thought that it was a genuine greeting from a friend, but she didn't let just anyone grab hold of her. Craig had seen her refuse to shake hands sometimes – she had insisted on the traditional Thai waai and she would go no further.

The 'waai' is performed with the palms together like a child in prayer, with the finger tips near the chin or nose, depending on the amount of respect conferred and the elbows and upper arms held parallel to the ground– there is no physical contact. Many Thais still prefer this form of greeting only shaking hands out of politeness.

"Come on, girls, sit down, join us. Lek, will you have a beer with us? El what do you want, love, orange?"

"Not just now, thanks, Murray. El and I bought some ham, tomatoes and onions and we want to make sandwiches so nobody gets drunk too early. We want to do now, finished. We can drink later. OK?"

Lek had learned to trust tradition rather than her creative intuition when it came to composing the filling for sandwiches these days

"Yes, OK... I just wanted to buy you a beer and ask about your shop..." Murray looked a little hurt, but it hadn't been meant as a snub, it was just that they wanted to get the work out of the way so that hey could relax too.

They started making their sandwiches on the next table and Ben joined them when she was able.

Lek spoke to Murray: "What you want to do for your birthday this year, Murray?"

"I don't know. We could have a little party here in Ben's if she say OK."

Lek asked Ben. "She say 'Good idea'. Do you want?"

"Yes, I want. We five can have a small party, can't we? I have brought loads of Canada salmon and crab that I catch over there. Make lovely food, put in jar for keep long time."

Murray and many other falang were in the habit of talking to Thais like babies. Murray didn't do it all the time, but he lapsed into it now and again. Craig found it irritating and had to say something as he usually did. Lek didn't like it either, but she was far too polite to criticise an older man publicly.

"Murray, do you have to speak to Lek like that? She speaks English very well, as you well-know. When a falang speaks like that, it just tells Thais that it is acceptable speech. They are never going to learn to speak English properly from you or anyone else that speaks that silly pigeon English to them.

"I know you don't do it all the time, but at least where Lek is concerned, please try not to do it at all. I want her to learn to speak English well, not like you're talking to her."

"Yeah, sorry, Craig, sorry, Lek. It is just a habit. Most Thais that I know only know a few words so if you don't speak like that you have to repeat yourself several times and then they don't understand anyway..."

Lek frowned at Craig, so he said, "Thanks, Murray, it's just that she has tried so hard to learn a decent standard of English from me and this sort of drivel is just confusing for her – for all Thais really.

"What would you think, if, after years of copying the way your wife spoke Thai to you and you were really proud of yourself, you found out that she had been speaking to you for ten years like a two year old and that your perfect Thai was at nursery school level?

"You would be more than a bit cheesed off, right? Ten years hard work to talk like a two year old? Well, that is sort of what it was like when Lek went to the UK with me. She didn't know that normal people don't speak like tourists in Pattaya. She had to relearn nearly all of her English.

"So, let's raise the standards. Speak normally, properly and give them a chance to learn real English. If they don't understand something, they can ask."

"Yes, but they don't do they? They think they will lose face by admitting that they don't know. You see it every day..."

"Yes, your right. It drives me bonkers too, but at least you're doing your best by speaking well, eh? If they don't want to learn, then 'up to them' as they are so fond of saying."

He could see that the women were following every word while pretending not to, but they gave no indication of what they thought of the discussion. Craig guessed that they were pondering the criticism of Thai ways. Thais are very sensitive to any criticism – personal or national.

Lek curtailed the silence

"You asked about our shop, Murray. It was my friend Ayr's idea. You don't know her, but we in school together 35 years ago. Maybe more. We have many people come in the shop and some people ask us to go to parties. At the parties we meet some falang.

"If you want, we can ask falang come here for your birthday too. Do you want?"

Murray was always keen to meet other foreigners because he was alone in his village too and being retired had a lot more time on his hands than Craig.

"Yes, that is a good idea, Lek. Can you do that?"

"Sure, I bring some here before already. If you come here, maybe you see them after school finish or on the weekend. Ben has met some of them too.

"OK, Murray, I will do that tomorrow."

∞

They arranged to meet at Ben's between twelve and twelve thirty the following Saturday afternoon. Most people didn't know each other or had met once. Lek was the common link really although Lek brought Ayr along too as she always liked to meet new people and her English was very good too. They left one of Lek's brothers in charge of the shop.

Lek and Craig arrived early so that they could make the introductions, Murray, El and Ayr arrived at about the same time, but Ben had already been working for seven hours by then. She asked if they wanted the shop closed to the public as she had already sold to her target customers and there was not much Thai food left for sale, but nobody thought that necessary and quite a few passers-by were surprised and delighted to see a falang birthday party in full swing in the middle of Phichai.

Ben laid the tables out so that the head table could seat a dozen and then the next table could accommodate a further eight, while three smaller tables at the far end could seat four each. No-one had a clue how many people would come, but it was odds-on that there would be enough seats for guests and passers-by.

Murray had been very generous with his fish and crab. He brought a rucksack with six one-litre preservation jars of salmon prepared in two different ways, and crab, plus a large pack of home-smoked salmon. He had caught and prepared all this himself while in Canada and then carried it back to Thailand. El put the rucksack out of sight so that she could control how quickly it came out.

Meanwhile, Craig and Murray sat drinking a beer and Lek, Ben, El and Ayr sat on the next table, chopping, peeling and preparing food for the table. Some would be cooked Thai style, some European and there would be hot and cold dishes including chips, salad and sandwiches.

Murray was the first to spot a small group of people by the police station outside. Two white faces and two Thai, looking over shyly. He jumped up and went after them.

"Hello, falang. You come to party. My name Murray. Are you looking for Ben's shop?" They nodded. "Come with me, over here." They followed. Murray was always so keen.

When they entered the café, Lek called them over, waaied and introduced them to everyone. Craig and Ayr had met them before.

"This is Mike and Su and this is Jeff and Ma. Mike and Jeff are teaching at local schools. Mike is from Australia, right? And Jeff is from the UK. Why don't you men go sit down over there and get out of the way. Su and Ma, you come and join us... You know Ayr and this is our friend Ben. This is Ben's Coffee Shop."

It was typical, the men and women rarely sat together or not for long anyway. Some of the Thai women found it difficult to follow conversational English, so they preferred to sit with other Thais. However, even at all Thai parties, the sexes usually split into two groups.

Minutes later, Ron and Soom, and Steve and Nid got the same treatment. Ron was also an English teacher from the UK, but Steve was a retired businessman from Germany. He lived in his wife's village to the west of Phichai and had been there for decades. He was the nearest one to Murray's age group. His English was almost flawless and he and Murray hit it off at once, although Murray got on well with everyone really anyway.

Steve had not met any of the men seated around him, the teachers had seen or heard of each other before, none of them had met Murray, which was not surprising as he had been in Canada for the last six months and Craig had met two of the teachers briefly. It was a pretty mixed bunch, but everyone made an effort and Beer Chang soon broke any ice that there had been.

The ladies started to bring over the food now that there was a group of well-wishers already and took it in turns, roughly, to join their husbands and meet the others. However, most of them were happier to be on the ladies' table speaking Thai. The exceptions were Ben, Lek and Ayr, but they wanted to make sure that the wives had a good time too, especially as this was the first gathering of the local falang community in Phichai.

Murray was in his element, not because he was the star of the show, that was not the point, he liked to meet other falang and he frequently tried to get commitments from the others to meet up every Tuesday morning which was market day which was impossible for the teachers or and Saturday morning.

Everybody thought it would be a good idea, but no-one wanted to promise to meet up regularly. After a few more Changs and a stomach full of food, they did commit to something.

For the moment, they agreed to recognise Ben's as the official clubhouse of the 'Phichai Falang Society', with Murray as it's unelected chairman until someone challenged him, which no-one ever would and promised to call in when they were in the area to see who was about and leave any messages for the others with Ben.

The women talked about what it was like to be the partner of a falang. Ma and Su had not met any partners of falangs that they could talk too before and they were astounded and relieved that other women in a similar situation to them had the same experiences.

"They are so different from us, aren't they?" said Su.

"In what way?" replied Ayr mischievously.

"Well, they say they like Thai food but won't eat it. Mike tells everyone that he loves Thai food, but I have to make it really bland for him. It's not real Thai food at all. 'Not hot, not nice' is what my Dad used to say. Mike has a quarter of a chilli in his food and calls it curry!"

The ladies burst out laughing so spontaneously and so loudly that the men stopped talking and looked over. "Have you noticed," said Murray, "that the girls always seem to be having a better time than we do?"

The ladies covered their mouths with their hands to hide their laughter, "And they can't eat Thai before the evening... they eat these sandwich things! That's not real food, is it? I don't know... I'd go fishing with that stuff."

And they all laughed again.

"Craig used to be like that, but after eight years, I've got him up to one chilli per meal – baby level!" And they all laughed again.

"We went to a pub in Barry last time we were over there, O Briens, and this man, not much more than a teenager, really, asked me if it was true that Thais could eat whole raw chillis. 'Sure,' I said, then he pulled packet of fresh chillis out of his bag. 'Here we are', he said, 'prove it'

"One of the men we were sitting with, Ray, said, 'Don't worry, Lek, you don't have to prove anything'. 'I don't mind,' I said and ate four one after the other. You should have seen their jaws drop. Then the young man tried one not to lose face. One little bite and he was running to the toilet to wash his mouth out. It was so funny, but I didn't have to buy another drink for hours. Well, Craig didn't anyway."

"Oh, they are funny. Really." Uproar again.

Ma said, "I love my old man, though, funny as he is. You know, I wouldn't swap him for a brand new Ferrari, if someone offered... No, I couldn't afford the tyres, let alone the insurance..." and off they went again.

Ron watched his girlfriend, Soom, laughing with affection, but he lowered his voice to speak to the men around him: 'You know, it's a waste of time coming here, to Thailand, I mean, if you're looking for some sweet little pussy cat to marry. There are no domestic cats here, they're all bloody tigers – Thaigirls, I mean" and he laughed at his own joke. The others knew that he was right though. Thai girls might behave extremely politely, but you cross them at your peril as friends of Craig, Murray and Steve had found out to their cost.

Ron laboured the point until people wondered whether everything was all right between him and Soom at home: "Yes, if you want a domestic pussy cat, you get one from your own country, but if you want a wild one, come to Thailand, where domestication is just a veneer."

People smiled thinly and Craig changed the subject.

"Does anyone know any other foreigners around here. If you do, why not phone them up to come on down? We might as well meet everyone while we've got all this food laid on. Murray had met others but had no contact details; Steve said he would bring a few more people next time he came to Phichai. Jeff was the only one who called a friend but his friend was too busy to come.

Meanwhile, Ben was setting up her new karaoke system. It was only a small, home unit, but it was plenty big enough for the shop. Lek and the other ladies loved karaoke and so did Steve, but the other men would have preferred to have been able to carry on talking without shouting.

As the women, got a little drunker, Lek suggested buying a bottle of lao deng – red Thai whiskey, as beer was too fattening. The others readily agreed.

Craig suggested that the ladies came to join them and Lek started to move their stuff over, but if the truth be known, they knew that they would have a better time on their own. It was just that it seemed a little selfish as it was Murray's birthday party.

As it started to get dark, Ben produced the birthday cake that El had bought for Murray and everyone sang 'Happy Birthday' in the Thai style, which is to the same tune as in the West, but with the refrain 'Happy Birthday to You' repeated over and over and over. Murray blew out the candles and El cut the cake while Ben passed it around.

Many passers-by stopped as the song was being sung and some even joined in as it is the standard birthday song throughout Thailand. Murray gave a short speech and everyone applauded. He offered all the strangers who had stayed a while a free drink, but many had a train to catch.

Everyone agreed that Ben's Coffee Shop was the most central place for the local falang community to get together, and, being right next to the train station and the bust stops, it would be easy to get to for those who didn't want to take their cars or didn't even have one like Craig and Lek.

Murray could see that Ben was starting to wilt by seven o'clock so he thanked everyone for coming, thanked Ben for hosting his party and making it all go so smoothly, thanked El for organising it and bade everyone a good night.

Everyone there had had a great day out. Some, like Craig had spoken more English on that one day than in the previous month and in their joviality and cups, they all agreed to meet up the following Saturday.

Ayr, Lek and Craig shared a taxi back to Baan Suay leaving their motor cycles to be collected the following day.

Craig took a tin of Chang with him to drink on the journey home.

# 14 ANOTHER ONE BITES THE DUST

Over the following weeks, Craig, Murray and Ron became increasing friendly. Either Ron or Murray would arrange to meet up and then one of them would collect Craig for a drink after work and return him home later, or they would meet him in Nong's shop, sometimes completely by surprise.

However, Ron soon became bored with going to the same places and wanted to start exploring the villages nearby. Craig had never done that, not having transport, but Murray had some local knowledge so every now and then they would go looking for somewhere different to have a beer.

This was all right for a while, but Craig could not really afford the time to drink and go driving around. Going for a drink at Nong's in the evening or Ben's some Saturday's was a way of getting out of the house and relaxing. It was not an end in itself, it was not intended to relieve boredom. Not only that, but Lek started questioning him about where they went and whom they met.

In fact, it was all quite innocent at first, but it did become clearer as time went on that Ron's real intention was to look for a different kind of fun. Craig stopped going with them and later so did Murray, because they were getting too much hassle at home from their wives. Hassle that they didn't deserve since they weren't doing anything wrong.

Lek became a real nuisance with her questioning, until one day she let it slip that Soom was worried about what Ron was up to.

"How do I know?" replied Craig, trying to play the innocent, but Lek saw right through him. "You know, because you know as well as I do what all men get up to given half a chance. I wasn't born yesterday, you know. I saw thousands of falang men tourists in Pattaya and I've seen thousands of Thai men up here. You're all the same."

"I resent that remark," Craig blurted out, trying to sound offended, but knowing all the while that she was right about ninety-five percent of men.

"I am not accusing you, Craig. We have been in the village for years and no-one has ever complained about you doing that sort of thing. I am just trying to find out what Ron is doing, because Soom is a nice girl and a good friend and she is worried. I am not accusing you or Murray of anything except that you know something and you aren't telling me."

That was all true, of course, but Craig didn't want to be the one to put the finger on Ron and destroy their relationship only to find out later that Ron hadn't actually 'done anything'.

"Look, darling, I have seen him talk to girls. I have talked to girls, for Heaven's sake, but I haven't seen him do anything more than that... and neither have I by the way."

"OK, I am not worried about you really, but I do know that you are clever with words and you only tell me that you 'have not seen him do anything'. I do not think that you stand in the bedroom or the field and watch him making love with ladies, so you tell me nothing. It is so, or not?"

"I suppose so... yes, you are right, but he has not told me anything either. I just got bored going with him so often and not having time to write my book and articles for my web sites. He is retired here and he hasn't got much to do. He only has a few hours teaching every week. He is bored, whereas I am not.

"Then there was you nagging me about where I was going and what I was doing every day... It was just all too much, so I cut back on leaving the village. Nong's is good enough for my purposes."

"Good, I like this idea. It is good for me too. I can see you there from my work and if you have problems, I can help you. When you are far away, I cannot help and I worry about you. You know that you have problems sometimes when you try to speak Thai. Nobody speaks English good in the villages around here. They are only farmers. Some never see a falang before and think you are very rich. Maybe dangerous for you, so I worry."

"Yes, OK, Lek. We can't have that, can we? I'll just stay cooped up in my cage where you, your family and all your friends can keep an eye on me. I'll try not to have too much fun, all right? Happy now?"

"Don't be like that, telak... we can have fun together, you and me."

"Yes, OK, I didn't really mean that." And he didn't either, well some of him did, but he had become used to the isolated life and he didn't really want to go gallivanting around the countryside with Ron. Not only because of the money and his work either, but because he wasn't so interested any more. He sometimes wondered whether he had become institutionalised.

As it happened, Soom, Ayr and Lek knew more than Craig about Ron's little pastimes, but they were not saying much either. It was strange how many foreigners thought that nobody knew anybody just because they didn't know anybody themselves.

For a start, the way that the educational system was organised meant that most villages had schools for the under-twelve-year-olds, but after that, they had all had to go to the only High School in the area, the one in Phichai, so most people in any age group knew each other from school for miles around.

Then there was marriage. People didn't only marry within their village. People married school friends; people they had met in town in a karaoke bar or a restaurant or at a fayre. Lots of people ended up moving out of their village to another one nearby when they got married. This produced a huge network of informers and the unwary falang would have no idea who they were or that they were even related by marriage.

Once Craig and Murray had left Ron to his own devices, he became bolder and started taking other women, much younger women out. However, he was not only taking free-lancers out, he was sleeping with the staff at organised brothels. He became quite famous amongst a certain group of ladies. Often he would take on two or three at a time just to show off.

The girls were not used to such flashes of cash and so were easily very impressed with Ron after usually going with farmers who would try to haggle them down from two hundred and fifty Baht to two hundred and who were sometimes successful, if business was slack.

Some boasted about 'their falang' boyfriend named 'Lon' and it didn't really take long for this news to get back to the three friends although Soom was the last to hear, because she had lived in the UK for a few years and had lost touch with people.

One woman agreed to meet Soom and tell her a story, so Ayr picked her up one afternoon and the three of them drove to meet the woman in her village not far away.

"Hello, Khun Din, these are my friends Lek and Soom," said Ayr.

"Yes, come in my dears. Welcome. Please take a seat," she gestured to the table on which she was already seated. Khun Din was not particularly well-mannered, but then being considerably older than the friends, she could get away with it. They all noticed that Khun Din, her house and her garden were a bit shabby.

"You want to know what I know about the falang they call Lon, eh? OK, well I won't ask why you want to know, but I will tell you anyway. He is knocking about with a girl much less than half his age who lives a few doors down there." She pointed down the lane to the left of her shack.

"A right little hussy that one is, I can tell you. Everybody knows what she's like around here. She don't care for no-one but herself. She don't care who she hurts or whose life she ruins.

"They say that that is because she don't have long left to live herself, if you get my meaning." The old woman lowered her voice to a whisper, "She's got those AIDS. 'Ad 'em for years, she 'as, and she can't shift 'em. She's been to the doctor and the 'ospital, but she's run out of money.

"She's tried the old remedies. She's eaten live toads and geckos, but nothing... So, she said 'sod it', so they say, 'I'm going out with a bang!'. And I reckon she's been banging everyone who don't know her story ever since." She laughed loudly at her own joke.

"Well, I sees her with his falang Lon, they said 'is name was, and they looked pretty close friends. Disgusting it was. He had his hands all over her, right there outside my 'ouse and she let 'im. In broad daylight, I tell you! Disgusting. She needs stopping, she does, before she gives all the randy men for miles around some of 'er AIDS. Filthy, no good dog of a woman."

They wanted to get out of there as soon as possible, so they made an excuse to leave. They got off the table and waaied, although it was obvious that the old woman was enjoying her moment of importance.

"Here Khun Din, thank you for speaking to us so candidly, said Soom, "I want you to have this," and she produced a bottle of whiskey from her bag. "I don't suppose you drink yourself. I had bought it for my Dad, but I want to give you something. I can get him another. If you don't drink, you can share it with your guests."

The old lady's eyes were sparkling as she indicated for Soom to put the box down on the table beside her. As they were leaving, they turned to smile one last time and saw her putting a cloth over the box of whisky. She didn't even notice them.

Once they were driving away, Ayr said, "Sorry you had to hear it like that, Soom," but Soom was already sobbing quietly. "What are you going to do about it?"

Soom sniffled and blew her nose into her handkerchief. "I don't know yet, but I suppose that the first thing that I need to do is get an HIV/AIDS test done, 'though if I've got it, it's too late to worry about it now.

"Ron and I have not had full sex for ages, so I might be all right. I was too shocked to ask how long this has been going on... but we haven't done anything like that for months... too busy arguing." She sobbed again.

"Are you going to tell him that you know?" asked Lek.

"I just don't know yet. Are there any other surprises to come?"

"Not that we know of, eh, Ayr?"

"No, not really... just that Khun Din's husband, my great-uncle Dan, died about a year ago and their only child ran off with that girl and never came back. They went to Bangkok together, but when she came back, he stayed there. We don't know whether he's sick or not, but the family thinks that maybe he is and that he's too ashamed to come back. It makes it very difficult for his mother though and she is quite bitter about the whole affair."

"So, she might just have been being spiteful about her neighbour?"

"I don't think so. She probably enjoyed telling tales on that girl, but I would say that what she said is true. Or at least , she thinks it is. Yeah..., sure..."

"Do you have time to stop for a drink somewhere, my friends?"

"Sure, we could stop in Ben's for an hour, but we'll have to get back then. Are you all right to get a taxi home from Phichai, Soom?"

"Yes, it's not far. Thanks. I could do with the company at the moment and I could do with a drink too. After all, it's not everyday that you get told that you may have a deadly disease, is it? Perhaps we could toss a few ideas about too..."

It was three thirty when they parked up outside Ben's, but they had phoned ahead to ask whether she wanted to close early and she had said 'no'. They were welcomed into the café, which was empty since all the food had already been sold. Ben was sitting at a table alone, drinking an iced coffee.

Soom explained her predicament to Ben in a hushed voice after four bottles of Chang had been put before them.

"Well I never...!" said Ben truly shocked. "I would never have guessed it. You poor woman, even if you are not ill, and let's all pray that you're not. Why do men behave so foolishly? For what? A bit of sex...

"What's this woman's name? Does anyone know her? Where did she catch HIV/AIDS?" asked Ben.

"No, not really," replied Ayr. "It seems that she had been living in Bangkok with relatives since she was a child. He name might be Jill. Maybe she got it down there."

"She is not really important, is she?" put in Lek. "What are you going to do about Ron? The way I see it you have two choices. Tell him that you know and see what he does or kick him out."

"There is a third, there must be. I want to teach randy Ronny a lesson that he will never forget," said Soom, "but the first thing I must do is get a check up in Phitsanulok. If I am not infected, Ayr, can I stay with you for a week or two? I have an idea."

"You can stay with me anyway, it's not that easy to get HIV/AIDS from non-sexual close physical presence. What do you have in mind?" Soom let the others in on the scheme that was forming I her mind.

∞

A few days later, Soom went to stay with Ayr with only an over-night bag of clothes. "What did you tell Ron," asked Ayr.

"I told him that I had to go to Bangkok to see a dying relative and that I would be away for a week after she passed away or a fortnight if she hung on. It was so funny. He pretended to be upset, but I could see him scheming as I spoke. He's planning all sorts of shenanigans while I'm away. I know it. He drove me to the bus station in Phitsanulok early this morning and left when I told him that the bus would be an hour late.

"Then I took a taxi to the hospital, took the test and came here. They said the results would take three days. I told them to send them here, as you offered. It saves me going back, doesn't it?

"Have you asked Craig to tell Murray and Ron that he will be bogged down in writing for two weeks so they should stay away?"

"Yes, he's done that. He thinks that Ron hit you and that you don't want to see him for a couple of weeks. He's on our side, so don't worry about him."

"OK, we're all set up at our end. Now for a few days waiting for the test results, during which I am going to be rat-arsed most of the time on this," she held out 20,000 Baht. Spending money, courtesy of my darling Ron and a credit card 'should I need it'."

Soom's days followed a pattern. She would get up with a hangover, eat, shower and get dressed, drink a beer in Nong's and then a man would collect her and bring her back an hour or so later. Then she would hang about the shop and go for a beer with Craig when he was ready at about four thirty. Soom often insisted on paying for everything, but it was only in Nong's shop in Baan Suay, so the bill was never very high and certainly never a thousand Baht.

The letter that she had been waiting for from the hospital arrived on the fifth day and everyone was relieved to read that she was HIV negative. That night she really went to town and spent twice the normal daily amount, because she bought a drink for anyone who came to the table for whatever reason, even if she didn't know them. The relief was obvious to everyone who knew what she had thought she might have had.

On the tenth day, Soom made a phone call to her brother to start the next phase of her plan. That evening, while driving home from a karaoke bar drunk, Ron was involved in a serious road vehicle accident, was breathalysed, found to be intoxicated and taken to hospital in Phitsanulok with a broken leg and multiple lacerations.

It was the following afternoon before the police could trace anybody who knew him and then Soom received a phone call from her brother who had been summoned to the police station to help trace her. Soom acted distraught and promised to be in the hospital before her husband woke up in the morning, which she was.

"Oh, Ron! What have you been doing, you silly man? I told you to take care and not to drink too much before I left. Look at you now!" Tears rolled down her cheeks.

Ron smiled weakly. "I was stupid. I didn't see the other car... but, Soom, I'm all right really. A broken leg and a few cuts. I'll be all right, really I will. Don't worry. The insurance will cover everything and after a few weeks in here with no beer, I'll have dried out. When my leg is better, we'll go somewhere really nice together... Koh Samui! You like it there don't you? I'm so tired, sorry, love..."

"OK, darling... I'll wait an hour and then get off. I want to go home and pick up some clothes and then I'll be back. You'll probably still be asleep."

When Ron was asleep a few moments later, Soom took one last look at him and left the room. She asked the first nurse she saw where she could check her husband's belongings. When she had seen the plastic bag, she was satisfied and called a taxi to take her home.

Soom looked around the house and opened a few windows to let the smell of stale beer and cigarette smoke out, then she went into the bedroom collected a few things and got back in the waiting taxi.

"Baan Suay, please..."

Soom smiled at the thought of how things had worked out.

"Oh, driver and stop at a bank along the way, please, any bank."

At Baan Suay, Soom stopped off at the shop, paid off the taxi and asked him to return at noon the next day.

Her return was followed by another long party for which Soom picked up the bill.

"How is Ron?" asked Craig.

"He's all right," she replied, "as well as can be expected. They have him drugged up to the eyeballs because he has a nasty break in his right leg. He'll live, although he'll probably be in hospital for at least a month. He's not so young any more, so it could take longer for the bone to knit despite the pins they've put in.

"That's what the nurse said. I didn't have time to wait for the surgeon to finish his rounds. When I got home to change my clothes, he had left the whole place wide open, you know. Probably as drunk as a lord from the moment I left. Still, he's in the best place for him now, isn't he? That's what people always say and in Ron's case, it's true. Excuse me, I want to thank Ayr for putting me up."

She gathered Lek as she walked to the shop where Ayr was still doing something.

"Aren't you finished yet, Ayr? I'll tell you what, your job is too much like hard work. You could make a good living out of what I just did. Ron's in hospital and I have his credit cards. I've taken a million baht already and there is plenty more where that came from. What's more Randy Ronny will be stuck in hospital for at least another month." She grinned at them.

"I only helped you because of how he treated you. It's not right to wreck someone's life just because you can. If I hadn't known that he messed you around and gambled with your life, I wouldn't have been party to this. Not that I did much anyway, really."

"Same goes for me," said Ayr. "Ron deserved it, but I wouldn't want to see it happen to all falang."

"Maybe not," she said and left the partners to lock up.

The following day, Soom left with the taxi she had booked. She had told everyone that she was going to hide out in Pattaya for a few months, but she told the taxi driver to head off to Chiang Mai and 'stop off at a bank along the way'.

∞

A couple of months later, the full story got back to Ayr and Lek of how Soom and her brother had arranged for a girl to get Ron particularity drunk and then dump him at the end of the night. Driving home, another accomplice had waited for him and forced him off the road into a tree and then called the police.

Soom had emptied both his credit cards and then sold them and his passport on the black market. When Soom had made a statement to the police in Chiang Mai, she had said that she was drunk in Baan Suay at the time of the accident where she was recovering from the shock of finding out that her husband had been playing the field and almost given her AIDS.

Ron was arrested when he was discharged from hospital and imprisoned for driving while under the influence and being without a passport. After a few days, the embassy had persuaded the police to drop all charges, given the fact that no-one had been hurt except Ron and he was deported on a flight paid for with money wired over by his brother. When he complained that his wife had stolen all his money, they pointed out that there was no proof of that, since that house had been left open for weeks and he had given her the PIN's anyway.

The cards were later confiscated in a shop when a young Cambodian woman was trying to use them to buy jewellery. This put Soom firmly in the clear.

Ron was banned from ever returning to Thailand again as an 'undesirable alien'. Within six months, Soom was back living in the house with a falang that she had met in Chiang Mai, but no-one ever met him, because Soom didn't want him to find out what had happened to her last one.

# 15 IN SICKNESS AND IN HEALTH

Craig was spending more time with Lek at that time than he ever had done since a month after he had met her. For many years, he had felt like a dog in a wheel turning a spit or a buffalo tethered to a plough, while Lek went off and did God-knew what. He had always trusted her, that had never been an issue with them, although the recent episode with Ron had caused him trouble, but it had seemed to him often that he was the only one pulling the plough.

Lek had not been able to find work because there was none in Baan Suay except back-breaking farm labouring or self-employment. Lek had tried a few things, but basically they had not had the money to try a decent venture. The return of Ayr had changed all that and given Lek the chance to prove that she was not a wastrel lady of leisure.

She was putting all the hours in that Craig usually did and found the time to cook for and socialise with him and she was making more money than he was, even though she had only just started her business and Craig had been working at his for eight years.

In Craig's favour, he was not jealous of Ayr and Lek's success, he was proud of them and in Lek's favour, she never mocked him for his lack of it. In fact, now that their money worries were over, even if only temporarily, they were both or even all three, happier than they had been for years and years.

Craig went to the shop if he wanted breakfast, which was not often since they ate Thai and he preferred toast and coffee. They usually ate lunch together or, if they were away, he would go to the local kwitiau cafe, go without or they might leave him something. They also always ate something together in the evening and had a few drinks either at Nong's, the house or the shop.

Despite all this, Craig often thought of Ron and his Fate. He didn't know the full story and he thought it better not to ask, so it was never mentioned, but it was clear to him, that if a Thai wanted a falang to go, then that falang would go.

One way or another.

Despite being happy, he was no longer the bread-winner and he wondered if that fact would decide his own Fate one day.

The balance of power in their relationship had changed. Lek no longer needed him to provide her with money and status or pay for Soom to go to university. In fact, in a few years, when the house money ran out, he would become totally dependent on Lek and her share of the business. He had heard rumours about Thai women and their money and guessed that he would be finding out for himself one way or the other over the next few years.

He thought that he knew Lek well enough, but not well enough to stop him worrying a little on a regular basis. Money changed people, he thought, how much would it change Lek? Would he be forced to go home with his tail between his legs á la Ron in a few years time?

That would be a wicked twist of Fate after all that he had done, for sure, but it was out of his hands, so he decided to do the only thing he could do and leave it to his Karma.

If Thailand was just a side-track in his journey through life, he would find out soon enough and if Lek was the instrument used to teach him that lesson, then so be that too.

∞

Craig spent many hours at his desk before a computer screen typing, and as often as not, his lunch break reading a book too. Lek was always warning him that he would 'wear his eyes out'. Craig didn't believe that this was possible, but as he grew older, he did notice that his eyes became tired sometimes and that if he worked very long one day and didn't sleep well, that his vision was slightly blurred the next day. This had been going on for several years, which was why Craig dismissed it. A good night's sleep always fixed the issue.

Craig's problem was though that he was not always capable of getting a good night's sleep. However, he had been like that since he was a child. Four or five hours sleep had always been ample. No matter what time he went to bed, he would wake up four or five hours later, maybe six if he had drunk too much, and there never was and never had been, any way that he could get back to sleep again.

He had spoken to doctors about it over the decades. Some had said that it was just the way he was, and others had offered sleeping tablets, which he didn't want. His parents had said that he had an over-active mind. It was the best explanation he had ever had, so he stuck with that, since the professionals hadn't come up with a better explanation.

His rationalisation now, since he couldn't talk to anyone about it, was that, since all muscles become weaker as one gets older, it stood to reason that the muscles controlling the eyes would get weaker too. He thought that the solution would be to get some stronger glasses the next time they went to a big city, since there was no optician's near Baan Suay.

One morning, Lek was standing behind Craig in his office while he was peering at his screen.

"Your eyesight is getting terrible, darling. You can hardly see what you've written, can you?"

"No, but it's because of the bad light and the fact that I didn't sleep very well. I probably need new, stronger, glasses too. I'm just getting old. It's not a problem..."

"Well, my Mum is a lot older than you and she doesn't squint to read from a few inches from the paper."

"Maybe she doesn't, but we were not all born with the same standard of equipment, were we? We are not all the same"

"Perhaps not, but some people look after what they have and you do not. I have been telling you for years to take regular breaks from the computer."

"Ye-as and I do... Sometimes."

"Yes, but not often enough and not for long enough and when you do, you usually read a book! How is that resting your eyes?"

"Well, how is looking at a tree resting them then? Images are still going in, aren't they?"

"Well close them then! But, you don't have to think much when you see a tree, do you? When you read a book you have to think, so by looking at a tree, you rest your brain and that is important too. If you close your eyes, you can rest your eyes and your brain, so that is even better."

"What about if you think? You still see things and have to think about them, or not?"

"Look, up to you, but you are not young man now, you should rest your eyes and your brain more often."

"I'll tell you what. Sort it out with Ayr and we'll go into Phitsanulok for the day and have our eyes checked. Yours and mine. We can take a taxi, the bus or a train, I don't care. Obviously it can't be a Sunday though."

"OK. Deal. I'll talk to Ayr and we go soon."

They went to their appointment at the Phitsanuwed Hospital in Phitsanulok on the following Tuesday.

Lek needed glasses, but of the weakest kind. She accepted the judgement on her age gracefully and admitted that her eyes had been aching a little over the past few months, but when it came to Craig, it was a different story.

"I don't know how you can see at all," exclaimed the doctor. "The right eye, is particularly affected, but the left is bad too."

"I will admit that it has been pretty difficult to see details recently. What is the matter, doctor? It is just age-related, isn't it?"

"Yes, you are senile."

"Well, I've been called mad before and crazy, but never by a medical person...," joked Craig, his knowledge of Latin suggesting what the optician meant.

The optician opened a drawer in his desk and leafed through a book... Yes, here it is... You have 'Premature Senile Cataracts'."

"Oh, I see, or don't actually... How did I get them?"

"We will never know for sure. It could be your blood if you are diabetic, it could be the strong sunlight, but basically, we don't know."

"What can I do about them?"

"We can cut them away for you. They cannot be dissolved and will only get worse. Your eyesight will continue to get worse until you take action and my professional opinion is that you will not have long to wait before you are blind in your right eye. The left one will follow later."

"Oh! Thanks a lot."

They were advised to make an appointment at the desk when they paid the consultancy fee.

"What do you think about that, telak?" asked Lek when they were outside the office.

"I don't know. I guess we ought to make an appointment and get it sorted out as soon as possible, eh?"

"No, not now. Let's go home and think about it. I want to talk to some people. Not good news for you, neh? I told you about computers."

"All right, he didn't say it was due to computers, so don't go braying about that just yet. We can ask next time. Let's get home, I fancy a few beers in Nong's before I go blind and can't find my bottle."

Lek smiled at his feeble joke, but really felt very sorry for him.

A few days later, Lek had consulted with 'her people' and decided that Craig should have another opinion and that it should be from the best hospital and doctors in the land, which meant a trip to either Bangkok or Pattaya. Lek really wanted to go to Bangkok so she could see more of Soom, but she conceded that it would be better to go to Pattaya because it was easier to get around and the hotels were cheaper, so she phoned the Bangkok-Pattaya Hospital for an appointment in four days and went into Phitsanulok for bus tickets.

∞

The surgeon at the hospital agreed with the diagnosis, but offered an alternative remedy.

"I can cut your old lens out and put a plastic one inside your eye," she said.

"That sounds horrendous," replied Craig. "Won't it hurt a lot?"

"The operation will not hurt at all because there are no pain receptors in the eye itself. You will be under a local anaesthetic for the duration of the operation, in order to preclude any discomfort. After that, we will monitor the situation, but you will only get better. The operation lasts twenty to forty minutes usually. Any questions?"

"Can I get cataracts again after this? And was it caused by watching a computer screen too much?"

"Unlikely, not the same kind, anyway and no. Why do you ask about computers?"

"Have a chat with my wife, please, doctor..."

Lek put her questions and voiced her concerns in Thai and the doctor put her mind at ease.

"OK, your wife understands the situation clearly now. Do you want the operation?"

Craig looked at Lek. She nodded 'yes'.

"OK, doctor. When can you do it?"

She looked at her watch: "In thirty minutes..."

"No, I don't mean 'how long', I mean when."

"Yes, so do I. I only have one more appointment this afternoon. That will take fifteen minutes. We can start after that."

"Sorry, doctor, but I need to prepare myself for this. Psyche myself up... and I need to know whether the insurance will pay for it."

"I understand, but my staff will check with the insurance people. It sounds better coming from them. I'll get them to phone you later on today, but be prepared to have the operation at eleven tomorrow morning, if you want it. Just confirm with whoever rings you later,

"Any more questions? No? Mrs. Williams? None either? All right, if you will excuse me..." and she was gone.

A nurse led them down to reception where the details of their insurance and phone numbers were taken. Lek was given a hospital patients' card for Craig and they walked out of the hospital rather shell-shocked.

"What do you think of that, Lek? The speed... I've never known anything like it."

"Do you want to have it done?"

"Yes, but that is not what I am talking about. Maybe you don't understand... I am from the UK, as you know, and we have a National Health system, which is free except for taxes, but you have to wait for operations. I know a lady who had to wait two years for the removal of her cataracts and here, I can have a completely new lens this afternoon! It is mind-boggling to me."

"You pay, you can have what you want."

"Yes, OK, but a few days ago, I was told that I might soon be blind and today, I am told that I will have near-perfect sight by this evening..."

"All right, that is not what the doctor said, but as good as..."

"Thailand very good, neh?"

"Yes, I love the place, that's one of the reasons why I live here, but this is something else. Oh well, let's go to your cousin's for a few beers and wait for the phone call."

"You cannot drink too much, neh? Or no operation tomorrow."

"I know, I know."

When the phone call came from the hospital shortly after six-thirty, it was to say that the insurance company had accepted the claim and to offer a ten o'clock appointment which Craig accepted. Five minutes later, the insurance company phoned to check that the claim was legitimate and confirmed that the bill would be met by them.

The operation, whatever it entailed, for Craig was not quite sure, was set for the following morning.

If he did not drink too much.

∞

The surgeon took one last look at his eye and sent him to the waiting room, where a nurse dripped a solution into his eye every three minutes for half an hour. Lek was present to keep him company.

When he was deemed ready, he was taken away by wheelchair and Lek was told that she would be able to see him in two hour's time.

The nurse helped him strip off and don a surgical gown which didn't wrap around him completely, leaving him naked from behind. He heard several nurses giggling as he walked to the operating room. He didn't mind that, but was grateful that no other patients were able to see him.

The operating table was a chair and the equipment looked like something out of Star Trek, but he felt more relaxed when he saw the face of the surgeon that he had met before and trusted.

Then a nurse tied his arms to the chair.

"Sorry, Craig, but it is to stop you interfering with me when I am busy."

"But I would never do such a thing...!"

"Ah, so sorry," she chuckled, "No, I mean, many people want to put their hand up, when I cut their eye. No, that does not sound right either. Am I saying it good? They try to defend themselves..."

"Yes, I understand, don't worry." They smiled at each other.

Then the nurse put another gown over him and then a face mask, so that only one eye was showing, a clamp held his head in place and a gadget kept his eye open. Then the surgeon loomed into view.

"Can you see me, Craig?"

"Yes, doctor."

"Good, look into the light, please, and relax."

A very bright, almost painful light was directed at his eye and he had no option but to look into it since his head was clamped in place and his eye held open.

"OK, I am about to begin."

Craig heard a pump and thought he saw a scalpel. Cracks like in a shattered window appeared in his field of vision and then he lost his sight.

"Can you see me now, Craig?"

"No, doctor..."

"Good. Please do not be alarmed, that is how it should be."

It felt scary to be blind, even if it was only in one eye, but he was not really afraid. He had total faith in this woman and wondered if she had put other foreign patients at ease with her references to being 'interfered with', since he knew that many people came to Pattaya from abroad for surgery because it was so good and so cheap.

She was fiddling with his eye, but he had no idea what was going on. At least it was painless.

"What can you see?"

"Nothing, doctor."

"And now?"

One of the most beautiful visions he had ever beheld was six inches from his face and he wanted to kiss her.

"I can see you, doctor."

"Good, I thought you might. Everything has been a success The nurse will prepare you to go home and I will see you tomorrow morning. Good day, Craig."

The nurse undid the clamps and untied his arms, cleaned his eye and put a dressing and a cover over it. Then she helped him into a wheelchair and took him to the post-op waiting room, which was far more scary than the operation that he had just undergone.

There were road accident victims crying out loud in pain or trauma, people in bloody bandages, all sorts of things. Craig was the fittest person there and was desperate to get out. After fifteen minutes, he signed himself out and the nurse called Lek to persuade him to stay put, but he would not, just could not stay there.

Thirty minutes later, after a little paperwork, they were sitting in a bar in Soi Buakhao drinking a beer or at least Craig was. Lek was ashamed of him for not staying in the hospital until he was told he could leave and for drinking so soon after an operation.

"I do not know how you can have such little regard for yourself!" she said in exasperation.

"It's not that, Lek. I had no anaesthetics, I am not on tablets, not on antibiotics, nothing. Therefore, there is nothing for this beer to hurt but my liver. Therefore, nothing has changed in that regard since yesterday. Did anyone tell you that I shouldn't drink?"

"No, but they said that you must not hurt your eye..."

"Yes, but isn't that a bit like saying 'I wouldn't cut my finger off, if I were you'? It's a bit bloody obvious, isn't it? I promise that I will not get drunk and fall over. How is that? I'll go even further, three beers and we go back to the hotel until tomorrow."

Lek reluctantly agreed.

When they got back to their room, Lek unpacked all the items that she had been given to treat him with and started reading the post-op after care procedures, which they had also been given in English. Craig was pleased to see that there was no mention of beer in there, but Lek was hoping there would have been.

"Lie back and let me look at your eye. He did as he was told and Lek very, very carefully removed the eye-defender and padding.

Then she squealed and looked away.

"What is it, Lek?"

"Your eye, it is... er, horrible" She fetched him a mirror from her handbag. There were tears in her eyes.

"Mmm, I see what you mean," he tried to joke, but it went straight over Lek's head. "I can assure you though that it looks far worse than it is. It doesn't hurt at all. Not in the slightest and I can see out of it, although light does hurt it, as it says on that piece of paper. In fact, light really hurts. It's like a knife."

His eye looked like an eight-ball, but the spot was red not white. It looked three times it's normal size, was the colour of Guinness and had a large, dilated red pupil. It was the best example of a black eye that he had ever seen and it was very scary. Well, it would have been, if he had seen it on anyone else, but since it was his own, he knew that it was painless.

Lek would only look at him through the corner of her eye.

"What's the matter, darling? It doesn't hurt, not one little bit, I promise you."

"I believe you, but it looks horrible and some Thai people believe that if you see something horrible, you can get the same... I don't want the same. You look like ma ba – wolf, maybe werewolf like in your story."

"Thanks very much."

When he growled at her she jumped off the bed, so he started howling.

"Stop it! It is not funny."

"It's the tablets, they're driving me mad!"

"You're not on any tablets!"

"Oh, no, you're right, I don't know what happened to me then."

"It is not funny. You are sick and you must take it seriously."

"Yes, dear."

Lek cleaned the eye, put the drops in and then replaced the dressing and shield.

Craig went to sleep and Lek sat guard over him. She was worried that he might take the eye shield off and stick his finger in his eye, which was one of the dangers written on the instruction sheet. Poking a finger in the eye could cause an infection, the biggest post-operation danger, which could yet cost him the eye.

The next day, the doctor said that she was pleased with the eye, but that he must be very careful not to get it infected. As a precaution, he was told not to shower for a week and to keep the dressing on at all times, except when putting drops in. However, the surgeon spoke more to Lek than to Craig, because she was brimming with questions.

"Doctor, Craig went drinking yesterday after the operation. Will that hurt his eye? And he says he is going to start work on the computer this afternoon and have more beer!"

"All right, Khun Lek, I understand your concerns, but neither the beer nor the computer will harm him in moderation and since he has a patch on, working on the computer could not hurt his eye anyway, but I will have a word with Craig for you."

"Khun Craig, your wife is concerned about your drinking and working," Lek was frowning and nodding at him like a mother saying 'I told you so'. "While there is no additional danger to drinking in moderation for recreational purposes now, I cannot condone it, although many believe that a glass of mild beer a day helps keep the kidneys clean.

"The danger to you is over-indulgence leading to additional injury to your eye and resultant infection, which could still lead to you losing it. I cannot stress that too much. As for using a computer, although it cannot cause you any harm, it is best not to put much stain on your eyes since they are weak, so you should take your wife's recommendations seriously and rest for at least ten minutes every hour. Don't forget that you only have two eyes and neither of them is very strong."

Lek nodded in agreement, her face having been saved.

"I'll see you in seven days from now. Goodbye, good luck, listen to your wife and take care of that eye." A nurse appeared to show them out and the doctor went back to her computer.

"A week, Lek! We have to stay here another week. What about Ayr and your work?"

"I don't know, I will phone Ayr when we get back to the room."

"The bar first, you mean. Same tactics as yesterday. Same agreement."

Lek reluctantly agreed, took him to the same bar at the top or Pattaya Plaza on Soi Buakhao, 'Oo's Bar', and left him to go to the beauty salon.

Craig soon got talking to someone as he usually did.

"Someone punch you in the eye then?" asked a man called Jerry.

"No, nothing like that, I had an operation yesterday." Craig explained the details.

"Get away with you. You're having me on. Show me."

Since Lek was not there to complain, Craig removed the shield and padding. He opened his right eye slowly for full effect. The man shuddered.

"Oh, my God, look at that!" and as he said it, the strong Thai midday sunlight reflected off a passing car window straight into his eye. He winced like Dracula being caught out of his coffin at sunrise and let out a yelp of pain. The man almost fell off his seat and Craig quickly replaced the pad and shield.

"What was that all about?"

'The light. My pupil is very widely dilated by the antiseptic drops I put in there and since I no longer have a cataract, all the light just floods in there and it hurts like a stabbing. I won't be doing that again in a hurry, I can tell you. I'm glad my wife wasn't here. She would have had a fit. Jeez, that hurt, really hurt."

Lek squared her absence with Ayr, and her mother and brothers filled in for her whenever they could, but the following week at the hospital, when they were told that they would need to come back once a week for another month, Craig wondered what would happen.

Lek spent a long time on the phone and since the conversation was in Thai, he only got half of it and maybe even that was wrong. When she hung up, Lek explained.

"I will stay with you. It is not worth going home every week. One day up, one day back. For what? Ayr agrees. There is no problem. She says I should stay here and take care of my husband, her friend, and I agreed. The family said they would help Ayr as much as possible and I believe them.

"So, my darling, I am staying with you as your nurse and wife and you, my husband and patient, must do exactly as I say. At all times. You agree?"

"Yes, darling, most times..." but he was relieved to finally know that Lek would be with him money or no money, in sickness and in health.

# 16 A TREE FALLS ND TIME STANDS STILL...

The three friends were sitting in Nong's shop one Sunday afternoon having something to eat and drink, as they usually did, because Sunday is a day of rest for many in Thailand as it is in the West, although not for Christian reasons. Not only that, but being a stone's throw from their own front door, they could see if any customers came without having to wait inside. It really was the perfect location for their shop.

Ayr said, "I was just looking at my driver's license, I think it has expired. What year is it?"

Just then, as Craig and Lek were looking at each other in amazement that someone didn't know what year it was in August, and Ayr was looking at Craig for an answer to her question, there came a loud groan from across the road. Ayr and Lek turned to look, Craig was facing that way anyway.

A large coconut tree moved, gave out a ripping sound, then a crack and, slowly at first, but gaining speed like an old movie, crashed to the ground, it's tip landing not five metres from them. It's coconuts spilled across the road like the contents of an artic lorry in a jack-knife accident.

"Wow, I have never seen anything like that before. Have you?" Both women shook their heads.

"Awesome!"

"Quick, count the coconuts," shouted Ayr, "We can put as lottery number." She and Ayr jumped up to count the coconuts.

"It is 2013." said Craig to himself.

"Fourteen coconuts," said Ayr, "Write it down somebody, before we forget."

Men were already tying a rope to the tree to drag it off the road and out of the way of any cars and farm vehicles that might pass. As the tractor started to drag the dying tree away, it groaned again and rasped along the concrete surface.

It was making a deep impression on Craig.

"Er, 2456." said Craig.

"What?"

"The year, it is, er, 2456 in Thai."

"Oh," said Ayr, "Are you sure? Anyway, I need it in English."

"In English it is 2013, add 543 for Thai. Oh, not 2456, sorry, 2556."

"Thank, you telak."

"Wait a minute! I was a hundred years out in the Thai date and you didn't even notice! If I had asked someone the year and they had said 1913, I would have known instantly that it was wrong, but you did not. The tree was amazing, but so was that! A hundred years out and neither of you noticed..."

"Oh, don't go on about it, Craig, it is not important." said Lek.

"Maybe not, in the scheme of the universe, but it explains something to me. The Spanish may have invented the word 'manyana', but the Thais have developed the concept to the extreme. A hundred years out! Not just an hour or two... Oh, my God!" But neither of them was listening to him any longer.

"I suggest we go somewhere later. What do you think? Wait until, say, four-thirty and then go somewhere for a few hours."

"I'm easy." said Craig.

"Where? It's Sunday all the shops are shut" said Lek.

"We could go for a drive and eat somewhere..."

"I'm all right here. I don't fancy driving about for the sake of it." said Craig. Lek didn't seem too enthusiastic either since there wasn't much chance of shopping.

"Well, we'll just sit here then, shall we?" said Ayr.

The other two nodded.

"I know what we ought to talk about, if we have nothing to do," said Ayr, "Wills!"

"Will's what, for Buddha's sake?" said Lek, using her new word.

Ayr caught on, but not because she understood the word 'sake'.

"Well, we have a business now, what happens if I die tomorrow. It could happen, think of Goong... What then? Where does my half of the business go to? Where would your half go, Lek?"

"What sort of arrangement do you both have, if say, Craig dies? Sorry, Craig, but you are older than Lek."

"No, that's all right, we have never talked about these things, have we, Lek?"

"No, I find them depressing..."

"Sure," said Ayr, "But it won't stop it happening, will it?"

Lek hung her head and shook it, "I suppose not... Actually, I met a woman once who was having enormous trouble because her foreign husband had died while on a trip back home, but he hadn't made provisions for his girlfriend of nine years.

"Listen, Ayr, let's just speak about this in Thai, because I don't want to bother Craig with it at the moment, if ever. It would be nice if he thought of it for himself."

"Are you all right, Craig? Sorry if we must talk in Thai, but it is about money and business and we are not sure of the English words."

"You carry on, don't mind about me. I'm still thinking about that tree falling... I've never seen anything like that before. You could order another beer for me though, when you're ready."

"OK, darling, thank you. Nong!

"Anyway, like I was saying, this woman, Nan, was going out with her man for nine years, he had retired a year or two before and they built a big house ten kilometres from here. It is a real stunner and cost about five million Baht. You don't do something like that if you don't love someone, do you?

"So, that was not in question. A few months before he went home to sort his house over there out, I don't know, rent it or sell it, he bought a large new four-wheel drive jeep costing one and a half million, but wanted to pay for it in instalments.

"He also signed a long-term lease on a shop to start a business – again, I don't know what he wanted to do.

"Anyway, he stepped off the plane, felt a bit queasy, went straight to hospital and died! Just like that! Within twenty-four hours of leaving Nan he was stone dead!"

"Wow, it just goes to show, doesn't it?..."

Lek waited for Ayr to finish.

"Show what?"

"Eh?"

"Show what? 'It just goes to show what?"

"It just goes to show that you never can tell."

"Yes, I suppose it does, but the lesson is to make sure that debts are covered, because now Nan is left with the upkeep of a huge house and the lease on a shop and instalments on a car to pay every month with no money coming in. She also wanted to build up a college fund for her daughter, but that may not happen now at all.

"She is in a real mess. No Thai would buy the house in her village and it would be next to impossible to find a foreigner to rent it. She can't sell the car because she would lose too much and she has no use for the shop.

"Nan is at her wits' end. It's a total disaster. And, of course, her boyfriend died. She's trying to get them to send over a bone to remember him by, but they are Italian and don't speak English well. Nor does Nan anyway and she only knows about two phrases in Italian."

"Yes, I can see how bad that would be," said Ayr in a very distracted fashion as if she was deep in her own thoughts about something else.

Lek ploughed on, "If he had taken out life assurance to cover his commitments, Nan would not be up the creek without a paddle or if he had made a will or if they had gotten married... But as it is, all his money will go to his Italian family and Nan will be left to struggle alone...

"Are you listening to me at all, Ayr? Ayr?"

"Yes, I am listening, my dear Lek, but none of it affects me really, does it: no husband, no boyfriend, no foreigner, no daughter, car's paid for..., but maybe we ought to have some agreement between us. Something on paper, done officially and you ought to get Cr.. your old man to make sure that you won't be in the same situation if he dies suddenly."

"Well, we are married, so I am in a stronger position than Nan, but yes, we did ought to have something more concrete on paper."

"OK, wait..., er Craig, can I talk to you a moment, please? We want some advice. You know me and your wife have a business together... well, what do you think of insurance? You were in business before, neh?"

"Yes, but not in Thailand, I don't know anything about how it works over here."

"Ah, I see, we don' know too much too... but in the UK, you have insurance with your family? What if one family, say, brother in the family die... What happen?"

"We didn't have life assurance through the firm,' though all the professionals advised us to get it, but we thought that they were saying it just for the commission. Maybe it would be a good idea in some cases. Not every business set-up is the same – not every business has the same requirements, er, needs. Your business is not the same as ours – ours was run by one family, yours is run by two partners.

"However, you ought to think about what would happen if one of you dies suddenly. If Lek dies tonight, I suppose I get her half, unless she makes a will or other arrangements. If I am even allowed to inherit it by Thai law... We, or at least I, don't know anything about these things.

"In our case in Wales, if someone, a shareholder died, our arrangement was that the firm would have to be revalued and those shares bought back by the firm at market value. They could not pass outside the family. Maybe you could do something like that.

"If Lek died, you would have the first option to buy her shares from whomever she had left them to..."

"Will you please stop saying 'if Lek died'? It sends a shiver down my spine. I know that I will die one day, but it can't be soon, I have too much to do."

Craig had temporarily forgotten how superstitious Lek was – how superstitious all Thais were.

"Yes, sorry, telak. We could just say 'if Ayr died'..."

Ayr leaned over and slapped his hand, "Don't pick on me now. Anyway, if Lek, you know what, maybe I would like to have you as my partner, Craig..."

Now it was his turn to feel uncomfortable.

"So, what we are saying," continued Ayr, "Is that none of us know anything about the legal implications of matters that could directly affect our lives at any time. Is that right?"

They both nodded.

"Well, in that case, I suggest that we all get down to Phichai to see a solicitor before anything horrible happens to any of us. Is that all right with you, partner?" Lek nodded. "And with you, Craig?"

"Me? What do you want me there for? I won't understand a word of it."

"You will have to be there to sign your will, won't you?"

"What will?"

"You just said that you thought that it was a good idea to get things straight on paper in case someone died suddenly... That includes you in your relationship with Lek. You will need a will too, so we might as well do it all at the same time and save time and money.

"Good idea or not?"

They both nodded again and Ayr winked at Lek, who smiled her gratitude back as surreptitiously as she could. As for Craig, he didn't know that he had been had, but he would have agreed to go anyway as he realised that it was a necessary thing to do to secure the future for them both.

They agreed to leave it to Lek to make the arrangements, had one more beer and then went home as the sun started to go down.

Ayr went back to her flat, presumably to watch television, Craig went back to work on his web sites, but Lek, instead of pottering around the house before getting an early night, as she had taken to doing on rare occasions like these announced her intention to call on their neighbour, Nok, a woman who had become a close friend over the years.

Nok was in her fifties and divorced. Her only child, a daughter was now living in Bangkok. She had no social life, no visitors and only went out early every morning to sell the small cakes that she made each evening. It took her an hour to sell what it took her two hours to make but it raised enough for a frugal life. Lek liked to call in and talk with her whenever she had time.

Despite her circumstances, Nok was plumpish and jovial. Craig and Lek often heard her singing over the garden wall that separated their houses and sometimes she would call out to Lek, although no-one actually knew why she did it or whether she knew that Lek could hear her. Craig often heard her from his office even when he knew that Lek was in the shop.

They were not cries for help or he would have gone to investigate, rather they sounded as if Nok just wanted to use someone's name and Lek's was the only one she felt comfortable with. If she had used her daughter's, people might have thought she had gone doolally tap.

Craig suspected that she was a little mad from the loneliness anyway, but at least she did get out for a while every morning to push her handcart through the village until her delicious cakes were gone. Sometimes, they found a bag containing two or four cakes hanging from a branch of a tree that spanned their communal wall.

Lek said that Nok had said they were for each of them to eat with their coffee in the morning, since she had been able to smell the coffee that Craig had been brewing every day for years. Lek sometimes reciprocated with a small bar of chocolate or some fruit that was in season, unless they had been to Pattaya, when she would bring Nok back something unusual.

Craig remembered once when she had come to one of their parties and a friend had asked her whether Craig drank too much whiskey or fought with Thais. Nok had looked at her questioner and at Craig very carefully before answering, 'No, but he does drink beer'. Craig thought that she had taken far too long to reply, but their marriage had hit a few rough patches, so Nok must have heard that and Craig was given to understand that her ex-husband had been a hopeless drunk who liked beer when he had enough money for it.

Still, despite that, she always said 'hello' to Craig and sometimes sent him her home-made cakes, so she must have had some regard for him and Craig liked her too, even if she was a bit potty.

When Lek returned home two hours later, Craig was glad to see her. He had not got a lot of work done, but instead had put BBC Radio 4 on the Internet and listened to that while he thought about the tree falling and watched shadows move around in Nok's house. He presumed that the shadowy figures were his wife and Nok, but he hadn't tried to see or work out what they were doing. He never had been a particularly nosey person.

"Have you had a good night, telak?" asked Lek.

"So, so, not bad, not good and you?"

"Yes, it was fun. We drank some home-made rice wine – sahto in Thai. I think that I am a little bit drunk. It is a lot stronger that beer, you know..."

"Really, you don't say? Wine normally is." He hadn't meant it to come out like that, because he didn't begrudge Lek her pleasures and he regretted it instantly. "You had a good time then," he tried to add quickly to cover his mistake.

"Yes, telak and..., oh, I forget, I am drunk, Nok send you a small bottle of wine to try. She makes it herself. We made some tonight, but you cannot drink it for a month. You must wait a month. Or three weeks sometimes, Nok said. Wait one minute."

Lek returned with a small plastic milk carton of about 150ml volume. "Here, Nok send for you."

He took a sip. It was quite good after four or five pints of beer.

"Mmm, yum yum," he said, "Please thank Nok for me in the morning. Say that I enjoyed it very much."

"OK, telak, choop, choop, I mus' go get ab naam now and go to bed. I am very tired."

'I don't know about tired, drunk definitely', thought Craig, but he said nothing. He also thought that it would be better to drink his wine before going to bed too, because he was sure that it wouldn't taste any better the following day.

As Craig finished listening to a play on the radio, he could hear his wife singing in the shower, he drank his rice wine slowly and then finished off his beer before switching the router off and going to bed himself.

It was an early night all round and the first for a very long time.

# 17 THE BUSINESS TRIP

The following morning, Craig awoke to the sound of Lek being sick in the toilet. He hoped that it was not morning sickness, but he would have laid money on it being the result of a bad hangover.

"Are you all right in there, my darling?"

"No, I am dying. What did you give me to drink last night?"

"Me? I bought you a few beers as usual. This has nothing to do with me."

"Please, pass me my pho...," but she broke off to throw up again. "My phone. I must phone Ayr. Tell her I cannot work this morning, because I am sick."

"As sick as a lord, we say."

"Just give me my phone, I cannot learn English now."

"Here. I have noticed that your English gets worse when you're drunk. I noticed it last night again too."

"Why don't you get out of the bathroom and make your coffee, I must speak to Ayr."

"Your wish is my command, telak."

Craig put the coffee on, then went into his office and switched the router on again. Out of the window, he could see Nok's hand hanging a small plastic bag in the tree six yards away. It looked like a mail bag for a large scale 1930's railway set.

When Lek emerged from the bathroom, she definitely looked decidedly ill.

"You look awful, love," said Craig. "Can I get you anything? Coffee? Tea? Paracetamol? Sahto?"

"Oh, no more... I remember now... Nok's sahto. How on Earth can she get up in the mornings?"

"I imagine that she doesn't mix a few pints of it with a few pints of beer. She is probably much more used to it than you are and she probably drank less than you. That would be my guess.

"Or are you pregnant?"

"I would rather be pregnant for nine months than have this for another hour or two."

Craig pulled up a chair for her, fetched a coffee and paracetamol tablet and fed them to her.

"Thank you, my dear," she said. "I don't have to go in, but I want to do my job, you know."

Craig nodded sympathetically. "You'll be all right in an hour. Eat something – your rice soup – and take another tablet and you'll be fine."

Although Lek drank a fair bit, it was unusual for her to feel this bad, so Craig knew that she must have drunk quite a bit of rice wine. He had felt the small glass that he had had, but it was well-known that one should not mix the grape with the grain.

She finally left for work three hours later at eleven o'clock, more or less just in time for lunch after spending four hours asleep on Craig's office floor. As he got up to show her to the door, something gave way in his bowels and he had to rush to the toilet. He suspected that the sahto had finally burned a passage through his gut and was trying to get out, but it was not going to wait for anyone or anything.

When Craig walked around to the shop for lunch, since they had not come to him, he saw them already sitting in Nong's, although without drinks so he suspected that they had arrived only a few moments before him.

"How are you doing, ladies?" he said as he sat down. "Fit, Lek?". She fired him a dirty look.

"Hey, it's not my fault that you have a stinking hangover."

"Maybe not, but having to listen to your stupid jokes does not help, OK?"

"OK, just remember that the next time I have a hangover, all right? What is good for the goose is good for the gander..."

Ayr took over quickly. "I told Lek that we'd come here for lunch and have one for the road..."

"Where are you going?"

"Nowhere..."

"Oh, you mean 'a hair of the dog'! Yes, good idea. 'A hair of the dog that bit you', but I think beer would be better than more of Nok's wine. A small glass of that stuff last night just burned its way through me like the chemicals they use to unblock drains."

"Soda fai"

"I don't know what they are called over here, but if 'soda fai' – 'electric soda' or is it 'fire soda' – means caustic soda, then yes."

It was your idea then to come here then was it, Ayr?"

"Yes. It usually works for me. I had a lot of times like this in Pattaya, I can tell you, but it is not wise to have a hair of the dog too often or you may become an alcoholic. I saw that happen to a lot of the girls too. It is very bad for the skin and the eyes.

"After some months men do not like you any more and you lose your job and then it is very bad for the lady. Maybe take drugs, steal or must go home and hang your head in shame like a bad dog."

Lek's head was resting on her hands flat on the table, her eyes open, looking at him, but not maliciously now. She was wondering what he was making of what Ayr was telling him about their mutual past.

In fact, Craig wasn't thinking about their past, he rarely ever had done, he was just thinking about how beautiful and how vulnerable Lek looked like that. It would have made an heirloom of a photo.

They had three plates of different styles of food and one of rice which they shared, accompanied by one beer each and all went back to work. It was one of the shortest lunch breaks they had ever had.

Ayr and Lek went back to the shop. Lek looked a little better for the food, but she said that she still felt awful.

"Come back to the shop with me, Lek," Ayr had said putting her arm around her and winking at Craig, "and you can have a nice easy afternoon in the stockroom." Lek allowed herself to be led away by her oldest friend.

"See you at five-ish, Craig, I don't think Lek will want any overtime today, even if I could get her to stay awake." Ayr didn't mind though, they had been through a lot together over a long time and although she did not call Lek 'Big Sister' as often as she had used to do, she still had a lot of respect for her and loved her like a sister.

For his part, Craig wished that he had brought his laptop with him, because he knew that he could finish his novel in four or five hours, but since he had promised not to work on it at home, he could only write it in Nong's shop. If he had known this was going to happen he could have finished it that afternoon. He decided to go home and get his gear and return to the shop.

When he got back, he put his laptop down and arranged his notepads around it, took his red Biro, blue Biro and pencil out and fired up the computer. As he waited for it to show his desktop, Craig hoped that the ending to his story would not change again. Several times now, an ending had seemed so obvious only to have become improbable as he approached it. The ending to his book was proving as difficult to grab hold of as a poisonous snake.

He took the only sensible course of action he could think of and ploughed on. If the characters in the story, which were also in his head wanted the book to end as they wanted and not how he wanted then so be it, he thought. He had never had this problem writing any of the thousands of five-hundred-word articles that he had written, but then there were not any characters in them and although the characters in his novel were not real, it seemed that they didn't know it.

He found it amazing how they told him what they wanted to say and do, yet they were keeping the ending secret even from their biographer. Sometimes, he wondered whether writing this book had finally driven him around the twist.

While Lek was asleep in Ayr's flat, she received what she considered an exciting phone call. It was an all expenses paid trip to Bangkok by plane in order to attend a sales convention on fertilizer. Tickets were available for both partners including accommodation in the hotel, two sharing, but with an optional upgrade. It seemed that most businesses were run by man and wife teams. Ayr accepted for them both, thinking that she could always go alone if Lek couldn't make it.

At five o'clock, Ayr woke Lek up and they retired to Nong's to sit with Craig. Lek was feeling a lot better but not up to drinking or eating anything but paracetamol. As they made the sign visible that told customers that they were seated next door and locked the door, Ayr told Lek her news.

"Isn't it great? We must be doing something right. What do you reckon?"

"Yes, it's excellent news. Are you going? When is it?"

"Yes, of course I'm going and I booked you in too. It's on Saturday."

When they sat down, Craig was just turning his laptop off and handing the extension lead back to Nong.

"Have you been here all afternoon?" asked Lek.

"Yes, but not drinking loads as you might think, I wanted to finish my book and I have. Just over eighty thousand words. Finished. Today.

"How was your day? Lek?"

"Wonderful, thanks. I'm glad you finished that book though. Ayr has some good news too."

"Yes, we, Lek and I have been invited to a company do in Bangkok on Saturday. They pay for flights and hotel and everything. Isn't that great?"

"Yes, good for you. Are you going?"

"Sure I'm going, but I don't think that Lek has made up her mind yet."

"Lek?"

"I haven't thought about it yet. I only heard five minutes ago. We can talk later, Craig."

He was happy with that, not that he would try to stand in the way of her going on a free trip either."

"OK," said Ayr, "to success." and they clinked their bottles together despite the fact that Lek had said that she hadn't wanted one.

∞

When Saturday morning came, both women were ready by seven 'clock. The plan was for Ayr to drive them to Phitsanulok Airport for the ten forty-five flight to Don Muang airport in Bangkok, where they would take a taxi the short distance to the Bo Bae Tower Hotel. Craig couldn't see them off because Ayr wanted to leave the car there and he didn't like driving in Thailand anyway, despite the fact that the traffic flowed on the same side of the road as in the UK.

Ayr looked thoroughly excited to be going and Lek looked suitably sorry to be leaving Craig behind until he was out of sight and then she couldn't wait either. Craig thought about going to Nong's and getting drunk, but it seemed such a sad-bastard thing to do when his wife would only be gone for thirty hours.

He was still tempted though.

His plans for the period were to proofread his book and then proofread it again, although that would probably take him a week not a Saturday. Then he had to work out how to get it self-published and actually do it. He guessed that he was looking at ten to fourteen days.

Lek and Ayr were singing as they drove to the airport, which was about sixty kilometres away from their village. Neither of them had flown for several years and both were looking forward to their adventure together.

They arrived at eight thirty, locked the car up, checked in and went into the departure lounge with just their handbags. After a quick check up in the ladies they went to the bar in order to start as they meant to continue – in top gear. They both opted for caution though and took a vodka flooded with fresh orange juice.

They really looked the part of jet-setters as they sat in the window of the lounge awaiting their thirty-five-minute flight to Bangkok. There was no time to serve a drink on the plane even though it was only a small Thai Airways jet and they touched down in Bangkok at eleven twenty-five. They were in the hotel just before noon.

Lek wanted to phone Craig to tell him that she was all right, but she had to phone her mother instead, because he didn't have a phone. When he sounded happy enough, she promised to phone again later, although they both realised that that would be a hit or miss affair.

Craig went back to work and the ladies registered with their hosts and booked into their room. The person in charge of the guests from the company which had invited them, took the receipts for the flight tickets and the taxi that Ayr offered him, entered them in a book and promised to reimburse her later. They were given RFID name tags in exchange for a glimpse of their own ID cards and a sample signature each. These cards, the representative explained, would entitle them to free meals in the restaurant and free drinks at the bar until noon on Sunday.

He wished them sanuk, waaied them and let them go to their room where their luggage was already waiting.

"Wow! How about this then? Is this the life or isn't it?" whooped Ayr as she flopped down on the bed.

"It certainly is nice to be appreciated for all the hard work that we have put into selling all that stuff. We have done well, but you know what? I miss Craig already. I know that it sounds stupid, but I do."

Lek idly took the schedule off a bedside cabinet and read aloud:

"Lunch from twelve to one-thirty. Welcome drinks in the main hall at two pm. Sales lah-di-dah until five; then free time until seven when dinner and dancing starts.

"So, I'm going to have a shower first, unless you want to and then I guess that we had better go and eat. What do you say?"

"I say that that sounds a good plan to me and while you're in the shower, I'll check out the mini bar."

Lek unpacked her small bag, undressed and put a hotel towel on. Her shower cheered her up a little, but she couldn't help feeling guilty about being there while Craig was at home working on his own. When she went back into the room, Ayr was sitting on the bed in her towel and shower hat sipping something orange.

"There's yours over there."

"What is it?"

"Vodka and orange, darling, only the best today and tomorrow. Well, tomorrow before noon anyway." She giggled to herself and went into the shower where she could be heard singing.

Lek took a sip, but it was really strong and she wasn't in the mood. She had got dressed and was putting on her make-up when Ayr came back.

"That's better," she exclaimed. "I know we weren't travelling for long, but it always makes me feel grubby."

"Yes, I know what you mean," replied Lek and went out onto the balcony with her drink. "Great view from here. You can see right out over nearly all Bangkok." She wanted desperately to get into the right mood so as not to spoil her friend's weekend.

When they were both ready, they went down to the restaurant, which was giving a buffet lunch. The choice was quite extensive with two soups, eight Thai dishes, some European items, boiled and fried rice, bread, butter, cheese, biscuits and lots of different fruits. There was literally plenty of choice to suit every palate and Lek and Ayr ate their fill, as they normally did.

In fact, they refilled their plates twice, before going to the bar located outside the conference room to await the first function of the day. When they sat at their allotted table of six men and themselves, Lek whispered to Ayr:

"I didn't like to say anything in the restaurant, because it could have been a general service area, but there are a lot more men here than women, aren't there?"

"Yes, I was thinking that too. The guy who invited us said that the rooms were doubles because many businesses are man-wife teams, but I don't see many wives. Maybe they've skipped the boring bit and gone shopping?"

Lek and Ayr received lots of attention from the men at the table and plenty of glasses of wine, which was just as well because the speeches about the company's new fertilisers were not riveting.

Still they had accepted the company's shilling and so they felt honour-bound to sit through the boring speeches and PowerPoint presentations. In fact, it was only the wine that made it bearable, but since they had their own expense account they were not reliant on the six men at the table.

After two hours, they went to the ladies.

"Oh, my Buddha," said Lek in exasperation, "they certainly get their pound of flesh, eh? If I'm ever invited again, I'm going shopping too. Shall we disappear or go back in?"

"There's less than an hour left, so let's just have some more wine and then go and watch a bit of TV, shall we?"

"OK, after you," replied Lek taking a deep breath.

The room was applauding when they retook their seats. Something about increased sales. The men at their table looked at them and applauded them too, but the partners didn't know why. It seemed that they had missed something relevant.

When the meeting closed, they made excuses not to join the men from their table at the bar and returned to their room.

"Ayr, I'm going to have a nap. Can you ask room service to call us at six thirty in case we both fall asleep, please?" and she was out like a light as she had always been able to do.

∞

When they went down to dinner, they were both regretting not having brought something more formal to wear, because they passed many women in beautiful black, sparkly evening gowns. However, when they walked into their function room, people were more normally attired which would have put them at ease except that the ratio of men to women was about four to one.

The friends looked at each other and knew that the single women would be expected to keep the men without partners busy. The skills of men-management that they had learned in Pattaya would come in useful again.

They were shown to their table, at which were seated the same six men, still single, from a couple of hours before. They all stood up until the ladies had sat down. Ayr and Lek looked at each of them as they would have done in 'Daddy's Hobby', that is, in such a way as to make them all feel special, but without favour.

The men fawned over them and did what they could to anticipate their every desire, but it was like water off a duck's back to Ayr and Lek who could see right through them, although they knew that it was not the time to let them know that, while they remained polite.

So they smiled and laughed at their jokes and even told a few themselves, especially Ayr. In fact, it was just a charade for Lek, although Ayr was actually enjoying being the centre of attention of a group of men again... 'and why not?' thought Lek, 'she is single and can do what she likes'.

Everything went fine during the meal and for a little while afterwards too, but when the dishes had been cleared away and the jazz band began to play, the earnest drinking started too and with that confidence on the part of the single men, who wanted to try to make an early conquest before the few available women had 'been taken'.

Lek and Ayr were used to it and had no problem dealing with it, but whereas Lek fended them all off, Ayr played a few along. Sometimes, she needed an accomplice to keep busy the friend of the one she was interested in. Lek found it fascinating how her friend had changed from Bolshie cynic, man-hater to predator, since she had finished working the bar in Pattaya and made some wise investment decisions.

Lek, on the other hand, had only ever wanted one or two things, namely a man to love who would love her back and some sort of financial security. Both of these were within her grasp already and she was happy with what she had. She felt glad that she didn't need or want to roam from man to man to feel fulfilled, but then, she had never been like that. She wondered whether it was born into some people.

"Come on, Lek, I want you to meet Shy. Shy, this is my friend Lek, we are here together." Shy waaied and asked if he may sit down in Ayr's seat while she was dancing with his friend.

"Certainly," she replied in a calculated, distant tone. She watched Ayr dance and wished that she had not done this to her.

"Where are you from?" asked Shy.

"Pattaya," lied Lek.

"It is a very fine city, but I prefer Jomtien."

Lek studied Shy. He was about forty-five, handsome, light-skinned, suggesting an office worker, well-groomed, suggesting personal hygiene and wearing an expensive suit and shoes. His accent was cosmopolitan, upper middle-class Bangkok, He may or may not have originated there, but he almost certainly had been to university in Bangkok.

"Jomtien is lovely."

"Why are you here? Er, excuse me, I am glad that you are, but this does not seem to be the place for a woman from Pattaya."

Lek had to fight very hard to keep an old fear down.

"What makes you say that?"

"It is just that this firm makes fertiliser and there are no longer any farmers in Pattaya."

Lek's fears ebbed, "Does a crab have to live in the sea? Does a bird live on the wing? We have cars in Pattaya, we can visit the countryside as and when we please."

"Yes, of course, how stupid of me. Can we start again, please, Lek?"

"There is no need to start again, there is no problem."

"I just feel hat I have upset you in some way and I want to make amends."

'No,' thought Lek, 'you are used to getting your way with women but now you realise that your tack was not right with me and you want to try another approach.'

However, she said: "Shy, you seem like a really nice man. I think my friend likes your friend, but I am happily married. I am not looking for a shag, I am just going to get pissed tonight for free and then go and see my husband tomorrow and you can make of that what you want, because I don't care."

Shy was taken aback, but he laughed out loud. "I like you, Lek, and I would like to shake your husband's hand, because he is a lucky man and maybe some of it would rub off onto me."

He got up and left in search of another woman.

Lek called the waiter and asked for their first bottle of wine, because so far they been drinking donations.

"Red, please. Rioja, if you have it otherwise Chiang Mai, please."

The boy brought back a bottle of Thai red from Chiang Mai.

"Thank, you." She gave him twenty Baht. He bowed low and waaied high, both signs of high regard.

When Ayr returned from dancing, she asked what had happened to Shy.

"Don't ever try to palm me off with anybody ever again, Ayr. Do you understand me? Do you?"

"I wasn't, Big Sister, I only 'parked' him with you Why, did he upset you? If he did I'll go and flatten him right now."

"No, Ayr, it was nothing like that, it was just... Ah, look forget it, but please don't park anyone on me again tonight – I'm just not in the mood. In fact, it was quite funny! I think I shocked him a little, but then I tried to because he was a plonker. Guaranteed married. The sort of man you instinctively feel uncomfortable being in the same room with. Like a mosquito in the toilet.

"Anyway, how are you doing?"

"Oh, not sure yet. There's plenty of choice isn't there? I reckon that I've got the choice of ten or twenty and the night is young. Are you all right here, darling?"

"Yes, go on, Ayr, enjoy yourself. I'm all right."

Ayr led her worried partner back on to the dance floor.

Lek had said that she was all right, but she should have said that she was bored rigid, if she had wanted to tell the truth. She wasn't interested in a Saturday night fling with anyone let alone an ageing sales representative for fertiliser looking for a one-night stand while his wife was taking care of the kids at home.

It hadn't been an issue for her while she was working in Pattaya, because she, or someone very much like her, was doing a job and there were thousands of other girls doing the same and men were flying thousands of miles for some fun for a few weeks before going back to their boring lives.

This was different and she didn't like it one little bit. All right for Ayr, though, she was single and didn't get to have much fun out of sight of her friends, critics and family in the small-minded society of their village.

She thought about leaving early and going to bed, but then had to chuckle to herself when she thought that that was what most people in the room had on their minds.

Then she saw them in a different light. It was just like the firm's annual party. It was likely that a lot of the people there had known each other for years. Lek and Ayr did not because they were newbies. They had been invited because they were new and doing well and had beaten so many sales targets or because they were a few extra women to have at the male-dominated party. Or some sort of combination of reasons. It didn't matter really, she would not be joining in the fun and would never come again.

She looked over to her right at Ayr who seemed to be enjoying being the centre of attention of a group of men. Ayr waved when she saw Lek looking over. Lek nodded back quickly and then looked away before the men had followed the direction of Ayr's wave.

"Not your cup of tea, this sort of thing, is it?" said a voice from behind her left shoulder. She turned to look before answering. It was the elderly man who had been sitting next to her all evening. He was dressed in a black dinner jacket and red bow tie. They had said 'hello' a few hours previously, but had not had a conversation.

"You can say that again! No, it is not. Never has been really."

"Nor mine. At least, not for years... I used to enjoy it more ten years ago, I suppose, but I only attend now because it is expected of me. Do you mind if I ask you what you do for a living, Khun Lek?" he said reading her name from her table place marker.

"My business partner and I have a farming supplies outlet."

"Very nice. Do you enjoy your work, your partner and you?"

"Yes. In fact, I would rather be behind the counter there now that sitting here... No disrespect intended, of course."

"Don't worry, dear Lady, none taken, I assure you. These days, I would rather be sitting in my garden than anywhere. There were times when I would work fifteen to twenty hours a day building up the business and there were also nights when I enjoyed all this kind of thing too, but when all is said and done, it is only your loved ones that matter."

"Yes, I agree with you, Khun Dtum. Well said, but please don't think badly of my partner, she is single and has always enjoyed a good party."

"Have no fear, I wouldn't dream of it."

"And what do you do then, Khun Dtum?"

"Same line of business as yourself, but I started fifty years ago. That's all, just a little further down the road than you are at this moment, but stick with it and with your attitude, you will go far. Thailand is in for big changes. It will become very important in the agricultural sector. Internationally too. In Asia first, but later globally.

"The world will always need food and as scientists create faster-growing strains or rice and other crops, those with the right kind of land in the best places and those with the farming supply stores nearby to service them will make lots of money.

"You mark my words and come back and tell me if I'm not right in ten years time, if I am still about."

"Oh, I am sure that you are right. My partner has been telling me the same for the last six months."

"Then you have a very intelligent partner. Hang on to her, because most partners are crooks. They see the money start to come in and then don't want to share it any more. That is another fact of life that you should remember, if you decide to take up with anyone else on a different business venture.

"But listen to me! I apologise for lecturing you at a party, even a bad one, when you are so obviously doing so well already."

"I'm afraid, I'm getting tired, Khun Lek, so I will bid you good night. It has been lovely to meet you. You have brightened up an otherwise dull evening for me."

"Thank you. It has been lovely talking to you too, Khun Dtum and thank you for taking the time and trouble to give me your advice. I will be sure to heed it well."

Khun Dtum stood up, bowed slightly, but waaied high, turned and walked away, leaving Lek alone again in a room full of people.

Lek wanted to leave as well, but she felt that she couldn't go so soon after Khun Dtum had left in case people thought she was running after him. She was stuck for a while because the Ladies toilets were outside in the corridor too, so she looked at her watch, counted the minutes down and watched Ayr putting on a show.

Lek thought that twenty minutes ought to be enough, so after ten, she motioned her friend over.

"Look, Ayr, I think I'll go to bed, all right? You don't mind, do you?"

"No, not at all. I can see that you're only putting on a brave face – your old bar face. You might fool everyone else, but not me, just like I could never fool you. We've been together too long, haven't we?"

"Yes," replied Lek and she squeezed Ayr's hand, "we have and I could not have had a better friends than you and Goong. Anyway...., I take it that you're staying here as it's still only ten thirty-ish?"

"Yeah, might as well, eh? I don't get to go to many parties like this, so I've got to make the most of it. The guys are talking about moving on when this place closes. I may go with them or may not. I haven't had a night out in Bangkok for... oh, years, ages."

"OK, then, you go back to your friends and I'll go to bed. See you when I see you. Take care and don't forget to phone me with his hotel room number if you go back there..."

They both laughed at their old Mama San's number one rule if they found a boyfriend.

Lek went back to their room, had a shower, got into her towel, put the TV on and laid down on the bed. She looked at the time, eleven o'clock. Craig would still be working... Craig, oh shit, she had forgotten to phone him and her mother would have gone to bed two hours ago.

It didn't make her feel any happier, but she fell asleep.

Lek woke up at seven, showered and dressed to go down for breakfast. As she was finishing her hair there came a few light taps on the door. Lek opened it to see Ayr leaning against the door frame.

"Good morning. How are you?" Lek stepped aside and her friend entered the room.

"Oh, I'm fine, just dog-tired. I don't know where we went, but I think it was great fun. Taxi here, taxi there. You know, three flash Harry's and me. I have to get some sleep now though. You going down for breakfast?"

"Yes, don't forget that check out is at eleven."

"OK, wake me at ten-thirty then, please."

Ayr was asleep on the bed as Lek went out the door. As she passed reception, she asked for an alarm call in their room at ten-thirty and went for breakfast. She was not surprised to see that there were not many there and that most of those who were, were couples, presumably married couples. A few people nodded to Lek as she collected her food and went to sit at a small table alone.

After breakfast, she went to the hotel shop to look for something to give Craig. It was all over-priced, but she wanted to get something, especially after forgetting to call him. She made a mental note to do that at nine o'clock. She picked out a small, but very well-made penknife. She bought that and a newspaper and went to sit in the lounge window on the ninth floor with a fantastic view out over Bangkok to read the paper.

Lek was just killing time now, she only wanted to get home, so she kept her head in the paper until nine, when she rang her mother to pass her phone to Craig, then read again until ten fifteen when she went up to wake Ayr.

They checked out after a light lunch, thanked the company rep for inviting them and took a taxi to the airport.

They were back in Baan Suay by two o'clock. Ayr had enjoyed it, but Lek said that she would never do anything like that without Craig again. Craig welcomed them back with open arms.

Especially Lek.

He loved his penknife and told Lek not to worry about not having phoned him. He didn't ask any questions about the 'business meeting' but did enquire about the journey back.

Lek wished that he would ask so that she could say that nothing had happened that he would disapprove of. Otherwise she was unsure how to work it into conversation without it sounding out of place, but he never did ask.

# 18 CRAIG'S BOOK

By the time Lek got back from her business trip, Craig had managed to almost finish reading his book for the first time, because he had done nothing in the thirty hours that he was alone but read, except for six hours of sleep in the early hours of Sunday morning.

When they arrived back, Craig was sitting in Nong's reading his novel on his laptop.

"Hello, my dears, nice to have you back. Sit down or whatever you're going to do, I've nearly finished reading my book. Want some beers after all that travelling? Or have you got jet lag?"

"I'll have one with you," said Lek, "but I think that Ayr might have a touch of jet lag."

"I'll have one too. I'm all right, it's just that I get a headache from cabin pressure."

"Oh, right, well you two keep yourselves busy while I carry on, won't you?"

"What is your book called, Craig?" asked Ayr out of genuine interest.

"'The Vampire Families' Alliance' – it's a horror story set in a Welsh seaside town."

"Which one?" asked Lek, "Barry?"

"No, not Barry. I don't actually say where it is, but in my head, I imagine that it's in West Wales. Somewhere remote – somewhere nobody ever goes because it's a long way," he translated.

"Now, I'm sorry ladies, but we writers are very busy people, I'm sure you understand."

Lek did, but the joke went straight over Ayr's head.

"Is it all right if we stay here, if we keep very quiet?" she asked.

"You may talk, by all means, just not to me. I need to concentrate."

He flicked his head as he thought an artist might do and brushed the three hairs on the front of his head out of his eyes. Lek slapped his hand.

201

"He's only joking, Ayr, take no notice. He's probably lived on beer alone while we were away and it has made him a little crazy."

∞

It took Craig another five days to read the book the second time. He found it really heavy-going. Having written the book over the previous eight months, he knew the story inside out. He had also only just finished reading it, so re-reading so soon afterwards was excruciating. He hated having to do anything twice at the best of times anyway.

However, he just got on with it, breaking the monotony from time to time by learning more about the publishing industry, formatting, his work and organising a cover for it, which he had done on the Internet. He decided to self-publish it, because he had read that traditional publishers were under severe financial pressure and so weren't taking on unknown authors who hadn't won major prizes for writing.

And he hadn't even won a minor one.

He hadn't even published anything yet.

Craig decided to go with Amazon's CreateSpace first because it seemed quite straightforward, so he downloaded a template from their resources and shoehorned his document into it.

It looked pretty good and he was very proud of it, but as with his web sites he had no-one to show it off to. Everyone knew what a book looked like and his looked like a book, but they didn't see all the research that had gone into making that happen. Same with the web sites – they didn't just make themselves, he thought.

It was a thankless task and not even Lek had the time to listen to him blowing his own trumpet.

When that job was complete, it was a book or a virtual book which would be put on the virtual shelves in Amazon's on line book shop. He felt a great sense of pride and couldn't wait to show Lek.

Then he read about Amazon's Kindle and after a few hours learning and more editing, his book was available as an ebook and a print book.

He now had to await approval and then a further few days before it would show up on Amazon's web site.

He couldn't wait.

When approval and a listing came through a few days later, he rushed around to the shop to show the girls his book on Amazon.

They made all the right noises, but he could tell that they weren't very impressed..

He emailed the page reference to his family and to Murray, but Murray was the only one who made encouraging noises. He promised to buy the book immediately.

Craig hadn't thought of that so he ordered two copies for himself right away so that he would have the first two copies of his book ever made. It would take a month for them to arrive from America and again, he couldn't wait.

Craig now realised that if he didn't promote his book himself, very, very few people would ever even know that it even existed. He soon realised that he would have to split his time between his web sites and his book He had spent the last eight years honing his skills as an Internet marketer, so he started by building a web site for it as a showcase.

He wasn't surprised to find that the domain name had not been taken, but he also realised that that was more by accident than design and resolved to bear it in mind if ever he wrote a sequel.

When he had finished the web site, Lek was a little more appreciative of the work he had put into it and he felt a lot happier until she asked how many books he had sold.

"Five," he replied, not wanting to point out that that included the two he had bought himself.

"Five? In three days? After working for eight months? Are you selling everywhere in the world?"

"Yes."

"So you sell five books to seven billion people? How much money do you get?"

"$3 per book."

"So, you made $15 in eight months? Writing does not sound like a good business to me."

And he couldn't really argue with her, despite the fact that she had put the thought to write a book into his head in the first place.

Lek could be like that sometimes – a real ball-breaker without even trying, although she had said it without any malice.

Craig decided to split his activities into two distinct parts, since there had been a lot of truth in what Lek had said no matter how much it deflated his ego and hurt his pride. From now on, until he had five sales, he would spend until noon promoting his book and the rest of the day promoting his web sites. This would work out to roughly five hours on the book and ten or twelve on the web sites, if his time in Nong's was included, when he often wrote anyway.

His copies of the book arrived by the afternoon post about a month later. It was one of the most wonderful feelings he had ever had in his life to hold those books in his hands. He turned one over very carefully, studying first the front cover and then the back. He read his name on the front and on the spine and then opened it.

'"The Vampire Families' Alliance" by Craig Williams'.

He slowly flicked through the pages looking for errors and blank pages, but it was perfect. Absolutely perfect.

Craig had never had any children, but he thought that he could at last understand what it must be like for parents to hold their first child in their arms.

He practically ran to the supply shop, the first time he had moved quickly for years.

"Lek, Lek, look at this!" Ayr was tidying shelves, but he wanted Lek to be the first to see it. She came out of the shop's kitchen.

"What's all the fuss about? Is the house on fire?"

"No, but look at this." He offered her the book with both hands, which is the respectful way to give a gift in Thailand. The gesture was not lost on Lek – it triggered an automatic response. She took it in both hands, bowed her head slightly and lowered her eyes to the book.

She too studied first the front cover, but not being able to read English, she was unsure what Craig had just given her, until she turned the book over and saw the author's photo above the blurb.

"That is you," she said looking Craig in the eyes. "This is your book?"

"Yep!"

She studied it again in more detail and hugged it to her heart. Ayr had come over by then.

"What's going on?"

"It is my husband's book." Lek was still hugging it to her chest as if trying to read it's contents with her soul as she did with letters from Wales. She seemed reluctant to hand it over to Ayr, but did so.

"You did this, Craig? You wrote this and made this book?"

"I wrote it and had the cover made and the printers made the book, but yes, it is the book that I have been working on for the last nine months. And am still working on it, if you count promotion."

"Amazing," said Ayr softly, "I know a man who can write books. My friend, Craig."

This was a wonderful feeling for Craig and he had never known anything like it.

Ayr examined his photo on the back cover.

"It is not a good photo. You are more handsome than that. Who took this photo?" She looked at Lek.

"Yes, who took that photo, it is not good enough," agreed Lek.

"I don't remember who took it. I found it on my hard drive. You are on the original too, Lek. I think that it was taken in Laos last year. Anyway, I just cut you off and used that."

"That is not good enough to go on my husband's books. Where will you sell this book? Go on tell Ayr."

"It's on sale at Amazon all over the world."

"There! My husband's book is on sale all over the world with a photo of him looking like a tramp on it. Can you change the photo?"

"Yes, but not on that particular book and that is the first one ever made."

"It is OK for the first one, but we must take a professional photo of you looking like a writer as soon as possible."

Lek came through the counter and pecked him on the lips, Ayr kissed him on the cheek at the same time.

"Well done, my telak," said Lek, I must go show all my friends. Is that all right for one hour, Ayr?"

"Sure." She smiled at Craig as Lek rushed out the door holding the book to her breast again.

"Come on, Mr. Writer, I'll buy you a drink. I doubt if we'll get much custom on a Friday afternoon anyway. We have a new bell now, did Lek say? No? I can switch it on here, like this and when someone opens the door or steps on the mat, it rings a bell outside. Good, eh? We can make it ring inside and out, just inside or just outside. Now I won't be frightened of going to the toilet if I'm here alone."

Ayr activated the alarm, pushed the door open, took Craig's arm, as she did sometimes, and they walked to Nong's shop.

However, she didn't say anything to Nong about the book, that would not have been correct as it was not her news to tell, itching though she was to do it.

Lek arrived within the hour as promised, which was unusual for her, but the reason was that she wanted to tell Nong before Craig bungled telling her and spoiled the effect. She sat down and waited for the beers to arrive so that she had Nong's full attention.

"Nong, do you know what Craig has been doing here for the last few months?"

"Drinking beer and playing on the computer?"

"No, that is what everybody thinks, but we are now ready to reveal the truth about what he has been doing. You see, he needed to keep it secret, in case someone stole his idea."

Nong sat down, caught in Lek's web, Even Ayr wanted to know what was coming next. Only Craig was missing out.

"Well, a few months ago, sitting right here at this very table in your shop, he had the idea to write a book. He told me that he had a dark tale to tell of vampires, werewolves and witches that live in his country.

"Wales is an old and mysterious place, like Thailand and people still believe in these things as we do here. As you do don't you, Nong?"

She nodded, leaned in closer and looked at everyone in turn in a conspiratorial manner.

"At first, I told him to be careful about writing about such things, but he said that I should be brave because the story of witches and dark spirits had to be told. I could tell that his words were true, so I encouraged him to continue.

"Now, that mystical story has been revealed and is on sale to the whole world and here is the very first copy of it." Lek picked it up off her lap and put it in Nong's eager hands.

"Oh, my Buddha... What a scary picture on the cover. Craig wrote this while sitting here? Right here?"

"Yes, didn't you, telak?"

Craig heard his name and instinctively answered 'yes', but he didn't know what they were talking about.

Nong looked at him in awe and turned the book over. She studied the photo and then went back to the front "Craig Williams" she read slowly pointing to each letter as she did so. That surprised the friends because they had no idea that Nong could remember any English from school.

Nong handed the book back to Lek and got up repeating the words 'dee – good'. She soon returned with three beers and said "Nong buy beer."

Craig felt really good when he heard about why Nong had bought them a drink and he made sure that she knew it.

Lek spent the rest of the evening telling everyone who came to Nong's shop some variation of the story that she had told Nong. Some people were in a hurry so she had to give an edited version, but later on, after tea time had passed, some of the older women got to hear an embellished version as Lek honed her own skills at story-telling.

Everyone that heard the story looked at Craig as if it were the first time they had ever met him. Everybody waaied him, some of the younger ones wanted to shake his hand and some even wanted to buy him a drink.

Lek and Ayr moved on to whiskey after a few beers, so when their friends or customers came past, she would offer hem a shot to keep them there as she related her account of why Craig had had to write that book.

Lek also knew that she had told the biggest gossip in the village when she had told Nong who was giving her own version when people made it past Lek.

He had a fan club although none of its members were capable of reading a sentence of what he had written.

# 19 WOOLLEN WEDDING ANNIVERSARY

In the period between Lek and Ayr's business trip and Craig's book launch, some people had noticed that Lek and Craig's wedding anniversary was coming up. Lek was notoriously bad on dates, finding it fascinating that some people, like Craig and her mother, 'had space in their heads', as she put it, to remember dates.

Craig did indeed remember that they had gotten married seven years previously on the 20th November and so did Lek's mother, although she couldn't remember how long ago it was. Craig looked 'seven years of marriage' up on the Internet and besides reading about the 'Seven Year Itch', he learned that it was associated with wool.

A gift of something made of wool hardly seemed appropriate in a country as hot as Thailand, thought Craig, but then they probably didn't use the same symbols in Thailand anyway. He decided to ask Ayr for some help, since he still could not communicate with Lek's mother very well.

They had not celebrated their wedding anniversary the previous year because they had been on the point of splitting up and had had no money. Looking back on those awful days now, Craig realised how near they had come to being single again. He was exceedingly grateful that that had not happened, although Lek had never mentioned it again, as if it had never happened. She was very practical like that.

She could analyse a situation, decide on a solution and carry it out without looking back, only changing the solution if the original cause warranted it. Craig often wondered what they would both being doing now, if he had not sold his home in Wales, but it was almost certain that they would not be together.

Lek could even be living with someone else after a year. It was an uncomfortable thought, but a distinct possibility nevertheless. And where would he be? Mouldering in his flat alone in Wales wishing he had taken some sort of action to save their marriage? Or perhaps drunk in a bar somewhere every night moaning about how fickle women were? He had made the right decision to support Lek, Soom and his marriage by selling his home, he knew that., but it was up to Karma from here on in as he had no more resources behind him.

He wanted to give Lek a really good party to show how much he appreciated her, but he also knew that he couldn't do it alone or without Lek knowing what he was doing. Lek knew everything about his daily activities. Everything, even without trying, which she usually did. Her family and friends had gotten so used to telling her where Craig was and what he was doing in the beginning of their relationship, that they did it as a matter of habit now and Lek did not discourage them.

He had no privacy, but that didn't bother him either. He doubted whether anyone in a Thai village had any privacy anyway. There was not that much to talk about, so the carryings-on of a foreigner were more interesting than most topics.

Craig reasoned that if his intentions were good, then that would be enough to demonstrate his feelings to Lek, so he took a walk around to the shop to see what the ladies were up to.

"Good morning, Ladies, how are things today?"

"Oh, we have been quite busy this morning, but we have a lull now so we were going to have a coffee. Do you want one?" asked Lek.

"Sure."

"OK, go and sit outside, I will bring it to you."

He picked up a brochure on the way out. It was in Thai, but he found it impossible to sit and do nothing these days. He would try to decipher some of the words. He was getting quite good at it. However, he put it aside when Ayr came to join him a few minutes later.

"Ayr, do you know that it is our anniversary on the 20th?"

"I knew that it was soon, but no, I didn't know when exactly. The 20th of this month or next?"

"This month! Next week! I would like to do something, but cannot do it alone, can you help?"

"For sure, but we must tell Lek, because she will know anyway."

Just then Lek came backing out of the door carrying a tray with three mugs of coffee and some Thai cakes.

"Craig wants to give you a party for your wedding anniversary, Lek. Isn't that nice of him? But he doesn't know how to do it. He asked for my help to keep it a surprise, but I said that that would be impossible because you know when a beetle breaks wind in this village.

"You know more than even Nong about what's going on in this place. True or not?"

Lek sat down. "Are you trying to say that I am nosey?"

"Me? Yes."

"I am not nosey, I just like to keep abreast of events. I like to know what's going on. That's all and I am not a gossip like Nong."

"No, that bit is true at least. You are not a gossip, but you are extremely inquisitive. To the point of nosiness."

Lek pretended to be hurt. "Anyway, Craig," she said turning to her husband, "so you want to give me a party. You have never done that before. Why now?"

"Well, last year was pretty bad for us and we didn't celebrate, so I thought we might do so this year. Nothing big, just a few friends in the garden, that's all. Don't you want it?"

"Yes, OK, why not? It will mean a lot more work for me and Mum while you sit and watch, but OK, sure. The 20th, right?"

Craig nodded and looked at Ayr forlornly. She smiled back. When he had finished his coffee, Craig went back to work, leaving the ladies sitting there.

"Why did you have to say that to him, Lek? It sounded very bitchy."

"What? It's true, isn't it? He gets the idea and feels great about it, but hands all the work over to me, my mother and maybe you! Am I supposed to feel grateful that he has had the idea that I can organise my own party? Come on! If he could take it on and do the whole job that would be another thing, but not just saying 'why don't we have a party?'."

"I still think that you were a bit harsh with him. He came around looking for my help, I told you about it and you sent him away with a flea in his ear. It makes me feel bad too."

"Well, I am sorry about that, but Craig could do more too... He makes bullets but wants everyone else to fire them. I'll make it up to him later... Sometimes, I don't know what gets into me, you know? I feel that I spoke the truth, but there was no need to hurt his feelings, I suppose."

"Come on, let's get back to work. What is done is done."

In between serving customers, Lek and Ayr tidied the shelves, dusted and discussed the forthcoming party.

"It is actually a very good time to have a party – in late November. It is the start of the party season, so, you give yours first and get it out of the way and invite all the people that will give parties that you want to go to. That way they have to invite you back. Clever, eh?" said Ayr.

"Yes, that is why I married Craig seven years ago. I was thinking about how easy it would make the party seasons for the rest of my life."

"Yes, all right, but I wouldn't put anything past you. So, who are you going to invite?"

"I don't know, the only four I am certain of at the moment are Craig, you, mum and me, but look, I'll put this sheet of paper here on the counter and we can add names to it as we think of them. The shop is going to have to give some sort of party over the next six weeks... we could combine our anniversary do with the firm's party, couldn't we?"

"Yes, we could do... very romantic, but I don't think that that was what Craig had in mind, do you?"

"He'll be OK about it as long as he has his beer and someone to talk to, he won't care. Let's do that and I'll sound him out later in Nong's. We can have it here too and retire back to our place when our guests have gone home. How does that sound? Better?"

"Yes, better. Craig has to put up with a lot living with you, doesn't he?"

"I suppose he does, but I'm obviously worth it too, or not? At least he thinks so and that's all that matters, isn't it, at the end of the day?"

"I suppose it is, yeah..., sure."

When they met up in Nong's at the end of the afternoon, Lek explained her idea to Craig. "What do you think? Would that be all right with you? We have to have a shop party anyway and this way, we could start at, say, two o'clock. Most people will go home at six or seven and then we can go back to our place to carry on with whoever is left."

"OK by me," said Craig, "it's your party. I don't even like them, you know that, I was only thinking of you." He was still a bit miffed.

"Fine that's settled then." Lek pretended not to notice that he was still sulking a little. "That is a very good solution all round. We kill two birds with one stone and get invited to loads of parties between then and January."

"Whoopee!" said Craig and looked at Ayr, who felt sorry for him, but thought that Lek was onto a good idea. Craig did too really, but could not show it yet.

They had a week to organise things. Lek wanted the stand-up comedian rep that had entertained them last time to come back, so she phoned him. He said that he would be delighted to come and agreed, but he probably would have come anyway, being in the trade. Lek also ordered food in the form of a buffet for the shop and Lek's mother said that she would prepare a few dishes for their home party. She suggested that they cook more food ad hoc, since they didn't know how many would be going on to the house.

Craig soon lost his attitude and Ayr soon saw that Lek had been right. Everyone was running around organising the parties and Craig was just sitting behind his computer as usual. Everyone's workload had increased by twenty-five percent and his by zero, just as Lek had predicted.

Lek confided to Ayr that she was worried about Craig because he seemed totally incapable of doing anything for himself any more. "He just sits at his desk all day and half the night like a big brain. I'm afraid it might explode one day." Ayr had laughed, but Lek had not been joking.

Lek phoned Murray, Jeff and Steve's wives to invite them for the afternoon party, but only Murray and Mike said that they would definitely be able to make it. Ayr organised the stage, dancing girls and music.

When the day arrived, they were ready on time and eagerly awaiting guests from the village and roundabouts by one thirty. The party was due to start at two.

Murray and El were the first to arrive with their large cooler box full of ice and Chang. "How are y'all doing?" He leaned forward to shake Craig's hand, then waaied Lek and Ayr. "Everything all right, ladies?"

They all waaied El, whom, being older than them, they called Pee El. "How are you, Pee El?" asked Ayr, "So nice of you to come to our party. We don't see nearly enough of you."

"No, I am not the party type, or at least, I do enjoy a party, but I don't go to many. I'm more of a home bird. I like my house and my garden. You know..."

"Well, we're so glad that you came today," said Lek. "Craig, why don't you take Murray and Pee El to the table by the stage and then get them a drink?"

"Sure, this way. What would you like to drink, El?" She was younger than Craig.

"I'll be along in a moment. I haven't seen the shop before, so I'll just browse and chat with Ayr and your wife, if you don't mind. You go outside with Murray."

Craig was about to ask Murray what he wanted to drink, but Murray tapped his cooler, so they just went outside. When they had sat down, Murray opened two bottles from his box.

"How many times, Murray, have I told you that you are not expected to bring your own drink to any party that we invite you to? It makes me feel mean, but cheers anyway. It is nice to see you again. Are you keeping well?"

"Sure, my friend, sure. It's good to see you again too. Hey, your missus and Ayr have got a great set-up here, haven't they? First time I seen it. So what is this party in aid of then?"

"The girls wanted to give an end-of-year party and I wanted to have a wedding anniversary party. It has been seven years today."

"Seven years since that party in your garden? Seven years already? My, oh my! I would have guessed two or three. Doesn't time fly? And how long have you had this shop?"

"This is nothing to do with me. It's purely down to the ladies. I have nothing o do with it at all."

"You don't do the books on the computer?"

"No, Lek taught herself how to do that, or she went to school to learn how to do it on paper and then taught herself how to do it on computer."

"Well, isn't she the bright little thing? I always knew that she had the intelligenics. What does Ayr do?"

"It was all Ayr's idea. She has a great business mind. Who would ever have guessed what was inside that pretty head, eh?", he joked, but in vain.

"Ain't that a fact. She's done well for herself now. That's for sure. I hear people talking about this shop and Ayr and Lek all over the area. They got a good reputation."

"Thanks, Murray, I'll be sure to tell them that if you don't." They took a slug of ice-cold Chang beer and then Craig continued, "What was the full story with Ron and Soom, do you know? Nobody tells me anything."

"I don't know whether I know the whole story either. You know what the Thai women are like, they only tell you what they want you to know, but I heard that Ron was fooling about and so Soom planned to get rid of him."

"What kill him?"

"No, literally get rid of him. Make him go away. Make him leave the area or even the country."

"Ah, I see. Lek said that he had lost his visa and so had had to go home and I had wondered what was stopping him getting a new one."

"I think Soom stole all his money and then told the police that he was penniless, so they deported him for vagrancy. I think, but I don't know, so be careful what you say."

Guests were arriving every moment now, but they were all to do with the business, so Craig was not expected to socialise with them. When Mike arrived he called him and Su over, but Su wanted to stand with El and the others so that left the three men to talk alone.

"We were just talking about the swift departure of Ron, Mike. Do you have any details, Murray and I know sod all between us."

Murray handed him a beer and opened it for him.

"I only heard that he had AIDS, got arrested by the police for drink-driving and deported. Is that right?"

"I didn't know about the HIV/AIDS or the drinking and driving," said Craig, "Did you, Murray?"

"I may have heard about a car crash, but I don't really remember at this moment."

Mike continued, "He was shagging some piece in a village nearby, caught AIDS and cheated on Soom the length and breadth of the province. She got to hear of it and had him nobbled in revenge. Soom has disappeared. Maybe she died of AIDS or is in a clinic, I don't know."

"The poor girl," said Murray. "I hope she's not dead, I liked her." The other two nodded in agreement and fell to thinking about the Fate of their erstwhile friends.

From time to time, Craig felt obliged to get up and say 'hello' to other guests, so he had to leave Murray and Mike alone, but since not many people there spoke any English at all and they had all come to see Lek and Ayr anyway, he didn't have to stay away long.

Lek seemed to appreciate him trying, but she too knew that they had not come to talk to him. Lek and Ayr were feeling very proud of themselves being in the limelight, especially when they both went up on stage to welcome those that had taken the trouble to attend that afternoon.

It was the first time for Lek since their wedding, but she took to it like a duck to water. She told jokes and made people laugh. She inspired Ayr and they became like a comedy double act for the fifteen minutes they were up there, although they had planned to speak for no more than two or three minutes.

"I don't know what they are saying," said Murray, "but just look at the crowd. They got 'em all on their side and no mistake."

Mike, whose Thai was a lot better said, "I can't say that I understand everything that they are saying, but I can tell that it is funny and it sure is going down well."

Craig felt immensely proud of Lek.

And she was proud of him, because unbeknown to Craig, she had brought his book along in her bag and whenever conversation flagged, she would bring it out and tell people what a brilliant author her husband was. Craig didn't realise this for a few hours, but when he did, he borrowed the book to show Murray and Mike.

"Yes, I have ordered one, but it hasn't arrived yet. I'm really looking forward to it. Impressive cover, eh, Mike?"

"You wrote this, Craig?", he asked somewhat disbelievingly.

"Yes, don't sound so shocked."

"Well, I never! An author in our midst..."

"I have written one book, yes."

"I don't know anyone else who has written any and I am fifty-five and been in education all my life, so take it from me – writing even only one book is an achievement. Well done. Congratulations! I'll have to get a copy too. Where? Amazon?"

"Yes, Amazon, Kindle, all the normal outlets, iBookstore, Apple, Nook... All that lot."

Lek and Ayr had invited a hundred guests, most of whom came from the village and they had also been invited to the anniversary party back at the house later. The others consisted of ten suppliers' reps and their top thirty customers from elsewhere. The mixture worked well, because most people knew each other already and practically everyone either knew someone or had heard of someone else.

The comedian did his act after the girls had been dancing for thirty minutes and Lek and Ayr had given their welcome speech. He really brought the house down with his topical jokes about farming and local farmers he said that he knew. No-one believed him for one moment but they couldn't help laughing all the same.

He even told a joke about 'falang', but although the three caught the word and the glances in their direction, they didn't get the joke. Not even Mike. Lek later said that it hadn't been insulting, but she wouldn't translate it either.

The party-cum-publicity stunt was obviously doing the business a power of good. Everybody was laughing, drinking or eating and some were even dancing. However, at five o'clock as if the bell had rung in a school, most people thanked their hosts for the invitation and left. There were only about twenty left by five-thirty and half of those looked as if they could hardly stand.

Ayr told the DJ and his girls that they could go home too, so she paid them off and they started to dismantle the stage.

"Are you coming around our house for a few more. It is our wedding anniversary today?" However, Craig could see from their expressions that they were not really interested.

"OK," said Murray, we'll come for an hour, but it doesn't do to be driving around these country lanes in the dark. Too many drunken kids on motorcycles."

Mike nodded in agreement and Craig knew that they were right.

"OK, an hour it is. Thanks, guys. We might as well go over there now and get out of everybody's way. What do you think?" They nodded in agreement – it was his party after all.

Murray put his cooler in his pick-up and Craig said to Lek: "We are going around the house, OK? We'll wait for you there. Great party, darling!"

The three men walked around the corner to the house that was known locally either as 'Lek's House' or 'The Falang House'. Craig opened the garden gate and let his friends in, but no sooner had they sat down than they all realised their mistake – or at least Craig's. It was like being on a pub crawl, leaving a busy, happy pub and going into a dead-miserable one. Spirits plunged and they all wished that they were back at the shop although no-one dared say it.

They played with the dogs, Bpom and Bpouy, but it was no good. They had made a big mistake. It was thirty minutes before Su and El showed up and they wanted to go home.

"Come on then, I'll walk you back," offered Craig. When they got back to the shop, Ayr and Lek were just finishing off with the comedian and the DJ. "Oh, we were just on our way!" said Lek.

"Don't bother," said Craig. "It's boring round there. We would be better carrying on here or sitting in Nong's."

"Sorry, telak, but I could not stop everything and follow you."

"I know. Don't worry, it was me who was stupid. I know that", but in his head he was thinking that that would be the last time he tried to organise a party ever.

"Come, sit down. I'll get you a beer. Murray, Mike, you want one too?"

They looked at their wives. "OK, I'll have one more quick one but then we have to be hitting the road."

Lek fetched the beers, and sat down to chat. The women on one arc of the table and the men on the other, but the atmosphere was lost.

They were just going through the motions.

Craig decided to give Lek the presents that he had bought for her the next day. The cake would keep too. She had received enough presents and cake anyway to make his gifts look insignificant.

# 20 THE PARTY SEASON BEGINS

The previous evening had gone well, although people had gone home earlier than expected and those that had ventured back to look for the party at their home were redirected to the supply shop and to Nong's. Lek didn't even know that Craig had made an effort to get her a few presents and a cake until she looked in the fridge the following morning.

Unusually for after a party, none of the friends had a hangover either. When Lek got up at her usual time of six thirty, Craig sprang out of bed too to give her the things he had bought.

"We didn't have much time to talk yesterday, my darling," began Craig, "so I didn't tell you I had these for you."

Lek took the bag of gifts in two hands.

"I am very sorry, Craig, but I didn't get you anything. I didn't think it was that kind of a party. Ten, yes. Twenty, yes, but before that is not important here.

"Yes, I had sort of gathered that over the last seven years, but in the West, married people usually mark every anniversary somehow, so I thought we could do it too."

"But yesterday's party was not so much about us, it was more about the business. I feel bad now. Why you not tell me what you had in mind?"

"Don't worry about it, Lek. I only bought you something small."

Lek opened the bag and the first parcel.

"Gloves? These are gloves, aren't they?"

"Yes..."

"And... socks?"

"Yes."

"Thank you, my dear, but I don't understand. I never wear these things before. Do you want me to start wearing socks?"

"No. I know that you don't normally wear them, but we have been married for seven years and in the West that means that you must give something made from wool. It changes every year. I tried to find out what you do in Thailand, but Ayr didn't know."

Lek opened the final parcel. "Ah, gold earrings. I like these very much. Thank you my telak."

She put them on and kissed him. "I love you, telak," she said and kissed him again.

"I love you too, but look the gloves and socks are not a joke. You are always scared of getting 'black skin', so when you go outside on your motorcycle, you can wear these and cover your skin. Good idea or not?"

"Yes, very good, telak," but she sounded sceptical.

"Come on, Lek, let's make a coffee and eat some of our anniversary cake in the garden."

They put an arm around each other and went out into the early morning light. The dogs were used to seeing Lek up and about at that time, but Craig rarely went outside unless it was to leave the property. They seized the opportunity to say 'hello'.

Craig put the box containing the cake on the table, let go of Lek and sat down while she put the coffee on.

"I'm really sorry that I messed up your ideas for our anniversary party, telak but I just did not know that they meant so much to you."

"Don't worry about it really, Lek. The truth is that I don't care that much about parties and you should know that by now. OK, I did get a little upset when things didn't go right, but it didn't last long and is completely over now.

"I think it is better that your firm got some good publicity or goodwill out of the party. Honestly. I did what I would have done if it had been our party anyway. I sat and talked to Murray and Mike. That's good enough for me. I'm no good at organising parties anyway. I have never put one on in my whole life and so I am not going to start trying to learn now, not when I have an expert like you."

Lek sat down with the coffees and took the piece of cake that Craig had cut for her straight from the box.

"This is very nice. It is lovely. Who did you get to make it for you, Pong?"

"Yes, he was very helpful. There are a couple of pizzas in the fridge that he made for us too. Shall I get one?"

"No, it is all right, telak, I will eat this and then go to the shop. I don't want Ayr to be cleaning everything up on her own, but when you come over for lunch, you could bring a pizza and three slices of cake, say four slices, one for Nong and it will save us having to cook. OK?"

"Sure, see you at one."

Lek looked around quickly and then kissed Craig. "I can leave you to put these few things away, can't I? Otherwise the dogs or next-door's cats will be into them. Oh, and you could feed Bpom and Bpouy too. There's rice in the cooker and scraps in the fridge. Bye"

Craig waved her goodbye and watched her go out the gate. She blew him a kiss when she turned to pull the gate to. He had enjoyed breakfast with Lek even though it was a very short one and resolved to do it more often. Craig probably spent less than five hours a week in the garden, but looking around himself now, he couldn't understand why.

It was a beautiful garden full of fruit trees and bushes. The smells were fantastic and although it was a little overgrown in places because Lek didn't have as much time now as she had had, it did not detract substantially from the garden's overall appearance. It was just a beautiful garden that had been well-planned and well looked after.

He sat there and had more cake and coffee to savour what had been just outside his office window for so long, yet that he had not seen for what it was. A fragrant, and largely edible, labour of love.

Craig sat down to his daily routine, the first part of which was to check his email. He usually received more than five hundred every day, but his spam filters were pretty accurate now, so about four hundred of those never saw the light of day. The rest were filtered into various folders, so that he had an idea of which were the most important and which could wait.

After answering anything from close friends or family or anything to do with money, he would check his PayPal account for web site sales and his book publishing accounts with Amazon, CreateSpace, Kindle, Lulu and Smashwords. Only then, would he get on with any work that might advance his situation, but all that usually took only twenty to thirty minutes so it was not a large slice out of his fifteen-hour day.

This day had a very unusual surprise in store for him, he had sold a hundred and eleven copies of his book on Kindle as ebooks and eight print copies on

CreateSpace. One hundred and nineteen books over night while he had been sleeping! Craig was flabbergasted. He knew that some books sold ten thousand copies a month, but he had never imagined that one of his would reach a hundred plus in one day.

He couldn't concentrate on work, he had to tell someone and that someone could only be Lek, so he showered and took the dogs with him for a walk to the shop.

Taking the dogs for a walk in the village was always risky, because the other dogs considered the road outside their houses as theirs too and didn't like other dogs walking on it, but Bpom and Bpouy were pretty good at looking after themselves in a fair fight.

As it happened, they made it to the shop without causing a canine disturbance, so he left them to wait for him outside while he went in. Both the ladies were busy, so he had to wait. After ten minutes, he went out the front again and walked around the back of the shop followed by his dogs and put a bowl of water down for them. They flopped down in the shade gratefully after drinking their fill. Craig pulled up a chair too and waited for Lek to have time for him.

He was in no rush. He was savouring the sales and wondered whether it was a flash in the pan. A group of school friends perhaps in the mid-West or even in Birmingham back home. All it took was for one influential person to like his book and recommend it to the people who admired him or her and flash! A hundred sales and then those one hundred telling their friends and bang! A thousand sales and then those people suggesting it to their friends and wallop! Ten thousand sales!

Craig dreamed of a viral explosion of sales taking in millions of readers overnight, or over a week anyway. While he was fantasising about becoming a millionaire in a weekend, he was staring into the distance, towards the rice fields that surrounded Baan Suay kilometres deep. Hundreds of thousands of acres of rice and hundreds of thousands of readers. All buying his book and he didn't have a sequel to satisfy them with.

That would have to be the next task, but it could not take eight months like the first book. One, two or three at most... but what should he write it on? The same genre... had to be... he was becoming famous, in his imagination, for his magical, mysterious, vampire stories, so the sequel would have to be more of the same, as they did with films.

"The Vampire Families' Alliance" parts one, two and three and then Steven Spielberg could turn them into a film and he would have to go to Los Angeles to act as a consultant to the director. It would be terribly disruptive to his current lifestyle, but he would do it for the sake of his art.

"Ars Gratia Artis" he was thinking when he was awakened from his reverie by Lek standing opposite him.

"What are you smiling about and what are you doing here at this time of the day too? Is the Internet down again?"

"No, my sweetheart, nothing like that. Everything is wonderful. How are things with you? Are you happy in your work today? Are you having sanuk?"

"As much as always, yes, I, we always have a good day at work, but what brings you here this early and with the dogs too?"

"Sanuk, my dear, pure sanuk, but I didn't have anyone to have sanuk with except the boys here and I wanted to share it with you."

"I don't really follow you... Is everything all right? This is just... so, unlike you..."

"Yes, that is truer than you realise." He stood up, started to sing, took hold of Lek and started to dance with her.

"What has happened?"

"I sold one hundred and nineteen books last night while we were sleeping."

"What? At $3 each that's $357?"

"Yep, or 10,710 Baht in one night."

Lek cheered and Craig joined her. It was loud enough to bring Ayr out of the shop.

"What's going on? Party time again? Drunk already?"

Lek explained in Thai.

"That's fantastic! Congratulations, Craig!" Ayr leaned in and kissed him on the cheek.

"Thanks you, ladies! Thank you fans!

"I don't know whether that was a one off event or whether it is a trend. It might not happen again, but it was certainly great to have it happen once. OK, I won't keep you from your work, I had better go back and write another masterpiece, just in case. It's no good trying to hold back talent... Talent will out. It will find a way. Come on, boys, home time," and he left.

Lek kicked him in the backside as he turned to go.

"That is really god news for Craig, isn't it? It sort of gives you confidence to go on, something like that does. Success breeds success, as they say and it is true.

"Actually, we did quite well yesterday as well. We took over 20,000 Baht, so we made almost ten thousand too, minus a few expenses like DJ, the girls, food and drink, but still... pretty good and we have had our turn in the party season, so we can sit back and let the others invite us from now till the New Year.

"Talking of which, we received six real invitations yesterday and quite a few promises, so I reckon that you are going to have to be selective which ones you are going to attend. Me, I'm going to all the parties I can. I love this time of year."

"Yes, I won't want to go to more than one or two max a week and one will be enough for Craig... unless he's on a high this year I suppose, because of his book. To think that a couple of weeks ago, I was thinking that he had been a fool to invest so much time in writing a book, because it had only sold... I don't know, five or six copies."

"Each to his own, isn't it Lek? We will have to work every day to keep our money coming in, but that book could still be selling in a hundred years time. Soom's child may get to earn from that book and any others that Craig writes. Just think about it... Ten books all earning for ten or twenty years... It's not a bad prospect, is it?

"I would be encouraging him for all I'm worth, if I were you."

There was a silence. Lek had not thought of the books like that, but she could see the benefits now. Ayr had not only said those things to show Lek a possibility but also to help Craig get more support from his wife, whom Ayr thought could be a little harsh at times, especially where Craig was concerned.

"Come on, we can't stand around here gossiping all day," said Ayr, "Let's go inside and do it where it's cooler and have a cup of tea. We can finish off that cake too. We should have offered some to Craig, shouldn't we?"

"Don't worry about him and cake... He bought one for our anniversary party that never was. I discovered it in the fridge this morning. I felt quite sorry for him. He's going to bring some around later and a pizza."

"In that case, we might as well throw this stuff out, unless you want any of it."

"I'll have a small piece of cake with my tea, but I'll take the rest home, if you like and give it to the dogs. It saves putting it outside where it might attract rats."

They sat down after putting all the excess food into a bag and had a break. Ayr showed Lek the invitations they had received the day before.

"This one will be a good one. Do you remember Jon telling us what he has planned?"

Lek nodded with her mouth full of cake.

"You should not miss that one and this one should be good too... then there's the Phichai council offices party... we have lots of friends there, so you can't miss that. Craig will know a few people there too, so he will enjoy that, won't he?"

Lek nodded again, the cake being a bit too dry to swallow easily. She sipped her tea to help it go down.

"Yes, you're right on all counts... Sorry about that, but this cake has dried out a bit. Maybe we should have kept it in the fridge overnight, but I guess we were all too tired to think about it really. I know that I wasn't drunk but I was worn out. Stress, I suppose."

∞

There were good parties and better parties in this season of party seasons, but the most influential by far was the one given by the Phichai Borough Council to a select group of two hundred people within the council office grounds. You needed to know someone with influence in the council to receive an invitation to buy a ticket.

Lek, Ayr, and partners, had received their invitation from Nic, the mayor of Baan Suay who had been allocated a table of twelve that he could fill up with whomever he saw fit. Since both he and his wife had been very friendly with Ayr and Lek all their lives and since Ayr and Lek were the indisputable 'Entrepreneurs of the Year' in Baan Suay, it was no surprise that they were asked to attend. It was quite a big honour.

Such an honour in fact that the ladies found it necessary to buy new outfits and to make Craig wear long trousers and a long-sleeved shirt for the first time he could remember for years, since in Thai society, formal clothing should not expose bare arms or legs. Sandals are perfectly all right, but T-shirts or shorts are not.

This is why November and December were such popular party months. The excuse for the parties might be the coming end of the year or the immanent new one, but the real reason was that the cooler nights made wearing 'formal' clothes more bearable.

The other peak party season was in April, one of the hottest months of the year when formal dress would be unthinkable in temperatures of forty or forty-five degrees Celsius. The average temperature in the last two months of the year was twenty to twenty-five degrees.

This made garden parties much more popular with the ladies and the gentleman and the long clothing provided additional protection from the omnipresent and ubiquitous mosquitoes, which were also reduced in numbers by what the Thais called 'the cold weather'.

Lek and Ayr knew about three-quarters of the guests, but Craig knew only four: Lek Ayr, the mayor and his wife and luckily for him they were sitting at the same table.

The tickets were available to invited guests only, but they still had to be paid for. The cost of the tickets, however, was negligible in financial terms at two hundred Baht a head, which included two bottles of whisky and four bottles of beer. More alcohol was supplied when the original quantity had gone.

The real cost of the tickets, at least as far as Craig was concerned, was having to listen to an hour of speeches from local government officials. Still, he did his best to appear interested and tried to follow what was being said out of deference to his wife and friends.

The food was in the style called a 'Chinese Table', which was typical of such parties. However the quality was marvellous. There was no dish on the table that Lek recommended that he not try because it was either too hot for him or made from cheaper cuts of meat or offal. And if the meat as good, the fish was even better and the fried rice was just about as good as Lek's best.

In fact, Craig had not had a better Thai meal in his whole time in Thailand and Lek and Ayr agreed, that it was of the highest quality. However, it was the council's flagship do of the year and Phichai was the second biggest town or city in the province so it was to be expected in a way.

There were dancing girls as usual, a small band and a disc jockey for in between sets. Most people danced for the last few hours of the evening after the majority of the food had been consumed.

When the party finished at midnight, more than half of the people on the mayor's table were not in the mood to go back to Baan Suay, so Nic and Jan suggested that they go to a karaoke bar to dance until two am. It was all or none as they had gone to the party in three cars, so everyone went, but they were fit for nothing but sleep when they arrived home at three o'clock, so they all wended their ways to their own homes from the mayors home where they were dropped off.

Some people were not at all pleased to have to get past the packs of snarling dogs that guarded the streets after dark – the same dogs that were totally harmless during daylight.

∞

Lek and Craig soon tired of the seemingly endless round of parties, each one almost identical to the last. Craig stopped going anywhere that Lek did not insist he went to. Then Lek stopped going unless Ayr said that it would enhance their business. Ayr loved it and would have gone out every night if she had anywhere to go. As it was she was attending about four functions a week over a radius of twenty kilometres from Baan Suay which approximated to their reach business-wise.

Craig knew that the same would be going on in the West, but the excuse would be Christmas parties or firm's do's. He wondered whether that was why it had started in Thailand, but without the reason being Christmas, since ninety-five percent of Thais were Buddhist and didn't celebrate it.

Whatever the reason, it was obvious that most people thoroughly enjoyed the cool party season.

He knew that Lek's mother would give a New Year's Eve party for the family, so he thought that he might try to provide a surprise for them. No more cakes, they had never really gone down very well, since his cakes were drier that the average Thai cake stuffed and plastered with sugary synthetic cream. He wanted to make a few gallons of wine.

He had never seen a demijohn in Thailand, but they did sell water in very tough plastic containers of the same shape. They held twenty-two litres though, not the five and a half of the demijohn. Two of those would be enough for any party and although there would not have been enough time in the UK to accomplish the task, the hotter weather in Thailand made fermentation a cinch.

Craig had made wine in the UK many years before, so he had a rough idea of what to do and he found precise recipes for the exotic fruits available on line. Within one afternoon, he had about 45 litres of wine ready: twenty-two of pineapple and twenty-two of mango. His only qualm was having to use bread yeast instead of the real McCoy, but he reasoned that that would only be an issue for the first batch. The local bakery supplied him with the yeast he required free of charge. No-one had ever asked them for any before.

Every single one of Lek's friends and family went to have a sneak peak at the fermenting wine, because none of them had ever seen anything like it before either. It was all he could do to stop them trying it while it was still fermenting and more than once he thought that someone had had a go at it while he was out, but he could not be certain that it was not due to evaporation because of the superior degree of heat. The fermentation in the early afternoon was so intense that it resembled boiling, cloudy water.

The aroma travelled for a hundred yards sometimes, although not many people knew what the new, unknown smell was.

Lek was fascinated. She had drunk wine before many times, both before and since knowing Craig and she had drunk it in Wales, but she had never stopped to wonder how it was made. She had assumed that it was some complicated process involving expensive machinery and vast knowledge.

"That is it? Four hours work and you have 45 litres of wine making itself with nothing more to do until it stops bubbling?"

"Yes, that 's about right. We have a fly in the West called a vinegar fly or a fruit fly and if they get in there then you lose everything, so it is very important to keep checking the top. It is a seal that allows gas out, but nothing in. When the gas stops blowing out, air can get in, because this is not a perfect seal, so we must know when that happens and act quickly, but that's all."

"Then you wait for it to clear – all the white stuff, the yeast sinks to the bottom and then we can put the wine in clean bottles, throw the rubbish away and start again. It s quite simple really as long as you keep everything very clean."

Lek took it upon herself to look out for the cessation of bubbling, which Craig predicted would take place within seven to ten days at the current ambient temperatures.

# 21 A CHANGE IN FORTUNE

A few days later, Lek's mother ran into the shop, saying that there would be some important news on the TV at one o'clock, in five minutes time. Ayr fetched the portable from their rest area, plugged it in on a stand behind the counter and switched it on. They sat around waiting anxiously for the state news programme to begin.

"There has been widespread flooding up north," prompted Lek's mother, "and rumour has it that there is a lot of water heading our way. Khun Chan across the road had a phone call from her son-in-law this morning... She's a terrible gossip, but she might be right. It has been known once or twice before...". She grinned at her own witticism.

However, the news broadcaster confirmed Khun Chan's prediction. There had been unexpectedly higher than normal rainfall in the north from Chiang Mai to Lampang and in the north-east from Nan to Laos, which had been compounded by flooding in northern Burma and southern China.

Several dams were holding most of the excess water back, but would not be able to contain it all and if it continued to rain, all future water would have to be released into the rivers, which would probably cause flooding as far south as Phitsanulok and perhaps even four hundred and fifty kilometres further south in Bangkok.

It was unexpected news, but similar floods had happened before roughly every six or seven years. Ayr turned the TV off.

"Bad news, very bad news... We may have twenty-four hours, give or take five or six hours..." said Lek.

"What do people normally do around here when a flood comes, Khun Pang?" Ayr asked Lek's mother.

"Nothing really, Ayr. Baan Suay is on a small mound, so even very bad flooding has never entered the village. People lose a crop usually... Any animals that are tethered in the fields will drown. Nobody has ever died though. Sometimes the government gives a little compensation per rai, but it's not much two-fifty to five hundred Baht per rai, but the farmer loses five or six thousand profit per rai."

"You're a farmer, what do you think can be done to save the crops? I mean, if we could help someone save five thousand Baht per rai, he may pay us half for doing it."

"But the crop is worth ten to twelve thousand Baht per rai, I only meant that the profit would be five to six thousand after harvesting it."

"Yes, I know, Khun Pang, you were very clear and I understood you, but if I saved your crop, would you rather have three thousand Baht or two hundred and fifty Baht compensation?"

"Well, when you put it like that, my dear, I would take the three or three and a half thousand, naturally."

Ayr noticed the price hike and grinned at Lek's mother who soon smiled back.

"Well, that is what we must try to do then. Come up with a way of saving the crops or at least most of them and make ourselves some money at the same time."

"Any ideas?"

"Well, we did laugh when old Jer down the road took a boat into his fields during a flood about ten years ago and he and his son cut the rice underwater by hand and put it on the boat. When it was full, they pushed the boat to the road and transferred the rice to their tractor.

"We laughed at him at the time, but he reckoned that he saved about three-quarters of his crop."

"Well, we could do that, Khun Pang. I think you've found the way to make some money out of this impending disaster."

"Wait a minute, though, Ayr, they haven't said that it definitely will happen yet, have they?"

"No, but we know that it probably will, don't we? Anyway, I have an idea, based on Khun Pang's story about Jer, which will pay for itself quickly if the flood hits, but which will make money anyway if it doesn't, although it will take longer in that case.

"Khun Pang, could you pump your friend for more information about the coming flood and keep us informed?

"I wouldn't use our money without your consent, naturally, Lek, but I have a feeling about this one. So let me explain, but this has to be kept very secret – only the three of us may know or we'll lose the advantage and lose the chance to make some fast money and be heroines in the farmers' eyes for years to come."

When Ayr had finished laying out her plans to the  other two, Lek's mother's lower jaw was hanging open and Lek, who had come to expect brilliance from her friend, was beaming with pride.

"You're a bloody genius, Ayr! Oops, sorry, Mum."

"No, you're right... Ayr is a bloody genius. I couldn't have put it better myself..." Neither of the friends had ever heard her swear before.

"I would love to come in with you, but I don't have the money that you two business women have and I couldn't put any energy into the venture, so I'll just stay retired and wish you the best of luck. But I suggest you keep that TV running all day and all night, so that you've always got the latest information."

"You're right, Khun Pang. We need ideas and this one was yours really, wasn't it? We want you in with us, don't we, Lek? It will be a lot for two, and so whatever percentage you put in, you'll get the same percentage out. That's fair, isn't it?

"In fact, you have done all the work so far. Your idea and your inside information from your friend... the weather report and you have a great deal of local farming experience that we can use."

"You can have that free, darling... but OK, I would love to be in. What's next?"

"I'll need to make some enquiries out of the village and we'll probably need to make some snap decisions… I'll be in touch later on today. I'd better go now, so I'll take the company credit card, the ATM card, my passport as ID and... my driving license... Oh, and my Thai ID... I think that's all I'll need.

"I'll ring my Dad on the way, so if you will run the shop, Lek, and keep me informed about any changes in the weather that your mother may uncover, I can listen to the radio... er, I think that's it. I may be back tonight or otherwise tomorrow morning. Good luck, ladies!"

"Good luck, Ayr!," they shouted as they waved her off then Lek's mother went over to talk to her friend.

Lek was pretty sure that all the farmers would have heard the flood warning by then, so she was not expecting anybody to come in looking for chemicals that would be washed away when the flood hit and she was right. The only customer bought a fan belt for the PTO on his tractor in anticipation of having to use it to pump water more than normally pretty soon.

He hadn't thought through where he was going to pump the excess water to though, thought Lek, if the whole surrounding area was a metre under water and the river had burst its banks. However, she sold him the belt anyway and didn't ask the question that might have embarrassed him.

Lek thought about how she could help the local farmers and possibly promote their new scheme without giving the game away before all their pieces were in place. She opened up their web site in the HTML editor that she had been learning to use for the last six months or so. She was by no means proficient, but she could add wording to the site and copy and paste information into it.

So she started to write an article called 'Flood Warning'. Basically, she just wrote down in her own words what she was hearing on the TV and added some of her own advice that her mother had mentioned like, 'Do not tether animals near the river' and 'Beware drinking too much and sleeping in the fields for the next few days'. When she was happy with it, she created a new page on their web site, pasted the article into it and uploaded it to the web. Then she sent an email to all their subscribers to check their web site immediately for important flood information.

When Craig came over for his lunch, Lek told him that she didn't have time to stop that day, because there had been a severe weather warning. Craig had heard it on the World Service News broadcast over the Internet, but it hadn't occurred to him that it might affect the people of Baan Suay.

"That's not a problem, telak... Are you working on your web site? That's great! And to think that not so long ago, you wouldn't even look at a computer. What are you doing?"

"I'm writing an article about the flood warning for our website... telling farmers to beware and giving a bit of advice. Nothing much. I'm taking a leaf out of your book, I'm using any opportunity to get people to come to our web site."

"Good girl! That's the way. Is there anything I can help you with?"

"No, not really... I'll upload this in a minute and then I'm done..."

"You could think about making half-hourly news flashes. You know, you listen to the news every half hour, well, you've got it on constantly anyway, so every half hour you can write four or five lines and every hour email your list.

"Then stop emailing unless something really good or something really bad happens, because you don't want to annoy your list and the ones who go there will already know that you are updating your site twice an hour. Say that on your site too and leave the old news up with the date and the time and put underneath each entry the name and location of your shop and web site. Then if anyone copies the message to a friend, you have sent a free advert.

"You could also do a search for a free news ticker. They exist in English but I don't know about Thai. You just copy their code into your web site and the latest news streams in from the news agencies or the government whoever, but still do your own news bulletin too."

"OK, thank you, they are good ideas."

"All right, Lek. I'll be off now and make some sandwiches. Is there anything you want me to do?"

"No, I am not hungry yet."

"I didn't mean about food, I meant about the flood!"

"No, there is nothing you can do, but the water will not reach the village or at least not the inside of the village. At least, it never has so far. No, it is not the human population that is in danger, it is their livestock and rice crops.

"OK, see you later, darling."

Within ten minutes of sending the first batch of emails, Lek was receiving replies. The one or two at first soon turned into a flood itself, until it levelled off at about one every five minutes. She was being asked all sorts of questions by local children whose parents didn't have time to explain what was going on to them and even from people much further away who had done a local search to gain more information and found their web address at the top of the list for the area.

One man in America wanted to know whether his uncle was still alive, but the village was miles away and Lek didn't know the family. All she could do was reassure the man that the flood water had not hit their region or that village yet. It was satisfying that she seemed to have quelled the man's fears in the USA.

There were also enquiries about government aid, which Lek had no idea about, and possible rescue services for people trapped in isolated locations. She couldn't help there either, but it gave her the idea to track down all the first aid and rescue organisations she could find and list their contact details on their web site together with the phone numbers of local fire stations, police stations and hospitals.

She got on with that by Googling the required services. It was a simple thing to do and used up her time, but she also realised that if someone were in a panic and knew that all the numbers they needed were on their web site, they would be easier to find. She had all the phone numbers listed and had sent out an email to the list within the hour.

Lek was very pleased with the idea that that hour's worth of work could save lives over the coming days or even weeks, for no-one truly knew when a flood of this nature and magnitude would subside.

After having had just the one customer all afternoon, Lek started to pack up and close everything down bang on five o'clock. She determined to take the laptop to Nong's so that she could continue her site updates, knowing that Nong's, like every home in the region would have the TV on the news channel.

As she was locking the front door and about to pull the shutter down, a flat-bed lorry pulled up.

"Sorry, I'm a bit late missus. I got here as soon as I could. I wanted to get home early myself tonight, but I won't get home till well after six thirty now..."

"Yes, what a shame. How can I help you?"

The driver hopped out of the cab and started searching his pockets.

"It was a last minute order, so I stuffed the delivery ticket in my pocket. I knew I should have put it on my clipboard... ah, this is it. Is this 'North Farming Supplies'?"

"'Northern Farming Supplies', yes, the name is on the sign up there."

"I see. Is there a North Farming Supplies' in this village?"

"No, not yet."

"OK, I see and would you be a Khun Lek William'?"

"Yes, that is correct."

"Well, a lady, a Khun Ayr, told us to deliver these to you. OK, Da, unwrap 'em. Don't worry about payment. That has all been taken care of."

Lek watched as Da slid the first twelve foot punt out of the back of the wagon.

"Six 12' plastic punts with paddles, two each. Where do you want 'em?"

"In here, please," said Lek. "Wait a moment while I open up. I was just leaving." She opened the sliding doors and the men carried the light-weight boats into the shop. They stacked neatly down the centre aisle, leaving just enough room to pass by.

"If you will just sign the docket, missus, we'll be on our way. Taking the family on a trip are we?"

"Yes, something like that," replied Lek as he climbed back in the cab, waved and sped off.

Lek turned to gaze at the boats: five blue and one yellow and was again in awe of how fast Ayr could move. She locked up again and sat at the table in Nong's. Craig was only minutes behind her.

Nong brought two beers over and was positively itching to ask about the boats, but could see that Lek and Craig were talking and she was too polite to interrupt. She put the beers down and 'busied herself' a few feet away waiting for her chance.

"How has your day been, Craig?"

"OK, fair to middling. I've sold another sixty books today so far. How has your day been? Is the web site all right."

Craig had never thought he would be able to ask that question in Baan Suay, especially of his wife. Never in a million years. It just went to show, he thought, you never can tell.

"Yes, fine. In fact, I'm taking a leaf out of your book. I have my laptop here," and she lifted her bag onto the table, "and I am going to carry on working on it right here like you do."

Craig was flabbergasted but couldn't help smiling with pride.

Nong saw the gap in the conversation as Lek was getting ready to log on.

"Er, Lek was that boats I saw being delivered to your shop just now?" Craig didn't understand, but then he rarely did and didn't mind.

"Yes, Ayr ordered them, which reminds me, I ought to give her a ring."

"Boats, eh? For fishing?"

"Boats," replied Lek, "for going on the water and doing what you like in. Fishing, yes, if you want."

"Are you renting out fishing boats now then?"

"I am not at liberty to divulge our business intentions at the present, I'm sure you understand, but all will become clear soon. Say, have you heard about the flood waters?"

"Of course, I have! Everyone has."

"Could you put the TV nearer so we can see it and hear it. I want to know what's going on. Catch up with any developments."

Nong scuttled off, put a small table not ten feet away and moved the TV onto it.

"Is that all right? I'll sit with you if you don't mind and we'll watch it together. There's not much business tonight. Everyone is battening down the hatches and moving their animals to higher ground. You're lucky you haven't got any land, aren't you? Ayr has though, hasn't she?"

"I don't think that anyone who was brought up a farmer like I was would count herself lucky that she hasn't got any land and nor do I. I would love to have some land, even if it did get flooded once in a while. In fact, Craig and I have been thinking about buying a few rai, but it will be after the water has gone back down now."

"Yes, Ayr has land, but I don't know what stage the rice is at or what she is going to do about the water. How about you?"

"I've only got ten rai, but it's rented out, so it's not my problem."

"Excuse me a moment while I phone Ayr." She dialled the number, saw Nong watching her and so got up and moved out of earshot.

"Hello Ayr, where are you now? … OK, six punts arrived an hour or so ago, we've stored them in the shop. Will you be back tonight?"

"No, I haven't finished yet. I'm wandering around now looking for likely prospects, but now that it has gone six, I don't expect to have any problems. Did anyone see the boats?"

"Nong did, but the shop has been empty all afternoon. I've been putting flood information on our web site and emailing our client list. It might be worth you leaving a trail of business cards behind you and telling people that they can get the latest local information from our web site. I'm updating it every half hour."

"OK, fine, will do. Look, regarding storage of the boats... I saw how they do it in the shop. They put an eye-bolt in the path at the front and back of the boats and it the wall directly above them. Then they thread a heavy chain through the rope-holes at each end of the boat and padlock the chains. We will need to get that done... Can your brothers...?

"No, forget it. We haven't got the chains, bolts or locks and your brothers will have enough to do as it is. I'll bring the gear back with me in the morning and I'll ask Dad to drill the holes. He can do that. Drag him out of retirement for an hour, eh?

"Look, I'll get on. Leave the shop locked up in the morning till I get there if you like, if the boats are in the way, but you will have to be there as normal because there will be more boats coming – only four though. We have bought the lot for miles around." She laughed loudly at the other end of the line and then said, "I'd better go now, I want to get this sorted out as soon as possible and get to bed for an early start back tomorrow morning.

"See you at nine or ten-ish. Bye."

"Bye, Ayr, see you in the morning," replied Lek and she went back to the table where Nong was trying to explain to Craig about floods, but was wishing she hadn't started.

"That was Ayr, eh, Lek? Is she all right? Not coming in tonight, is she?"

"No, I'm pretty sure that she'll not be in tonight, Nong. She has a meeting somewhere out of the village, so will not get back until after you've closed for the night."

Lek was very good at not lying, but misleading people into forming the wrong conclusions all on their own.

"Two more beers, Nong, if you please?" Then to Craig after she had left: "I have never known anyone as nosey as that woman in all my life. She really annoys me sometimes."

Craig was slightly taken aback, since it was not often that Lek criticised anyone no matter what she thought of them and she had often told Craig to keep his negative opinions about other people to himself. It was interesting, he thought, but he didn't comment.

"Where is Ayr?" he asked instead.

"She has gone on a fact-finding mission. We need to know more about this flood that is hurtling down upon us. We need to know how big it is and how deep the water will be here..."

"Are you worried about human life now then?"

"No, not yet. The loss of human life is still unlikely, but you never know. There are some very stupid people about. Ayr will be back in the morning. We will know more then, but in the meantime, we need to gather as much information about the weather conditions up north and the effect they will have on the river levels around here as possible.

Oh, by the way, I put a list of the phone numbers of the local emergency services on our web site, and the bulletins, as you suggested. I haven't found a 'news ticker tape' in Thai yet, but I will look now again and update the newscast too. That should take another beer after this one, if Nong leaves me in peace, so you just get on with whatever you have to do for a while, will you, Craig? Sorry, if I can't talk to you much tonight."

"Don't worry about that, Lek. You cannot know how happy it makes me feel to see you working on a computer on the Internet and really working, using the Internet for its true purpose, not just for games. You make me very proud. If I can help, just sing out."

"Thank you, telak, but sing what?"

"Don't worry about what to sing. Make something up. I'm right here, I'll hear you anyway."

Lek lowered her gaze to the screen and Craig's mind drifted to the plot of his new book. He wished that he had brought his own laptop with him at that precise moment, but he was more than capable of just 'living in his head', as he called it, for a few hours. He retreated inside, but his eyes watched Lek.

Lek had one part of her mind on what she was doing and the other on the TV. The newscaster was saying that there was not likely to be a break in the rains in the north for at least forty-eight hours, which meant a vast volume of water was heading their way. The extraordinarily heavy rainfall on tens of thousands of square kilometres of land was heading straight for them.

When Lek had written and posted her report to their web site, she phoned her brother Long:

"Hi Long, what do you make of the flood?"

"It is coming all right, sis, make no mistake about that. I'm down by the river now inspecting my lowest fields. Ngat's here too. It is really weird. The river is rising as you look at it and the water is swirling and dark … with mud, we think, but the weather is fine. You don't normally get a flood when the weather is fine, do you? It's rally weird... no other word for it, but the water level has risen a foot in the last few hours. Three or four feet more and my lowest field will be too wet to work.

"Don't know how long it will take to get that high, but at this rate, my guess, our guess is nine or ten o'clock tomorrow morning. There is no hope for this field though because the rice is four weeks off harvesting anyway, so it is just lost, but the fields three or four or five hundred metres away are ready to cut. They could be saved, but my guess is that you won't be able to hire a harvester from tomorrow for any amount.

"It looks bad, we may easily lose the lot."

"Shit, that bad eh? Will you keep me informed of what's going on, please, Long? I'm putting the information on our web site to help keep people up to date."

"Sure, we're both going to sleep here tonight. Not that it will do any good, but watching it happen seems a better alternative somehow to just walking in on it tomorrow morning."

"Just take care, that's all. Losing the crops is bad enough, but losing my brothers would be too awful."

"Don't worry. We'll sit up talking till midnight and then take it in turns to sleep. We've also rigged up a flood alarm bell. It was Ngat's idea. It's really quite good. Six empty spa water bottles tied together on the end of a string that passes through a bent twig stuck in the ground at both ends. The bottles will float, right? Well, that will pull the string which will release a peg which will cause a weight to knock a plastic beaker of water over us. Ingenious, or not?"

"Yeah, brilliant, but still take care. Don't fall in the river if it's that fast. Goodnight, say hello to Ngat for me and don't forget to call me if anything happens. Any time of the day or night, OK?"

"Will do, sis, see you tomorrow."

"Goodnight," she whispered into the lifeless phone.

When Lek had finished what she was doing and the third beer, they decided to go home.

"I have never seen you doing computers before, Lek. Where did you learn that? From Craig?"

"I have been 'doing' computers for about a year, but there is such a lot to learn that you never stop learning. Yes, Craig taught me. He's such a good teacher, so patient. Goodnight, Nong."

"Goodnight both, see you tomorrow," she responded hopefully.

Once home, it was usual for Craig to work for a few hours while Lek watched TV in bed, but this night, for the first time ever, they worked on their computers side-by-side. Craig was doing routine maintenance on his web sites, because Lek had dragged the TV to where she could watch it and it put him off writing.

Not that he minded, it was a milestone day. Almost another meeting of their minds on a different level. Something that Craig would never have put any money on.

They showered and went to bed together at midnight, when Lek realised that her audience would then be fast asleep. She also wanted a very clear head for when Ayr returned in the morning.

# 22 THE SANUK EMPLOYMENT AGENCY

Lek slipped out of bed as quietly as she could at the first sign of dawn, at about five thirty. She was anxious about her brothers, but she didn't want to ring them in case they had gone home to bed already. She could see lights shining in other houses and hear the pom-pom-pom of women crushing spices in their giant pestles and mortars. She put one of Craig's shirts on over her nightie as she often did and went straight to her computer, something which she had never done before first thing in the morning.

The fact that she was behaving more like Craig was not lost on her. She fired it up and read her emails. There were only a few, but that was what she had expected, most people would have gone to bed before her and were only getting up now. The majority of the Internet-users were teenagers who went on line on their parents' behalf as far as the shop was concerned.

Lek had decided in bed, that she would copy and paste all the recent emails that she sent and received about the flood to the web site, so that people could read the history of the event. She remembered when Craig had asked her about the history of Baan Suay several years before and she had had to admit that no-one knew, because no-one had ever written anything down. This record, her record, would be the first known social history ever written about her village and she was very proud to be its curator.

She emailed the list that she was on line and said that she would be at her computer for most of the day, if anybody wanted to contact her, although she did not yet know whether Ayr had anything planned for them or not.

By the time she had spruced up the web page to copy the messages to and rewritten the introduction stating what the purpose of the page was, it was light outside and she could hear farmers in their tractors moving off to work, or more likely, to inspect the damage if any.

Her brother had been right. Normally, if there was a flood, you had an idea whether it was better or worse because of the amount of rainfall, but in this case the rain was falling hundreds of kilometres away and their only sources of information were the news and the river.

Craig was standing beside her.

"Addictive, isn't it?"

"Good morning. What is?"

"Don't give me all that 'Good morning. What is?'..."

"Yes, it is. I could never understand, not for nine years, how you could sit there hour after hour and not get bored or tired, yet I have been sitting here for almost two hours now and the time has just flown by.

"That reminds me, I can phone Long now."

With that her mobile rang.

"Hello? Long? Thank Heavens! How are you both? I wanted to phone as soon as I got up, but I thought you might be sleeping."

"Morning. We are fine. We've been awake for a couple of hours now too, but I wasn't sure about you. Anyway, the river burst its banks near our lowest field about thirty minutes ago and it's slowly creeping towards our walk-wall. It's spreading out far and wide now, so the rise is not so fast, but I reckon it could be over our wall in an hour or so.

"We were all worried about the water and drowning and all, but that is not a problem. Guess what is? Snakes! There's bloody hundreds of 'em. They must have been living on the river bank or between us and the bank and now they've been flooded out, they're heading for higher ground.

"It's not a huge problem, yet, but I reckon we ought to get out now. Wow, look at that one Ngat. Sorry, there's a big retic coming over the wall now. He's got to be fifteen metres long. A beautiful animal. I ain't scared of them, but you don't know what else is on its way. There will be cobras for sure, so we'll get up on the road now while we can still see where we're walking. We've been waiting for some decent light to see by.

"We'll be home soon, so don't worry. I see other people arriving now, so we may stop for a chat. Make that an hour. See you."

"Bye," she replied, but he hadn't waited for her.

"That was Long. He and Ngat slept in the na last night, but they're coming home now. The river has burst its banks and there are all sorts of snakes escaping the water. He said he can see them coming over those little mud walls we use to separate the fields. You know what I mean, don't you? They're only about a foot high."

"Yeah, yeah, I've seen millions of them. Don't know what they're called though. Not even in English. "So, the flood is here or at least the first wave is." Lek did not get the pun, but she would not have found it funny even if she had.

"Can you put the coffee on and take care of yourself this morning? I have to tell people what Ngat just told me." She sat down and started typing.

"Sure, I usually do in the mornings anyway," he mumbled and then louder, "Do you want a coffee?"

"Yes, OK, thank you," she replied without looking up.

By eight o'clock, Lek had packed her computer and was heading to the shop. She rang Long as she walked:

"Where are you now?"

"We are still here watching the water creep up the road. You know where Village Lane meets the river? By there. There are about fifty of us here and more arriving all the time. The river is creeping up the road inch by inch. It'll be over our wall any moment now. I think the walls will hold, but not if they are totally submerged for any length of time and that will mean a hell of a lot of work for everybody affected.

"Imagine it, thousands of four-hundred metre walls! Maybe hundreds of thousands of them. Just one thousand is nearly half a million metres of new wall. Dear me, five kilometres! I don't like to think about it."

"How are the snakes?"

"Oh, they are long gone, but God knows where to. The water will push them towards the village, but there is still a very long way to go."

"See you then, I'm at the shop now."

Lek put up the shutter and unlocked the door. She peeped inside and saw the six boats lying there, so she sat down at the table outside and phoned Ayr.

"Good morning! How are you today? Did you get a good night's sleep?"

"Good morning... No, not really, but I'm fine and we'll be all set to roll at nine o'clock. A bit later than I said... sorry about that, but it was a late night. That means that we won't be there much before twelve.

"How're things with the flood? I've had the TV on all night, but I didn't see much about it."

Lek related all that she knew.

"Well, it seems like we acted just in time, doesn't it partner? Listen, I phoned my Dad a few minutes ago and he said that he would come round with a drill and make some holes for us later on this morning, but I don't know exactly when. It's like pinning down jelly, but it's not so important either, is it?"

"No, not at all. I planned to sit here and wait for you anyway. I'll make your Dad a cup of tea when he gets here. We'll be fine."

"Yes, I'm sure you will. Well, I have to go down for breakfast now and then get our chains and things – and a tarpaulin, I nearly forgot that. We can't have our boats getting wet, can we?"

"Pardon?"

"Sorry, only joking. Strong sunlight is not good for plastic apparently and the tarpaulin also protects them from nosey thieves, not that we suffer from them in Baan Suay. Still, if it takes a tarp and chains to make us look professional, then a tarp and chains we shall have, I say."

"Yes, sure. I'm certain that I'll see what you mean when you get here. I can't wait. Drive carefully, Ayr, bye."

Lek shuffled past the pile of boats and plugged her laptop and the percolator in.

"First things first," she muttered to herself as Windows played its tune. "Now, where were we? Emails..."

She read a few emails, fetched a cup of coffee and then resumed, copying all relevant emails and her replies, where she had worthwhile help, to the web page as she went.

The American Thai was back looking for an update on the situation and a few kids sent emails to the effect that their fathers had gone down to the river and reported back that it had burst its banks in several places now.

Lek tried to tell Long's story about the snakes as a warning, but with a funny spin and she was quite proud of her journalism. She put the TV on, but it didn't give much information on the village either. Lek's mother rang to say that Khun Chan's source had said that it was still raining up north with no sign of cessation yet. He had added that the government was trying to hold as much water back as the Sirikrit Dam near Uttaradit could hold, but that it could never retain all the rainfall indefinitely.

Lek was beginning to see a bigger picture. How other factors might come into play in the unfolding saga of the flood.

Lek wanted to hang a map of the area on the wall and chart the flood areas, but she didn't have a map and didn't know how to get one from the Internet. She made a mental note to ask Craig how to do it.

Ayr's father arrived at eleven thirty and insisted that they carry one of the boats outside so that he knew he would be drilling in the right place. Lek offered to loan him a tape measure, but he said that he didn't 'like them' because they were too 'prone to errors'. They carried a boat outside and Lek was surprised how light it was – a strong man could easily carry one on his back for quite a long way.

They laid the boat down where Lek thought it should go, which was half-way down the wall that faced Nong's shop, right opposite the inside of her shop. It was as good as telling her to keep an eye on them.

Lek plugged his extension lead in, gave him a chair to stand on if he should need it and went back inside to put the kettle on for his cup of tea. When it was ready she took it out to him, since she could hear that he hadn't finished drilling. It seemed that Ayr had already described to him what the job entailed, so he was happy to get on with it alone.

"Here, you are Khun Paw. A nice cup of tea for when you are ready. If you want another, just let me know. Ayr should be here soon."

He smiled at Lek, but didn't stop to speak. She couldn't help thinking that he looked awfully frail.

No sooner had Lek sat down at her computer, than Ayr's pick-up drew up outside the shop with a scrunch of tyres on the dust and grit. Lek rushed out to greet her friend, but she stopped in her tracks when she had full sight of the vehicle. Ayr was grinning at her through the open driver's side window.

"What do you reckon?"

"Um, yes, very nice... but who are they?"

"They're our workforce. I said I was going to get some boats and some workers, well the boats arrived yesterday, or half of them did anyway, and here are the workers."

"I thought you were going to hire local labour."

"Yes, well, I thought about that, but local labour is scarce, isn't it and they will all want to help their families. These guys are ours, so we hire them out to whomever we want." Ayr jumped out of the truck.

"Come on guys, down you get, this is your new bosses' office. This is our village and this is your other boss, Khun Lek. Leave your stuff in the back for now and I'll take you to your quarters later.

"Anything you want them to do, Lek?"

"Mmm, your Dad is round the side there drilling holes, I suppose they could take these boats out of the shop..."

"Yes, good idea." Ayr repeated the instruction and they jumped to obey." I'd better take these things to Dad and say hello. Has he been here long?"

"No, thirty minutes or so. I just took him a cup of tea." She stood aside as a blue boat came out of the shop towards her and darted after her friend. "Er, where are they from?"

"Mae Sot. I was near there last night on my travels and one man I was talking to said that there was a bit of a drought in Mae Sot and that there was a lot of unemployment. Ironic, isn't it? We're flooded and they are parched. Not that Mae Sot is good farming land anyway – too much rock and it's higher up and colder than here.

"Nice city though and great nightlife. Me and the lads here were out nearly all night. Yes, Dad, that's just right. You're doing a grand job. Here are the eye-bolts, the chains and the tarpaulin. The bottom boat has to lie on wood, so that it doesn't scratch on the concrete path."

"Yes, all right, I'm not senile and I wasn't born yesterday neither."

"Yeah, sorry, Dad..."

"Nong, can we have a case of small Cokes, please, ice and a case of half-litre waters too."

She handed a thousand Baht note to one of the young men and he jogged over to collect the order from Nong.

"They're a great bunch of lads. They'll do anything for you."

Lek and Ayr went back into the shop, Ayr turned to shout over her shoulder, "Take a seat in the shade, lads and have a drink of something. We'll be out later. Have a rest, you're going to need it. Oh, and by the way, this is my father, your new landlord."

He turned around and looked at them like a cobra eyeing it's prey.

Once inside, Lek made Ayr a cup of coffee and they sat down.

"Go on then, tell me all about it."

"I set off to do what we agreed: buy ten or twelve boats and secure some experienced farm labour. I didn't know where to go for the boats, but Dad gave me an address just the other side of Phitsanulok, so I went there first. No problem, but they could only let me have these six. They said that they had a few more in another outlet in the direction of Mae Sot, so I went there and I bought another four, all they had in fact.

"I got talking with the boss and he told me about how dry it was and how there was no work in the area, so I asked him to deliver the boats, or punts, or whatever they are, today, and I drove on to Mae Sot, which was only about twenty kilometres further.

"That was when I spoke to you. I was thinking about labour and chains and things and wondering what to do next, but I didn't know the place well and I was feeling hungry, so I went into a cafe for a beer and some noodles. There I got talking to the boss again. He remarked on my accent, I told him what I was doing there and he made a few phone calls.

"Two of the guys outside are nephews of his and they organised the other eight. They're all farmers' sons with experience, but without work. The boss of the noodle bar, called his nephews in and told them that they could go with me, but that they had to behave etc, etc. He gave me his card and said that if I had any trouble with any of them at all, to call him.

"Also, if we want more like these, to call him. Between you and me, I just think that he just wants me to call him, but we were lucky, weren't we?"

"Yes, it certainly seems so. How much are you paying them?"

"We, darling, this is a joint venture, remember, but that is neither here nor there really. I offered them 200 Baht a day, six days a week and Sunday if they wanted it. They nearly bit my hand off. I could have got a hundred men.

"Anyway, the two brothers, the gangers, if you like, are called Da and Bot, I'll introduce you later, so if you want, you can just tell them what you want done and they will pass your instructions on. I phoned Dad last night and he said that they could sleep in the old rice barn. It's secure and dry, but we will have to dig a couple of toilets, or rather, they will have to, and Dad will charge them 20 Baht a night each.

"That is cheap enough and they are happy with that. Then they will need a campfire to cook on and socialise around, but they are here to work, earn money and send it home. This is not a holiday for them, they know it and are grateful. Like I said, if we need another ten, twenty or thirty, I only need to pick up the phone. Not even that – just tell one of the brothers."

"Two hundred a day is cheap, isn't it? I mean for experienced farm hands?"

"Ah! That is what we think, because labour is scarce here, the farmers are not poor and they pay three hundred, even three-fifty sometimes, but these guys usually work for one-seven-five to two hundred a day when they can get it!

"They are over the moon. Really, you can ask them. Come on, let's introduce you to the team." Ayr led Lek outside by the arm to where the young men, between the ages of seventeen or eighteen and about twenty-five, were sitting under Nong's tree, smoking cigarettes.

"Hello, gang, I'd like you to meet my partner, Lek. Khun Lek or Pee Lek to you. You take as much notice of her as you do of me, all right, because she is paying half your wages. Any nonsense and you go back home.

"Anyway, having said that, will you call out your names, one at a time, so that we know who you are?"

They introduced themselves to Lek and Ayr's father and waited to be told what to do. Instead, Lek asked whether they had any questions.

Bot put up his hand, "A few of the guys are wondering what we are going to be doing, where we will sleep and eat and things like that..."

"And when we get paid," added Da.

"OK, fair questions, although I did tell you all that stuff last night, those of you who can remember what we did last night." There was some embarrassed laughter. "Anyway, we can run through it again.

"We are due a flood in this village, in fact, it has already started, so you will be needed to cut rice by hand, but sometimes under or at least, in water, but I'm sure you can do that. I promise that it will not be dangerous.

"You will sleep in a big barn on my father's farm on the edge of the village over there, but it's only ten minutes walk from here. You will eat there in the morning and in the evening. Food that you prepare yourselves, but if you are good, maybe some of us will help you out sometimes.

"Lunch times, you will eat on the job with an hour's rest break. If you want snacks, cigarettes, tobacco or anything like that, there are several shops in the village, but Nong's here is about the best.

"As far as pay goes, we will sub you two hundred Baht each today and then you will be paid weekly, minus the cost of your accommodation, that is, Dad's barn.

"You won't be working today, but you will get paid for it. However, I will first take you to the barn to drop off your stuff, then we will go to look at the flood and the fields and then we will eat and the evening will be yours to do as you wish, but think on this carefully! This is our village, we live here and you are our guests, but if you make a nuisance of yourselves or embarrass me, Lek or my family or anyone, you will be up the road without a moment's hesitation.

"Da and Bot, I am relying on you to make sure this does not happen. And, my partner's idea not mine, anyone who stays the course, until we are out of this crisis, will get a bonus, 'though I cannot say how much that will be, because it depends on how hard you work.

"OK, pile aboard, let's go see your new home.

"Are you coming Lek?"

"Er, no, not this time, I'll look after the shop and meet Craig, but I'll go with you to the river later. Ring me when you leave and I'll be ready and waiting."

"Bye, see you soon."

When Craig came to take Lek for lunch, she had to decline again, but she asked him to show her how to get a local map. He downloaded Google Earth and started it up.

"Now all you do, is type the map references in here and the programme will take you there or, if you don't know them, type in the name of a city, like Phitsanulok, which he did, and then scroll north or north-east, zoom in like this and press print. It's that easy, when you know how."

Lek took the black and white print-out and started to colour the river with a blue pen.

"Look, Lek, I'm going to have a beer and a cake or some crisps in Nong's and then I'll go home, so I'll come back at about five and see what you're up to. OK?"

"Sure, sorry, telak, but it is a very difficult time for us now. I tell you everything later on."

"OK, my dear, I don't mind, really."

Lek raised her face to be kissed and Craig obliged willingly.

Ayr's call came about twenty minutes later, so she locked up, checked on the boats and went to sit with Craig until the car arrived.

"We are going down to look at the flood, do you want to come?"

"No, thanks, I'll have one more and get off home, I want to write a few articles, but I'll be here later, like I said."

"OK," when Ayr pulled up outside the shop, she waved and Lek drove up to her. She hopped in, with the team in the back and they drove off, leaving Craig to wonder who all the young men were. He supposed that they must be family of Ayr's.

Ayr drove them around the village, stopping sometimes to shout something to the boys in the back if she thought it would help them orientate themselves and then she drove out of the village down River Lane. The boys in the back knew no different, they were amazed at how the rice fields stretched for kilometres into the distance, swaying waves of green, but Lek and Ayr had never seen a tenth as many people on the road as there were that day.

When they got to the far end, they stopped a hundred metres short and walked the rest of the way. At least the last six hundred metres of the road was under water and small children were playing in it. The sense of doom and loss that they had been expecting was completely absent. Nobody had seen anything quite like it before even during other floods, because they had occurred during monsoon periods.

The boys caused quite a stir among the villagers, because they were total strangers, but no-one asked Lek or Ayr who their new friends were. Lek decided to cause a stir of publicity, so she called the team over and pointed at Long's field which was now almost completely submerged.

"OK, lads! Listen up! Tomorrow, your first job will be to take the boats into that field and harvest the rice before it rots."

She saw that some farmers were also taking notice, but not enough, so she repeated it in a far louder voice than she needed too, pausing for dramatic effect and looking villagers in the eyes, as she explained how they would achieve the task and what they would do with the rice.

"And when you have finished that field, we will have more for you. Ayr has fields that are in danger and so do many of these good folk standing around you now, don't you my friends?"

There was a murmur of agreement, so she continued.

"We know the government's record in helping farmers, don't we? We can lose months of hard work through no fault of our own, so our firm, Northern Farming Supplies, which you all know and many of you use already, will be able to supply experienced labour, these fine, strapping young men, sons of farmers all, to help you get your crops in.

"If you want any further details, call into the shop, you all know where it is, in the heart of Baan Suay, and pick up a leaflet. Or look on our web site and get in touch. Send us an email, why not join our newsletter? And I will personally keep you informed of all the news I hear from farmers like yourselves in our shop everyday.

"You cannot rely on the TV news. We all know that. They try to paint a big picture, but they don't know what is going on right here on the spot like we do. And let us be fair, how can they? I am not here to criticise the government or the news services, just to offer an alternative.

"OK, my friends, we have to go now and prepare for our first big salvage operation tomorrow."

Some people clapped, a few even cheered and others bade them farewell. They all made their way through the small crowd feeling like heroic gladiators leaving an arena.

"That should give them something to think about," said Lek as they drove away. "Now I had better get back to the shop and produce those leaflets double quick."

They high-fived and laughed.

"That was pretty good for off the cuff," said Ayr. "You watch them come in later on. We had better get some sort of rota worked out so that we don't double book the boys or the boats."

On the way back to the shop, they discussed what they would call the new agency, but they both found that one name said it best of all.

Lek got right to work on the computer, first making an A4 poster for the window of the shop. It said simply:

"Need More Labour or a Boat in a Hurry?"

Call us now on!

0665-805079667

or email us on

lek@behind-the-smile.org

See our Facebook:

http://facebook.com/LekInPattaya

or visit our website

http://northernfarmingsupplies.co.th

"THE SANUK EMPLOYMENT AGENCY"

She stuck that to the window with blue tack, and then reduced the size to B5 and printed fifty sheets, two to a sheet, which she cut in half and finally, she copied and pasted the whole thing to their web site.

She had a whole advertising system ready for the off within thirty minutes and she was feeling very proud of herself.

Next she went to Nong's and bought twelve exercise books, then reduced the size of the advert again to four per sheet, printed four of them off and cut them up. She stuck one to the front of each notebook and marked them 00001 to 00012. These would be the company's personnel records, but she also wanted to set up a spreadsheet for the company too.

When Ayr returned with the boys an hour later, she handed them each a book, numbered 00003 to 00012 and told them to write their names on the first line, date of birth on the second, ID card number on the third, followed by their address. Lek and Ayr did the same. Then Ayr gave them two Baht each and Lek made them sign for it in their books.

"OK, boys, you are free to go, but don't get into trouble and don't get too drunk. I'll see you in the morning at The Barn at seven thirty, so be ready to leave by then or you walk to work and lose money.

"If you want to hang around outside here, that's OK as well. Enjoy yourselves."

# 23 OPERATION 'SALVAGE'

Lek was straight on the computer again the following day. She posted the relevant emails to the web site, answered those that required it and left those which concerned their new agency until she could talk with Ayr at eight o'clock.

Ayr, for her part, drove to her Dad's for breakfast, left her car there and used his old Thailand tractor to take the boys to the shop. Everybody was quite excited, it was like a school outing on a charabanc.

Ayr stopped outside the shop and turned the engine off.

"Wait here, lads, or sit in the shade under that tree, if you like, I won't be long."

She went inside. "Good morning, how's business? How's the flood?"

"Well, the flood has risen another two feet in Long's first field and has travelled another 600 yards inland, but there is no business, as such... JUST 15 EMAIL ENQUIRIES!!!"

They bounced up and down for a while like cheerleaders.

"OK, that's good enough for the first day. Now then, what do we do about it? Long's first field is by far the worst affected, but his rice is only fit for fodder... It would've been more impressive if it had been ripe for harvesting... Still, we could put half the team with two boats down there, just to show what we can do. Maybe Long will give us half of what he sells it for, but I'm not worried about that too much.

"It's a great place for people to watch us or them at work. And then, I have a field that is ready for harvesting. It's not wet yet, but probably will be tomorrow. I will pay the going rate to have that one saved.

"If we get a client before the end or the morning, we can pull the guys off Long's field and put them straight to work on the new job.

"What do you think about charges?"

"We usually work on double and this is a crisis, so four hundred Baht per day per man. Say, a thousand Baht a day for two men and a boat, otherwise a

257

boat is three fifty a day to rent on its own, but priority for boats must be with our own team."

"That sounds good to me. Write it down. Oh, and give me that stack of flyers, I'll hand them out."

Ayr went outside, "OK, lads, load up two boats and four paddles and let's get started. Before we go, Da, check in that case over there at the front of the flat-bed. What's in it?"

"A load of machetes..."

"That's it then, we're off."

She dropped half the men off at her field with Da because they passed it first. They took a machete or a hand scythe and a clean twenty-litre paint bucket each. They didn't really need any instruction as they had all been doing that type of work since they were twelve or so.

Ayr drove on slowly through the crowd, people had come to call this walk 'going to the beach', and dropped the others off a few hundred yards from Long's field which was by then invisible, although they knew that it was the last rai on the right. Bot and his team put everything in the boats and paddled off under the gaze of the onlookers.

Ayr handed out leaflets and then drove back to the first field, where she had to leave the Thailand for the rice. She talked with people, felt that they were interested in their salvage operation and then cadged a lift back to the shop with friends a little while later.

"Well, Lek, the boys are working and earning money, so that's the first hurdle jumped, although there never was any real doubt that we would be able to find work for them, was there?

"While I think of it, you should tell Long that his team has already started harvesting, so they will need a 'Thailand' to put the rice in or it'll be double handling."

"OK, I'll do that now."

"Long? The boys are already cutting and need transport for the rice. You're already there? Right..., OK. Bye.

"He's already on to it. He says that they are doing a good job, but are making it look more like fun than work. Apparently the water is four feet deep. They paddle out to where they have to be, dive in, tie the boat off on a swathe of rice stalks, cut the rice until the boat is full and then paddle it back to Long. Easy."

"Yes, that's the ticket..."

"He also said that they are catching quite a few frogs underwater and the crowds 'on The Beach' are buying them for a hundred Baht each."

"Enterprising, aren't they? When we have teams of two per boat per field, they will be able to triple their wages...., so we will have to make sure that they are working for us most of their time... Still, it is a good incentive for them to stay with us.

"How about the flood and what are the enquiries like?"

"The rain may be easing off. It is intermittent, but it hasn't stopped for more than twelve hours for a week yet. They are trying to contain all the rain they can behind the Sirikri Dam, but that doesn't help rain that falls directly north of us and the dam is nearly full anyway, so they may have to let some water go in a few days, which will obviously affect us.

"Then it seems that the Phitsanulok Dam is under pressure from all areas, including Bangkok, of course, not to let more water through than they are already doing, which our farmers say, is not enough. There is a lot of conflict there and you can even hear them talking about it in the village..."

"Yes, I have. I think they have a good point too."

"Then, we have a request for two boys and a boat for this afternoon and three for two boys and a boat starting tomorrow and… well, enquiries are coming in all the time..."

"Do you think we need more men, Lek? We have our ten boats now and I don't think it's worth looking for more. I reckon they've all gone by now and been back ordered until after the New Year."

"I think that we can wait two or three days to see how things pan out. We don't want to call in more labour and then be stuck with them, although it doesn't look like that would happen. Why not phone your admirer and tell him you may need ten more in three days, then he can start asking around?"

"Yeah, good idea, 'though I don't think there will be any problems with labour, not if they are earning good wages on a regular basis.

"It's the farmers I was worried about. They are a mean bunch and our rates may just be a tad high. The way I work it out, a farmer will just about make a profit using our labour because they have to thresh the stalks too, which a harvester normally does automatically. Has anyone said anything about that?"

"No, but, on the other hand, if they are going to make some money by using us, they are still better off for two reasons," said Lek. "Firstly, the flood will not last more than a month and perhaps less, so the flooded rice will not rot away completely, which means that when the water subsides, they will still have to have the old rice cut away before they can plant new, because the Rotavators we use around here are not heavy enough to turn a field of rice into the ground.

"And secondly, this is called 'The Rice Basket of Thailand', isn't it? Because we are the only area that can produce three crops a year. Therefore, if we take a big hit, the..."

"Price of rice has to rise!" they said together.

"So," continued Lek, "if the prices rises sharply soon, as we agree it must, then the farmers will have an incentive to use us to bring the stuff in."

"Brilliant, Lek! I think you're right. In fact, I'm sure you're right. OK, that has to be our counterargument, if anyone starts chopsing about costs, although no-one has yet, that has to be in their minds and someone will sooner or later.

"Good. I like to be prepared. What do you want to do today?"

"I was going to sit here, keep the web site going with live info; answer emails; sell coils of rope and fan belts, because we're not selling much else, and take orders for the guys. Why, is there anything you want me to do?"

"No, there is no more for you to do. Maybe you could print me out some more flyers to put in the car. No, this is the best place for you today, but there is nothing at all for me to do here, so I thought that I'd go down to The Beach and try to drum up some trade.

"As you said, we are only selling rope and fan belts, but is there anything else we could sell... specific to the current conditions?"

"Cheap fishing gear: rods, nets, line, hooks, that sort of thing maybe..."

"Yes, that's what I was thinking too. I'll pick up a handful of things while I'm out and we'll see how it goes."

Lek handed over the B5 flyers and set the computer to print out another fifty double adverts.

"OK, Lek, see you for lunch at one?"

"Sure thing! I'll either be here or there. You can double as our 'roving reporter' and send me 'on-the-spot bulletins' about the state of the flood for the web site."

"Yes, OK, will do. See you."

"Bye for now".

Ayr had kept her word and phoned a few updates through to Lek to be used on the web site, but when they met for lunch, she had even more, although less pertinent news.

"Lek and Craig, you really have to come down to The Beach and see what's going on down there. Our lads have got them eating out of the palms of their hands, almost literally. They've been catching frogs, snakes, rats and fish, while they were working, stuffing them into nets and now they are selling them in their lunch break.

"They have invited the three of us and my family to eat at their first 'Wild Meat Party' cooked Mae Sot style at Dad's house tonight. They said to turn up any time after six thirty.

"Isn't that something? They are inviting me to dine at my father's house. I don't suppose they have looked at it like that yet, but it is nice of them to invite us, isn't it?"

"Yes, it's sweet, said Lek, "it shows that we chose the right name for the agency too, because they wouldn't have invited us if they weren't happy. You know, I know that my mother has been worried about feeding the team, but when she gets to hear about this, she can rest easy. Have you eaten rat, frog and snake before, Craig?" asked Ayr.

"Well, they eat frogs in France and I tried them there a few times before I ever came to Thailand, but they only eat the legs. And I have eaten them here, but I can only eat the legs, not everything, like Thai people.

"And I have eaten rat and snake here too, but the way it's cooked, it's hard to tell what you are eating. We call it 'Bush Tucker', or the Australians do anyway – all the bush tucker here is prepared in the same way and tastes the same to me. It could just as well be chicken."

"We can tell, it's just you that can't, don't worry about it." put in Lek.

"I'm sure that you are right, but I definitely cannot tell the difference the way it's cooked here. When I was first offered rat, I expected to see a skinned rat on the plate, not tiny pieces of minced meat. The same with a snake, I expected to see cutlets, like with eel, not minced meat.

"Can we take some fruit with us, if we are going, because I'll eat the fish, and rice, of course, but I'll skip the rat and snake and eat fruit instead."

"Sure, we can do that. Dad has plenty of fruit there anyway. You only know this part of Thailand, eh, Craig?"

"Well, I know Pattaya, obviously, that's where I met you both, but Lek and I have been to Mae Sot, and Udon Thani on the way to Laos, but we didn't eat any local food as far as I know, did we, my dear?"

"Yes, we did, but only food from restaurants, not the real stuff that the locals might cook and eat at home. Like you can go to a restaurant here run by people from here for people from here, but you will never see rat, snake or frog on the menu, or maybe frog, sometimes, but people eat it at home every month."

"We don't."

"You don't, you mean. I used to cook it sometimes when you were working and either eat it alone in he garden or take it to Mum's and share it. Mum cooks it whenever Long or Ngat give her something since she doesn't go out working in the na any more."

"There you are then, Ayr, the answer to your question is a straight yes and no. Are we going there tonight then?"

Lek said, "Yes, I think we ought to since they invited us. Ayr?"

"Yes, I'm going, but I couldn't really say no anyway."

"No, nor could I as their joint employer, but you don't have to go if you don't fancy it, Craig. Ayr and I will be just fine with ten strapping, homesick young men to mother, won't we, Ayr?"

"I'm looking forward to it, I am."

"Yes, me too," said Lek.

"OK, I'm in too. Ayr, can I put a case of Chang in the back of your car for tonight?"

"Sure you can."

∞

Lek and Craig went to the boys' party on Lek's motorbike since it wasn't far. If the worst came to the worst, they could leave the bike there and walk home.

On arrival, Lek went into the house that she had known all her life to talk to the family. Ayr handed him a cold beer and invited him in too, but he declined and went to sit with the men from Mae Sot. They welcomed him over, waaied and bowed very politely and smiled a lot, but as he had expected, no-one spoke a word of English, although that was not quite true, one boy kept holding a bottle up towards him and saying 'Happy'.

Craig soon got tired of saying 'happy' back to him every few minutes, but realised that he meant well and so let it go until he himself got tired of saying it.

The team, as they were described, had built a large but low fire, so that they could all sit around it and hold sticks with bits of meat or fish stuck on the end in the fire, but for this occasion, four of them had delegated themselves as chefs and were cooking with pots and pans closer to the fire, while others peeled, cut, chopped and otherwise prepared food for cooking.

Two others were tam-tamming spices in heavy pestle and mortars.

One boy held up a dead rat by its tail and shook it at Craig. They all laughed and even Craig managed a smile. Then another held up a dead snake and repeated the gesture, with the same result.

Craig was beginning to wonder what he had let himself in for, when Lek and Ayr came to his rescue.

"Are you all right there, Craig?" asked Lek.

"No, not really, but I'll survive. They're just having fun. Are you going to sit with us now?"

"Yessss, don't worry, I won't leave you on your own for long. We did ask if you wanted to come in and say hello to the family, didn't we? You refused, didn't you?"

"Yes, OK, I've learned my lesson then. I can't talk to them and vice-versa. They don't speak English and they don't seem to understand my Thai. I can't follow theirs easily either. Is it a different dialect?"

"Yes, it's not a lot different, but it is different, yes. More in accent than in words. Their tones are slightly different. It's not easy at first even for us or them, of course."

"Right... so, none of us can talk to each other?"

"No, I didn't say that. We can talk, only you cannot."

"Oh, that's all right then, isn't it?'

"It is OK for us, yes."

He knew she was only joking in her practical, straight-faced style.

Lek's equivalent of a dry sense of humour.

The team put on a great spread, they used all of Ayr's mother's plates and dishes and then started laying their food out on banana leaves. There were dozens, perhaps three dozen dishes laid out between the thirteen of them and as one plate was emptied, someone replenished it. Craig was not counting, but it seemed that every boy cooked at least one dish, probably his own personal favourite.

One thing that he did notice though was that they tended to eat straight from the main serving plate with their bare hands, which Lek had told Craig was a big social mistake. He pointed it out to her since there wasn't much danger of embarrassing any of the team.

"It is not right, er, polite, to eat like that in company, but it is still common practice in some parts of the country and with some kinds of people all over Thailand. I should think that half of these guys have done national service, well, they probably ate like that when on a field trip. I don't know. Some people do it here too, not at home, but if they stop for lunch in the field, they just dive in and don't care about manners.

"It might not be 'nice' but it is pretty normal, especially with a gang of boys like this. Don't worry, I always put your food on a separate plate. I know you don't like this."

"Well, you are wrong, actually, I wasn't complaining, I was just wondering if it was a cultural thing, because Muslims eat like this."

"They are not Muslims, they are Buddhist..."

"I didn't say they were Muslims, I just meant..., Oh, forget it. OK, it is because they are country people working together and do not have to show good manners."

"Yes, exactly. Not because they are Muslims."

"No, I never thought they were Muslims."

"Well, why did you say they were then?"

"I didn't...I wish I'd never started now. Look, can we just forget about Muslims for now and get on with the meal?"

"Yes, a very good idea."

Lek and Ayr talked and laughed a lot with the young men, while Craig observed and drank beer.

One of the things that he noticed very clearly, was how respectfully they treated Lek and Ayr. He guessed that this was because they were twenty years older than the boys and because they were their bosses, Thai society still being very hierarchical, much more so than any Western country he had ever been in.

At some point, after they had had their fill but were not yet completely stuffed, some of the boys started singing and one or two got up to dance. Craig took his lead from Ayr and Lek who not only clapped during some of the songs, but also applauded loudly at the end of each one.

After half an hour of this and no doubt several bottles of Lao Khao, two of the boys asked their bosses for a dance. The one who asked Lek, looked at Craig for permission, which he granted without a second's thought. There was no touching in Thai dancing, not that he would have minded anyway, it was up to Lek whom she wanted to dance with and how she wanted to do it.

Lek and Ayr put on a good show, whirling around with their arms in the air in traditional Thai style and all the men either danced or clapped them in encouragement. Most of the men looked over at Craig and made some sign of appreciation concerning the women – a thumb's up or a nod – and they were good too, but then he had known that for years already.

At eleven o'clock, Ayr said that the party had to close down because her elderly parents wanted to get to sleep. There were no complaints and Ayr promised that they could have a later party every Saturday night, if they kept the noise down on the other six days. They were satisfied with that.

The boys cleared the things away, and a few of them set about washing up. Everybody waaied everybody else and then Ayr, Lek and Craig went home.

A very good night was had by all, even Craig.

∞

The following day was even better for the agency, although they were making a lot less on the farming supply side. When the partners met in the shop after Ayr had dropped everyone off at work, she called Lek outside to help her unload the car.

"I got a few things yesterday... the ones that we were talking about and a few others that I noticed the boys were short of. Then I realised that farmers use these things in the na too, so why not stock them ourselves?

"We have: collapsible, one-man, spring-steel mosquito nets and blankets for use in the sala in the fields; those army-style cooking sets, where the pan is a plate and there's a tin cup, knife, fork and spoon inside; fishing rods, line, hooks, nets and keep nets; plus a few sheath knives and assorted penknives."

"What do you reckon?"

"Proper little Army Surplus Store now aren't we? A Scout Shop."

"Yes, Camping Supplies, I suppose. If I ever see a couple of cheap two-man tents, I'll get those too. We can hang them on the wall, or off the ceiling like they do in Bangkok."

"Yes, why not? I think that the more choice we have, the more diversity we cover, the less a disaster like the flood can affect us, as long as it's all related to farming... but yes, farmers often sleep in the sala in their fields at night as well as in the day. These things are all useful," said Lek.

"About those extra men for the team, what do you think today?"

"I think that we may as well get another ten right away. The other guys are doing so well with the free food that they could support their colleagues easily enough. They'll sort themselves out. They probably all know each other anyway. Half of them might be related..."

"Oh, I know that some of them are for sure. If someone came to you with employment for a few bodies, wouldn't you ask your own family first? I know I would and I'm sure they did too, but that's all right... there's nothing wrong with that... in fact it works in our favour, they will stick together... more co-operation, less fighting... Yes, it is a good thing.

"All right, I'll phone Romeo after nine o'clock and see what he can come up with. If he can get them to Phitsanulok, they can get a train to Phichai and I can pick them up from there. It might be worth telling him to look for another ten too, just in case."

"Why not? The water hasn't stopped rising and it doesn't cost us anything, does it?"

"No, and I have told the boys that we do have that they only get paid for the days that they work, but that they can sell their catch too, although they can't live in Dad's barn unless they work for us.

"That puts a stop to the wise guys before any nonsense starts."

"Sorry?"

"Well, if they are making more money catching and selling animals, someone might want to start doing it full time and I don't think we can allow that."

"Ah, yes, I see... No, you are quite right... that's a perk, not their sole reason for being here.

"One small point, while we are talking about their catch. I noticed last light that someone had killed a python..."

"Yep, I saw that too. Thanks for reminding me. I will point out that we are strict Buddhists and only eat poisonous snakes. They'll have been taught that too, so they will understand. I'll say that it would upset my father and other village farmers.

"Anything else before I check on our workforce? Oh, I'll help you put all this stuff up on display this afternoon, so you don't need to do it all yourself."

"I don't mind doing it, but if someone wants to buy something, I don't know how much you paid for it, so I'd have to wait anyway."

"Yes, OK, we'll do that after lunch. See you then."

"Yes, see you," said Lek softly to herself as Ayr was disappearing out of the doorway. A sudden flash of a thought disturbed her but she couldn't grasp it at first, then she realised that that was what it must have been like for Craig for all those years. Craig stuck inside working while she was outside in the fresh air and sunlight.

She had never seen it from Craig's point of view before.

# 24 CHRISTMAS AND NEW YEAR

In mid-December, a fortnight after the flooding had begun, the waters were still rising near Baan Suay. Long's field, was now at least six feet under water and it was estimated that over a million Baht in crops had been lost by that one village's farmers alone, despite the best efforts of the Sanuk Employment Agency, which had grown in strength to thirty men and women, most, but now not all of whom came from Mae Sot.

The Team and the ten punts that the firm controlled were in permanent employment. The agency was now the prime earner, since the farmers saw little point in tending crops that might rot later underwater. However, the agency had sparked other farmers to try to emulate their salvage operation and some were quite successful at it.

The problem for most farmers was labour and age. Ninety percent of the village youth had already left Baan Suay to seek higher education or better-paid jobs in the cities of Thailand and they found it impossible to drop everything and rush home to help save the family business. Not only that, but farmers who had once been fit and wiry, had been sitting behind a wheel driving farming machines that couldn't work in water deeper than a few inches for far too long. They were no longer fit.

With the best will in the world, most farmers were stuck, well and truly stuck fast and the only help that was readily available was the agency, so the agency thrived and grew at an alarming rate. It frightened Lek, but not so much Ayr, to think that the agency had not even existed three weeks before, but now employed thirty-three people, including its founders.

However, many people had good reason to be glad of the agency besides the employees and the farmers that it assisted. Several families built service industries that could not have existed if it hadn't been for the agency's work.

The stalks of rice needed threshing and not many people could remember how to do it. Many of the old, retired farmers were called back into service to give demonstrations or to teach the lost skill. Then, some families still had an old belt-driven threshing machine that could be run off a PTO. These old wooden contraptions had not been used for nigh on forty years, but once serviced they were faster than doing the job by hand.

Some women made cakes and pots of tea or tureens of curry and rice and sold them to the agency staff in their rest breaks. Some even bought fish from the workers, cooked them and then sold them back to them. There was also a constant crowd 'on The Beach', paddling and even swimming to whom the ladies sold their wares.

A few farmers who only had fields that were now under water became fishermen and supplemented their income by selling fish. There was definitely a large financial loss being suffered by the local farming community as a whole, but they had seen hardship before and knew better than to wait for government handouts or physical support.

In short, they just got on with their lives and made the best of the bad situation.

Ayr and Lek's social standing, face, for want of a better word, rose dramatically and so would that of Lek's mother have, perhaps even more so, if she had allowed her partners to tell people that she was also part of the team, but for reasons known only to herself, she wanted to stay out of the limelight.

However, the three women each played their part and ran the firm very well between them. Lek did almost all of the administration and so became a permanent feature in the shop. She kept the spreadsheets up to date and accurate, she handled the advertising, although the need for that had dwindled, and she kept the information on the web site current.

She had discussed with Craig whether each firm should have its own web site or not and they both thought that they should, but that it was not a priority in the short term. Lek had that on her 'To Do List', but she was looking forward to designing and actually creating the new website, when she had time.

Ayr handled the staff and the purchasing. She was great with the Team and they all loved her – most as a favourite aunt, but she suspected that one or two had a secret crush on her too. She took them to work in the Thailand every morning, had lunch with them every now and then and took them home in the evening. She even ate with them in the evenings quite often and made a point not to miss the Saturday night campfire feasts, which were gaining quite a reputation in Baan Suay and the surrounding area. Most people had heard of the Team from Mae Sot and some girls from roundabouts actively sought an invitation to a Saturday night party.

All of the new lines that Ayr had come up with were selling well. In fact, they were outselling their traditional lines of fertiliser and feed in those very unusual times. The camping equipment was a great hit with the locals. The fold-up mosquito nets were a real boon to those who regularly slept in their fields when expensive pumps needed guarding and refuelling at night. Light-weight aluminium pots, pans, plates and mugs sold like hot cakes and so did small primus stoves and the small tins of gas needed to run them.

It seemed that everyone had taken up fishing as a means of supplementing their income and diet. The villagers had been keen fishermen and women before the flood but now, many of them had little else to do all day with no rice fields to tend. Despite all these extra anglers operating around the village, the supply of fish, frogs and snakes was not reduced, Some said it was because fish from upstream were being washed down to them, but others pointed to the fact that there were now thousands of tons of rice underwater for the fish to feed on.

Some people specialised in netting fry, which the locals had always encouraged to grow in their fields in order to reduce the mosquito population. A local delicacy was fish fry omelette and always had been. Another popular egg dish was omelette made with the tiny freshwater prawns that also thrived in the shallows of the rice fields. The population of these prawns also exploded and omelette of one kind or another was now more common than rice as a main food source.

Lek's mother, Pang, played the role of doting grandmother to the Team and she was very good at it too because she really did care for those young people, about half of whom had never been away from home before. Some of the men had done national service, but they had still been 'looked after', this was the first time that they were 'on their own' a hundred miles from home and that went doubly for the six girls that had also joined the workforce.

Pang did little errands for them when she was in Phichai, showed them how to mend their clothes when they got ripped, helped them get over minor ailments and even spoke to their mothers back home, when asked, to reassure them that their 'little Johnnie' or 'baby Susan' was still alive and well. She was everyone's surrogate mother or grandmother and everybody loved her because she truly cared.

There had never been even one incident caused by the guest workers or even one complaint about them in the three weeks that they had been working in Baan Suay and that made everyone associated with the new company very proud too.

Many of the workers who had seen this job as a temporary stopgap to the unemployment problems at home and the local disaster that was the flood, were now hoping that they might find permanent jobs in Baan Suay. It had long been Ayr's intention to start an agency 'one day' and she had seized this unexpected opportunity to get it off the ground early, but whether the company would survive long term was not at all certain. In any case, it was unlikely to continue at its current size, but they knew that that was out of their hands. They would just have to 'wait and see'.

None of the Team wanted what they had to end, but they all knew that the flood situation would not last forever. A few of them asked Ayr if she could try to find them more permanent work after the agency no longer required their services. She promised to help all those that she could.

The agency added quite a bit to the work lives of Ayr and Lek and so it gave Lek the perfect opportunity to drop out of the party circuit without causing offence. After all, it was basically only the farming community that was suffering, life in the towns like Phichai went on as before. The government offices, banks and shops were unaffected although retailers did register a drop in sales, due to the farmers' loss of income.

However, Ayr did not give up her parties unless there was a pressing need to do so. She worked all day from seven in the morning until at least six in the evening and then was either with Lek and Craig in Nong's, with the Team at her parent's or at a party. She was rarely in bed before one a.m. when she would fall into bed exhausted only to be woken up by the alarm six hours later. She was getting less sleep now that at any other time in her life. Lek and her mother were both concerned about Ayr's health. She looked well and seemed happy, but they thought that she wasn't taking enough care of herself.

And the water level was still rising, presenting more opportunities for work to the agency. Ayr called in another ten, but pointed out that they would probably only be needed for a week or two, although she had no evidence to base that assumption on. The barn was big enough to hold a hundred, so that was not a problem, but sanitation was, so Ayr hired a small digger and a driver to dig three more toilets, two for the men and one for the ten women. She also bought 'toilet tents' to erect around them to replace the temporary wooden sheds that they had cobbled together.

She also had one large communal shower constructed which was large enough to accommodate ten. The women were allocated their times and the men theirs, anyone using the showers outside heir allotted time periods risked being intruded upon by a member of the opposite sex. However, the Team were all good friends and the scheme worked very well. Farmers were used to having very little privacy and so respected their own and other peoples'.

One day, there was an announcement that the Sirikri Dam was approaching capacity and would have to release a large volume of water over the following twenty-four hours and even longer if the rain in the far north didn't subside soon. Nobody had any idea what this would mean and the authorities were not offering a prediction. However, they were soon to find out. The water lever rose by two feet over night and hundreds more fields disappeared under water as the high water mark raced ever closer towards the village. The small patch of road by Long's field that had once been called The Beach, was now considered deep water and the Beach had shifted a kilometre nearer to the village.

This was breaking point for the farmers who besieged the council offices in Phichai on a co-ordinated rally with banners, placards and chants. A notice was glued to the front door of the civic offices which read:

'We the farmers of this area, the people who voted you into a job, hereby swear, that none of us will ever again vote for anyone who now holds office if the water level does not recede within one week'.

It was a difficult time for Ayr and Lek, because their gut feeling was with the farmers who were their family and friends, but they didn't want to be seen to be threatening the powerful local politicians. They played it by ear and did what they could to both support the farmers and stay in the background but it was not easy.

Within three days a 'solution' was found. They would open the Phitsanulok Dam and let the same volume of water flow past as the Sirikri Dam had, that way they thought they could pass the buck up stream. It worked for the farmers in and around Baan Suay, because the water level receded to below where it had been when Sirikri had opened up, but the fields and cities south of Phitsanulok flooded.

The government of Phitsanulok could do nothing but hold their hands up and remind the southern cities that at least they had been given three weeks warning to strengthen their flood barriers. The flood water travelled all the way to Bangkok where large areas of the suburbs and even Don Muang Airport were feet under water, but not that many of the northern farmers or politicians had much sympathy with them after having lost so much money.

Far from costing the agency business, the receding waterline created more work for Ayr and Lek because the farmers did not expect the local politicians to stand up to pressure from Bangkok for long. They were sure that the Phitsanulok Dam would soon be closed again and that the water would rise above where it had been, so they wanted their rice cut right there and then or before if possible. The forty members of the Team were working flat out, twelve or more hours a day, seven days a weeks.

Lek could barely cope with all the enquiries and they certainly couldn't fulfil all the requests for hired labour. It was a very stressful time for everybody. Everybody except Craig of course who was totally unaffected and so carried on as normal.

One evening in Nong's when the three of them could get together, Lek and Ayr discussed the local situation with one of the best sources of local information, Nong herself.

"Three beers, please, Nong! What do you reckon on the flood now then? Will it get worse again or are we finally seeing the end of it. Or at least the beginning of the end of it?"

"Well," she said taking a seat, proud that someone was actually asking her opinion before she gave it to them anyway. "Well, as I see it, they may close the dam in Phitsanulok for a little while, but they will reopen it to let all this water go out to sea. They have to.

"The farmers around here are fed up with the politicians; the politicians are scared of losing their jobs and they have already burned their bridges with Bangkok by flooding it once, haven't they? Then there's the traders. I don't know if you know, but I try to get along to the Chamber of Commerce meetings in Phichai when I can, which is not too often because it's in the evening and being a single woman, I don't like being outside the village after dark.

"Anyway, I went to the last one and the shopkeepers in Phichai are going crazy about the loss of sales they are suffering because the farmers have cut back. That has not become public knowledge yet, because the traders were asked not to show public support for the farmers... but they back the farmers all the way and more.

"In fact, they are quite cheesed off. Everyone has such sympathy for the farmers, but the shopkeepers don't get a mention! They won't be putting up with that for much longer, I can tell you. If the Farmers' Union said the right things to the traders' associations, you'd see rallies and protests such as no-one has ever seen in these parts before."

"Divide and rule," said Lek, it always works, doesn't it?"

"Of course," said Ayr, "Why didn't I see that before?"

"Don't be too hard on yourself, Ayr," said Lek. "Why would you think of it? Why would any of us? We're farmers..." and she broke off as the realisation of what she was saying dawned on her.

"No, Lek, we were born farmers, but we, you and I stopped being farmers twenty-odd years ago when we got on that bus to go to Pattaya, and we stopped being whatever it was that we became there when we came back here. I have some land, but do I farm it? No, I hire other people to do that for me. I may know how to farm, but do I want to be a farmer? No, not on your Nelly!

"No, we are traders now, Lek. 'Business people' to put a nicer name to it and we deal in labour and materials. Our hearts may be with the farmers and they are the ones who pay our wages, but we are not farmers. We need to learn to think further than the next dawn or the next monsoon. Much further.

"We were lucky this time, but you cannot rely on good luck forever. It doesn't work like that, does it. Sooner or later, good luck always turns into bad luck."

"What are you going to do, Ayr?" asked Nong.

"The first thing I am going to do is have another beer. Who'll join me? Lek? Nong? Craig, sorry we have left you out of everything, but it's only boring local politics. Do you want another?

"Three and one for yourself, please, Nong."

When Nong had left, Ayr whispered to her friend. I just had a brainwave. How would you like to be a politician?"

"Me?"

"Yes, you. Why not you? Look at all the thieves, liars and scallywags we've got now and everybody loves you."

"Why not you? It was your idea."

"My history is a bit too close for comfort, I think, but you have been here for eight or nine years. That's plenty of time. You are a bedrock of the local community now, whereas I am still an unsure bit of driftwood."

"I have always thought that I would like to be an assistant councillor."

"Mmm, well, I wasn't thinking of starting quite that far down the ladder. That job is all right if you're twenty-five or not well-off or something, but you deserve a position on the district council and then on the Provincial Council. You're forty-one years old and partner in a couple of thriving businesses, come on!"

"It will take a lot of work, Ayr, and I wouldn't know where to begin."

"Well, you're right there on both counts, but we can find out, can't we? Don't tell anybody anything yet, but when you get the time, look it up in the government documents on the Internet. It'll be on there, won't it? Qualifications, application form, salary, duties. I don't know anything about it either, but we can find out, can't we?"

"Yes, sure we can. No harm in looking, is there? Do you really think that I could do it, Ayr?"

She touched Lek's hand, "Yes, Lek, I really think you can do it and I really think that you can do it really well. Quiet now, fog horn is coming back.

"As I was saying... Christmas tomorrow, isn't it, Craig? Oh, thanks, Nong.

"Cheers my dears, here's to an exciting future!"

∞

The following day, Lek and Craig exchanged presents, but Lek still wanted to go into work, which was not unexpected, since she didn't celebrate Christmas and never had done. Nobody did in Baan Suay, with the possible exception of Craig who had started the 'tradition' eight years before of doing a 'pub crawl' around the village on Christmas morning.

"I'll walk in with you, Lek" said Craig. "I can't work yet. I'll make my annual tour of inspection of the village early, maybe come back, have a sleep and then try to work later."

"Inspection of the village? Piss up, you mean!"

"Well, if you have to put it so crudely, yes. Christmas comes but once a year and has to be celebrated."

"Yeah, yeah, I hear the same every year. Come on then, I want to get an early start. I've got some research to do and a web site to build."

"I'm right behind you."

Lek knew that something was wrong as soon as she turned the corner. The Team was sitting in the Thailand and the shutter was still down on the shop. She ran ahead as fast as her shoes would allow.

"What is it? Where is Ayr?" Da appeared from around the side of the building. "Where's Ayr?"

"I don't know Pee Lek, she didn't pick us up this morning. Her Dad gave me the keys and so here we are."

Lek was pushing the shutter up and unlocking the inner door. She called Ayr's name but there was no answer.

"Ayr? Are you in there?"

She hurried on through the counter and knocked on Ayr's private door, but again there was no answer. She let herself in gingerly.

"Ayr, are you all right?" She could see a figure on the bed, so she put the light on.

"Ayr! Are you all right?"

Her head lolled towards Lek, she looked perfectly normal, but was a very peculiar colour. She groaned softly and vomit oozed out of her mouth. Lek pulled her onto her side, head facing down over the edge of the bed.

"Da, quickly, tell Nong to phone an ambulance. Quickly! Emergency! And send someone for the village nurse."

The nurse arrived within minutes, but they were very long minutes to Lek. The ambulance turned up amid a storm of dust with its sirens whooping and lights flashing. The paramedics put Ayr on emergency life support apparatus and then wanted to check some details like her full name and her insurance company. Lek showed one of them the card from Ayr's bag, tucked the bag under her arm and then got in beside Ayr when they pushed her stretcher into the ambulance.

"Craig, I don't know when I'll be back, but I'll phone you in Nong's later. Take care of yourself and don't drink too much!"

Then they were gone.

While Craig was wondering what to do next, Nong spoke to him.

"Ayr mai sabai? Is Ayr sick?"

"Kit wah, ther mai loo, I think so, but don't know."

"Ah, better get men to work. I tell them for you?" she said in Thai

"Kapun kap, Nong. Khao mai kow jai pom. Yes, please, Nong, they don't understand me."

"Come on then, lads and lasses. Khun Ayr will be all right now. The best way you can help is by getting on with your work so that she doesn't have to worry about that. Come on, back on the Thailand. Da, do you have everything you need?"

"Yes, Pee Nong."

"Come on then, get them off to work. If you pop back here at lunch time, I may have some further news about Ayr for you."

"OK, thank you, Pee Nong."

And off they went too, leaving Nong and Craig and half a dozen neighbours looking on.

"Thanks, Nong. I go for walk around village now and I will come back to your shop at eleven or twelve o'clock. See you later."

Craig entered the desolate shop looking for keys. He found Lek's on a table, locked up and left on his annual tour, his heart wasn't really in it, but it was better than sitting at home alone.

# 25 MAYA - ILLUSION

Ayr appeared to be unconscious for the journey in the ambulance.

"What is the matter with Ayr, my friend there, please, Doctor?"

"I am not a doctor, I'm a paramedic. I'm afraid I can't say what your friend is suffering from. She looks delirious. What is her name, Ayr, you say? Do you know if she is on any medication?"

"Yes, her name is Ayr Boontar. Medication? No, I don't think so. She would have told me if she was. Probably on contraception though, if that's any help."

"Any details could be important. Khun...?"

"Lek, just call me Lek. Ayr and I never did go in for all the titles. Is she going to get well? Is it serious?"

"It is hard to say how serious it is until we know what she is suffering from, but there is no sign of internal bleeding and she is breathing comfortably now. We'll be in the hospital in seventy minutes, we'll know more then.

"Talk to her and hold her hand, if you like. Just watch the drip. I don't know whether she can hear you, you never can tell in cases like his."

Lek took her hand.

"Come on, Ayr, you're all right now. You're in an ambulance and we're nearly at the hospital. The paramedic is taking care of you, so you have nothing to worry about.

"I've got your handbag and the shop is locked up. I told Craig to put the team to work too, so there's no need to worry about anything in Baan Suay. I'll phone your Dad when we get to Phitsanulok

"Craig was going to take us out this evening. You know what he's like at Christmas. You'd think he was sixteen not nearly sixty, wouldn't you? Still don't you worry about that! I'll make sure that he takes us out another time, as soon as you are well again. Next week perhaps?"

She didn't look at the paramedic for confirmation because she was too frightened that he wouldn't give it.

Time passed slowly, but after an age of talking, there was a slight squeeze on her hand and Ayr's eyelids fluttered the tiniest amount. Lek couldn't help but look at the paramedic now, but he was smiling thinly and nodding, and that gave her confidence.

"We're nearly there now, my friend, ten more minutes."

Lek had to keep breaking off to dry her eyes, she was trying really hard not to make any sounds that would reveal her distress.

When the ambulance pulled into Phitsanuwed Hospital, Ayr was whisked away. Lek had never felt so alone in her whole life when she took a seat in the visitors' waiting room.

However, after a while a nurse approached.

"Khun Lek?"

"Yes," she jumped up, "any news about my friend?"

"I cannot say. I am sorry, but I have been told to ask you if you would like to sit outside Khun Ayr's room."

"Yes, please. Wait a minute. Is that a good sign or a bad one?"

"I'm really sorry, Khun Lek, but I have no information. Please follow me."

The nurse led Lek to a room on the seventh floor and pointed to a chair.

"Is Ayr inside this room?"

"No, she is still undergoing treatment, but it was thought that you would be better here. You will see when your friend arrives."

"OK, thank you."

"If you go to the Matron's Desk at the end of the corridor there, she may be able to find you a newspaper in the staffroom."

"Thank you again, you are very thoughtful."

Lek took her advice. Anything to keep her mind busy. The matron was happy to find a paper for Lek and pointed out the coffee machine. Lek took the paper and coffee back to her seat to wait.

At midday, Lek phoned Nong.

"Hi Nong, is Craig there?"

"He's just crossing the road now. How is Ayr?"

"There is no news, which, I suppose is good news like they say. I'm outside the room where they will move her to when they're done fixing her up."

"Well, that's good news, at least they expect her to be wanting a room and not a … er, a bed in Intensive Care or something."

Lek knew what she had been going to say – 'a slab' or 'a drawer' in the morgue.

"Yes, that's true, Nong. Is he there yet?"

"Yes, putting him on now. Lek..."

"Hi Lek, how are you and Ayr?"

"I'm all right, just sick with worry and that bloody stupid Nong going on about mortuaries. I'm all right really. As for Ayr, there is no news yet. She is still with the doctors. Oh, we are in Phitsanuwed. I'm standing outside the room that she will recover in."

"Well, that's good news, isn't it. A recovery room means an expected recovery. Oh, I am glad."

"That's what Nong said. I suppose you're right. I wish you were here darling. It is so lonely waiting on my own."

"I'll get a taxi in now, if you like."

"No, best not, but you could come in this evening at say five or six o'clock. Could you lock up the shop? There are some spare keys..."

"I've already done it. I found Ayr's keys and locked up this morning."

"Ah, good. Could you go back with my Mum. I'll ring her now, she can choose some of Ayr's clothes and you can bring them in later. Is that OK?"

"Sure. What time?"

"It's just after twelve..."

"No, not what time is it now? What time shall I meet your mother?"

"Oh, I see, er, say, about three-thirty, so you can get a taxi at four-ish. I'll get Mum to organise that for you. Ayr has a private room, so it doesn't matter too much. Look, I had better go, I'll speak to you later. I love you, choop, choop."

"I love you too, choop, choop. Bye."

Lek watched the lift arrive. Three nurses pushing a gurney followed a doctor out and towards her. She stood up and as they pushed the bed past her, she saw Ayr. Their eyes met and Ayr gave a weak smile. Her eyes and face were a little puffy and drained of colour, but at least she was conscious.

"Please give us a few minutes to put Khun Ayr Boontar in her bed, then you can come in."

Lek used the time to make two swift phone calls. One to Ayr's father and one to Nong so that the whole village would know within the hour.

The doctor was the first to leave. Lek nodded and waaied him respectfully, but he was heading for her, so she stood up.

"No, please remain seated, er...Khun Lek, is it?" he asked consulting his clipboard. He sat down next to her.

"I understand that you are a very close friend of Khun Ayr. Would you mind helping me with my enquiries?"

"No, doctor, not all. How can I help?"

"Well, did Khun Ayr go to a party last night? It was Christmas Eve and she may know some foreigners... that sort of thing?"

"My husband is a foreigner, so if there had been a Christmas Party, we would have known about it. No, I don't think so. We had a few beers after work and went our separate ways at about seven-thirty."

"All right, this is rather delicate, but is Khun Ayr an alcoholic?"

"No! No… I don't think so. She likes a drink and she still acts like a woman half her age, but alcoholic? No. Drinks too much? Possibly. Probably, even."

"Thank you for your candour. Does she make or sell illicit whiskey? 'Moonshine' as it is sometimes called, or 'Lao Bpa' - 'Jungle Juice'?"

"No, doctor, definitely not, she doesn't have to do things like that, she is quite well off."

"Thank you, well just one final question: has Khun Ayr been overdoing it recently in your opinion?"

"Most definitely, yes, doctor. We have all been very worried about her, but at the end of the day, I suppose we all just thought: 'Well, that's just the way Ayr is' and let her get on with it."

"Thank you very much. You have been most helpful. You will be able to go in and see your friend in a few moments. I have to be going now."

"Uh, wait a second, doctor. Is Ayr's condition serious? What is the matter with her?"

"I think that I will have to let Khun Ayr tell you about her condition."

"Well, will she recover?"

"Yes, in all probability, if she really wants to. I do have to go now. Very nice to meet you, Khun Lek. Bye."

No sooner had she sat down than the nurses came out smiling at some private joke.

"You may go in now, Khun Lek. Khun Ayr can see you now."

"Is she all right?"

"She's all right..." and they giggled again, hands before their mouths as they scurried past.

Lek entered the room cautiously, but there was no need. It was a large room with an en suite bathroom and a small worktop for preparing 'things'. There was a coffee machine a 42" wide-screen TV hanging on the wall opposite the bed and a huge picture window at the far end of the room. Ayr was sitting up in bed watching her.

"Not bad, is it? I've stayed in hotels worse than this," said Lek.

"So have I, much worse."

"So, how are you?" asked Lek as she closed the door behind her and walked over to the bed.

"I'm all right now, thanks. I just had a funny turn, that's all."

"A funny turn!? None of us thought it was very funny this morning and I didn't notice you laughing!"

"No, I suppose not. Thanks for all your help."

"No problem. I've got your bag here." She put it down on the bedside table between them and sat in a chair, which she dragged as close to the bed as she could get.

A few moments passed.

"Come on then, partner, out with it. What caused this funny turn of yours?"

"It's nothing. Really!"

"It was not 'nothing really', what was it?"

"It is a condition called A.P. It occurs in our family sometimes, but I am the first to suffer from it for generations. It's nothing when you know that you are at risk, you can control it very easily..."

"A.P? I've never heard of it. What, is it something like diabetes or cholesterol?"

"That's it! Not as serious, but something like that. There is no need to worry about it."

"Ayr... we have known each other for a very long time and I know that you are not telling me everything. Now what is it?"

"Oh, all right, if you promise not to tell anyone... alcoholic poisoning. Go on, you can laugh now."

Lek tried not to, she knew that alcoholic poisoning could be very serious, but she had to laugh at how her friend had tried to conceal it. She was also considerably relieved. It started as a grin, became a chortle and turned into a laugh. Ayr started laughing too.

"If you tell anyone, I swear I'll give it to you."

"You can't give someone alcoholic poisoning..."

"Well..., I'll give you something, I will..."

They laughed again and Lek moved forward to hug her friend.

They cried like only close girl friends can.

When they drew apart, Lek said,

"You have been working too hard. I knew it, but I didn't make a fuss. That was wrong... I should have made you slow down... Sorry, Ayr. I could see it, but I did nothing..." She took a brush out of her bag and started to straighten her friend's hair.

"Don't beat yourself up, Lek, it wasn't your fault. Remember what Nong was telling us about the Phichai traders? Well, when you went home, I went house-calling. I went to a few traders and a few farmers I know and just chatted about the mutual problem, the flood, that the farmers and the merchants faced.

"I went on about 'what a shame it was that we weren't facing this crisis together' and 'how much stronger people would be if they realised that we are all on the same side'. You know all that sort of stuff. I said it in such a way that they thought of the solution for themselves.

"You could almost see the Red Flags waving. Anyway, I must have gone to at least seven houses and had drinks in each one, mostly lao khao, which I can't say that I like, but I had to be sociable. Pretending to be maudlin and bemoaning the lack of co-operation only helped my cause.

"I was getting really good at it... people were phoning their friends and talking about 'their new idea' of co-operation between the farmers and the merchants. It was great and then I went to my uncle's house, you know, the one with the shop on the main road? Well, he wasn't in, but I hadn't seen my cousin for ages so I told him and his pals my story. I was really getting into it by now.

"Anyway, they were drinking some rot-gut lao bpa that they had bought for fifty Baht a bag. The five of them had a bag each and each person had flavoured his bag with his own favourite herbs, spices, flowers and bark, you know, as they do. Well, I was going through my routine, quite tipsy by now, I will admit, and they were all nodding and agreeing and passing me their lao to taste, which I did.

"The next thing I remember was seeing you and wondering where I was."

"Oh, Ayr... that stuff is lethal and on top of everything else? You're lucky you didn't die."

"Yes, maybe, Lek, but that's Karma for you, isn't it? Just look at our lives... We were schoolgirls thirty years ago and what did we want out of life?"

"Just the same as everyone else, I suppose," replied Lek, "to find a nice husband, a rich one, if possible, get married and have kids… to live a happy life in the village and build up the farm like our parents had done."

"Yes, exactly, but where were we ten years later? All right, you had a go at the 'family life dream' and it didn't work out for you. That was a shame, but you got a smashing daughter out of it. Anyway, ten years, not even that, after being schoolgirls we were working in a bar in Pattaya. You, me and dear old Goong.

"Three ordinary girls working in a bar in Pattaya, selling ourselves. And for what? You went there because the 'family farm dream' hadn't worked for your parents. You went there to rescue them and you did it.

"Goong and I went for the adventure, but the point is that weeks before that, we had no idea that that was what we would be doing!"

"That's true. I was so ashamed at first until I learned to pretend that it was not me doing those things… and I had the goal of paying off the bank..."

"Yes and you did that and when you had achieved your goal, you got out."

"I was lucky, I wanted to get out so that Soom would not be ashamed of me and I met Craig at the right time..."

"It was not luck, my dear, it was Karma. You deserved what you got. An opportunity was placed before you and you took it, with no inconsiderable risk to your own future if you remember."

"True again. If it had all gone pear-shaped with Craig, I might have lost my respectable job as cashier and been working in front of the bar again, but you helped me out there too."

"Yes, a little, but I could have taken the job off you, or I might have met a man and had to let someone else take the job and that person might not have let you have it back. Anything could have happened, but you took the risk and it paid off – Karma, you could not fail. It was written.

"In the same way that your Fate as a schoolgirl was not to have a happy village marriage and nor was mine or Goong's. Just look at what those years of hardship have brought you. Your failed first marriage brought you a lovely daughter and your crappy bar job found you a fantastic husband, who has encouraged and, I guess, largely paid for that lovely daughter to go to a lovely university.

"How many families in our little Baan Suay can say that their child is at one of the best universities in Bangkok studying computers? I'll tell you: none, zero. That's how many. And why is your daughter there? Because of your history."

"It is true, that wherever you are in life, you do not have to stay there..."

"You're darned right, you don't! We all have to make decisions and as often as not we come up with the wrong one. That puts us on a road, we may not like the road when we can see it more clearly but there is no going back on the road through life. All roads will take you when you are going. What do they say? 'All roads lead to Rome' and that is true."

"Yes," said Lek, "It's just that some are more crooked, some are not so well-paved, some have got potholes and some have got brigands. You will never always choose the right road, but you can learn to avoid the dangers."

"Exactly, and if you don't like the road you are on, take the next exit."

"One of life's most persistent illusions is that we are stuck where we are right now, because we are not. Changing one's lifestyle is difficult, as it is for a cart to leave the ruts in a well-worn lane, but we can change things for the better or for the worse and the choice is ours, so it's no good blaming anyone else for our own bad choices."

"No, you could have done that, Big Sister, when your husband was cheating on you and your family suggested that you went to Pattaya to help out, but you didn't. Goong and I were so proud of you for that even in those days."

"Do you often think of Goong, Little Sister?"

"Sure, every day, several times every day. I often feel her presence and once or twice I have thought that I have seen her, but when I take a better look, she disappears."

"I wish that I could see her, Ayr, but I do feel her nearby sometimes. Craig believes in ghosts. His parents used to see them all the time and tell him about them. I'm a little afraid of them, but he isn't at all."

"Fear the living, not the dead' is a wise old Thai proverb."

That's what Craig says: 'If they didn't try to hurt you when they were alive, why would they start when they're dead?'"

"But, that's true, isn't it? People confuse real-life ghosts with the zombies in the films. It is not a clever mistake to make."

"Look at us now, eh? I stopped work in Pattaya ten years ago and am married to an impoverished writer and you finished in Pattaya eight months ago and are the genius behind three firms already: the shop, the agency and your farm. That is some achievement..."

"Ah, I had a long time to plot and plan and no-one to spend my money on. But look at me now! This is exactly what we have been saying: ex-bar girl turns good ends up nearly dying of A.P. on Christmas Day! How bloody stupid is that?"

"What now..", but Ayr's phone started ringing and she was fumbling in her bag.

"Hallo? Who? Oh, Ross! Nice to hear from you. Yes, I'm fine. Merry Christmas... Yes, no, now we have discussed this before and I have said 'no' before, so just enjoy your Christmas with your friends and I'll see you soon..."

Lek was reaching over for the phone,

"If that is Ross, I'd like to wish him 'Merry Christmas'."

"Ross, before you go... Lek, you remember Lek? Yes, all right, I thought you might... Lek wants a word."

"Hello, Ross, Merry Christmas," she got up and moved to the window. "Where are you now, Ross? Bangkok? Oh, you are in Thailand then... Are you coming up over the holidays? Sorry, can you say that again, please, there is a lot of noise at your end. A party? Mmm, sounds like it too.

"Right, I see... that is what she said, is it? Well, do you know where we are now? In Ayr's room in Phitsanuwed Hospital, in Phitsanulok. Yes, Ayr was rushed in this morning. We are all very worried about her. She looks pretty scary right now, yes..." Lek was looking at Ayr who was doing her best at miming Lek to shut up and hang up under pain of strangulation.

"OK, Ross, that's a good idea. You do that. Phone me on Ayr's number from the lobby and I'll come and get you. Bye."

"He will be here in a couple of hours."

"He what?! Why did you do that, Big Sister?"

"Because he loves you and you like him a lot, I can tell, and he is concerned about you. Are there any better reasons?"

"No, I guess not. Remind me that I owe you something. To be honest, he has been asking me for months if he could move in, but I said 'no'."

"But why, for Heaven's sake?"

"I don't want to shack up with someone..."

"Ah, I see. I understand that. The permissive society hasn't reached Baan Suay yet, has it? I agree, but where he comes from it is quite normal. He just hasn't given it much thought. Typical man, look for the easy way out. Have you told him that?"

"No, if he can't see it, then too bad. If it is meant to be, it will happen. As Goong used to say, 'It is all Maya, it is all illusion anyway'. Whether you are a schoolgirl with schoolgirl's dreams, a bar girl in the tourist industry with hers, a house wife with a housewife's dreams or a business woman with her dreams or a man, it doesn't matter. Not really, not in the long run.

"It doesn't matter because no-one can make things happen in the way that they want. Parents can want a child and so have one, they made that happen, but what if they got a girl, but wanted a boy, or wanted a genius but didn't get one? What if you want a fast car, work for years and get killed in it the first time you take it out?

"Dreams are Maya. The whole world is Maya. You don't see the same world that I do and no-one sees the world as you do. We all live in our own little worlds. All wanting to be like someone else, some film star, pop singer or millionaire. We want to be like them but in truth we know nothing about them. We only see the image that their PR person creates for them.

"Goong was right about Maya, she was right about many things, but I didn't always see it or understand it at the time..."

"No, I had several long chats with her about Karma and Maya just before she died. One saying she had that I particularly liked was: 'When the student is ready, the teacher will appear'."

"Yes, brilliant."

"She used to say that the world is a university, one of millions in the universe and that life on Earth is just a permit to attend that university. I wish I knew she was here now."

"I can't definitely say that she is, but it wouldn't surprise me in the least."

"Nor me. God bless, you Goong".

"Oh, I forgot to say, Craig is coming in later, well, soon, actually, he'll bring in some clean clothes for you."

"Lek! I'm shocked at you! You let your husband rummage through my underwear drawer!? Sexy, though, what?"

"No, as if! I asked my mum to pick some things out and put them in a bag for him."

"Shame, it would have been interesting to see what he had chosen."

"Ayr, you never change, do you? Which is why you are stuck in here."

"And if I were not stuck in here, I would not have lover boy flying up to see me, would I?"

"That's true...," then she looked her friend in the eyes. 'Surely, not even Ayr would do a thing like that,' she thought, 'make herself sick to force her paramour into action'. "Ayr?..."

"What?"

"It's OK, I won't ask, because I do not want to know." Ayr smiled and looked out the window. A Thai Airways flight from Bangkok was passing the window. "That could be him now."

Bangkok was only thirty minutes by plane.

"Yes, strange isn't it? It will take Craig three times longer to get here from the same province than it will Ross to travel four hundred kilometres."

"It is the new age, even in Thailand, but do not forget that whatever the image and no matter how newfangled, it is still only an image, it is still only Maya."

Twenty minutes later, Ayr's phone rang again. It was Ross in the lobby. Lek quickly ran the brush over Ayr's hair again, straightened the pillows and blankets and hurried down to meet him. Lek looked around and spotted Craig first, he was talking to a man, Ross, as she approached, she heard Craig saying:

" ... you're dead right! They are women and a half they are, it is a pity you never met Goong. There used to be three of them. What a handful! Inseparable they were. They used to call themselves the Three Musketeers.

"Oh, hello, darling..."

"Talking about us were you...?"

"Only good things, I assure you, Lek. Look who I found...", interjected Ross.

"Yes, so I see. Are you all right, telak?

"Yes, sure. How is Ayr?

"She's over the worst. I think the drugs have given her some sort of high. I'm waiting for her to fall asleep any moment."

"Come on then, let's go up."

"Er, Ross, no flowers, chocolates, presents?"

"I didn't have time... shi... sorry."

"Here, give her these, they'll do more good coming from you than from me," said Craig.

"Thanks, mate."

More illusion, thought Lek, but perhaps less than the illusion that Ross is about to walk into in a moment, but she said, as they were walking, "You told me on the phone that you love Ayr."

"Yes, I have for ages. I've asked if I can move in with her several times, but she keeps knocking me back. I don't know why though, I think she likes me really... deep down."

"Oh, she does. She is in love with you. She told me this afternoon, but she won't just live with you..."

"You mean... she might marry me?"

"Of course that's what I mean. Look, living in the village is not like living in Bangkok, Pattaya or Sidney. We don't have the permissive society yet. If you want to live with her, you will have to marry her."

"Crikey! I never thought of that." He kissed Lek on the cheek and then looked sheepishly at Craig, who just shrugged his shoulders.

"How can such intelligent people be so stupid?" asked Lek of no-one in particular, and no-one answered.

Lek pushed the door open and let Ross enter first. Ayr had lowered the top half of the bed and was lying down flat now with her eyes barely open.

"Oh, my Ayr! What has happened to you?" She opened her eyes a little wider. Ross threw the flowers on the bed and draped himself across her chest squeezing her shoulders. He began to weep.

"You will never have to face another day like this alone ever again, my dear. Please marry me and let me take care of you for the rest of our days?"

Ayr winked at Lek over Ross' shoulder, "Yes, my darling, I will marry you. As soon as I can get out of this place. I thought you'd never ask."

Ross picked himself up, tears still running down his cheeks, but smiling from ear to ear. He looked at Lek, "Thank you, Lek. Thanks for everything. I am the happiest man in the world." He kissed Ayr again.

Lek said, "We had better be going then. Knowing my Craig, he'll be wanting a Christmas beer or two. We'll stay in a hotel nearby tonight and pop in and see you before we go back to the village tomorrow.

"See you both. You're doing the right thing, I know you are. Come on, Craig, let's go for a beer."

"First things first," he walked over to the bed and kissed Ayr on the cheek. "Congratulations and get well soon. I brought you a get-well card, but it should have been an engagement card instead." Then he shook hands with Ross, "Congratulations, mate, I'm sure you will both be very happy. Welcome to the gang!"

"Yes, of course." Lek did the same and then they left them to it.

As they walked out into the hospital car park, Lek said:

"They will be all right now, won't they Craig?"

"Yes, I'm sure they will be."

"And we will be too, eh?"

"We still have an exciting future ahead of us, my dear.

"Who knows where it will take us?

"No-one, I guess, but wherever it goes, we'll go together."

"So, where shall we go now then?"

Lek slipped her arm around his waist and Craig put his arm around her shoulders.

"I don't mind. Nearest quiet bar will do me. Are you hungry?"

"Is Buddha a Buddhist?"

**The End**
(for now)

Look out for the fourth book in the trilogy:
"The Lady in the Tree"

Please leave a short review where you bought this book. This kind of feedback is extremely important to authors and other readers, so please make your voice heard, and join me as my fiend on Facebook and Twitter.

Thanks,

Owen.

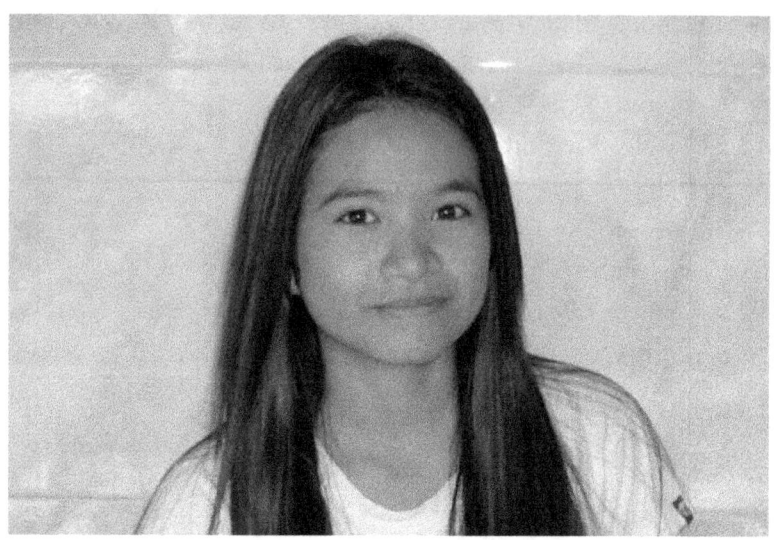

# GLOSSARY

Ab Naam: a shower, as in to take a shower

Ayr  : The third of the three friends who went to Pattaya together

Baan Suay: Lek's village

Baht: Thai currency worth 2p or 3c; 15.2 grammes of gold

Bangkok Post: Thai daily, English-language newspaper

Beou: Lek's cousin and owner of Daddy's Hobby

Ben  : a half bottle of whisky

Ben's Coffee Shop: in Phichai

Bum: the daughter of the owners of a shop by the Wat

Chalita: Lek's sister, married to Deo, living in Bangkok

Chang: Beer Chang; an elephant; a tradesman or contractor

Choop: a kiss

Craig: Lek's Welsh husband from Barry

Daddy's Hobby: bar in Pattaya where Lek worked for ten years

Deng: red

Geek: a lover, mistress, or fancy man

Goong: Lek, Ayr and Goong had gone to Pattaya together

Gumnan: mayor, Nic in Baan Suay; wife's name is Jan

Hong Naam: a WC

Kapong: tin (of beer, milk etc)

Khao: white or clear; rice; food in general; a mountain; to enter

Khun: Mr., Mrs., master or miss – usually used with the first name

Kuwat: bottle (of beer, milk etc)

Kwitiau: noodle soup with vegetables and meat(balls)

Lek  : Leynou Suksawat (full maiden name)

Lao : Thai 'whisky': lao deng is red and sweet, lao khao is clear and rough; lao bpa is home-made and can be lethal – literally 'jungle spirit' because of the traditional sites of the illegal stills.

Loy Krathong: 'Millions of Boats', the Thai day for romance, in November

Mapang : plum mangoes, an expensive crop in Thailand

Na: a rice field

Naam Ya: literally 'medicine water' or 'medicine soup'

Neh?: Thai equivalent of 'eh?'

Nong: said to younger people or those of lower social status. Also a name

Pattaya: Asia's most popular resort for Westerners

Pee: a mark of respect to one who is older or of higher status

Phichai: the nearest town

Phitsanulok: nearest city

Pee: a ghost or spirit

Rai: 1,600 m², a standard rice field (na)

Ross: Ayr's friend

Saan: court as in courtroom

Sala : a rough construction with no walls for sitting in

Sanuk: difficult in English: pleasure at work; joy; maybe 'hwyl' in Welsh

Satang: a worthless coin nowadays, 100 to the Baht

Songkhran: 14-16 April – Thai New Year

Soom: Lek's daughter by her first marriage

Suan: a garden or a market garden

Tuk-tuk : a motorbike taxi with two small bench seats in the trailer

Telak: darling; dear; sweetheart

Udon Thani: a large city in Isaan, north-eastern Thailand

Vientiane: capital of Laos

Waai: traditional Thai gesture for 'hello' or 'goodbye'

Wat : Thai Buddhist Temple – there is at least one in every village

Bonus:
Chapter One - Volume Four

# THE LADY IN THE TREE

Book Four in the Series

## Behind The Smile

*The Story of Lek, a Bar Girl in Pattaya*

### 1 TROUBLE AT T' MILL

"It's just got to be some kind of mafia… I can't see who else it could be…"

"Who's got to be the Mafia, Lek? I don't follow you," asked Craig eventually having to give up on his writing because Lek was driving him mad with her incessant mumbling, hunched over her laptop at the other end of the desk.

"Someone is trying to ruin our businesses, aren't they? Little, niggly things like petty theft started about two weeks ago… yes, about two weeks after Ayr went to Australia to get married, but I didn't think too much about them, because that sort of stuff happens, doesn't it, right? But when we started having real problems the other day… It's as if they were testing us with the thefts, and now that they know that we are a ma.., er woman down, they are hitting us hard. They know that I'm rushed off my feet and can't be everywhere at once.

"They also know that I don't have a man who can help me."

"Thank you very much."

"Well, it's true, isn't it? A Thai man would be able to help. He would know people, he would understand, he would do something to help… but what can you do? Write a story about it? Put it on your blog? You don't know how things work in Thailand, you don't know anybody and you don't even speak Thai.

"Therefore, I am left on my own to take on the mafia without a husband to help me."

"If you put it like that, I suppose you've got a point, but you don't paint me in a very good light, do you? I'm just some useless storyteller who can't help his wife take care of business."

"It is truth…"

"All right, so it's the truth, but I wish you wouldn't keep rubbing it in. I have my pride as well, you know."

"I am just calling a spade a spade… There is nothing wrong with that, is there?"

"I don't suppose so, but you could call me a nice, useless old spade to soften the blow. What has happened, and who are these Mafioso, anyway?"

"What is 'Mafioso'?"

"Italian Mafia personnel, why, what are you talking about?"

"Not Italians, that's for sure! The mafia, you know, crooks, thieves, bandits, bullies, the Thai mafia. When Thai people say mafia, it is not Italian Mafia, it is just local criminals, bullies, mafia… Anyway, I told you before, but you always too busy to listen me: they pour paint on Ayr's car, go in her flat and sho.. the shop, make problems in the na… I told you."

"Yes, sorry, you did. A bit more than coincidence, eh? Have you been to the police?"

"See, you don't understand! Go to the police, what good is that? I go already, but without evidence and proof, they can do nothing."

"No, I suppose not, but isn't it their job to get evidence?"

"See, you just don't understand, do you? If it was a murder, they would have to investigate, because they can see a crime… but not in cases like ours. The mafia can say that I started it and they are coming back at me and who knows… maybe they pay police to look somewhere else…"

"The other way?"

"I must give them some proof… something that they cannot ignore… then I can get some help.'

"Yes, tricky, isn't it? Can't your brothers help?"

"I give up with you sometimes, I really do… look, my brothers' wives don't want them getting involved with the mafia for me, and as their big sister, neither do I, and secondly, I don't want them to think that we can't handle the problem on our own, or we will both lose face… and you will look like a pussy. I am trying to save you from that, not that you can help anyway.

"That is why I have no-one to turn to but Ayr. She would know what to do."

"I see, that hopeless, is it?"

"I am afraid so. All those years ago, I thought that having a falang husband was the best thing in the world, who would have thought that I would regret it one day?"

"Charmed, I'm sure! Are you saying that you regret marrying me now?"

"No, darling, but at this precise moment, a Thai husband would be more use to me."

"Funny, isn't it? You don't want your Thai brothers to get involved with the mafia, but you wouldn't mind if your Thai husband had to have a go."

"Not funny, no, but that is part of his job, not part of a brother's job. A brother has his own wife he must fight for… and I have you. It is a shame, but that is my Karma."

"I wish you would stop saying things like that, you'll be giving me a complex soon!

"Hey, I've got an idea! You could take a Thai lover and he could do all your fighting for you!"

"I have already thought of that, but I am too old now. Only old men like me now and they cannot fight good."

"Oh, I was only joking… Did you really consider taking a lover to fight your battles for you?"

"I have to consider every option, telak, but I didn't want to have to do it, not really. Anyway, that idea is no good, so we can forget about it. Water under the bridge, as you say."

"I don't think we do, but I know what you mean. So, I am lucky that I am married to an old woman, who can't get a young lover then?"

"Haven't I always said that you are lucky to have me, Craig? Nothing has changed and I still love you too. We are lucky that they haven't shot us yet, but maybe that will come later, if we ignore their warnings. What do you think?"

"I don't know, I have never been in this predicament before, and, like you have said many times, I don't understand, so I'm afraid that you are quite right, you are on your own for the time being, my dear… Look, if you want to ask your brothers for advice, I don't mind if they think that I am a pussy… just ask them not to say it too often, eh?"

"No, I'm afraid that that option is out too."

"OK, let's try something else then. When is your other, not so useless, partner coming back from Australia?"

"Next week, I think, Why?"

"I was thinking that we could order a few things off eBay from China, security devices and things like that, but it might be better if Ross and Ayr brought, or even sent, them back from Australia. I'll phone or email him later. By the way, have you told Ayr about any of this nonsense?"

"No, I didn't want to spoil her wedding, but maybe is all right to tell her now."

"'It is all right'…"

"What?"

"Not 'is all right', 'it is all right'."

"What is?"

"Never mind, look, why don't you put her in the picture and I'll have a chat with Ross? We oldie falangs may not be able to grapple with the Thai mafia, but maybe we can get some evidence so that our wives can go to the police and get them to do something about it.

"Does that put your mind at rest a little, telak?"

"Yes, telak, you may not be a brave Thai warrior, but you are not a stupid falang either, are you?'

"Er, thank you, I think. OK, well, let's get on with that, then I can get back to typing this novel up. What are you doing tonight, Lek?"

"I will go in the other room and phone Ayr and then go and sit in Nong's so I can keep an eye on the shop for a while. Do you want to come and keep me company?"

"Yes, I'd love to, give me some time to get to a sensible place to stop and I'll come and join you, but look, don't go fighting with any mafia until I get there, you know, so I can take photos for evidence."

Lek poked her tongue out at him and left the office. Craig flicked over to Skype and selected Ross' account.

"Hi Ross, how's married life? Good, good, when are you coming back here?.... Ten days? Was that Ayr I just heard? Say hello from me. OK, look, we've been having a spot of bother over here. Lek thinks it's the local mafia hired by the competition, but there's nothing she can do about it without evidence… Oh, the shop's been broken into, wilful damage, that sort of thing, but no personal violence.

"You may know more about security devices than I do, but I was thinking about a security system for our house and one for the shop that you could extend into Ayr's flat, or you could have a separate one for that, that's up to you. I want ours to have battery back up with a solar panel charger…. Yes, that's the idea… Can you manage that? Everything wireless, OK? PIR's too and a CCTV unit, no make that two for us and at least two for the shop and, er, two for Lek's orchard, but there's no electricity there, so they will have to be solar. I don't know if this is possible, but I would like low-light cameras for the orchard… no, there's no lighting there, and I don't really want to put any either. No, if a light comes on, they will cover their faces and scarper. I want to catch them red-handed.

"Can you do all that? Do you have time? You might want to check with customs as well. Maybe send some of it back to us, and the shop and Lek's mother's address, Ayr will know what that is.

"OK, mate, sorry to be the bearer of ill tidings, but these things happen, apparently, not that they ever have to me before. Perhaps someone is jealous of falangs' wives making a few bob… Lek didn't say so, but it could be the case nevertheless. You know what they're like, they never tell you everything anyway, do they?

"OK, Ross, give my love to Ayr, we'll be looking forward to seeing you in ten days. Yes, OK, will do, I'm going to see her now, and don't worry about the situation here, we're doing what we can and are holding the fort. The security cameras will be a great deterrent, I hope, unless some bugger shoots them out, but it's worth a go.

"Lek? Tell Ayr she's fine. She's coping really well, you know her. In fact, she's sitting sentry duty outside the shop right now, but she has to sleep too and can't be everywhere. I'll suggest we get some of the boys to help tomorrow, but it's too late to do that this evening. Lek only just told me what's been going… this saving face thing can be a real pain, eh?

"Oh, well, you've got all that to come then, my friend and good luck to you with it. Bye for now, see you."

Craig flicked Skype off and went back to Word, then he looked down at the rough book of his current novel for the next sentence to copy up. He couldn't be bothered, the call of a beer was more inviting than the desire to add another thousand words to his computer copy. It was rare for him to feel like that, typing up work that he had already written out in longhand seemed like the worst job he had ever had. He knew what was coming next in the story, hated doing things twice and still couldn't type after thirty years. He seemed to have a mental and a physical block on typing.

He stood up, left everything running as he always did, locked the doors and walked around the corner to Nong's shop. It was only a couple of hundred yards away and she would want to close at nine or nine thirty, so he could catch up on his typing then.

"Hello, Nong, sabai dee mai, kap?" he asked, as he walked down off the road. She was dealing with a customer, but she held up a thumb to say she was well, and then a finger to ask if he wanted a beer. He nodded back. He laid a hand on Lek's shoulder and then sat down opposite her at the new picnic-style, double-bench table that she had just had made. A piece of oilcloth had been nailed to the top of it to protect the hardwood, presumably from spillages and any rain that might blow in under the roof since there were no walls on the little shelter. He noticed right away that condensation from Lek's bottle had created a puddle on the cloth, whereas it would have dripped through and dried up without the cloth. He wouldn't have the heart to tell her that the oilcloth was a bad idea.

"No mafia yet then, Lek?"

"Ha, ha, ha, ha, ha! They will come at three or four o'clock in the morning, not when everybody can see them!"

"Yes, I think that you are right. Would you like another beer, my dear?"

"I'm not sure, let me think… I could just sit here, stare at this empty bottle and waste my life, or I could have another one."

Nong brought Craig's beer.

"Lek auw eek kwat nung duay, kap – Lek wants another bottle too, please." It was obvious that Lek was in a bad mood.

"Cheers, my dear!" They clinked bottles. "I rang Ross and ordered a few security systems. He'll bring some back with him and post the others. The video cameras work on movement, so we will always be able to see anyone hurting your business. Ross says he'll post them the day after tomorrow and they will bring the rest in ten days,

"So, what do you think? That should go a long way to solving your problem, shouldn't it, telak?"

"Yes, Craig, very good. You do know that I was only joking about taking a lover, don't you?"

"No, I didn't really, but I bet it did cross your mind as an option, didn't it?" He watched a dark cloud pass over her expression. "I don't mean that you considered doing it... I just mean that the option probably crossed your mind and you said 'no' immediately, which I am sure you did, because you are a loyal and faithful wife, I know that."

She smiled enigmatically, but did not give a reply, although he knew that he was right. After ten years of living with her, he knew that Lek thought of most things.

When Nong brought Lek's beer, Craig tried another idea.

"Khun Nong, khun loo layoo wah Ayr mee penha tee baan? Phom yahk wah mah khun bai non tee baan khun Ayr wahn nee, OK, mai?."

Nong looked at Craig quizzically, and then at Lek, who said it properly.

"He's trying to say: 'You know that Ayr had a problem in her house,' – he means the break-in – 'I want your dog to sleep in Ayr's house tonight, OK?'."

Craig knew what was going on and listened carefully, as he always did, but couldn't notice the subtle changes Lek had had to make to render it intelligible to a Thai who didn't know him as well as Lek.

"Is that what you want, Lek?" asked Nong.

"It is not my idea, but it might help."

"Yes, all right, when do you want to put him in there?"

"Mmm, have you fed him yet, and what time are you going to close?"

"I fed him two hours ago, and I will probably close at nine, but if you buy a few beers, you can still sit here and drink them. That is not a problem. Things are pretty quiet tonight, eh?"

Nong called Milo over and picked him up. He was a fully-grown, chocolate-coloured poodle cross, which stood a foot tall, but he was brave and would bark at anything that moved within four yards of him at night.

Milo would be the ideal guard dog, not because he was much of a threat, but because he would make enough row to wake the neighbours up, should anyone try to enter the shop."

"Will you be safe without Milo, Nong?" asked Lek.

"Yes, I've still got my 38 under my pillow and I can scream louder than Milo anyway."

Nong and Lek walked over to the shop with Lek and dropped Milo inside the door as Lek opened it.

"I'll just pop inside and put some water down for him. Thanks ever so much." Nong started back to her shop, pleased that she could help out.

"No, problem, any time. I hate thieves.. the bane of my life, they are… kids nicking sweets, their parents taking petrol and forgetting to mention it… You've got to have eyes in the back of your head when you've got a shop like mine, you know…" She walked off still muttering.

"OK!" Lek regretted triggering one of Nong's hobby horses, because she could go on about petty thieves for hours. However, it did give her an idea.

She locked up and rejoined Craig.

"You really should run these ideas past me first. You know that I don't like people to think that we can't cope on our own, I lose face again now a little bit. Thai people don't tell people everything or ask for help – only from family. I don't like Nong to know everything."

"Jesus, Lek! She already knows you had a break in! She already knows that there is not much you can do until Ayr gets back, so what is the problem? She lent you her dog? Big problem, eh?

"I just solved a problem for you… OK? Now, tomorrow you can get two of the boys to sleep in there and give Milo back! In fact, you should have organised that today already! Capiche? Lighten up will you?

"Not everyone has got a scorecard at the ready to deduct points from your face-count whenever you do anything."

"Are you finished ranting now? That is what I said, you do not understand Thai people, because that is exactly what they do, especially in a village. Oh, they don't have score cards like in ice skating, but they have very good memories… believe me, and so do I."

Craig knew that he shouldn't have made that last remark, because he did believe her.

"Yes, all right, love, I'm sorry for saying that, I didn't really mean it, but you can't criticise me for not helping and then shout at me when I do. It's not very fair, is it? I might just as well crawl behind my desk and stay there – and say nothing!"

"Sometimes, it would be better, I think so too… I was just talking to Nong and she has a bee in her bonnet about theft from her shop, so why don't you order one of those security set-ups like they use in the 7/11's and sell it to her. You said you could order one from China through eBay, didn't you?"

"OK, but she is a bit mean, what if she doesn't take it?"

"If she doesn't, one of the other shops will and there are at least ten well-off families that might as well. In, fact, order two or even three, with video cameras that can be linked to the Internet. Don't worry, I'll sell, you just install them. You can do that, can't you? Good, no-one else around here is doing it yet." Lek started to enumerate the likely local customers under her breath in the strange way she had of counting on her fingers starting with the thumb on her right hand. "I think we can sell at least ten, maybe fifteen, telak, what do you think? Good idea or no?"

"It sounds good to me, I'll order them tonight. I know that many, many people in the village are on the Internet now, because I get so many Facebook friend requests from people here. Last year there were only a few in total, but now there are a few every week. Yes, it sounds like a very good idea."

"Internet is still new here, people don't know about eBay and don't have credit cards and don't trust to send money to China to someone they don't know for alarms. They don't understand yet, but Thai people are not stupid, they will learn quickly, we must do it first."

"Yes, OK, telak, I get the picture. I'll get on to it as soon as Nong kicks us out of here."

∞

The next morning, Lek got up at six fifteen, as usual, showered, made a bowl of rice soup for breakfast out of leftovers and took it in a flask to their shop, Northern Farming Supplies. She was normally there by seven anyway, but she wanted to let Milo out before he got desperate and had an accident. She opened up, set him free and sat at the small concrete table outside to have her meal.

They had two gangers running their workforce, Da and Bot, both of them from Mae Sot, as were most of the workers. Da was slightly senior, so she phoned him.

"Good morning, Da! Everything all right?"

"Yes, Khun Lek, we are already out. We've got the guys out in the fields as arranged yesterday… rebuilding the boundary paths between the plots and we've got two teams cutting rice."

"Good, good. Look a few things have cropped up, so when you've got everyone settled could you come up here to the shop? Bring Bot with you too, will you? You'll have to phone him and let him know, because I am a bit busy right now. What time? Oh, before lunch, say, tenish…. Yes, righty-o, you do that then, ring Bot and then call me back. See you, bye."

She took her bowl into the shop, swilled it and the flask out under the tap, put the coffee machine on, and then had a quick look around for dog muck, but there was none, so she clicked the computer on and started her day's correspondence.

Most of the emails were junk as usual, but there were a few offers from new suppliers that had to be looked into when she had more time. She quickly created a few rules that would direct them to the Suppliers' Folder in her Inbox in the future and dragged and dropped those emails into the folder manually. Requests for work were dealt with in a similar fashion, and then she came across an email the like of which she had never seen before.

"Get out of the rice business! If you don't get out, we'll TAKE YOU OUT! You have been warned!"

She had to read it a few times before it sank in that it wasn't a joke and that it really was addressed to Ayr and her. It crossed her mind that Nong had a gun as well as a dog that she might need to borrow, but she put a brave face on, took up her ledger and started stocktaking.

Meanwhile, Craig was getting up too. He clicked on the coffee machine as he headed to the bathroom. The two mugs of water that he had put in there the night before had boiled by the time he came out, so he made his first mug of instant, took down the biscuit tin, and went into his office. He always left the laptop running, so he only had to move the mouse to bring it out of hibernation. He too ate his biscuits – three with each of the two mugs of coffee – drank his coffee and answered his emails, most of which were junk too, the same as for every other Internet user in the world.

He had nearly finished, when Facebook beeped to say that he had a message. It was Lek.

"If you have time, please come to the shop. I want your advice. Love Lek x"

It was an unusual message for Lek, but it didn't sound urgent so he drained his coffee, went for a shower and got dressed. Then he poured another coffee, left it there to cool, locked the house up and walked the several hundred yards to the shop.

"What's the problem, Lek? Everything OK?"

"I not sure, take a look at this email, telak. It came this morning, or last night."

He wanted to correct her English, but sensed that it would not be a good time.

"That's not very nice, is it? Do you think it's serious? The timestamp says it came at one eleven this morning."

"I don't know, but I think that I have to treat it as serious because of what has been happening, don't you? I tried to ignore it when I first read it, but I can't, it keeps coming back into my head. What do you think we ought to do about it?"

"Let's take a closer look. Sit down in front of the screen." He pulled up a chair and sat to her right. "OK, right-click on the email item in the list, that brings up the metadata, let's see what that can tell us. Email forgers and spammers usually blur this data so they can't be traced… and? Hey, these people haven't done that! Well, well, well. It shows that we're either dealing with amateurs or fools. OK, put the cursor in that data, click 'Control A' and then 'Control S', open Notepad, put the cursor in there and click 'Control V'. Good, now save it to the desktop. Now we have a copy of where the email came from and when.

"Now we can think about what we're going to do with it.

"First, we can check who their ISP is… TOT, and who supplied their email address, and that is there, their website is called thaifarmingindustries.com and it is hosted by HostArmada, so, we can report them for abuse to those people and we can report them to the police as well. How far do you want to take it?"

"What do you think? I'm new to all this, I don't know?"

"To be honest with you, this is the first time I've had to deal with a cyber death threat too, but I imagine that the procedure is the same as for spam. Oh, there's another thing we can do, get their web site delisted at Google by issuing a DMCA."

"A DMCA? You do what you think you can do, but try to make it look like it don't come from us, OK? How you say, anonymouse?"

"Yes, that's close enough for today. OK, I think I can manage that. If I were you though, I would use any contact I had in the Thai police force to find out how to report this, because it is serious abuse. They may be stupid, but they may be violent as well. So, if you like, I'll email this metadata to the house and deal with it from there, while you scour the Thai police web site to find out how to report this. I can't do it because it won't be in English. There may be a few other things we can do too, I'll have to have a think."

"Will you be all right here alone? Do you want me to bring my laptop here and stay with you?"

"No, it's not worth it, I'll be OK. If they want me, they'll get me, there's not much you can do about that. Thanks though."

At that moment, Da and Bot came in behind them and Lek jumped. Craig was worried for her.

"I'm sorry, Lek, but you can't work here under these conditions. I've got an idea, why don't you tell Da that you want two of his biggest men to work around the shop until Ayr and Ross get back?. They can repair those holed punts, repaint the outside or dig a garden for you. Plant some flowers — anything so that you are not here alone"

"I'll think about it, telak..."

"No, you won't, you will do it! I want to hear you tell them now. I can't work at home knowing that you're jumping out of your skin every time the doorbell rings. Go on, tell them."

Reluctantly, Lek did as she was asked, but without giving Da a reason why. Da said that he would have them there after lunch, so Craig went home.

The first thing he did was address the problem of the death threat. He had taken it more seriously that he had let on to Lek — he was really very worried about it, but he knew how far he could go was limited.

He did all he had told Lek he would do, but also left a request for help message on the FBI web site, because the site was hosted in America. Then he wrote an anonymous message complaining about a death threat from the owner of the web site on the Thai police helpline, giving the man's address.

Craig pulled his rough book into eyesight and changed to Word to continue typing up when he had one more idea to help Lek and ease his mind. He took down Bpom's lead, and walked him around to the shop.

"Here, Lek, our last precaution, Bpom wants to help as well."

"Aw, Craig! I haven't got time to look after him, serve customers and do everything else, please, take him home! Besides, two men will be here after lunch, so there really is no need."

"Tough, you've got him now, and if you refuse, you'll hurt his feelings. Look, he's on a lead and we can tie this length of rope," he said, taking a hank of rope off a shelf. "to that and tie him to the back door. That way, you won't get any surprises from Ayr's flat –you can forget about it. You'll only have to watch the front door and the boys will help there… All right, love?

"I am satisfied that there is nothing more we can do for now, OK, so if you take Bpom, I will go home and leave you in peace. Good, I'll tie him up around the back, give him some water and get out of your hair. I love you my dear, and don't want anything to happen to you, because I don't know what I would do without you."

"All right, all right, you win, I'll see you in Nong's for a beer at seven, as usual. Now go, please, go and do some work."

"OK, I'm going, bye telak, I love you."

Lek blushed at such a demonstration of affection before strangers, and Craig, realising it too late, made a rapid exit past a bewildered Da and Bot out of the front door with their dog.

# ABOUT THE AUTHOR

Author Owen Jones, from Barry, South Wales, came to writing novels relatively recently, although he has been writing all his adult life. He has lived and worked in several countries and travelled in many, many more.

He speaks, or has spoken, seven languages fluently and is currently learning Thai, since he lives in Thailand with his Thai wife of ten years.

"It has never taken me long to learn a language," he says, "but Thai bears no relationship to any other language I have ever studied before."

When asked about his style of writing, he said, "I'm a Celt, and we are Romantic. I believe in reincarnation and lots more besides in that vein. Those beliefs, like 'Do unto another...', and 'What goes round comes around', Fate and Karma are central to my life, so they are reflected in my work'.

His first novel, 'Daddy's Hobby' from the series 'Behind The Smile: The Story of Lek, a Bar Girl in Pattaya' has been followed by four sequels, but his largest collection is 'The Megan Series', eighteen novellas on the psychic development of a young teenage girl, the subtitle of which, 'A Spirit Guide, A Ghost Tiger and One Scary Mother!' sums them up nicely.

As Owen puts it:

'Born in the Land of Song, living in the Land of Smiles'.

Please leave a short review where you bought this book. This kind of feedback is extremely important to authors and other readers, so please make your voice heard, and join me as my fiend on Facebook and Twitter.

Thanks,

Owen.

PS:

You might like to visit our web site:

https://meganpublishingservices.com

# Other Books by Owen Jones

**Alien House**
*A Story of Love, Hope and Alien Intervention*
-

**Andropov's Cuckoo**
*A Story of Love Intrigue and The KGB*
-

**Annwn – Heaven** - *series*
**A Night in Annwn**
*The Strange Story of Old Willy Jones's NDE*
**Life in Annwn**
*Thhe Story of Willy Jones's Life in Heaven*
**Leaving Annwn**
*Returning to Earth on a Mission!*
-

**Asian Shorts**
*An Anthology of Short Stories Involving Asians or Asia*
-

**Behind The Smile** - *series*
*The Story of Lek, a Bar Girl in Pattaya*
Volume I: **Daddy's Hobby**
Volume II: **An Exciting Future**
Volume III: **Maya – Illusion**
Volume IV: **The Lady in the Tree**
Volume V: **Stepping Stones**
Volume VI: **The Dream**
Volume VII: **The Beginning**

## Daisy's Chain
*A Story of Love, Intrigue and the Underworld on the Costa del Sol*

-

## Dead Centre - *series*
## Dead Centre
*Not All Suicide Bombers Are Religious!*
## Dead Centre II
*Even The Wrong Can Be Right Sometimes!*

-

## The Bull at the Gate
*The Day the Sky Fell !*

-

## The Disallowed
*The Story of a Contemporary Vampire Family*

-

## Fate Twister
*The Strange Story of Wayne Gamm*

-

## The Bull at the Gate
*The Day the Sky Fell!*

-

## The Ghouls of Calle Goya
*When Malice Results From Good Intentions!*

-

## The Psychic Megan Series
*A Spirit Guide, A Ghost Tiger, and One Scary Mother!*
## The Misconception
## Megan's Thirteenth
## Megan's School Trip
## Megan's School Exams
## Megan's Followers
## Megan and the Lost Cat
## Megan and the Mayoress
## Megan Faces Derision

Megan's Grandparents' Visit
Megan's Father Falls Ill
Megan Goes on Holiday
Megan and the Burglar
Megan and the Cyclist
Megan and the Old Lady
Megan's Garden
Megan Goes to the Zoo
Megan Goes Hiking
Megan and the W. I. Cooking Competition
Megan Goes Riding
Megan and the Radio One Beach Party
Megan Goes Yachting
Megan at Carnival
Megan's Christmas
Megan Catches Covid-19

-

**The Bull at the Gate**
*The Day the Sky Fell In !*

-

**Tiger Lily of Bangkok** – Series
Volume I: Tiger Lily of Bangkok
*When the Seeds of Revenge Blossom!*
Volume II: **Tiger Lily of Bangkok in London**
*The Tiger Re-awakens!*

-


Non-Fiction


**How to Give Your Dog a Real Dog's Life**
*(and make him love you for it)*

-

**The Eternal Plan**
*– Revealed*
(written by Colin Jones, compiled by Owen Jones)

-

## Authorship
*Publishing Your Book On You Own*

=

## Podcasting Mastery
*A modern means of mass communication!*

Plus 195 other self-education manuals.